To Mark,
Enjoy the suspens
Cris Anso
BEA 5/09

FIRST TO *Die*

Cris Anson

CERRIDWEN PRESS

What the critics are saying...

A Cerridwen Press Publication

www.cerridwenpress.com

First to Die

ISBN 9781419959622
ALL RIGHTS RESERVED.
First to Die Copyright © 2008 Cris Anson
Edited by Sue Ellen Gower.
Cover art by Willo.

This book printed in the U.S.A. by Jasmine-Jade Enterprises, LLC.

Electronic book Publication July 2008
Trade paperback Publication May 2009

Cerridwen Press is an imprint of Ellora's Cave Publishing, Inc.®

FIRST TO DIE

&

Dedication

∞

To my sister, whose heart is as boundless as the heavens.

Special thanks to:

∞

John McPhee for writing *The Pine Barrens* (Farrar, Straus and Giroux, 1967; republished by The Noonday Press, 1988). His loving exploration of the thousand-plus square miles of primeval forest and rich wetlands in south-central New Jersey helped me enrich the texture of *First to Die*. Now known as The Pinelands, the setting is as much a character as the people who move through it.

Trademarks Acknowledgement

ﾛ

The author acknowledges the trademarked status and trademark owners of the following wordmarks mentioned in this work of fiction:

Academy Award: Academy of Motion Picture Arts and Sciences

Acura: Honda Motor Co., Ltd.

BMW: Bayerische Motoren Werke Aktiengesellschaft

Chevy: General Motors Corporation

Coke: The Coca-Cola Company

Corvette: General Motors Corporation

Countess Mara: Countess Mara, Inc.

Dodge Viper: Chrysler Corporation

Dom Perignon: Chandon Champagne Corp.

Earthwatch: Earthwatch Expeditions, Inc.

Ford: Ford Motor Company

Fortune 500: Time, Inc.

Glenfiddich: William Grant & Sons Limited

Harvard: President and Fellows of Harvard College

Ivers Johnson: Henry Repeating Arms Company

Jockey: Jockey International, Inc.

Lexus: Toyota Jidosha Kabushiki Kaisha TA Toyota Motor Corporation

LPGA: Ladies Professional Golf Association

MedEvac: Center for Emergency Medicine of Western Pennsylvania

Meissen: Staatliche Porzellan-Manufaktur Meissen GmbH

Mercedes: DaimlerChrysler AG Corporation

MG: MG Rover

Miata: Mazda Motor Corporation
Monopoly: Hasbro, Inc.
Mylanta: Stuart Company, The
Palm Pilot: Pirani, Amin
Pepsi: Pepsico, Inc.
Philadelphia Eagles: Philadelphia Eagles LLC
Porsche: Dr. Ing. h. c. f. Porsche Aktiengesellschaft Corporation
Princeton: Trustees of Princeton University, The
Realtor: National Association of Real Estate Boards
Sabolich: Sabolich, Inc.
Shalimar: Guerlein, Inc
Sheraton: Sheraton Corporation of America
Smith & Wesson: Smith & Wesson Inc.
Sotheby's: SPTC, Inc.
Stolichnaya: PepsiCo, Inc.
Tarzan: Edgar Rice Burroughs, Inc.
Velcro: Velcro Industries B.V.
Victoria's Secret: V Secret Catalogue, Inc.
Yale: Yale University

Prologue

∾

The figure scuttling out of Simon Sutcliffe's house blended with the night—black knitted cap pulled down low, black gloves of surgical thinness, black jeans, black boots. Having slipped in through the kitchen door, the figure had found the basement stairs and headed unerringly to the gas furnace, made a few adjustments, then smiled in grim satisfaction. With tonight's forecast calling for the first hard frost of the fall season, the thermostat would kick on, calling for heat.

Heat that would not come. What would come, if luck held, was death.

* * * * *

"Oh, God, Carrie, I can't hold off any longer!"

"Yes you can," Carrie Sutcliffe murmured. Her sharp teeth nipped the skin at the crease of his groin. She wrapped a loose fist around his thick, heavy cock and stroked it slowly, balls to tip, as she knew he liked it.

To tease, she had insisted on a midnight swim first, the polyethylene dome and heated water holding back the cold October night. Now their nude bodies were slick with pool water and sweat as she knelt over him, her mouth inches away from the purple head of his cock. The sharp tang of chlorine overpowered the remnants of her trendy, expensive perfume. The soft whir of the filter mingled with the sounds of their harsh breaths.

"Damn you, woman." He thrust his hips up, his rampant cock searching for her mouth. After a long moment she let him find it, closed her swollen lips around the heat of him. His fingers grabbed handfuls of her jet-black hair, holding her head immobile, and he let out a groan of half ecstasy, half relief as he began fucking her mouth.

Oh lord, she loved to suck cock, loved the power she held over a man only minutes away from exploding into her talented mouth. In his half-dazed state he'd promise her anything, would do anything she ordered.

To ratchet up the tension a notch, she relaxed the muscles inside her mouth, lifted her head, and allowed his firecracker to slip out.

"Jesus, Carrie. What the hell—?"

With a throaty laugh, Carrie got to her feet, reached for his grasping arms to bring him with her. "Pillows. Come fuck me on the chaise."

"Bitch," he swore as he scrambled upright, his cock bobbling with his movement. Hauling her to his slick body, he crushed his mouth to hers, began stabbing his tongue inside her mouth, his hands grabbing her perfect ass and raising her up to grind her pussy against him.

Yeah, she thought. This was what she liked. The point where he'd die if he didn't stick his cock inside her right now. She clamped her legs around his waist and let him drive into her voluptuous, twenty-five-year-old body. She had yet to meet the man she couldn't wrap around her finger. She was especially pleased to have captured Simon. When she allowed herself to get pregnant with his child, he'd insisted on marrying her. With the birth of Kevin Harland Sutcliffe, she was sitting pretty.

The man humping her wasn't Simon, not by a long shot, but he could be very useful. And she intended to use him.

A slight noise caught their attention. The man went still, his breath coming in short gasps that she knew signaled he was seconds away from detonation. "Are you sure Simon's not coming home tonight?" he managed to rasp out.

In response, Carrie clamped her pussy walls around him with enough expertise to make him forget he was fucking another man's wife.

* * * * *

Simon Sutcliffe turned his green Lexus into the second of three driveways on the private road skirting The Pines, a family-owned golf club nestled at the edge of New Jersey's Pine Barrens. He'd spent the past two days hoping to entice a Fortune 500 company to lease space in a Class-A office building he owned on the bustling Route One Corridor near Princeton. When the negotiations had reached an impasse, he'd taken the last flight out of Detroit, eager to sleep in his own bed, with his son in the cradle nearby.

At six months, Kevin was the center of Simon's life. He'd given up his frantic pace of buying and selling properties and, at thirty-seven, had settled down. Soon Kevin would be saying "Da-da", toddle into Daddy's waiting arms, and Simon's heart would turn inside out with pride.

As to Carrie, her insistence on a hefty dowry should have warned him he'd be making a mistake marrying her, even though she was carrying his child. He'd given her half of his twenty-percent share of the holding company that ran the golf course and held other land for development. Hell, he'd have given her all of it, just to see and hold his son. But dammit, marriage and motherhood hadn't diminished, by a single molecule, her need to be the center of attention in any group of males.

Simon frowned as he negotiated the curve that led to the front steps of the carriage house he'd restored. A murky glow emanated from the vicinity of the pool. Had Carrie left the lights on? Surely she wouldn't swim after midnight and leave Kevin alone upstairs. He parked the Lexus at the curve and strode around to the back.

The translucent dome over the pool came into view. Simon saw Carrie's lush body silhouetted against a curved wall, her full breasts bouncing, head lolling back in ecstasy with her curly hair swinging, knees wrapped around the waist of a man who was pumping his hips into her.

"Goddamn!" Simon's vision exploded into blood red.

He started moving even before his brain reviewed his options. Outside access was from the other side of the house. He'd have to enter the house from the doors of his office that opened onto a private patio. He fumbled for his keys. He'd kill the son of a bitch. Cut his balls off, and then hang him.

Then he'd deal with Carrie.

He swept open the door and charged toward the back entrance. A pungent odor assailed his nostrils. It took him a moment to identify the smell. Gas. His blood chilled.

"Kevin!" He veered abruptly toward the stairs, took them three at a time to the master bedroom. "Kevin!" Gasping, eyes stinging, he scooped Kevin up from his cradle and smashed his foot through a floor-to-ceiling window for fresh air.

Frantic, he forced his brain to work logically. Was his son too young for CPR? *Oh, God, help me! Help Kevin!* He climbed out to the roof outside the window, cradling his son close to him. The rescue squad found him there, still trying to breathe life into his son, six months and four days old, with one tooth, a shock of black hair, and a cupid's bow mouth that would never smile again, his Tarzan pajamas damp with Simon's tears.

Chapter One

One year later

෨

The butterflies in Tamara Hart's stomach felt like bats frantically flapping their way out of a cave. She'd been so nervous last night that she hadn't pulled the alarm out all the way and had just gotten to the boardroom. Her first solo project at age twenty-nine and she'd almost messed up.

Her friend and advisor, Yvette Kai, gave her an encouraging smile. Yvette sat at the end of the walnut table nearest the projection screen making last-minute notes, looking coolly composed in a taupe power suit, her auburn hair pulled severely back into a neat chignon. Tamara felt a twinge of envy. Yvette, not Tamara, looked like the person in charge.

The combination of rushing, nerves and the heat in the windowless room had compelled Tamara to shed the jacket of her gray, pin-striped pantsuit while she attended to last-minute details. As the board members began filing into the room, she felt half-dressed and vulnerable in her white silk blouse—she was so harried she'd forgotten to don a camisole.

Harland Sutcliffe, sixty-six-year-old chairman of the board of The Pines, flashed her a warm smile as he took a seat. Tall with the erect bearing of a military commander, Harland was a handsome, charming widower with a lady-killer smile. Tamara offered a silent prayer for Harland, who six months ago had taken a chance on an unknown image consultant who had just started her own company.

The others either glared at or ignored her. Harland's son, the older twin Jack, had a bloated, dissipated look about him.

Bloodshot eyes and puffy lids sat above an aquiline nose and surprisingly sensuous mouth. It was no secret that he was a divorced, hard-drinking womanizer with a string of temporary bed-warmers.

Simon, the younger twin, had disappeared from The Pines before Tamara's arrival and was apparently gallivanting around the world. His wife, Carrie, slithered in wearing a tight cashmere sweater over impressive boobs and tighter leather skirt. She looked, as usual, ready for an audition as a hooker. Tamara assumed the marriage was dead, or else Simon would be protecting his turf — she'd often seen Carrie sniffing around any unattached male at the club.

The lawyer, Elliott Grosse, wore one of the impeccably tailored Italian suits he favored. Discreet facial tucks and regular visits to an expensive skin salon, as well as rigorous workouts in his home fitness center, disguised the fact that he was over fifty.

When the controller's stony gaze met hers, Tamara remembered Yvette's assessment of Marta Chudzik. "Speaking as an attorney who's handled a number of sex discrimination cases, I can tell you that Marta is a sharp individual with a keen mind and a lust for power. She's been there over twenty years and thinks she should be CEO."

"She told you that?" Tamara had asked.

"Didn't have to. I recognize the signs."

Shifting her focus to her presentation, Tamara rechecked the speaker's ice-water pitcher, the electronic pointer, and the slide projector. The bow holding her hair in place at her nape began to come undone. Blonde strands cascaded around her face as she bent forward to set pens and legal pads at each place.

"Honey, can you get me a cup of coffee before you go?"

The lazy baritone voice was so close, Tamara couldn't dispute that it was directed to her. She straightened, stiffened her spine — and looked into the most feral eyes she'd ever seen.

The predatory gleam in them softened when their gazes locked. For an instant she thought she saw deep into his soul, a bleak place where so much pain resided that he blanked it out in order to function. It reminded her of a TV program she'd seen of a wolf caught in a bear trap who gnawed his paw off to survive.

Then his whiskey-colored eyes raked across her face, her disheveled hair, her blouse sans camisole, and she fought off a shiver. He towered over her. His longish raven hair was wildly unkempt, as though he'd stuck his finger in a live electric socket. The black mustache and full beard completed a disturbing image of a man on the edge of civilization.

She wondered briefly if this was Simon Sutcliffe. Why else would his presence—or his Neanderthal attitude—be unremarked by the board members?

"Black, please." He smiled, even white teeth contrasting sharply with a skin tanned, no doubt, from a dilettante's life on the golf courses of the world. The smile did disturbingly attractive things to his eyes. The crinkle lines around them made him seem human.

Pulling the image of Yvette's ice-cool demeanor around her, Tamara held her head high with steely self-control and left the room sedately, scooping up her jacket as she passed the credenza.

Simon followed her exit with his gaze. He noted the tiny waist, the quiet sway of her hips, the long line of her legs in bell-leg pants and too-sensible flats, and thought it a shame that such a good-looking woman wouldn't wear miniskirts and high heels. He wondered if the blonde bombshell secretary was Jack's latest conquest.

Jack doesn't deserve her, Simon thought, surprised that he could feel protective of a woman who'd probably had a string of lovers. For an instant she'd looked vulnerable. Then shutters of ice had closed off that fragility and she'd stuck her chin out like a Valkyrie brandishing her sword and shield and daring mere mortals to challenge her.

At Harland's discreet cough, Simon turned and slid into the chair opposite his father's at the rear of the table, nodding to the woman at its head. "Go ahead, you can start."

Yvette gave him a half-smile, like the Mona Lisa painting behind bulletproof plexiglas, and said, "We'll wait until you're taken care of."

Simon felt a ripple around him. He resisted the urge to lift his arm and smell himself. He'd showered and shampooed his hair—three times. Before that, it had been a week since he'd taken a spit-bath in a basin, months more since he'd shaved. He wore a fresh white shirt he'd pulled out of a dry-cleaner's bag. So he was wearing jeans and no tie. So what? All his hand-tailored suits fit someone else. The trousers were two sizes larger than he was now, yet the shoulders were snug. The jeans were the only thing that fit.

When he'd arrived home two days ago, he'd been on the go for fifty-three hours. He'd barely caught the weekly flight from Petropavlovsk to Anchorage. That flight had taken him across the date line into yesterday. If only he could go around the globe a hundred, no, a thousand times a day, turning back the clock to October 14 of last year, the day before—

Damn! All that running hadn't diminished his pain one iota. He'd been a fool to think it would. He'd been able to submerge the vision of Kevin's tiny casket by working himself into sheer physical exhaustion. He'd gone from one godforsaken Earthwatch site to another, from outback Australia to Zimbabwe's black rhino quest to Russia's Ring of Fire—the more primitive, the better.

Neither filing for divorce nor the scientific research expeditions he'd joined could make him forget Carrie's betrayal and its deadly consequences. If he never came back to The Pines, that would have suited him—Jack was the heir apparent, not he. But they'd found the one button to push that would bring him back. The telegram said, "Harland had heart attack. Asking for you." Thank God it was a false alarm!

His gaze met his father's. Harland inclined his head toward the door. *It's your fault we're waiting,* he seemed to be saying.

I acted like a chauvinist, Simon thought sourly. It was seeing Carrie in this room that did it. That and the sexuality oozing from the blonde's every pore even with her icy demeanor. After a brief mental argument with himself, he rose and strolled out the door. He'd get his own damn coffee.

The blonde was walking toward him, carrying a creamy china cup and saucer. A twinge of disappointment lanced through him on noting the shapeless jacket buttoned up tight. "That suit doesn't fit," he blurted out.

She broke stride. Then her chin went up again. Ignoring his ill-mannered comment, she offered him the coffee, seeming to take pains to make sure their fingers didn't touch. "Black," she said the way a squeamish woman would say "bug".

"I've been away from civilization for too long," he said, giving her a disarming smile as he accepted the cup. "I spent the past few months digging around a dormant volcano."

She gave him a look that could peel the skin off a carrot. "Good for you." Then she walked brusquely past him and back into the boardroom.

As an apology, the one he'd given her was halfhearted, but her brusque rejoinder irked him. He followed her in, wondering if she'd be taking minutes of the meeting. The ribbon that had slipped down her shiny hair was gone. Her hair was pulled back into a tight braid.

All that showed beneath her pinstriped armor was a discreet bit of white silk at her slender neck. Again he wondered if Jack— Then he noticed his father's eyes following her every move with tenderness.

A jealous snake coiled in the pit of Simon's stomach. *Dammit, not Dad!* Jack, yes, he could understand, but if this too-sexy woman was Dad's mistress, if she had her claws in the one person he still cared about—

She stepped up to the podium. He sat down, hard, before shock made him fall down. The cup he held clattered on its delicate saucer as it thunked heavily on the table.

"Thank you all for coming," said the blonde. "For those of you who don't know—" and he felt her cold, cobalt-blue stare down to his sockless Docksiders, "my name is Tamara Hart, President of Avante Image Consultants. My colleague is attorney Yvette Kai."

Concentrating on keeping his mouth from dropping open, Simon glanced at the faces around him. Dad looked like a besotted lover, damn the woman's bones. Marta was tight-lipped, her arms across her linebacker chest in a body-language stance of "I'm from Missouri, show me". Jack looked as though he'd doubled his drinking in the year Simon had been away.

Elliott sat as a buffer between Simon and Carrie. After this meeting he'd collar the lawyer and find out just what the hell their status was. It shouldn't have taken a goddamn year to get a divorce. Adultery was adultery. Anger threatened to overwhelm him again. Simon forced his attention back to the blonde, who spoke in a cool, professional voice.

"One of the biggest questions was, should The Pines become a full-fledged country club, remain a private golf club, or opt for semi-private status, that is, build around the course and open it up to residents. My recommendations will—"

Jack interrupted. "If you've done your homework, Tamara, you know the zoning board's all but approved our plan, so your recommendation doesn't even enter into the picture."

"Mr. Sutcliffe—"

"It's okay, you can call me Jack in public. They'll understand it's nothing personal."

He said "personal" with such intimacy that Simon detected a slight reddening of Tamara's cheeks before she gave Jack a look that would shred steel. Had they been intimate?

Hell, why should he care? He made a show of nonchalantly sipping his coffee and watched the blonde's fingers lace tightly together. She leveled a cool glance at Jack. "Take your time, Mr. Sutcliffe Junior. I'm getting paid by the hour."

A flush crept up Jack's collar and onto his already florid face. He looked away.

Simon gave the blonde a "10" on guts and let the jargon— stock-keeping units, return on investment—wash over him. Until his dad asked her a question, addressing her as Miss Hart.

"'Miss Hart'? Come on, Harland," Carrie interrupted, a sneer in her voice, "we all know you've been screwing the consultant while the consultant does her best to screw the rest of us."

Sharp breaths were drawn around the table.

"I don't—you can't—" Tamara's fingers gripped the podium until her knuckles turned white. Her face slowly turned the shade of pink rosebuds. She stared at Harland, obviously waiting for a denial. But he merely leaned back in his chair and looked like a pampered cat that had just licked a bowl of cream empty.

Tamara wanted to evaporate. The concept of uttering a single word at this instant seemed foreign to her. Her cheeks felt fiery. Perspiration pooled between her breasts and under her arms. Hecklers she'd handled before. But Harland! How could he?

Yvette stood. "If you'll excuse us for a minute. Some of the slides appear to be out of sequence." She pried Tamara's fingers loose and with a forcible nudge led her out the door.

"How could he do that?" Tamara rasped when they had gained the relative safety of the anteroom.

"Calm down. He's testing you. Don't fail him."

"Testing— He's destroying me!"

"Tamara, look at me. Have you slept with Harland?"

"Of course not! He's like a father to me!"

"Then he has his reasons for not denying it. Obviously Simon's arrival has put everyone on edge. They'd been counting on voting his shares by proxy. Simon's a wild card. Harland's playing poker, don't you understand?"

"Poker?"

"He's bluffing to see who'll fold. Go back in there, hold your head up high and finish your presentation the dynamic way only you can. That little outburst from Jack just proves that Harland needs your help. Go with the flow. You can do it!"

Tamara's lower lip trembled. She hated it when she couldn't control an involuntary response. Why couldn't she have Yvette's iron will?

"You're a survivor, Tamara. After your accident, what you've gone through, nothing can faze you. You have backbone you haven't even used yet."

The accident. Even ten years later she still had nightmares about it. Her bad leg began throbbing. To take her mind off the pain, she closed her eyes, saw all the hostile faces. They wouldn't, couldn't triumph. She took a deep breath.

"That's it. Take another one. And another. Ready?"

"Yes." Tamara opened her eyes. "Those bastards don't know much if they think they've got me."

"'Atta girl. Give 'em hell."

The buzz of conversation ceased when Tamara opened the door. She felt all eyes on her as she walked back to the podium. The image of a steel rod through her spine kept her head high, her back straight. "Thank you for your forbearance.

We're all on the same page now. Harland?" He turned the projector back on and she nodded a thank-you.

"This recommendation concerns the bottom line." She picked up the remote. "Is anyone interested in a thirty-seven percent increase in golf course rounds a year?"

Good. That got their attention.

"Thirty-seven percent of all new golfers every year are women. A survey done by the LPGA in 2004 shows that most of the five million women golfers are part of a household with an income of over sixty thousand dollars a year. Most are professional working women.

"The Civil Rights Act of 1964 notwithstanding, a number of country clubs still prohibit women from holding memberships in their own names. Even without such restrictions, there are subtle pressures making women feel uncomfortable."

She flicked a slide full of statistics. "Fact. Every time a woman has called for a Saturday tee time at The Pines in the past several months, the earliest slot available was eleven a.m. When a man called, he could get one as early as eight—if, indeed, he didn't already have a standing tee time."

Jack snorted. "That's because women play so slow."

Tamara ignored Jack's comment. "On an ideal day with a professional playing at par, The Pines can be played in three hours, forty minutes. Fact. Sixty-two percent of the male members take over four and a half hours to play the course."

"No wonder. What's the average Joe's handicap? Twenty?"

"And sixty-six percent of the female members take four hours twenty-two minutes to play the course. Eight minutes less." She flicked another bar chart on screen to make the visual point.

"Where did you get such a cockamamie statistic?"

Tamara stared at Jack until he lowered his gaze. "From hands-on observation. Avante Image Consulting hired college students to track the starting and ending times of every foursome during fourteen spring and summer weekends."

"Bullshit! Women are always talking instead of swinging."

"Women don't play Bingo Bango Bongo on every hole." Bingo Bango Bongo was a betting game that Jack often won money on, and Tamara knew that everyone at the table knew it.

"The average age of male golfers at The Pines," she continued, "is forty-nine. For women it's forty. That alone gives them an edge in stamina and speed of play."

"But women can't hit as hard. They don't know etiquette, and don't know when to pick up their balls." Jack's comment brought a few snickers.

"Then give them a pro who will teach them, and build a range where they can practice until they feel comfortable enough to play The Pines."

As she successfully parried each of Jack's outbursts, Tamara felt her confidence building. She kept to her script, backing up each recommendation with statistics.

Finally she reached the most explosive item. She flicked Jack's land-use plan on screen. "The proposed development before the zoning board is a flat-out raping of the land."

The Pines' lawyer bolted to his feet and stalked up to Tamara. "Are you an architect? Land-use planner? Real estate developer? Can you back up that inflammatory comment? Which, by the way, I consider slanderous and will follow up in court."

Tamara swallowed around the dry spot in her throat, fought the urge to take a step backward. She was accustomed to smooth-talking, soft-spoken lawyers who radiated condescension, not hatred. She had to remember he was a shareholder, had a personal and financial stake in the outcome of the project. With great effort she wrenched her gaze from his hard, gray-eyed stare and forced herself to look each shareholder in the eye in turn. "Those words are a direct quote from one of the premier land-use planning firms in the East Coast. If you'll move, Mr. Grosse—" She looked at the lawyer. "I can give you each a copy of his professional opinion."

After a long moment, Grosse retreated a few steps.

"Thank you." Tamara picked up a folder from the table and passed out photocopies of a two-page letter.

"This is nothing but sour grapes." Grosse tossed his copy on the table. "This respected firm was one of the bidders. They're bad-mouthing our work because they didn't get the job. Our design firm is highly regarded. The zoning board has received our proposal favorably and is ready to vote on preliminary approval. What you're doing is too little, too late."

"I was hired to provide image-enhancing ideas and that's what I'm—"

"You're out of your element. You don't know the first thing about pro formas or business plans." The lawyer punctuated his statement with a finger stabbing the air between them.

"I know a bank doesn't want collateral," Tamara retorted. "It wants cash flow. From the time you move the first shovelful of earth until you sell your first house, how are you going to produce cash flow? I don't see how the cash flow of The Pines can cover the repayment schedule for the kind of loan you need."

Jack stalked around the table, trapping her between him and Grosse. "Image is one thing. I'll go for a logo change, sure, that makes sense. I'll even concede that we don't do enough to encourage women golfers. But I'll be damned if I let you bad-mouth a project that's been three years in the making."

"You've stonewalled me every step of the way," Tamara said, turning her barely contained anger at Jack, "so I can only generalize. However, it is not my mission to pronounce your proposed development viable or non-viable. My mission was to enhance the image of The Pines. And if you'll allow me, I have a few more slides."

Harland subtly cleared his throat. Both men returned, albeit reluctantly, to their seats.

Tamara's adrenaline level subsided to a bearable level. "Because of the environmentally sensitive nature of The Pines and its surroundings, five thousand units of townhouses and condos with no breathing room or sewage capacity is reckless endangerment. If The Pines executes the other image-enhancing initiatives proposed today, it can become a top-rated course."

She took a deep breath and unleashed the biggest gun in her arsenal, the one that could sink the other proposals. "You've seen the demographics earlier. An enormous pool of potential high-income buyers is available in this region. Therefore, I recommend designing and building an enclave of no more than fifty homes in the range of a million dollars."

The room exploded.

"Fifty homes?"

"A million dollars?"

"You're crazy."

The board began arguing, the decibel level rising with each sentence. No one deigned to ask her a question. Even though she had more slides to show, her presentation was effectively finished.

She was finished.

All she needed was one look at Harland's stoic face to know that she'd failed. She'd given him interim reports, but never had he indicated anything less than tacit approval. She'd poured herself into this project for the past six months, had searched her soul for the right recommendations for this land at this time, and had all but given up a social life.

And she'd failed.

The shareholders seemed to be unanimously opposed to her suggestions. She wouldn't even get the piddling job of logo design. Her bad leg throbbed. Her back hurt from keeping it so stiff.

They'd want her out of the company's cottage now. With a pang she realized how much she'd come to love the Pine Barrens area. She'd have to find another job. Why hadn't she softened her stance? She thought Marta agreed with the ROI argument, but even she had ice in her eyes by the end. Simon's expression was one of cynical boredom, as though he'd expected her to fall on her face. No surprise, given his male chauvinist attitude. Carrie's opinion didn't matter—she was lost during a business discussion. If attention wasn't centered on her, she zoned out.

Tamara stuffed her notes into her attaché case. Why should she care? She was washed up. Even Harland hadn't supported her. Polluting an aquifer or upgrading a golf course wouldn't make a difference one way or the other if she no longer lived here.

Simon's a wild card. Wasn't that what Yvette said? Did his opinion matter? *Was Harland playing poker?*

Tamara shivered in spite of skin heated from shame, from her failure before the board. She might as well polish her résumé tonight. She'd need it tomorrow.

* * * * *

Watching the bitch take charge of the meeting was a bitter pill. She simply had to be eliminated. Too much was at stake. Too many careful plans had been laid, too many dollars had crossed greedy palms. What had started with Kevin's death had to continue at all costs. No two ways about it.

Tamara Hart had to die too.

Chapter Two

ഇ

"Jesus Christ, that broad'll ruin us all!"

"Calm down, Jack. Here." Elliott handed him a double bourbon. He tossed it down in two swallows.

"Jesus," he said again. The tremors had stopped, but Jack's stomach was queasy. He glanced at his watch. Two-fifteen. He supposed they should order lunch. Instead, he tilted the bottle to his glass and poured.

"Sit down." Elliott snapped open his crocodile-skinned attaché case on Jack's desk and pulled out a pristine legal pad.

Jack slid into a leather chair, his only perk in this stinking tiny office he'd occupied for far too long. When the hell would Harland hand over the reins? Manager, said the plaque on his desk. What he was, was nothing. Harland still had the power. All Jack had was a view of the putting green.

"Let's start at the beginning. Harland has forty percent," Elliott said, writing the name in one column and the number in another. "You have twenty. Simon's twenty is split half to him, half to Carrie. My ten, Marta's ten."

"Who the hell sent that telegram?"

Elliott looked up, annoyance momentarily flicking over his surgically perfect features. "What are you talking about?"

"Why did Simon come home at just this moment? Who sent him a telegram saying Harland had a heart attack?"

"What do you mean?"

"Simon. When he burst in on me Friday night, he babbled about why I didn't go to the hospital to see Harland because of his heart attack." Jack couldn't understand why Simon still played adolescent at thirty-eight, calling Harland "Dad".

Elliott idly tapped his gold-tipped fountain pen to his lips. "A telegram. How many people knew where he was?"

"Harland kept the itinerary on his desk. Anyone could've looked at it. Hell, I looked at it. Made me feel good to know he was in some unpronounceable town on the other side of the fucking world."

"What exactly did the telegram say? Did he show it to you? Or recite the words?"

"I don't know. No. And no. Why would I want to remember the exact words? Anyway, how could that help us?"

"Just trying to sort out loyalties."

"Carrie's loyal." His mouth curved up in a half-smile, half-leer. "Of that I can assure you."

Elliott studied him until Jack began to fidget. What arrangement he and Carrie had was none of his goddamn business. If Elliott was jealous, fine. He'd seen the long looks Elliott gave Carrie when he thought no one was looking.

"And Marta?"

Jack's smile grew wider. "Marta has a special place in her heart for me. When she first came to The Pines, she needed a friend." He smoothed his thick hair back away from both sides of his head with his palms. "I helped her."

"You helped her? You were, what? Seventeen?"

"Showed her the ropes, told her who was who. Gave her a shoulder to cry on."

"And she's been grateful ever since?" Elliott's voice held a note of disbelief.

"I've been nice to her."

"So has Harland."

Jack shrugged. "He's nice to everyone. But I'm the one who had time to listen to Marta. She isn't exactly Miss

America, you know. Or even Miss Congeniality. She kind of treated me like a kid brother. I made her feel good, is all."

"I'll take your word for it. Now what about the planning board?"

"I got the chairman, Ramsey, in my pocket," Jack said. "His son caddies for us. I caught the kid in the locker room with Sheila what's-her-name, the one with the knockers, whose husband runs the bank that holds the mortgage on Ramsey's mansion. Happened to have my digital camera with me."

Jack held out his hand and rubbed the pad of his thumb against two fingers in the time-honored symbol for money. "We have four sure votes, which is a majority. Plus maybe the mayor. He hasn't bitten on my offers, but he owns the hardware store, so he's got to be pro-development."

"Good. Now. Let's get back to the shares." Elliott drew two boxes. Inside one he placed Harland's name and percentage. "Forty. If Simon votes with him," in the other box he marked Elliott, Jack, Marta, Carrie, "it's a stalemate. How do we get Simon's vote?"

"Carrie?"

"Good God, no. When Simon returned from Harland's, he turned apoplectic to discover she was still living in the carriage house." Elliott stroked his jaw. "I have to meet with him this afternoon about the divorce. I can feel him out."

"Good. Does he have a will?"

Elliott's eyes flickered with interest then banked behind his expressionless lawyer's façade. "Why?"

"If he doesn't, then his wife stands to inherit, right?"

"You aren't thinking of…"

"No, I'm not going to do anything. I'm just asking."

But the seed had been planted.

* * * * *

"Have you eaten?"

"Huh? Oh, Marta." Jack looked up from his desk at the Amazon who filled his doorway. Christ, did she need to wear shoulder pads under everything? Her black dress was double breasted, with wide lapels. The black orthopedic shoes looked like they belonged on a waitress in a greasy-spoon diner. She tried to act like a man. Cut her own grass, changed the oil in her sedan twice a year. Once she'd even told him she fixed a plumbing problem in the kitchen. "Haven't had time. Elliott just left. He's been here since the board meeting."

Marta sniffed the air then frowned. She walked all the way in, lifted the receiver off Jack's phone, and punched three digits. "Larry? Send up a club sandwich for Mr. Jack and a chef's salad for me. Thanks."

She cradled the receiver and sat heavily in the captain's chair opposite the desk. "Jack, don't you care for yourself?"

"Sure I care. I care about what's going to happen to this club if that interfering broad has her way."

Marta leaned forward, fixed a stern gaze on him. "You know what I mean." She eyed the empty rocks glass. "If you're going to drink, you need something in your stomach."

"Christ, Marta, not that soapbox again."

Marta sucked on her inner cheek. After a moment she said, "I've been over the numbers again. We should reach break-even in four years. That cash flow scare the Hart woman tossed out, that's just a smokescreen. She didn't deign to qualify that the mortgage would be interest-only until we sell the first unit. And we've all agreed to additional investments as needed to satisfy the bank. She was just trying to impress Harland."

"Do you think he's fucking her?"

She didn't bat an eyelash at his intentionally crude words. In fact, he'd heard her use them herself.

"He was certainly tolerant of her recommendations. But it's hard to read Harland sometimes. He keeps things too close to himself." Her lips thinned into a tight line. "Sometimes I think he doesn't trust my ability. Just because I don't have—"

"'Balls, said the queen, if I had them I'd be king.'" He smirked when her eyes narrowed. "That's right, Marta, I've heard you say that before. And you know what? It suits you. Make no mistake. When this thing gets off the ground and I'm in charge, you will definitely be my Chief Financial Officer."

"Thank you for your confidence. Ah, here's your lunch."

She signed the chit and reached for her Pepsi. Jack watched her pop the top and drink as heartily as a sailor on leave guzzles his first beer. He hefted his sandwich and took a bite. "What do you think of Simon coming back?"

"It was certainly a surprise. He's lost a lot of weight. And that hippie look doesn't become him."

"I mean in relation to the project."

"I think we have to appeal to the businessman in him. After all, he's amassed quite a tidy pile of investments. Educate him on the potential of this project. And the sooner, the better."

"He sure as hell wouldn't listen to any pitch from me."

"Let me do it," Marta said. "This project is as much my baby as it is yours. We may not see eye to eye on a lot of things, but Simon respects my ability. On another subject, are you going to Harland's dinner tonight?"

Jack snorted. "Are you kidding? That wasn't a request, it was a summons. Dinner jacket. Hell, just because Simon's back? Believe me, it won't be a welcome-home celebration. It'll be a free-for-all to hash over that broad's proposals."

"Should I try to reach Simon this afternoon then?"

"Yeah. He should hear our side of the story before any final vote. Oh, and Marta? He thought the divorce would have been final by now. He's not too happy to hear he's still a married man. So don't mention Carrie to him, okay? "

"Right. I won't."

* * * * *

"Thanks, Liddy. Send him in."

Elliott disconnected the intercom then slid a file back into his desk drawer, locked it, and slipped the key into his vest pocket. He rose when Simon walked through the door of the luxurious office that Elliott had spared no expense to furnish. The antique desk had been purchased at a Sotheby's auction. An inlaid game table near the marble-faced fireplace held a priceless Meissen vase. Image, he knew, was everything.

"Simon." He held out his hand. "Glad you could make it."

Simon briefly returned the handshake and sat in the indicated leather club chair.

"You've been a hard man to get hold of." Elliott had decided the best defense was a good offense. He opened the folder on his desk and handed Simon a half dozen envelopes, all stamped with variations of "Moved, Left No Forwarding Address" in as many languages.

"I tried to advise you before you left that suing for adultery with no one except the plaintiff testifying to said adultery, to say nothing of not identifying the co-respondent, would be nearly impossible to engineer."

Simon lifted a questioning eyebrow.

"Go ahead, open them. They're addressed to you." He handed Simon a letter opener shaped and decorated like a Toledo sword.

Simon read quickly through the missives. Then his jerked up. "'Not tantamount to adultery'?"

Elliott had known the New Jersey Superior Court case he'd cited in one of the letters would raise Simon's hackles.

"I don't believe this. 'Actual proof of sexual conduct other than intercourse with a third person is not tantamount to adultery under the statute as a ground for divorce.' Shit. I saw their silhouettes jerking like pistons. They'd been there long enough for the gas to suffocate my—" Simon crumpled the letter in a massive fist. He stood abruptly, lurched to the damask-draped window.

Elliott unscrewed the top from his expensive pen and busied himself with making notes to the file in his tight script. He was too discreet to have Simon turn around only to find his grief for his infant son on public display.

"I'm sorry." The tremor in Simon's voice was almost under control.

Elliott looked up. "Cognac?" He replaced the cap on his pen, set it exactly aligned with the edge of the leather blotter.

"Thank you, no. I'll probably have several tonight."

Elliott's barely lined face smoothed into a smile. His glance took in Simon's attire from the board meeting—jeans, wide black belt, Egyptian cotton shirt with the top two buttons open. "You're dressing for dinner?"

"Dad made a point of it, so I took my monkey suit to Farrell's for alterations early this morning." Simon glanced at the no-name, Army-style watch he'd used for the past year. "They close at six, so let's get on with our business, shall we?"

"Of course." Elliott gestured, and Simon took a seat.

"You have several choices, none of which are instant answers." Elliott lifted a manicured hand and held up one finger. "First is the no-fault. That takes eighteen months. We could argue that the clock was running the day you left the country."

He held up a second finger. "Willful and continued desertion for twelve months. Only Carrie, the deserted party, can initiate that ground. For that you have only two more months to wait."

"That makes me the bad guy."

Elliott shrugged.

"What else? I mean, other than that imprisonment or mental illness stuff."

"Only one. Extreme cruelty. But you need a series of incidents, a history, if you will."

"Christ, Elliott, my son died because she was fucking some other guy! If that isn't extreme cruelty, I don't know what the hell is!"

Elliott leaned forward. "Carrie's betrayal, in addition to your loss, has wounded you profoundly. Perhaps I can persuade her not to contest an extreme cruelty ground."

Simon jerked to his feet, began pacing on the hand-sheared Kirman rug. "Knowing Carrie, it'll cost me an arm and a leg."

"Your wealth couldn't have meant too much if you gave me power of attorney over your investments and walked away from it."

"Dammit, it's the principle of the thing, and you know it. That bitch used every wile known to Eve and then some." His voice took on a bitter edge. "She never loved me. She looked at me and saw dollar signs."

"Oh, I don't know," Elliott said softly, holding back a note of jealousy. "She really was crazy about you."

"Then what the hell happened? Where did I go wrong?"

"Workaholic?"

"No. I didn't spend any more time away than I had to. After all, she was carrying Kevin." His voice broke on his son's name.

"I have an idea."

It took Simon a moment to respond. "Yes?"

35

"I don't know how you're planning to vote on this image thing, or on Jack's land-use plan. You're probably still assimilating everything."

"Marta gave me a quick and dirty. She has a sharp mind."

"Then you know it's a go, if Marta says it'll make money. Vote for the project. Carrie's share would be enough to get her out of your hair the rest of your life. And your current assets would stay intact."

Simon said nothing. Elliott let him absorb the ramifications.

"She signs an agreement. Gets out of my house. Out of my life. Now." Simon's voice picked up speed and conviction. "The only contact I have with her is during board meetings. And you'll be the buffer, as you were today." He balled a fist, pounded the desk once. "No contact. Period. None. Nada."

"Let me try it out on her."

Simon stood. "I have to get to Farrell's. Thanks, Elliott."

"One more detail." Elliott rose and walked around the desk, placed his hand on the taller man's shoulder as he escorted him to the door. "If Carrie has to find alternate living quarters…" He let the implication hang.

Simon's gaze rolled to the ceiling. "I'll give her an allowance of three thousand dollars a month—"

"You haven't been paying attention to your wife's standard of living. It will cost her that much for lodgings."

"What?"

"My suggestion would be ten thousand a month. Of course," he added hastily, "I'll start with two and allow myself to be negotiated upward. Grudgingly, so she thinks she's bested us."

"Fine. It'll be worth a hundred and twenty grand to get her out of my life."

"A year."

"Whatever." They shook hands and Simon departed.

Back at his desk, Elliott allowed himself a smile. It had been so easy.

After his secretary left for the day, he unlocked the drawer and retrieved the file he'd been perusing when Simon arrived.

It was almost too hot to handle.

Chapter Three

ॐ

"Will somebody please tell me why I ever agreed to this?"

Tamara scrutinized her empire-style dress in the cheval mirror inside one of Harland's guestrooms. Its ice-blue shade made her eyes more vividly blue. Skinny straps held up the fitted bodice. The wispy skirt fell in graceful folds to her calves.

Harland had invited them to stay over. At the dressing table Yvette was applying another coat of mascara on her up-tilted brown eyes. They had adjoining rooms with a connecting private bath, but it was more fun to primp together.

"When Harland called this afternoon, I thought he was going to tell me to pack up and get out." Tamara ran a brush through her hair. She'd allowed Yvette to talk her into using a curling iron and had to admit she liked the way the soft waves framed her oval face. "I completed my report. My contract calls for the last third of my fee within a week. Why am I here?"

"To celebrate," Yvette said. "You did a fantastic job, kept your cool against some formidable goading. You gave them thought-provoking recommendations. They got what they paid for."

Tamara sat down on the crazy quilt covering the spindle bed. "I felt like a cue ball on a pool table, crashing into a racked pile of balls that caromed off each other."

"Exactly. Didn't I tell you Harland was bluffing?"

"You're mixing metaphors."

"It doesn't matter. I have a feeling tonight's going to be an even bigger explosion."

Tamara tipped the shield-shaped bottle of Shalimar and dabbed perfume behind her ears and on her inner elbows. "But why do we have to be there? To pick up the bodies?"

"Maybe Harland wants you to get to know his 'wandering son'."

"That male chauvinist? He made me feel like an Amsterdam hooker."

"Well, I understand he has been out of circulation."

"He had the nerve to say, 'That suit doesn't fit.' It's supposed to be boxy." She took an angry breath. "*My* suit didn't fit? This from a guy wearing someone else's baggy jeans. That white shirt with a monogram on the cuffs had to have cost two hundred dollars, but the jeans were bunched up like a dirndl skirt under that mock-Indian belt."

An amused smile played around Yvette's mouth. "You noticed quite a bit."

"And that hair! He looked like the Wild Man from Borneo."

A gentle knock prompted Tamara to snap her jaws shut.

"Ladies? May I escort you downstairs?"

"Harland." A look of panic flicked over Tamara's face. "I'm not ready. You go on, Yvette. I'll be down in a bit."

Yvette rose gracefully from the dressing table and disappeared into the hallway. She looked smashing, Tamara thought, in a beaded silver shell and black satin pants.

She went to the mirror and stared at her reflection. "You're a fraud. You should just plead a headache and go home." Then she sighed in resignation. No way could she leave Yvette to clean up after her. They were her recommendations. Yvette was only her advisor. She flicked navy mascara on her thick lashes then poked the studs of her pearl earrings into her pierced ears.

She jumped at the knock.

"Tamara? I would be honored to offer you my arm."

Yvette was right. Harland was up to something. Pasting a smile on her face, she opened the door. "Wow! You look great!"

And he did. With one hand on Harland's white-dinner-jacketed arm and the other on the balustrade, she glided down the fifteen steps. By now she was so accustomed to her bad leg that she didn't even worry about stairs. He led her to the spacious dining room, where a damask-covered table was set for eight. Tall, slender tapers rose from silver candelabra. Gardenias floated in small pools of water. Bone china in an intricate pattern and several etched wineglasses graced each place setting.

"The others will be along momentarily. Please allow me."

Harland pulled out a Queen Anne chair whose seat was covered in burgundy velvet. Its patina and those of its mates told Tamara they were the real thing. She settled into it as Harland slid it forward. "Addy wore Shalimar," he murmured, bending toward her. "I do wish she would have been able to meet you."

Tenderness filled Tamara's eyes at the unabashed sentiment. Mrs. Sutcliffe had died about six years ago she knew. Tamara turned her head and smiled at him. His lips grazed her temple.

"How touching."

Tamara's head snapped toward the sound of Simon's voice. His dinner jacket fit like the skin on an apple. His right shoulder rested nonchalantly on the doorjamb, his left hand was thrust into his pants pocket. He looked like the man leaning on a lamppost in the Broadway musical *Me and My Girl*.

Her gaze traveled upward. She did a double take. His shaggy black hair had been trimmed, no, styled with the right amount of sideburns, the length in the back just at the collar.

His clean-shaven face was all angles and planes and deep grooves. It was an austere face, almost ascetic, as though he'd spent the past year in penance and meditation. A vivid flashback reminded her of the pain she'd glimpsed in his eyes when they'd met.

Now those eyes burned as though looking at a candle flame through a glass of scotch. Tamara was conscious of an immense heat where his gaze rested, at the exposed swell of her breasts.

"Simon," said Harland, straightening. "Please sit at the place of honor. I assume everyone's following you in?"

Tamara's tongue felt like a shoelace that had knotted. Harland had positioned her to his left, Simon to his right. Simon would face her. She should have run when she had the chance.

The rest of the board wandered in. Harland seated the other twin to her left, Carrie beside him. Yvette was at Simon's right, Elliott next. Marta took the hostess chair at the far end of the table. Carrie's black dress was short, tight, and strapless, with what must have been a merry widow pushing up even more cleavage than Tamara exposed.

"Ah, here's Ilya." Harland nodded at the magnum of Dom Perignon the butler held and watched as he expertly poured the bubbly into crystal flutes. "To the pleasure of having both my sons with me," he said, lifting his glass. He sipped, apparently oblivious to the fact that his sons looked at each other with less than affection. Everyone dutifully drank to the toast.

Ilya returned, wheeling a mahogany cart bearing a soup tureen. Behind the thin, white-haired man was an equally white-haired woman carrying a silver ladle.

"Danuta, you made my favorite soup," Simon said, his angular face creasing into a grin that crinkled the skin around his eyes. His glance found Tamara. "Cream of winter vegetable."

Tamara thanked heaven and earth that she was seated. Simon's smile, when it warmed his eyes, could melt asphalt. Liquid fire raced straight down to her pussy. She paid inordinate attention to Danuta's deft motions as her bowl was filled.

Another wave of heat blanketed her. She lifted her lashes to find Simon staring at her. When their gazes collided, he insolently lowered his gaze to the cleft between her breasts. She had a powerful urge to tie her damask napkin around her neck. Equally powerful was the urge to have him suckle them.

"Tell us about Russia," Carrie said. "What did you do in the back of nowhere for the past three months?"

Simon's head jerked around. He glared at his wife at the far side of the table then leaned around Yvette. "Elliott, what about our agreement?"

Elliott set his silver spoon down, patted his lips with his napkin. "We're all interested in your experiences, Simon. You've seen and done things most of us never dreamed of."

"Did you see any lava actually flowing?" Harland asked.

With Harland drawing him out, Simon reluctantly related his adventures. Through the hearts-of-palm salad, the pappardella with wild mushrooms, the sorbet, the lobster and scallops Française, the three different wines, Tamara kept her gaze on her plate, hearing Simon's mesmerizing baritone discourse on Kamchatka, Hwange National Park's black rhinos, aborigines in Queensland, Brunei's rainforest. Not until the chocolate velvet did she realize he hadn't revealed anything personal for all his exploits. His vivid descriptions of exotic locations and alien cultures were devoid of interactions with people.

Surprised at her observation, she stopped with her dessert spoon midway to her mouth and looked up at him.

And found him staring at her. The flame from the low-burning candles reflected in his amber eyes. The heat of his gaze communicated itself directly to her pussy. A curl—no, a tsunami—of desire awakened, stretched like a cat, and demanded satisfaction.

God, no! Why had her treacherous body chosen this chauvinist whose opinion of women was lower than the snakes he'd studied in Brazil? Through gritted teeth she bit out, "When you get an eyeful, wink."

His mouth curled up in a predatory smile he must have copied while observing panthers, but he didn't avert his gaze.

In a low voice Jack said, "I'd rather have a mouthful."

Tamara felt as though a blowtorch had been aimed at her cheeks. Jack had spent most of the dinner leaning close to her, whispering in her ear so he could peer down her bodice. She didn't know which twin she despised more at that moment.

"What's going on over there?" Carrie demanded.

"Jack was just extolling the virtues of this charming little Chassagne Montrachet," Harland said, twirling his glass to the light and then sipping conspicuously.

"Let me tell you a story," he continued, glancing at Tamara. She silently thanked him for drawing the spotlight away from her. "About a little girl whose father died when she was still in pigtails. Her mother remarried so she could give the little girl a good home. The new father turned out to be a lazy bum, and the girl suffered from neglect when the mother had to go back to work as a seamstress in a dress factory."

Tamara took a sharp breath. The story was uncomfortably close to her own origins, but how would Harland know that?

"The other characters in this story are two brothers who grew up with every advantage. One grew jaded, because as the older, he stood to inherit everything. The other, in his brother's shadow, had to work hard for every success, for every bit of approval from his father."

"Harland, what the hell—?"

His sharp glance silenced Jack's outburst. "Both boys were given cars as soon as they reached legal driving age. One boy used it as the tool that it can be. The other drove fast, sometimes too fast, often while drinking. He got into scrapes and expected his father to get him out. The father always did."

The room was silent now. Harland had everyone's attention.

"When she was a month from her high school graduation, the girl visited another town. The prospect of a scholarship had her giddy. She was so excited after an interview with the dean of the university that her feet barely touched the sidewalk. When the light turned green, she dashed into the intersection, and was hit by a car. The driver never stopped."

With trembling fingers, Tamara reached for her water goblet. She felt as though half the Mojave Desert had suddenly lodged in her throat. Somehow he'd discovered her past. What did he have in mind? Why now?

"The boy, knowing he was in deep trouble, ran to his father. He'd been drinking, hadn't seen the light change, hadn't seen the girl until after she was flung over the hood of his MG."

"Jesus Christ, Harland, what are you doing?" Jack shoved his chair back and jerked to his feet.

Harland gave him a glacial stare. "Sit down. I'm not finished."

Jack snatched the brandy decanter and a snifter. His hands shook, and brandy splashed over his fingers as he poured. He tossed back half of it, breathed heavily as he glared at Harland.

"The girl lay in a coma for days. When she finally awoke, she was scarred for life. It was three years before she was able to go on to college. The boy never paid a penalty for his misdeed, because his father spent a lot of money covering it up. The boy never learned his lesson. He continued to drink more than he should." Harland leveled an accusing glare at Jack.

Jack defiantly brought the snifter to his mouth and swilled down the rest of its contents. "So what's the moral to this little fairy tale?" he sneered.

Harland looked at Tamara, whose face had drained of all color, then at Jack. "I want you to meet your victim," he said calmly. "She's sitting to your right."

Chapter Four

"No!"

Jack jerked to his feet, hurled his brandy snifter toward the far wall, missing Harland's head by inches. The shattering of glass in the sudden silence sounded as loud as a machine gun. "You son of a bitch!" Jack pivoted around Tamara's chair and came at Harland. "You told Mother you'd never throw it up to me. You said it was forgotten." He yanked his father out of his chair and grabbed him by the lapels. The chair toppled over as Harland stumbled against the unexpected assault.

Simon exploded into action. He came behind Jack, slung a hammerlock across his neck. "Get your hands off him!"

A strangled noise was Jack's response. His knuckles whitened as he held on tighter to Harland's jacket.

With his left hand Simon pulled his right forearm tighter, trapping Jack's Adam's-apple like a pecan in a nutcracker. "I broke a gorilla's neck once in a hold like this," he hissed.

Slowly Jack's fingers unclenched. He lifted his hands in the air as if a gunman had said, "Stick 'em up."

"You lay one filthy hand on him, ever again," Simon growled without easing his grip, "I'll kill you. Understand?"

Jack's head jerked up and down fitfully. Simon released his hold, gave Jack a shove in the small of his back. Jack staggered forward, bumped into Harland. His knees buckled.

Harland grabbed his older son and held him upright, as he had done for too long. Softly he said, "A CEO has to take responsibility for his actions, son. It's time you grew into the job."

Jack glared at him a moment then lowered his gaze. His throat burned. His upper arms burned where Harland still held onto him. His face probably looked like it was burning. Because it was. Burning with shame. And loathing. Not only for Harland, but for Simon, and for that blonde who'd haunted his dreams ever since he'd seen her limp body flying over the hood of his car like a doll tossed by a bored child.

For ten years he'd lived in fear of someone discovering his secret. And that bastard had just announced it in front of the entire board. He'd pay. By God he'd pay. And so would she. "I need a drink," he said, shrugging Harland's hands off him.

"Coffee will be served in the study in ten minutes," Harland said, straightening the hang of his dinner jacket. "I think we all need a break right about now."

The realization paralyzed Tamara—Harland had known when he hired her. He'd been the blurry figure urging her, day after day, to fight when she had lain in the hospital bed in a coma. Harland was the anonymous benefactor who'd paid her hospital bills, her college tuition.

Because his son had maimed her.

The memory of three years of pain, of death wishes before she climbed out of her despair and took advantage of the hush money he'd offered, had not dimmed. She thought she'd conquered her enmity toward the coward who'd fled, leaving her bleeding and unconscious in the gutter. But she hadn't. The rage, the bitterness, flowed back into her, leaving her hot with impotence.

"Tamara! Are you all right?"

Yvette's voice finally reached her. Shaking her head to clear the past, she roused herself, forced her focus on her friend. On Yvette's brown eyes liquid with concern, the full mouth drawn up in a tight line of tension. Her friend. Thank God Yvette was here. Was that why Harland had invited her? Knowing Tamara would need someone to lean on?

Warmth seeped into her fingers, making her realize how cold they had been. She glanced down to see her hands sandwiched between Yvette's.

"You look like you're trying out for the part of Morticia Addams," Yvette said.

Tamara turned her palms around and squeezed Yvette's hands. "God, I'm glad you're here tonight!"

"As your lawyer, I advise you to take a quick trip to the powder room. I'll come with you."

They rose and headed to the guest bathroom, Tamara almost staggering. Looking in the mirror, she ordered, *Get hold of yourself!* She forcibly pushed the horrible past back into a corner of her soul then breathed deeply.

"He's your anonymous benefactor," Yvette guessed.

"Has to be."

"Didn't I tell you he was playing poker?"

"Poker! That looked more like Russian Roulette to me. I don't know if I'm up to any more surprises tonight."

"But aren't you glad you know? Finally, after ten years?"

Tamara didn't feel quite as forgiving as Yvette probably thought she should. "I guess so." She sighed. "What a snake pit! Are you sure this is just a poker game?"

"Yes. And I have a feeling you're holding four aces."

"Will you stop that? I don't even play the game."

"You don't have to, honey. You're just the little white ball the croupier throws into the roulette wheel."

"More like a monkey wrench."

"Probably," Yvette agreed with alacrity.

When they returned, the dining room was empty. Yvette began walking down the hall toward the study.

Tamara bit her lip. She wasn't sure she could continue. Yvette had taken it in stride, but it wasn't her leg, her life that had been altered. Did Harland expect her, Tamara Hart, to look Jack in the eye and act magnanimous and forgiving?

"Ah, Yvette said you were here." Harland appeared in the archway, looking as calm as a spring morning. "It was time," he said, obviously to forestall the protest Tamara had been about to deliver.

"You're my benefactor."

"Yes." He seemed relieved that she'd figured it out. "Now I must ask you one more favor. Will you help me?"

Tamara stifled a sigh. How could she not? He hadn't been driving the MG. He'd done what he could to mitigate the aftershocks. The hospital bills, the college tuition, modest deposits mysteriously appearing in her checking account, the letters of encouragement. "Of course."

His lined face broke into a grin as he looked over her shoulder. "Ilya. May we have those?" Appearing suddenly from the darkened hallway, the butler handed the package to Harland.

At the sight of the objects Ilya had apparently retrieved from her bungalow while they dined, Tamara paled. She'd thought she'd already had all the shocks that the evening could hold. But she'd been wrong. What he was asking was nothing short of baring her soul.

"I—can't."

"You must."

"Harland, please. Don't ask this of me." She stared at him, at his outstretched arms. At the offering he was holding.

She felt the stinging at the backs of her eyes. She wouldn't cry. She didn't dare cry. She'd rather feel the hatred, the rage that had fueled her, that made her strive for success. "Don't make me vulnerable again."

"It's the only way to get through to him." Harland's eyes met hers in a test of wills.

Harland won.

* * * * *

Standing by the fireplace, Simon glanced around the study. Near the pocket doors Elliott was talking to Jack, whose hands were, thankfully, devoid of the ever-present rocks glass. Carrie was telling Yvette about the original oil painting of the pyramidal sixth hole at Palmetto Hall hanging over the desk. Idly he wondered where his father and Tamara were. Copping a quick feel?

Feeling suddenly disloyal, he hid his discomfiture by gulping down the rest of his brandy. They weren't lovers. They couldn't be. His father had drilled into him never to mix business with pleasure. But the memory of Harland skimming his lips across her temple at the dinner table gave the lie to his wishful thinking. The tender look she'd given him in return twisted something in Simon's gut.

Dammit, was he jealous of his own father? Tamara Hart had gotten under his skin as soon as they'd met, with that unguarded look of vulnerability before she'd become the cool professional again. He remembered the slick look of her upper lip after she'd sipped the wine, the way her tongue unconsciously licked it. Her softly curling hair had his hands clenching and unclenching with the urge to run his fingers through it.

What was the matter with him? He'd vowed never to let a woman take over his sanity after Carrie. But damn, Tamara looked delectable. Whenever she'd leaned forward to take a bite, his eyes had snapped to her of their own volition to see how much more cleavage she would show. When she reached for her wineglass, the movement rearranged the soft mounds of her breasts until his blood heated. As it was heating now. He poured another belt of brandy to quash the urge to fuck his father's doxy.

From the corner of his eye he saw Marta bearing down on him.

"Jack drinks too much," the controller said bluntly.

Simon stared in disgust at his snifter. Was he getting like his brother? He set it on the mantel, untouched. The mention of Jack forcibly reminded Simon that he'd been more preoccupied with a sexpot than with what had happened between his father and brother. "If he raises a hand to Dad again—"

"He doesn't mean it."

"Maybe when he's sober he doesn't. Which is when? Tuesday mornings in leap year?"

Marta was silent a moment. "It had to have been eating away at him."

"More likely what's eating away at him is cirrhosis of the liver. You could navigate by the road maps in his eyes."

"Simon, you're a compassionate man, put yourself in his—"

Simon snorted. "Sorry, Marta. I'm all out of compassion. Ever since Kevin—"

He jerked away. Undaunted, Marta maneuvered around to face him. "We all face losses," she said, her voice softer than he'd ever heard it. "Harland with Addy, you with Kevin. Even I've had—" Her voice broke. She changed direction. "Don't you think Jack's suffered for ten years knowing what he did? Do you think that maybe he's been afraid to be a leader because this kind of disclosure would bring him to his knees?"

Grudgingly, Simon looked at her. She had a point.

"Put yourself in his place. Why build something up when you know that some day, everything will explode in your face?"

Simon's voice rumbled with controlled anger. "I remember when he sold that MG. Said he got rid of it because a Porsche could turn more female heads. If he'd taken responsibility at twenty-eight, been a man—"

Those last words echoed in Simon's head. Who was he to talk about being a man? He hadn't been able to get it up since

Kevin died. Hadn't wanted to, until now. With a blonde sexpot who probably notched her bedpost with every conquest.

Dammit, they were talking about Jack, not about him. "If something happens to Dad, Jack will answer to me."

Simon watched his brother turn to Carrie, standing near the door. He looked like W. C. Fields on a good day with all the red capillaries along his nose. "He isn't capable of anything except—"

The rest of Simon's sentence died. The look Carrie and Jack exchanged curdled the brandy in Simon's stomach. Had his *brother* been fucking the mother of his son the night Kevin died?

Simon's attention was distracted when the pocket doors to the study rolled open and Harland entered. Against his will, Simon's gaze roamed behind Harland, searching for the woman who had put fire and blood in his cock. Tamara swung into the room, chin high, lips trembling. Determination, fear and vulnerability vied for dominance on her face.

Her eyes met his. Across the room he felt her I-dare-you challenge. Her nostrils flared like a filly eager to have her head to race whatever obstacle course faced her.

Swung. It took a moment for Simon's bedazzled mind to register the fact that her shoulders were hunched up, pulling the material of her blue bodice up to cradle her breasts even higher. He wrenched his gaze from her bosom and skimmed down the red sticks she was leaning on.

Crutches.

Down to her shapely—

Simon swallowed hard. Tamara had only one leg.

Chapter Five

✂

Simon's gaze skittered around the room. No one else had noticed Tamara yet. He had the insane urge to protect this magnificent, vulnerable woman from what she apparently already knew was in store for her, judging by the defiant jut of her jaw.

He could read it in her combative expression. Love me, love my stump. No wonder she'd erected such a shield! He focused an intense stare at her, hoping to convey what he couldn't put into words—that he knew all about pain, rejection, despair.

Her eyes widened in awareness. Then her mouth softened, parted to reveal the tip of a pink tongue that flicked nervously across her full lower lip. Her gaze dropped to his mouth. If he wasn't fifteen feet away, if others weren't in the room, he'd be at her side in two seconds. His fingers would capture her jaw, he'd lower his head, graze that soft, yielding mouth with his. He could almost hear a husky moan rising deep in her throat as he yanked up her skirts and stuck his cock inside her.

From his peripheral vision Simon saw Jack, deep in an argument with Carrie, fling out his hands. Jack pivoted angrily on his heel—and slammed into Tamara. The blood running heavy in Simon's veins dulled his reflexes, so that all he could do was croak, "Watch out—!"

Her crutches clattered to the floor. She fell backward.

Tamara landed on her coccyx bone and right forearm. Pain shot through her spine, her elbow. Detested tears sprang to her eyes. She'd fallen so often while learning how to walk with the prosthesis that she should be used to it. But she'd never get used to the utter shame of it, the feeling of helplessness, the vulnerability of a gimp in a two-legged world.

And, damn his hide, she'd never forgive Simon Sutcliffe for seducing her with his eyes, for taking away for the tiniest moment—just long enough to wreak havoc—the chip on her shoulder that kept the vulnerability at bay.

"Haven't you ever seen a woman fall down before?"

Her quivery question shocked her audience into embarrassed shuffling as Simon knelt before her. "Let me help you up."

"Don't touch me," she hissed.

Unintimidated, he placed his hands under her arms and lifted her effortlessly then eased her weight onto her good right leg. Regaining her balance, she reached for the crutches Harland held out to her. She couldn't, wouldn't think about Simon's big hands in such intimate contact with her bare underarms, pressing against the sides of her breasts. Impatiently she waited for him to withdraw, so she could put the impersonal titanium shafts in the place where warm, living hands caressed her.

"Move it," she barked, disturbed that her voice came out no stronger than a whisper.

His hands slowly slid down to her waist, leaving a trail of fire no less burning than his gaze. She tucked her left crutch first, giving her needed balance. With her right hand she swung the other crutch with all her strength. It smacked against his anklebone. "I said move," she gritted between clenched teeth.

A startled look flashed across Simon's face. Then he smiled a smile that said, "You're playing with fire and you know it." Its heat transmitted itself down to her phantom toes and all but melted her crutches before she managed to turn her gaze.

"Well, what d'ya know. Li'l brother got the hots for the broad who's going to screw us all."

"Shut up, Jack." Simon threw him a scathing glance.

"Going to make the same mistake again, li'l brother? Big tits, great ass, you gonna—"

Simon slammed Jack into the wall, pinned him there with strong hands around his neck. "I said, shut up."

"Having a woman like Carrie in your bed wasn't enough?"

"I wouldn't have Carrie in my bed again if she was the last woman on earth and my cock was as hard as those crutches."

"We've lost sight of the point of all this, haven't we?"

Harland's voice cut through the red haze in Simon's brain. He abruptly released Jack, who slumped halfway to the floor before snagging onto Elliott's helping hand.

"If you'll all take a seat." Harland sounded like the chairman of the board calling a meeting to order. Which, Simon realized, he was.

"Ah, the coffee." Harland opened his arms in a welcoming gesture to Ilya, who wheeled in the cart containing a silver urn and delicate cups. Danuta scurried around, serving coffee and petit fours. Then they withdrew.

Harland sat behind his desk. The others settled around the room. Only Tamara stood. Defiantly, proudly, on one high-heeled leg and two crutches, positioned at Harland's right hand. Simon thought he'd never seen anyone so magnificent. Her impenetrable façade was back, the chip on her shoulder plainly visible in the pugnacious thrust of her jaw, the hard stare at anyone who dared look at her with pity or distaste. Her blonde hair tumbled about her face in tantalizing disarray. Her cheeks were stained like summer peaches, a sensuous contrast to her earlier pale state when he thought she was going to faint.

Harland touched each guest with his trenchant gaze. "I paid Tamara's hospital bills, her college expenses, through a bank intermediary. I kept in touch with her by a post office box. It was no coincidence that I chose her as consultant." Harland let that sink in a moment. "And I'm changing my will."

Jack's cup clattered against the saucer. "What? Why?"

"When your mother died, she left you and your brother each twenty shares." Left unsaid was the further division of some of those shares. "I've decided to redistribute my forty percent of the holding company. I'm also restructuring the voting so that it takes a seventy percent vote of shares to go forward."

"This is the first I heard of it," Elliott said mildly. "Are you sure you've thought out all of the ramifications?"

"I have, and I'm prepared to go ahead."

Jack's face took on the pasty sheen of the china cups.

"We should discuss this first thing in the morning," Elliott said. "I can clear my calendar and see you at eight."

"I'm busy then." Harland turned to Tamara and smiled. "Tamara's going to show me her development ideas. We'll be on horseback most of the morning." He reached for the day planner on his desk. "How's four o'clock tomorrow afternoon?"

A look of annoyance flashed across Elliott's face but was quickly subdued. "That's fine. My office?"

"What are you doing with the shares?" Jack demanded. His fingers trembled and he clenched them into fists.

"A good question. What I have in mind is—" Harland paused dramatically, "ten shares to Simon, ten shares to you, and twenty shares to Tamara."

"What?" Jack shot to his feet. "Just because—" His face darkened. If looks could kill, Harland would be slumping in his chair.

"Harland, please," said Tamara. "Don't cause trouble in your family on my account. I'm flattered, but you've already done more than enough. I'll manage."

"I'll manage," Jack mimicked in a falsetto. "How long have you been scheming to get your hands on Harland's money? You've been sucking up to him for six months now. You must be a damn good fuck to have him give you twenty percent of two hundred million dollars."

"You moron," Tamara shot back. She hobbled around Harland's desk, perched on the edge near Jack's chair, set her crutches aside and yanked up her skirt. Holding her truncated leg with both hands, she said with barely suppressed fury, "Do you think this—" and she waved it in front of his face, "can get me twenty percent of anything, never mind two hundred million dollars? Just because you think with your cock, do you believe everyone else does?"

Jack scraped his chair back, a look of horror on his face.

"That's right, run. I can see it in your expression. You're not thinking, 'Jesus, I did that to her.' You're thinking, 'I tried for six months to get in that broad's pants. Thank God I didn't succeed.' Am I right? Dammit, am I right?"

Jack bolted for the door, his hands to his mouth.

With a mixture of satisfaction and revulsion on her face, Tamara watched him go. Then, as if remembering she had an audience, she raked her skirt down and picked up her crutches. "If you'll excuse me, it's been a long day and I'm tired." She swung herself toward the door, stopped and shot back, "Besides, it takes twice as long to climb the steps with one leg."

Harland had the grace to look abashed. After all, he'd forced her to expose herself.

Every eye in the room was riveted on Tamara's exit.

After a brief silence, Harland spoke. "Simon, would you bring Jack back? We're not finished with our board meeting."

Simon's conscience warred within him. He wanted to follow Tamara upstairs, to comfort her, to say she wasn't as alone as she thought. But he also knew that his father had provoked this scene for a reason. A desperate reason. And he intuited that Harland indeed had had, if not a heart attack, some intimation of mortality. Suddenly he was afraid of losing his father.

* * * * *

Goddamn him! Goddamn Harland, and Simon and Jack, and the whole rotten bunch of them!

Tears of fury burning the backs of her eyes, Tamara at last reached the relative safety of the guestroom. If Harland had wanted to show Jack what he'd done to her, he'd succeeded— in spades. And his goddamn sidekick son played right along, luring her with hot, amber eyes to get her to lower her defenses then—crack! Leaving her without a leg to stand on. Literally.

She didn't know which embarrassed her more, her unexpectedly hungry reaction to Simon's lustful look, or falling flat on her ass in front of all those people.

She'd forgotten how difficult it was to climb steps without her prosthesis. In Philadelphia she'd lived in an elevator building. The bungalow on the golf course grounds had only one step to the porch. Gingerly she lowered herself onto the double bed. Her back ached from the fall. She felt bruised all over.

No, dammit, it was her psyche that was bruised. The nerve of him! Studly boy-toy. She didn't want Simon's pity. Did he think she'd be grateful for the attention of a handsome man?

Why was she even thinking of that barbarian who may or may not be in the process of being divorced? And why had he shaved off his mustache and beard? To give him a veneer of civilization? She could at least bear his presence when he'd looked like a werewolf. Clean-shaven, he disturbed her on a number of levels that she didn't want to examine too closely.

Her high-heeled prosthesis on the floor near her overnight bag caught her attention. Ilya must have brought it up after Harland had cajoled her into removing it. She should just put it on, walk out of here, get in her Miata, and never come back.

Hell. Yvette had picked her up. She'd have to get someone to drive her home.

She'd known. Yvette had known something was going to happen tonight. "Oh, it'll be fun to stay over," she'd said. "I'll drive my Acura, because there's more room for our dresses." How transparent it all seemed in retrospect.

She didn't want any part of this gothic-Southern family. She just wanted to be left alone to lick her wounds.

As she'd been alone for the past ten years. Her stepfather had all but disowned her when he'd discovered how maimed she'd become—until her stepbrother had informed him of the anonymous payments she'd been receiving. Then he came sniffing around looking for a share. Thank God her mother had died not knowing what a lazy bastard Ike MacKinnon was.

Tamara shuddered. If he found out she stood to inherit twenty percent of a two-hundred-million-dollar development project, he'd be on her neck night and day.

But it wouldn't happen any time soon. Harland was a very robust sixty-six.

With all the new bruises, she hoped she could stay on a horse. Learning to ride had been part of her therapy and she'd had a leg made specifically for it, thanks to Harland.

Wearily she sat at the dressing table to remove her makeup then hopped into the bathroom to wash her face and brush her teeth. She slipped a Nature Conservancy T-shirt over her head and climbed between lavender-smelling sheets.

Sleep eluded her. It must have been a good two hours later when she heard Yvette in the adjoining bathroom. Then it was quiet again. Tamara strained to hear footsteps in the hallway.

God, who was she listening for? Had she had some vague expectation that Simon had stayed the night in his father's house and that he planned to sneak in and make good on the promise in his eyes by ravaging her?

The very idea that she could think such a thing angered her.

So did the fact that he hadn't done as she'd expected.

* * * * *

"Another nightcap?"

"No, I'm fine, Dad. Go to bed."

Harland rose from the wing chair in his study and bade him goodnight. Simon knew his father was comfortable having him stay alone and drink his fifty-year-old brandy, or go home, or sleep in the study or in his old bedroom.

The meeting hadn't lasted long after Tamara left. Dad had been intractable. Simon had been surprised at the vehemence with which Marta took Jack's side. Elliott, while remaining aloof, had seemed stunned that his client could be changing his will without consulting him, especially on top of the revelation about his financial support of Tamara over the past ten years. Harland in effect had told them that he didn't trust his own lawyer.

Simon brooded about that a moment. Did he trust Elliott? He hadn't had time to review the books on his investments under Elliott's stewardship, but he sure as hell hadn't gotten Simon the divorce. Was Elliott on his side or Carrie's?

Damn, he didn't want to think about Carrie. He wanted to think about the blonde whose vulnerability had reached out to him, whose mouth had softened at his look, whose brutally mutilated body was, at this very moment, lying in the spindle bed his mother had found on one of her forays to a country auction.

His blood quickened at the thought of Tamara's long, thick hair fanned out on a satin pillow, her smooth ivory skin naked under cool sheets, her breasts heavy in his hands, her nipples hardening under his tongue. He would start at her neck. No, behind her ear, and kiss and lick his way down her shoulders, through the valley between her exquisite breasts, squeeze and suck them. He'd move to her impossibly tiny waist, her navel. Then he'd discover if she was a real blonde, tangle his fingers in the hair that surrounded her pussy, then dip his head down and lick her clit—

Christ, he was as hard as a five-iron. What on earth was he thinking of? That woman had such a wall of ice around her, a dozen volcanoes couldn't shake it apart.

Ah, but what lava could flow. With that thought he vaulted out of his chair and strode out to the hallway. He took the stairs two at a time and headed straight to the doorway behind which the spindle bed stood.

Where Tamara lay.

Was she sleeping? Was she dreaming of him plunging his cock in and out of her wet pussy? Or was she, like he, restlessly awake and thinking of what might be?

He rested his head against the doorjamb, caressed the smooth cherrywood, wishing it were the curve of her sweet ass. His hand hovered an inch above the doorknob. This room had no lock, he knew. Should he?

Damn, he must be as drunk as Jack. His father's mistress. With an effort he pushed himself away from Tamara's doorway and stumbled down the hall to his old room.

* * * * *

"I don't like it, Elliott. You have to drag your feet on this will business."

Marta paced her sitting room in front of Elliott, who sat motionless on her mildly shabby sofa. "We simply have to change his mind. All the work, all our plans, the carefully cultivated contacts, everything's down the drain if he follows through."

"He'll never sign the papers," Elliott said.

Marta stopped her pacing, held her breath.

"There's too much at stake." Elliott stood, his eyes narrowing. "We'll have to consider more drastic measures than trying to talk some sense into him."

"Like what?"

A look passed between them. Marta knew Elliott felt as strongly as she did that Jack's plan was the right one. She also knew how much money Elliott stood to make on the deal. "I'll do anything you need me to do," she said. "Anything."

"I know," he said softly. "I'm counting on it."

Chapter Six

෨

"Thanks, Cliff. I haven't ridden Blackwing for a while. I hope he's not too feisty today."

The groom held the bridle while Harland mounted the gelding. "He'll be all right, Mr. Sutcliffe. Just give him his head in the jumps. He don't like to be led by the nose."

Harland covertly studied the nineteen-year-old. He could use some polishing. But his Aunt Marta wasn't exactly a paragon of charm herself. Thick-necked and sturdy like her, with dark brown hair falling in unwashed clumps over brown eyes, Cliff Johnson walked with a slouch and took his sweet time about everything.

Harland watched him help Tamara mount Jet Star. After the bruises she must have suffered last night in her fall, he wondered whether Cliff should have given her a less spirited mare.

She'd emphatically denied that anything hurt. If he'd learned one thing about Tamara, it was that she gave no quarter when challenged. The way she'd put Jack in his place had been magnificent. The confrontation only solidified his decision.

A slap on Blackwing's rump sent the horse into a trot. Tamara followed, looking quite fetching in snug black pants and riding boots, and a blue crewneck sweater that exactly matched the brilliant October sky as well as her eyes. They rode along a hard-packed trail through fragrant pitch pine forest. In the distance a woodpecker signaled in an avian Morse code. Blue jays squabbled nearby. Now and again they caught a glimpse of a chipmunk or pine vole.

"Cliff's a little sullen today, don't you think?" she asked.

"He's a good kid. Just needs some direction. Don't forget, he's been in foster care since his parents died, then that special school. Even though Marta, as his only living relative, adopted him, he probably feels strange."

"No wonder."

Harland chuckled. "Go ahead and say it. I know Marta is abrasive. To have a teenager thrust on you when you're on the wrong side of fifty must have been tough for her. She just doesn't like to show any of the softer emotions that women do."

"Is he dyslexic?"

"No, just a slow learner. He's doing fine at the stables full-time. He seemed to like it when he was here last summer."

"You're a kind man to give him a job."

"Hell, Marta is like family. She's been with us forever. She came here before the boys graduated high school."

After riding the path a while, Tamara led Jet Star through a clearing in the trees. "This is where I think the nine-hole course could go. There's a natural flow to the land, where the swampy lowland could be the rough, and enough high ground for Rees Jones or Gary Player to do a first-class design." They picked their way through the site, Tamara explaining, Harland nodding in appreciation. She'd done her homework.

Back on the trail, she led him to where the million-dollar homes might be situated, each with a view of either a current tee or green or the proposed nine-hole course. She pointed out what should remain open space and why, giving Yvette, as the Nature Conservancy's attorney, full credit for input.

They had been out about three hours when Harland reined in at a meandering cedar-tinted creek. They dismounted and ground-tied their horses, which immediately began lapping the cool water.

"I had Danuta pack lunch," he said, lifting saddlebags from Blackwing's withers. He led the way to a couple of large, smooth stones in a pocket of warm sunshine and unpacked a thermos of lemonade, a wedge of brie, Hoboken baguettes and several perfectly ripe pears. They ate leisurely, enjoying the smells of rich decaying leaf mold and autumn air, the scurrying sounds of small animals, and the occasional call of a pine warbler or towhee.

At length Harland broke the companionable silence. "I want you to reunite my sons."

Tamara's face showed her surprise. "Me? How?"

"My telegram may have brought Simon back home, but you've brought him back to life." He silenced her protest with a wave of his hand. "I've seen the looks he's given you. You've also ignited a spark in Jack, however misdirected it is. At least he's thinking about fighting for something he believes in, instead of going with the flow." He reached into a shirt pocket and withdrew a folded sheet of paper. "These reallocated shares—"

"Harland, I absolutely refuse to accept them. You're going against four generations of tradition."

"The tradition is for the oldest son to inherit the golf course. Just the land. Still, if I had it to do over, I'd have given each of them half, let them know they had to work equally hard," Harland said, a wistful note in his voice. "My own father set great store by tradition. As do I. Because of that, Jack just coasted through life, thinking the golf course was the whole ball of wax. What neither of my sons realized until their personalities were formed was that the holding company actually has all the power. Hence the judicious allocation of shares."

When she nodded in understanding, he continued. "Together they'll hold fifty percent of the shares. They'll need twenty more to do anything. You won't vote for Jack's sardine plan. I think Jack made a deal with Marta, so she won't side with Simon. Simon will vote the opposite of Carrie."

He handed her the paper. "There's all the permutations. The only thing that makes sense is Jack-Simon-Tamara. I'm counting on you to get Simon and Jack to agree to your plan."

"I don't see how that's possible after last night."

"Ah, yes, last night. What a temper!"

Tamara turned away, but not before he saw two bright spots of color bloom on her cheeks. "I have a habit of engaging my mouth before my brain."

"An attribute to be admired. You speak from the heart."

"I get in trouble that way," she said ruefully.

"I made another codicil that I didn't mention last night." Tamara's wary glance made him chuckle. "No one will take umbrage. I've not reduced anyone's inheritance or put anyone else out. It has to do with the place you're staying in."

The five-room bungalow, situated between a soybean field and an Atlantic white cedar forest, had been part of the farm that Harland bought, which contained his residence and Simon's carriage house. "Neither Jack's plan nor yours calls for building anything in place of it. So I have granted you life rights."

Her eyes widened. "Oh, I couldn't! You've done too much for me already."

"Please indulge an old man. No matter what you do in the future, whether you marry or move away or buy a house, you will always have this to come back to."

Tamara's eyes shimmered with tears. "Thank you. I've come to love it here. The sundews in the bogs, wild blueberries growing outside my door. Where else can you find seeds that won't sprout without a fierce fire to wake them up?"

"Have you ever seen a Pine Barrens fire?"

"No." She shivered as a cloud covered the sun.

"My grounds manager does controlled burnings in winter. If you get rid of the dry understorey—pine needles and leaves on the forest floor, the shrubs like sheep laurel and huckleberry—it makes the woods safer against fires started by careless visitors. Around here, fires can jump a mile."

"With all the underground water, you'd think there wouldn't be any fires."

"To the contrary. Drainage is so good through the Cohansey soil that water doesn't stay on the surface to keep the fallen leaves damp. Only place there's water is the bogs, where the water table is close to the surface." Harland's expression turned serious. "If you're ever caught in a fire, either try to go through it and get onto burned ground, or look for Atlantic white cedar. They like wet feet. You might be able to survive in the water."

Tamara rubbed her arms briskly. "It's too nice a day to think about fires."

Gazing into the distance, Harland was silent for a long moment. "Addy and I had a daughter two years before the twins. She died before they were born. They probably never even think about Kathye. But I do."

He let out a sigh. "All those long hours in the hospital, talking to you when you were unconscious, making you fight, watching you struggle underneath all those wires and machines, I kept thinking about Kathye, about how we'd been given a second chance. Because of Jack's involvement, Addy wouldn't let me disclose our identity. But we followed your progress keenly. When you finally decided to go to college, we rejoiced. When you graduated with honors, we celebrated.

"Before Addy died, she made me promise to take care of you, to treat you as our daughter." His voice broke on the word. "It's been a great joy to watch you at work. Your presentation yesterday made me very proud."

Tamara's brows furrowed. "But I don't understand. Why couldn't you just proceed with the plan? You're the chairman.

Between you and Simon, you have sixty percent of the votes. Why all these machinations with stock?"

He stared at her, letting her brain find the answer.

"Oh," she said. "It's Jack's future. You're forcing him to make decisions."

"Yes. Jack has always known he'd run the course. Although I wonder how much tradition means to him. I think he's being manipulated. He believes the five-thousand-condo plan is his idea, but I don't think he's in control."

"So you're using me to flush out the bad guy."

"As a catalyst, not a target." He packed the remnants of lunch back into the saddlebags and stood, scanning the cloudless sky. "I'm glad I didn't tell Elliott one o'clock. I may not even get there by four."

"I imagine he wasn't too happy to hear you'd made such momentous plans without consulting him."

"Elliott's not the only lawyer in New Jersey," he said cryptically. He didn't tell her what he'd recently learned about Elliott or the other reason he wanted to change his will.

They returned to their horses and mounted. Harland gave Blackwing his head, as Cliff had suggested. The spirited gelding surged forward, eager to run. Harland threw back his head and laughed as they galloped, Tamara slightly behind and to his left, her blonde braid flying, through tree-tunnels into sun-dappled shade and, at last, into the narrow chute punctuated by a series of jumps requiring steel-nerve timing. The first two were adjustable-height wooden fences, the last was the stone hedge marking the original property line of the farm.

"Last one over cooks dinner," he shouted over his shoulder.

At that Tamara spurred Jet Star while Harland drew back slightly on Blackwing's reins. He wanted them to take the jumps as equal partners, the way he and Addy had. White hair rumpled by the breeze, eyes alive with the sheer joy of living, he leaned forward into the jump, lifting himself off the saddle with his powerful legs. Blackwing landed perfectly. With his peripheral vision Harland noted Jet Star did the same.

Preparing for the second jump, Tamara leaned forward, aware that her form wasn't as polished as Harland's, aware that her stump throbbed. She had to be crazy to be jumping so recklessly after her fall last night. She hoped the Velcro glued to her left boot would adhere to its teeth in the stirrup.

A sliver of flashing light in front of the fence caught her attention just before she felt Jet Star's forelegs jerk. Then time seemed to stand still. She saw Blackwing buck and stumble. Harland hurtled forward like a bullet. His horse landed with a loud whinny on his forelegs, pitched forward before regaining his balance, then shied sideways and limped off into the woods.

Jet Star's rear legs caught the top board of the jump. Tamara could feel the mare twisting, horse and rider falling to their left. Frantically she tried to pull her feet out of the stirrups. Her left leg didn't obey the phantom command. With her left hand she jerked her boot free of the Velcro just as horse and rider landed in the forest humus. Jet Star's full weight fell on her short leg.

She must have fainted from the sharp stab of pain, because she gradually became aware of several things. Shivers racked her, the sun had disappeared below the trees, and silence surrounded her like a shroud. Tamara took stock of her condition. She lay on her left side, her throbbing cheek cushioned on layers of decaying leaves. Taking a cautious deep breath, she decided no ribs had been broken. She flexed her fingers. They worked. Her stump felt caught in a vise. Gingerly she raised herself on an elbow.

"Harland? Harland, are you all right?"

He lay unmoving, his neck wedged at an unnatural angle against the stone hedge.

"Harland!" She flipped onto her knees. Pain shot through her stump. Dragging her left leg, she maneuvered on her right knee and her arms, thanking every curl, every push-up she'd ever done to strengthen her upper-body muscles for the times when she needed crutches. She touched his cheek with a finger.

Harland's eyes flickered open. "You're okay," he rasped.

Tears blurred Tamara's vision. "Harland. I thought—" She clamped down on what she'd thought, afraid that giving voice to her worst fears would make them come true.

"Twins. Work together. Tell them."

"You're going to be fine. You'll tell them yourself."

"Need—help."

"Hang on. I'll be right back."

She scrambled to her feet. The pain in her stump caused her knees to buckle. She sank to the ground. The prosthesis. The space-age material could stand a lot of abuse, but twelve hundred pounds of horseflesh must have bent the socket out of shape. She touched the area. Her pants were wet. Blood. It wouldn't be the first time.

But she had no time to coddle herself. Harland needed help.

She tried to remember the lay of the land. The jumps were three quarters around the perimeter of the golf course from the stables. She thought the trail passed within yards of the seventeenth hole. Maybe there were still diehard golfers trying to finish before dark. With a last worried glance at Harland, she began crawling on hands and knees.

The stone hedge was about three feet high. Hoisting herself up with her arms, she managed to flop her bleeding left leg over the top, then her right. Then she was crawling again, her prosthesis dragging uselessly behind her. The light was going. The reds and yellows of sunset had transmuted to mauves and purples. God, no fool could still be playing.

Yes, they could, she told herself with a grim smile. There was no fool like a golfing fool. She'd seen them in snow, in hail, in wind that could rip a toupee off a man's head. She just prayed there were some fools there tonight.

A bobbing light caught her attention. A golf cart!

"Help!" She scrambled to a tree and clawed her way to a standing position. The pain in her stump almost knocked her back down. Tears scalded her eyes. "Help!"

The light made an arc, aimed toward her. She hopped to the middle of the trail, waved her arms, yelled again.

Then she fainted.

Simon jumped off the cart and ran toward Tamara's slumped form. His quick but thorough scrutiny noted blood seeping down the abraded left side of her face, dirt and leaves adhering to her clothing. She'd probably been thrown and Dad had gone for help. Dammit, she shouldn't have been riding in the first place.

He knelt at her side. Then he saw more blood. Her pant leg was saturated with it.

She moaned.

"Tamara, what happened?"

"Harland..." Her eyes tried to focus on his face. "We got thrown. Harland. By...stone wall. Get...help..."

"How bad is he hurt?"

"Neck...don't know."

He dashed to the cart. Thank God he'd taken Jack's, with the built-in cellular phone. He called 9-1-1, barked out orders, then called the pro shop and issued terse directions.

When Harland hadn't shown up for his appointment, Elliott had called Simon. His father was never late for a meeting. It had given Simon a funny feeling in the pit of his stomach, so he'd gone looking.

71

Tamara was struggling to sit up when he returned to her. Ignoring her groan of pain, he lifted her into his arms, strode to the cart, and settled her into the passenger seat. Then he pressed the throttle and ate up the distance at full speed. He killed the battery, vaulted over the stone fence.

"Dad!" He knelt down at his father's side, placed his lips on his father's cold cheek. Harland lay motionless under his lips. Simon pressed two fingers to his father's carotid artery. No pulse.

"No-o-o-o-o!" His cry was that of a wounded animal. Not his father too! Not so soon after losing Kevin! He wanted to give him CPR, but the angle of his neck told him it would be useless. "Dad," he whispered. Tears fell unheeded down his cheeks, splashed on his father's cold body.

The touch of a hand on his shoulder made him jump. He spun around, knocking the hand away. Tamara was on her knees beside him, her face tortured.

"You goaded him, didn't you," he spat out. "You made him ride too hard. Probably challenged him to beat you, a challenge you knew he couldn't resist." He streaked a hand across his face impatiently. It came away wet. "You killed him."

"You're wrong," she said, her voice ragged. She reached out to him again. "Neither of us knew —"

"Don't touch me!" He jumped to his feet and loomed over her. "You think because you're handicapped that I'll overlook it? Damn you to hell. If there is such a thing as hell." He didn't think so. He'd already had a hell on earth when Kevin died, and having his father die like this proved his premise. Hell was right here, right now. Hell was a woman who made him start to feel again, who made him think with his cock when he should have been watching out for his father. *Dammit, Dad had had a premonition. Why else would he have called me back?*

The chug-chug of the rotor blades claimed his attention. In the glare of lights the Medevac landed just the other side of the stone fence. EMTs jumped out and went into action.

Simon grabbed Tamara by one arm, yanked her upright. With a cry of pain she reached out to him for balance, but he seized both her upper arms and carried her away from Harland, set her down roughly to brace against a tree. "You stay away from him. It's too late to show your concern."

The chopper's lights limned the unscathed side of her face. He saw her lower lip tremble, saw her thick lashes spiked by tears. He didn't believe a bit of it. Acting. She was acting. Just like Carrie. He'd been a sucker for a woman again and had caught it on the chin. Shit. He was no better than Jack. Each of them with an Achilles' heel. Jack with the bottle, him with a vulnerable woman.

Vulnerable? He snorted. The woman had probably used her disability to worm her way into Dad's confidence, certainly into his pocketbook. Twenty percent. God, it was enough to make him want to vote his shares with Carrie.

What the hell was the matter with him? His father had just died at the hands of that woman and he was thinking about shares of stock! Why hadn't he stayed in Kamchatka? At least there he knew what was expected of him. Work, sleep. Work, sleep. No emotion. No feeling. No pain.

No love. No father's choked-up voice calling him Son. No arm around his shoulder speaking volumes of love without words. Dad. His father was gone. He hadn't told him that he loved him.

* * * * *

The interested bystander had long since blended into the darkening woods. Although the wire had tripped the horses, Harland had made it easy. His neck was already broken from the fall. All it needed was another yank, and crack! The sound of it had provided a thrill that would never be forgotten.

Harland had been eliminated with a very clever "accident". Luckily he hadn't signed his new will yet. They'd been in time.

But the woman. She had survived. She needed some other kind of accident or she'd screw up the whole thing.

Tamara Hart would get hers. And soon.

Chapter Seven

ဢ

The runny piece of fried egg fell off Ike MacKinnon's fork onto the cracked plate as he stared, mouth open, at the picture of Tamara Hart. Then he turned the newspaper around. "Hey, Vinnie, is that your cunt of a sister on the front page?"

"I keep telling you, Pa, my name is Vincent."

Eyes narrowed, Ike studied the boy combing his hair in the mirror over the kitchen sink. The spitting image of himself thirty years ago—sandy hair, bedroom eyes, thin blade of a nose. Medium height, average build. Of course, Vinnie didn't have the meat on him that bricklaying and beer put on a guy. Or the hard edge that living on unemployment honed. "You may be twenty-four, but you're still my boy. I'll call you Vinnie if I want."

He scooped up the egg and shoved it into his mouth along with a chunk of fried pork roll. "Take a look at this story."

Vincent slipped the comb into the back pocket of his tight jeans, sauntered over to the table, and picked up the paper. "Yeah, that's her, all right."

"Think that's the guy that's been sending her money?"

"Could be."

Ike watched his son grope for the chair to sit down. As Ike had predicted, the story had snagged his attention immediately and he began reading aloud.

"'NOTED PHILANTHROPIST DIES IN FALL

"'Harland Sutcliffe, 66, died yesterday as a result of a riding accident on a horse trail, part of a private golf course owned by the deceased. With him at the time of the accident was Tamara Hart, 29, a consultant who resides on the premises.'"

Vincent snorted. "Consultant. Hah! That's a euphemism."

"What's a you-you—?"

"Euphemism. It means a nice word for something else."

A cruel grin twisted Ike's mouth. "Like 'cunt' is a euphemism for 'daughter'?"

"Step-daughter," Vincent corrected.

"Whatever. I took her and her Ma in when they had nothing, and look at the thanks I get. Not a single dollar for her old man all those years since her accident." Ike shuddered. She'd been in rehab for months, then refused to come back home, not that he could have stood it. The remembered sight of Tamara hopping around on one leg made him ill. She'd rented a room with some family the hospital found for her when she started college in Philly. He hadn't gone to see her until she'd gotten a new leg and looked halfway normal. One thing he did miss was her cooking. Another was watching her bodacious tits bounce and sway.

He absently rubbed the sagging flesh protruding between his T-shirt and pants. He knew he deserved a better hand than life had dealt him. And that ungrateful little cunt might just deal him a new one—a good one.

Vincent continued reading. "'Miss Hart was injured in the fall from her own horse.' Can you believe she's riding horses?"

"She always had a mind of her own. Never paid me no mind." It pissed Ike off to think it. When he started sniffing around, she must have been fifteen, sixteen, and ripe as a New York call girl. He used to get such a hard-on just watching her on her knees pulling weeds out in the garden, her ass in snug jeans begging for him to grab, he'd have to jerk himself off. One day she'd kicked him in the balls and threatened to kill him if he ever stuck his hand inside her blouse again.

But that was all in the past. Ike turned his attention to the future. "I been to The Pines once after she moved there. It costs a pretty penny to join. What's it say about a funeral?"

Vincent scanned the article. "Doesn't. Says private services at the convenience of the family."

"Huh." Ike scooped the yolk up with the last piece of toast and shoved it into his mouth. "Looks like I gotta pay my daughter a little visit."

"Let me do it, Pa. She'll at least talk to me."

Ike scowled. The little bugger was right. If Ike was dying in a desert, Tamara wouldn't give him so much as a jigger of water. But maybe Vinnie could weasel something out of her. Growing up she'd had a soft spot in her heart for her younger brother. Vinnie used to run sniveling to her when he'd beat the shit out of him for not obeying fast enough.

Yeah, let them talk about old times. If Vinnie had inherited his old man's golden tongue, and he knew that he had, he'd talk her right out of anything Sutcliffe had given her. But Ike knew it wouldn't be enough for the way she'd treated him.

* * * * *

"Just what the hell were you trying to prove yesterday?"

Tamara's eyes jerked open. Simon noted with grim satisfaction her flicker of fear, of guilt, at his belligerent voice. Then her face shuttered. Even supine on the hospital bed early in the morning, her shoulders under the sheet seemed to square as if to balance the ever-present chip that, he thought, could power a nuclear submarine.

"Get out of here," she gritted out.

"Not until I get some answers."

Standing at the foot of her bed, Simon took in her condition at a glance. A raspberry-hued blotch covered her left cheek. Her eyes had the heavy-lidded look of sleep. The skin under them was the color of wet cement. A bandage like a tonsure held down her hair. The sheet vividly outlined the contour of her legs, one creating a tent where her toes stuck up, the other stopping abruptly a few inches below her knee.

The other bed was empty but rumpled. Its occupant might return at any time. He wanted to get this over with before they had an audience.

"Visiting hours start at one o'clock." Her eyes flashed fire.

"Tough. I want to know exactly what happened yesterday."

"Ask Lieutenant Kyrillos."

"Dammit, don't get flip with me. My father's dead because of you, and I want to know why. So I'm asking again. What the hell were you trying to do?"

"Nothing. We were just riding." A weary sigh escaped her. She turned her gaze toward the window. "Leave me alone."

He took two long steps forward. "Dammit, what did you do for five hours?"

"Get away from me!" She sat bolt upright and groped for the buzzer that would signal the nurse. The bleached white sheet fell to her waist. One tiny cap sleeve of a flimsy, peach-colored nightgown slipped off her shoulder, exposing more of her breasts than her gown had the other night.

He swallowed hard. "How can you wear stuff like that in a public place?" He didn't like the raspy sound of his voice, as though he wasn't in control of all his faculties. Well hell, he wasn't, because he wanted the gown to slip down further and show him what color her hardening nipples were.

Mentally castigating himself, he took a step back and reached again for his anger.

She jerked the sheet back up, abandoning the buzzer her fingers had just found. "It isn't public. The door was closed.

And I'll remind you again, visiting hours don't start until one o'clock. So please leave."

Her knees under the sheet shifted. Pain brought a shimmer of tears to her eyes.

Simon took a breath. Maybe his emotional pain was keeping him from seeing her physical pain. He should try to understand her point of view. Backing up to the foot of the bed, he put his palms out. "I'm sorry. Let's start again. How do you feel? Did you break anything?"

"Only my prosthesis."

"The bleeding on your leg?"

"I'm used to it. Until I got my Sabolich leg, I had raw sores every other month from the prosthesis. It'll heal."

"How long will you have to stay?"

She shrugged. The sheet slipped off her shoulder. She grabbed it and tucked it under her arms, pulling it taut across her breasts. Clenching his hands to stifle the desire to cup them, he forced his mind elsewhere. In the hallway nurses chattered, carts squeaked. The intercom paged a Doctor Goldstein. The antiseptic-pine soap smells typical of a hospital mingled in his nostrils with the residue of perfume and woman.

"Depends on the X-rays. I should know today." Her voice lowered, softened. "You have my deepest sympathies on the loss of your father. Harland was quite a man."

His father. She was the last to see him alive. Simon took a deep, steadying breath. "Was he in a great deal of pain?"

Her eyes filled with tears. "I don't think so. I—I think he must have been paralyzed. He could barely talk."

"What did he say?"

"Go get help," she said tartly.

Simon gritted his teeth. What had he expected? That Dad would have said, "Tell my son I love him?" He gave himself a mental shake. "And during the day. What did you talk about?"

"The primary purpose of the trip was to help him visualize the plans I proposed. I showed him where the housing might go, how the second course might be aligned. That kind of thing."

"How did you come to be jumping?"

Tamara's mouth moved upward in a ghost of a smile. "He said, 'Last one back cooks dinner.' And kicked Blackwing into a canter."

"And you couldn't resist the challenge."

"He was a good rider. I didn't challenge him. We were just sharing the moment."

"Why weren't you wearing helmets?"

"A lot of good it did Christopher Reeve."

He grunted. "Point taken. But my father had back problems for the past ten years. He had no business jumping."

"He was old enough to make his own decisions."

Simon glared at her. "What were you trying to prove?" He gestured to her nonexistent leg. "That you're as good with one leg as Harland was with two? That you could outride and outjump him? I'll bet he just loved it, the challenge of the chase with a beautiful woman young enough to be his daughter. One whose hospital, whose college he paid for. What else did he pay for? Was Jack right? Were you his trophy mistress?"

She grabbed the plastic glass on the nightstand, tossed it at him with impressive force. "Get out!"

The glass hit him in the chest and bounced to the floor. Water splashed a crazy design across his golf shirt under an open jacket. His eyes darkened. "You haven't seen the last of me. I'll get answers if it's the last thing you do for The Pines."

"I'm not doing anything else for The Pines," she retorted.

"The hell you won't. Marta tells me you still have one payment coming."

"If you're threatening to withhold payment, I warn you, my lawyer is better than your lawyer."

Simon fought to keep the amusement out of his eyes at the childish statement. "I'm sure you'll fulfill your commitment."

Her chin raised defiantly. "If you read the contract, you'll know I already fulfilled my commitment, which was to present my findings to the board. Let's see if you honor Harland's word by fulfilling the terms of the contract on behalf of The Pines."

"Is the publicity part of the contract?" he shot back.

"What publicity?"

"I suppose you didn't read the morning papers." He didn't even try to keep the sarcasm out of his voice.

"How could I? You woke me up."

"You're all over the front page—photograph, résumé and all. You must have a good PR agent."

"What's that supposed to mean?"

"Nothing much. It just looks like you used Dad's death to advertise that you're available to take on new clients."

She snatched the nurse's button and stabbed at it once, twice, then jammed her finger to it. "Get out, you cretin!"

"Jack asked me when you're planning to move out."

Her face turned as pale as the hospital sheet. Then she stuck out her chin and said, "As soon as I can pack. Would you please hand me my crutches?"

He felt a dangerous glint in his eyes and made no effort to hide it. "Gladly." He turned to the small closet, opened the metal door and lifted them out. Like a predator sensing a helpless prey, he stalked back to the bed, held them just out of her reach. "Here."

Her glare could have curdled milk. She had to know that he'd seen the flimsy little pieces of material clinging to her breasts. He wanted her to fling the sheet aside and grab the crutches. He wanted to see the curve of her hips, the dip of her waist under the clingy peach fabric. His eyes dared her to take the crutches and stand up.

"Get out," she whispered hoarsely.

"What's the problem, honey?" the nurse asked as she briskly entered the room. "Oh." She gave Simon a thorough once-over, then favored him with the kind of smile a hooker gives a prospect. "Visiting hours aren't until one o'clock."

"I was just leaving." He thrust the crutches at the nurse. "Your patient needs to use the bathroom." He stalked out, taking with him the image of Tamara propped up in the bed with her mouth open, those glorious breasts flushed, and daggers in her eyes.

Damn her! Damn himself for goading her, for wanting to rip the sheet off her and fuck her until—

Christ, he had to be out of his mind. The woman had just caused his father's death. Lieutenant Kyrillos had told him that sending Harland's body for an autopsy was simply a formality to verify that he died of a broken neck. But why did Hart's horse stumble too? Had she spooked?

Maybe Hart was such a poor rider that she bumped into Blackwing at the crucial instant. Maybe she couldn't control her horse because of the leg. Whatever the actual cause of the accident, the fact remained that she caused his father's death. No amount of runaway testosterone would change that fact.

He'd see that she was off the premises as soon as possible. Hell, he'd even pay someone to pack for her so she couldn't use her leg as an excuse. He wanted her out of there. Because she killed his father.

And so he wouldn't be tempted to lust after her.

* * * * *

Tamara's pulse still raced. Why couldn't Yvette have brought a flannel nightgown instead of one of the Victoria's

Secret specials that she'd splurged on after her divorce? At first Tamara had been grateful that she didn't have to wear those obscenely small hospital gowns that tied in the back and exposed half your bottom. But Yvette had less padding, and Tamara hadn't realized how much her breasts spilled out beyond the silken panels until she'd felt Simon's gaze on her bosom.

Damn Simon. She'd never met a man who could rankle her so much while at the same time making her wet between the legs.

Okay, so she understood the man's anger. His father had died violently. One minute he's laughing, the next he's dead and the son didn't have a chance to say goodbye. She could see how he'd concentrate his anger on her instead of on God, or fate, or whatever he believed in — if anything. From what she'd seen of Simon Sutcliffe so far, probably nothing.

Tamara smiled at the memory of the nurse's dumbstruck expression when Simon thrust the crutches into her hand. Then she'd closed her mouth and wordlessly handed them to Tamara. Of course, she'd refused them. It was easier to hop to the bathroom without them. It was only for longer treks that she needed them. She hated the crutches. It reminded her — and the world — of her vulnerability.

But she had no choice. Until the wound healed, she couldn't use the prosthesis, even with the stump sock.

Now she sat in the padded chair in Yvette's clothes, a rust turtleneck and jeans, the right cuff rolled up twice, the left pant leg pinned neatly behind the knee. She felt sure the doctor would discharge her. She couldn't wait.

The door opened. "Vincent!"

The sight of her stepbrother coaxed a wide smile from her. His sandy hair spilled over one eyebrow endearingly. His green eyes sparkled with mischief, as though he'd just let loose a mouse in the nurses' station. "Hiya, sis," he said. "Brought you a get-well thing." He handed her a vase holding a half dozen yellow roses with ferns and baby's breath.

"How'd you get in?" She looked at her wristwatch.

Vincent set the vase on the bedside table then bent over to kiss her forehead. "How do you think?" He gave her a lecherous look. "Nobody can resist me. I give them my patented drop-your-drawers look and they say yes to whatever I ask."

She laughed. "You're good for what ails me. How did you know I was here?"

"You're front-page material, kid."

"So I heard. You didn't happen to bring it, did you?"

"Sure did." He reached into the inside pocket of his leather jacket and handed her the first section of the paper.

The more Tamara read, the more she frowned. Some reporter had to be very enterprising to discover so much about her background. No wonder Simon had accused her of using it for PR. Then she felt an embarrassed flush heat her cheeks. She'd been reading about herself instead of Harland.

Half the page seemed to be devoted to Harland and the accident. A sidebar detailed his involvement in the community. She skimmed through the factual account of the accident, the comments from hospital spokesmen and the police. Lieutenant Kyrillos had said that an autopsy was being performed because of the nature of the death but that no foul play was suspected.

Foul play.

Something niggled at the back of her mind. A sliver of light flashing in front of the jump. Wire? Could someone have strung a nearly invisible wire at the narrow chute and yanked it up when the horses had committed to the jump?

Could that explain why both Jet Star and Blackwing had stumbled? But she hadn't heard the twang of a breaking—

"What?"

"I said, here's the doctor. Don't you want to go home?"

Tamara shook her head to clear it. "Sorry."

She pushed the flashing sliver of light to the back of her mind and set about getting discharged.

Chapter Eight

❧

"Why didn't you tell me about the accident last night?"

"It wasn't no big thing. Blackwing's thrown riders before. I didn't think nothing about it."

"But Harland dying from a horse jump." Marta's face creased into a frown as she drove Cliff to the stables. While she was sorry Harland died, more important to her was the police knocking on their door early this morning to talk to Cliff. "Didn't you wonder if he was all right when the horse came back alone?"

Cliff shrugged. "Blackwing always comes back to the stables. I just assumed Mr. S. knew he would and that he found himself another way to get home."

"What did you tell the police?"

"Not much to tell. Blackwing come back, I take off the saddle, walk him to cool him down, curry him, feed him."

"Did you inspect him for damage?"

"Why?"

"Harland was thrown while jumping. The horse obviously didn't clear the barrier. Did he have any cuts or bruises?"

Cliff's look said, *What am I, a veterinarian?*

"Cliff, I'm just trying to protect you. I feel responsible for you. If someone accuses you of neglect, I need all the facts to forestall a lawsuit."

"I didn't do nothing."

"I'm not accusing you of anything. I just want to be sure you tell me everything you remember."

"That's all I did for Blackwing."

She turned into the grounds and parked her sedan. They got out and she followed Cliff to the rolling doors. A shiny new padlock—a big one—had been installed over the entry. A piece of yellow tape fluttered on the ground, caught in a clump of weeds. Marta squinted to read the black printing. "Police lines, do not cross." They must have cordoned it off last night, she thought. Obviously they completed their investigation or Cliff wouldn't have been allowed to come to work.

Cliff pulled a key from his pocket.

"Is that the one the groundskeeper dropped off?"

"Yeah."

"Sort of like closing the barn door after the horse ran off," she muttered. When he opened the door, Marta entered behind him. The smell of horse manure stung her nostrils. She didn't know how the boy stood it day after day.

"What about the other one? The one the blonde rode?"

Cliff's face cracked into a grin. "She's built like a brick—uh." He cleared his throat.

"The horse, Cliff. When did her horse come back? Before or after Harland's?"

Cliff jabbed at the spaces between his teeth with a piece of straw he'd picked up. "I guess a short time after Blackwing. She was awful high-strung. Took me a few minutes after she come in just to get close enough to catch the reins."

"Did you examine that horse?"

He shrugged again. "I just did what I'm paid to do. I feed them and stall them. I have to wait until the last horse comes in before I close up. It ain't up to me to check them out for sickness or whatever."

"Show me the one Harland rode. I want to examine it."

"Why?"

"I'm just trying to protect you," she emphasized. "Bring him out into the light and we'll take a look."

Cliff hooked the bridle over Blackwing's head, stuck the bit between the animal's teeth, and led him outside.

"Hold him good, now." She'd tried riding once, but she and the horse hadn't seen eye to eye and she'd gladly given it up. She still feared the beasts.

Marta pushed up the sleeves of the Eagles sweatshirt Cliff had given her for Christmas, hitched up her khaki slacks at the knees and squatted beside the horse's front legs. Gingerly she ran a hand down from his knee joint to the knuckle then inspected the visible portion of the hoof. She moved to the other front leg and did the same. There was a scrape that looked like the hoof had struck stone. Cautiously she checked his hind legs.

Then she stood and probed Blackwing's chest, looking for hidden bruises. The horse whinnied loudly and shied away. Cliff hung on grimly to the reins. Marta scrambled backward.

"Jeez, Aunt Marta, what are you trying to do?"

Ignoring his comment, she said, "Okay, now the other one."

As Cliff led the gelding back to his stall, the sound of tires on gravel caused her to turn toward the parking area. She frowned at the Lexus. Simon. What was he doing here?

"I see we had the same idea," he said as he came up to her.

Marta nodded a tight greeting but said nothing.

When Cliff led Jet Star out of the paddock into the clearing, Simon said good morning to the groom, then reached into his denim shirt and fished out a sugar cube. "Here, old girl," he murmured. The mare lipped the cube from his palm and blew a stream of hot, moist air onto Simon's hand.

Crooning tunelessly to the horse, Simon slid his big hands across her face, her neck, down her chest. The horse danced nervously when his hand touched her left side. "Is that where you landed, baby? Does it hurt there?" She quieted under his soothing voice and he stooped and checked her legs. A few inches above the hoof he found dried blood. He got down on his hands and knees to study the diagonal wound. Only a few inches across, thicker than a knife would make, but not an abrasion from contact with the stone hedge or a board from the jump.

"Could be from anything," he said to Marta, who had stooped alongside him and was trying to see what had interested him. The computer that was his brain began clicking. He knew the head groundskeeper had strung high-tensile wire around the cornfields to keep the deer out. They also had fenced some areas in barbed wire to keep hunters out. She could have gone over that if she was spooked. Or snagged against a jagged stump hidden by ferns. Simon didn't think they had any machinery or old cars rusting away in an unused pocket of land, but it too was a possibility.

He inspected Blackwing under Marta's anxious gaze, finding nothing except bruising along his chest. He swore softly.

"What did you find?" Marta asked as she scrambled to her feet beside him.

"Nothing."

"What were you looking for?"

"Something to tell me why the damn horse didn't clear the jump. Dad wouldn't have jumped if he didn't have confidence in Blackwing. He'd have steered him to the beginner's path."

"You know how his back bothered him."

Simon stared out into the distance as Cliff led Blackwing back inside. The father that he remembered was robust. Had he changed so much in the year Simon had been gone?

"The past few months it got worse," Marta offered. "He shouldn't have been on that horse."

Simon's stomach muscles tightened. "Tamara," he muttered. She'd made his father think he was twenty years younger than he was, made him forget his back problems, made him jump.

She killed him, damn her blue eyes.

He spun on his heel and headed to his car. "Thanks, Cliff," he called out over his shoulder. "See you, Marta." He didn't see, as he pulled out onto the road, the worried look Marta threw after him.

A half-hour later, Simon parked the golf cart at the stone hedge. Inspecting the horses had told him nothing. Tamara had given him no clue. Had his father been careless? Had his back bothered him at a crucial moment so that he distracted Blackwing with a moan of pain or an inadvertent jerk on the reins?

He examined every stone on the top course for the scrape of a hoof. Nothing. Then he walked a few hundred yards down the riding trail. He pivoted and began walking toward the jumps, his eyes darting from side to side, reading the indentations in the packed earth. "Okay. They're riding along, two abreast." A few paces further, "Their stride lengthens. Here's where they spurred their horses." What was it Dad had said? Last one home cooks dinner. Simon's fists clenched. Were they sharing that cozy chore? Dammit, were they sharing a bed as well?

The first jump loomed. The eight-foot-wide wooden barrier stood about three feet high, with sturdy side beams holding adjustable crosspieces. The top board was at its highest setting. Simon saw where they landed cleanly on the other side.

As he walked to the second jump, a flash of light caught his eye. A length of shiny cassette tape, snagged on the middle riser, fluttered in the breeze. Had that spooked the horses?

Tracks behind the second jump scrambled in all directions. Where the EMTs had done—had failed to do—their job.

Simon dropped to his knees. "Dad," he croaked.

* * * * *

"This is some cute place you have here," Vincent said as Tamara hobbled on her red crutches into the bungalow before him.

Tamara swallowed hard. She wanted to tell her brother about Harland's promise to give her life rights to this "cute place", but he'd never gotten to sign his new will. She wondered how long before one brother or the other would be knocking on her door with the sheriff's eviction notice in his hand.

"What's nice is the peace, the solitude," she said. A small living room, furnished in early rustic, including a chair made of deer antlers, opened into a smaller dining room with a round oak table that seated four. A utilitarian kitchen, a no-nonsense bath, two small bedrooms, one of which she'd converted to an office, had been all she needed, as long as she had the outdoors to look at, to walk through, to inhale.

Now Harland was gone. Was Simon right? Had she goaded him into a jump he wasn't physically fit to make?

No, dammit. Harland died as he would have wanted to die, full of life, doing something he loved, instead of being hooked up to tubes and machines that did everything for him. And now he had joined his beloved wife. And Kathye, the child she, Tamara, was a substitute for.

"Hey, sis, are you all right?"

Tamara brushed away a tear. For the five years they'd lived as brother and sister—from her mother's remarriage to her accident—she'd always fussed over him. It was nice to be on the receiving end. Her glance found the yellow roses he'd set on the table. "Harland was a wonderful man. I guess I'm just feeling the impact of his loss."

"Did he leave you anything?"

She gave him a sharp look. "Don't be so crass." Then she turned away. He had left her nothing but memories. Her work here was done. She wasn't required to put any of her plans into action. What she did have to do was polish her résumé. She looked out the living room window at the cedar forest two hundred feet away. It was time to leave home.

While she wasn't looking, this corner of the Pine Barrens had become home. Had it been Harland's loving tutelage? Every time they'd been together he'd given her some new tidbit about its ecology that impressed and delighted her.

"Why don't you freshen up, and I'll buy you lunch at the club." Vincent flopped onto the high-backed early American sofa and picked up a golfing magazine from the side table.

Tamara did more than freshen up. In the shower she scrubbed off the hospital smell then washed her hair, gingerly working around the lumps at the crown. She toweled off, checked the extent of her bruises in the full-length mirror, and changed the bandage on her stump. She debated pulling her wet hair into a ponytail, but decided she needed to feel good about herself. Grimacing at the bruised and abraded left side of her face, she touched up her eyelashes with navy mascara, blew her hair dry and let it cascade in a shiny fall down her back. She dressed in a creamy silk blouse with cravat, navy slacks and jacket, and an elegant navy flat. She was glad she'd found The One Shoe Crew, which paired up one-legged people to share shoes.

Thirty minutes later, Vincent swung into the parking lot of the club. She'd wanted to show him that she wasn't helpless, but he was like a kid at Christmas on seeing her sporty Mazda Miata, which had been a gift from her no-longer-anonymous benefactor, so she let him drive.

She could feel members' eyes on her as she hobbled, chin high, on her crutches into the dining room of the club. She'd spoken to most of the members over the past six months, and not one, she'd bet, had had an inkling she used a prosthesis.

Vincent insisted on ordering a bottle of champagne to celebrate her release from the hospital. Tamara argued that it was desecrating Harland's memory to celebrate.

"He'd have wanted you to," Vincent said.

"He would at that," Tamara said, smiling.

"Well, it's good to see you up and about."

The smile froze on Tamara's face. Carrie Sutcliffe stood at the booth, her eyes all but eating Vincent up. He returned the scrutiny avidly, paying special attention to his eye level, which was about 34DD underneath her tight cashmere sweater.

"Vincent, this is Mrs. Simon Sutcliffe," Tamara bit out, emphasizing the title.

Carrie held out her hand. Vincent lifted it and brushed her knuckles with his lips. She giggled and said, "Call me Carrie. And you are?"

"Charmed," he said.

"Are you here to help our Tamara recover?"

It was all Tamara could do not to hurl. "I'm fine, Carrie. My brother just brought me back from the hospital because I didn't have my own car handy."

"You're so lucky. I'm an only child." She batted her mascaraed eyelashes at Vincent, who still clung to her hand and whose eyes still clung to her sweater.

"What a shame," Vincent purred. "Have you eaten?"

"No," Carrie breathed.

"Please join us." Vincent slid deeper into the booth without letting go of Carrie's hand. "I'm buying."

Carrie slipped in next to Vincent, gave Tamara a simpering smile. Then she gasped. "Your face!"

The abraded side of Tamara's face was to the wall, so Carrie hadn't seen it while standing. "I'm so sorry about your father-in-law," Tamara said to draw attention away from herself.

"My condolences to you as well." Carrie bobbed her head in acknowledgement then turned to Vincent. "Tamara was Harland's lover," she said in a stage whisper.

Heat flooded Tamara's cheeks. "That's not true," she rasped. But she was sure Carrie would take the blush as a declaration of something to hide.

The waiter arrived with the champagne bucket. "Shall I get Mrs. Sutcliffe a glass?"

"Absolutely," said Vincent.

When all three glasses were poured, Vincent lifted his flute. "To beauty," he said. "Blondes and brunettes alike."

"Oh, Vincent." Carrie snuggled closer under the pretext of clinking his glass then sipped while gazing into his eyes.

Tamara set down her glass untasted. Carrie didn't waste any time. She probably already had her thigh glued to Vincent's and her mind on his crotch.

"Is this a private party? Or can anyone join?"

"I thought you didn't want to be anywhere near me," Carrie snapped at Simon.

"Extenuating circumstances," he said with a pointed glance at Tamara. He leaned down and thrust out his hand to Vincent. "Simon Sutcliffe."

Noting Tamara had become flustered, Vincent decided it was Carrie's husband, not her late father-in-law, that his dear sister had the hots for. He also noted that the look Simon gave Tamara could melt asphalt under a snowbank. This could work all around. "Vincent MacKinnon," he said, shaking the bigger man's hand and enjoying the question in his eyes. "Sit down."

"My brother," Tamara clarified as Simon complied.

"Step-brother," Vincent corrected, giving his sister a hot-eyed glance. "We're not blood relations."

Beside him, Carrie stiffened. Across the table Simon raised an eyebrow. Good, thought Vincent. Both Simon and Carrie understood the innuendo.

"Vincent." Tamara's voice held a note of warning.

Which he disregarded. "I got my first anatomy lesson from watching Tamara take a bath," he said blithely, strengthening the innuendo. "Been learning and loving it ever since."

"Vincent, did you ever get a job?" Tamara's voice was near panic. How had the situation gotten away from her so fast? She hadn't seen her brother in months and suddenly she was surrounded by innuendo and—and Simon. His presence dominated the booth. He crowded her even though they weren't touching. She'd scooted as close to the wall as she could when he sat down. The crutches pressed into her hip. She wished she could put them between herself and him without being obvious.

The waiter returned and poured another flute. Simon raised his glass to Tamara. "You look—different from this morning."

Tamara felt her cheeks heat again as his gaze skimmed her body. Damn, why couldn't she control her reaction to this man?

"She was wearing this skimpy little—"

"Never mind," Tamara interrupted, her face flushing even warmer at the memory of Simon ogling her breasts under the peach negligee.

"You must have gotten there real early," Vincent said. "When I arrived at ten, she was packed and ready to leave."

A cloud passed over Simon's face. "We had...things...to discuss." He turned to Tamara. "And we're not done yet. I'd like an hour of your time when you've eaten."

"Sorry, I'll be busy. I haven't seen Vincent in months."

"Oh, you two just go right on," Carrie chirped. "I'll keep your brother entertained."

"I just bet you will," Simon muttered.

Carrie threw him a look that might have crumpled a lesser man. Then the hardness in her eyes softened. "Simon. You and I could still—"

"Excuse me. I just remembered a call I have to make." Simon slid out of the booth then stood and seared Tamara with a look. "I'll wait for you in the bar."

"I'm not going anywhere with you," Tamara ground out, knuckles white as she gripped the stem of the champagne flute.

"You haven't been cleared in Dad's death yet."

The blood left her face in a rush, making her feel dizzy. "By whom? It was an accident," she rasped.

"Maybe the police believe that. You still have to prove it to me."

She was denied the opportunity to respond by the sound of Yvette's voice. "Oh, good. This saves me a few phone calls."

Tamara looked up to see her friend approaching the booth. Yvette wore another power suit, this one in beige wool worsted with a double-breasted jacket and slim skirt.

"Glad to see you out of the hospital," she said to Tamara with a wide smile. "I need to speak to all the shareholders. I was meeting Jack and Elliott for lunch. But since you're all here, perhaps we should eat in the boardroom as a group."

Tamara smiled. Too bad Carrie wouldn't be able to use her wiles on Vincent. She'd have her brother to herself. "Fine. Vincent and I will be able to have that quiet lunch after all."

"Sorry to mess up your plans," Yvette said. "But it would be easiest if we were all together."

"You said shareholders. I'm only the consultant."

Yvette's face broke out in a smile the likes of which Tamara had seen only when The Nature Conservancy got a big bequest. "I've just returned from the probate office, where I entered Harland's will for probate. The new one he signed last week."

Chapter Nine

Did they all think Harland was stupid? Yvette wondered as she watched the board members settle around the same table they'd used only two days ago. None of them had wanted to order lunch when they'd heard the news, although both Elliott and Jack brought up their drinks, Jack's full of bourbon in an iced tea glass without ice. Did they think Harland hadn't known the currents swirling around him? The animosity that Tamara's mere presence engendered, never mind her findings? Had they really thought he'd announce plans to change his will without having already taken the steps?

The timing of Harland's death left a sour taste in Yvette's mouth. He'd known the risks, had confided his fears to her. It wasn't an accident. Someone around this table... She suppressed a shudder and cleared her mind. She was a good attorney and she'd represent her client to the best of her ability.

Elliott charged right in. "How do we know he was of sound mind and body when he signed this new will?"

Yvette knew she had to defuse him immediately. "Harland left several letters to be distributed after his death. One is for you." She pulled out a business-size envelope from her cordovan leather attaché case and handed it to Elliott.

He eyed her suspiciously. "Do you know its contents?"

"I do not. I am merely the conduit."

Elliott rose and left the room. A few moments later he was back. His stone-faced expression told her nothing. "Go ahead," he growled. "Let's begin."

"I'll give each of you a photocopy of the exact wordage," Yvette said, "but right now I'll just enumerate the points.

"First, the land on which the golf course exists is bequeathed to the oldest son, Jack, according to tradition." She noted the slight easing of Jack's tension, although they all knew the holding company controlled the land surrounding it.

"Second, after bequests to Danuta, Ilya, Cliff and a few others, Harland's estate, except the holding company shares, is bequeathed to his sons. They may pick and choose from among his assets as long as it is substantially equal. Absent agreement, everything will be sold and the proceeds divided in half."

Jack drank heavily from his glass, no doubt to hide his profound relief. It was no secret that he was cash-poor.

"Third, Tamara Hart is granted life rights to the bungalow she now occupies and no future development may impinge on that right." From the corner of her eye Yvette saw Tamara's mouth tremble, but she refused to embarrass her friend by announcing her unbridled approval in the form of a war whoop.

"Next, Harland's forty shares are being distributed ten to Jack, ten to Simon, and twenty to Tamara."

"I don't want them." Tamara snapped. "I don't want any part of this family. I'm here only because you're my friend and you asked me to be here."

"So give up your life rights to the bungalow," Jack sneered. "We don't want you either."

"This place is so big that I'll never have to run into any of you. I love the Pine Barrens. I just don't want anything to do with the golf course."

"Fine," Yvette said, trying to regain control of the meeting. "After we transfer the shares, you can sell them to the highest bidder, give them to The Nature Conservancy, whatever you want. All I ask is that you not paper any walls with them. It isn't fair to the other legatees to tie their hands."

She looked at each of the board members. "With this bequest, the shares line up like this. Jack has thirty, Simon twenty, Tamara twenty, and Carrie, Elliott and Marta, ten each." She paused. "And yes, the seventy percent rule is legal."

Yvette cleared her throat. "The last major provision concerns the two executors. They must function together or the provisions of the will are null and void and the estate reverts to specified charities. In other words, no one gets anything unless both executors fulfill their duties to the letter."

Jack darted a smug look at Simon. "Hell, we can work together, right, li'l brother?"

A muscle twitching in Simon's square jaw told Yvette that their animosity preceded Simon's return. She glanced at Jack. This provision would wipe the cat-that-ate-the-canary look right off his face. "The executors are Simon Sutcliffe and Tamara Hart with myself as attorney of record."

"What?" Jack jumped up. "That bastard! What's he trying to do, undercut me? Come on, Elliott, we have a will to break."

For once Elliott's carefully nurtured tan seemed to dissolve. "Settle down, Jack. Let's hear the rest of it."

"Settle down? He's made me the laughingstock of the club!" He glared across the table at Tamara. "I'll break the will. I'll break you, you conniving little bitch. You set him up. Fucked your way right into his fortune. I'll prove that he signed it under duress. Elliott? Are you with me? It wasn't just me he slapped in the face. How's it going to look among all your attorney friends that you let a woman lawyer steal your best client?"

Jack rounded the table and bore down on Tamara. "When I get done with you, you won't have a leg to stand on."

"I don't have a leg now, thanks to you."

Jack's face reddened. Tamara had been seated when he'd walked into the room. Obviously he'd already forgotten her disability. Then he rallied. "I'll take the other one, too, if I have to. You aren't getting my development!"

Elliott's hand on his arm diverted his attention briefly from Tamara. He strained against his lawyer, turning back to her. "You're dead meat. You just don't know it yet. I've waited too long, spent too much money getting everything lined up. I won't have some sexy twat screw up my plans. You hear me? You're dead!"

* * * * *

"Here. Drink this."

Simon set the glass of cognac in front of Tamara, whose face was still as pale as her blouse. With Jack's threat ringing in everyone's ears, Yvette had quickly ended the meeting. Elliott had dragged Jack out with the same effort it had taken Simon to move a stubborn mule in Guatemala.

Yvette hadn't wanted to leave Tamara alone with Simon, but he'd been adamant. He still had questions about his dad's death. He was determined to get some answers if he had to hypnotize them out of her.

Sitting down next to her, Simon gently pried Tamara's fingers loose from her stranglehold on the armrests of her chair. He took one clammy hand in his. It was soft, delicate, with long, slender fingers. His thumb stroked lazily across her knuckles as he willed warmth into her.

The contact penetrated her fog. She turned then snapped her hand out of his grip when she saw who held it. "I'm fine."

"Good." He reached for the snifter.

Tamara closed her eyes. "I never asked for any of this."

"Dad was like that. You wanted something too bad, you had to work for it. If he took a shine to you, he was generous. Did you know he paid for Ilya and Danuta's grandchild's schooling? That he set up a scholarship fund for the caddies? No, you wouldn't. He didn't brag about the things he did."

He held the glass to her lips. "You need to warm up."

She turned her head away.

"Fine," he said, setting the glass back down. "We can warm you another way." He placed a hand under her chin and gently moved her head to face him. Her lips were inches from his.

Her eyes widened in awareness. Panic flashed across her features. "B-brandy," she said.

With a provocative smile, he handed her the glass and watched the muscles move in her slender throat as she swallowed several tiny sips. Right there, at the pulse point, he thought, would be a good place to put his mouth.

He jerked to his feet. Dammit, he needed answers, not kisses. He couldn't allow this soft, vulnerable woman to get under his skin until he knew why his father had died. "Come on," he growled. "We're going riding."

"I can't ride without my special prosthesis."

"We can double up. I'll make sure you don't fall."

"Let's put it this way. I don't want to ride." Her hand unconsciously stroked her stump end.

"Does it hurt?" he blurted out. Hell, of course it did. Hadn't he seen blood on her pant leg? "Sorry. That was a stupid question. I thought recreating those last jumps would jog your memory. How about if we take the golf cart?"

"I'm not going anywhere with you. Vincent's waiting for me downstairs."

"Is your step-brother as predatory as he looks?"

"Preda— Where'd you get that idea?"

"I know lust when I see it. Carrie and what's-his-name can't wait to get naked together."

Her chin lifted. "It's none of my business what Vincent does. He's over the age of consent."

He lowered his voice to a whisper. "And you, Tamara, are you at the age of consent?" He bent forward, tunneled his right hand under her luxuriant blonde hair and pressed his palm against her soft nape. With his left he stroked her downy cheek.

His mouth brushed against hers. The first tentative contact sent electric flashes down to his awakening cock. Her meltingly blue eyes were wide with wonder and hesitation. His tongue grazed her full bottom lip. It felt like warm, living velvet. He pressed his lips more firmly against hers, moved his head from side to side in a delicious friction.

Her eyelids fluttered closed. He marveled at the thick curve of her lashes, the porcelain smoothness of her skin.

On one side. The abrasions on her left cheek mocked him.

Jesus, this woman was responsible for his father's death! How could he let testosterone overwhelm his sanity? He jerked his hands away and straightened. "We'll take Vincent with us if you're that set on seeing him."

Tamara blinked several times, as if waking from a dream. "Vincent?" she parroted.

"You're going with me to the scene of the crime, if I have to take Vincent and all the damn shareholders with me."

He knew the exact moment she came out of a sexual daze. Her eyes narrowed. She squared her shoulders, thrust her chin up. She centered herself in the chair, gripped the armrests and gracefully hoisted herself up to balance on her good leg.

He moved toward the crutches leaning in the corner.

"I'll get them. I don't need your help." She took several hops on her flat shoe, using the table for leverage.

"Don't be silly—"

"I've managed to reach my crutches for ten years without you, Mr. Sutcliffe. I think I can do it again."

After giving her a long look, which she returned without flinching, he pivoted on his heel and left the room.

Tamara struggled to keep her good knee from buckling. Dear God, the man could destroy her defenses with a touch! So featherlight it could hardly be called a kiss, yet he'd left her aching for the warmth of his mouth on her breasts, the weight of his naked body on hers. Was she no better than Carrie?

Simon Sutcliffe would be no one-night stand, she vowed. She'd had enough of faceless, nameless bodies as she searched for respect and acceptance but found only sleaze. Starting now, she'd allow no man close until he accepted her, warts and all. No romantic hiding beneath sheets or darkened bedrooms or too many glasses of champagne. He would kiss her from the stump up, or he'd not have her. Or so she told herself as she thumped down the stairs into the front hallway.

Simon entered the hallway from the restaurant. "According to the bartender, he left with Carrie about ten minutes ago."

Tamara gritted her teeth. Vincent would get an earful when she next saw him. How could he choose Carrie over her when she hadn't seen him for months? More importantly, how could he leave her to the machinations of this man whose amber eyes melted her very bones?

"Come on, I'll take you home."

"Thank you, but my Miata is here."

"Is it? The bartender said they left in a white Miata. Carrie doesn't have one. Does Vincent?"

Furious, Tamara realized he'd given the keys to the valet instead of to her. "Simple. I'll take a golf cart."

"Great. It's the best way to get to the jumps from here."

"You're not going to let go, are you? You're like a pit bull locking onto a man's ankle until it's shredded."

"Lady, you haven't seen anything yet. Until I know how—and why—my father died, I'll be a pit bull and a Doberman pinscher and a Rottweiler all in one. You can make of it what you will. But you're going to help me." He grabbed her arm. "Let's go."

Tamara dug in her heels — heel — and thrust out her chin. "You and what army will make me?"

After a long look in which Tamara saw him slowly bank the fires of anger in his eyes, he released her arm.

"I'm not done with you yet," he bit out as he stalked away.

Chapter Ten

ဢ

Trying to keep the tears at bay, Tamara leaned on her crutches and stared up into a sky full of low-hanging clouds. Fitting atmosphere for a funeral, she thought grimly. It looked like someone had wet a piece of watercolor paper and splattered it with splotches of black ink, which spread in unpredictable directions to cover the whole in shades of wet, luminous gray.

The Pines was closed today, with police posted at both entrances. A memorial service open to the public would be held later, but burying a man like Harland Sutcliffe was too personal to share with rude paparazzi and curious strangers.

No more than two dozen people had been invited to the tiny cemetery that had come with the farmland, where Harland was being buried next to his wife, his daughter and his grandson. It was one of the highest elevations of The Pines, surrounded by an intricate wrought iron fence and spectacular view.

Tamara recognized the head groundskeeper, chef, golf pro, Danuta and Ilya. Carrie and Elliott stood together as if lending each other support, but neither seemed especially sorrowful.

Stoic, unemotional Marta had brought Cliff, who seemed to be uncomfortable in his dark suit. Jack, for once, looked sober and somber. Simon's angular face was taut with grief, the skin stretched across his sharp cheekbones like rawhide that had been left in the sun too long. His eyes had a haunted look.

Last night Tamara had been exhausted, but had tossed and turned in bed for hours, her mind reeling from everything that had happened since the presentation. Harland's revelations, his death, his legacy. Vincent's unexpected appearance. And over it all, the smolderingly masculine presence of Simon Sutcliffe.

She felt Yvette squeeze her arm. She was grateful for such a staunch friend. Tamara had called her at midnight, and Yvette had driven over with bagels and hot cocoa and a sympathetic shoulder and had stayed the night.

The minister concluded the service. People murmured, "Amen."

"Amen," Tamara added, recalling the cold, blustery day a dozen years ago when a minister had said similar words over her mother's casket. She'd died of ovarian cancer, too harried by a stingy Ike to go to the doctor until it was too late. How she'd wished her mother had been there for her when she was learning to walk again, to cope with being different.

Now Harland was gone, the man who'd been her surrogate—if anonymous—father all these years, her guardian angel, the man she'd come to admire and love in the past few months.

Had she goaded Harland to take the jump? Oh God, she couldn't live with herself if she was responsible for his death. She stared into the yawning hole that wasn't quite covered up by the plastic carpet of grass. She felt a tear trickle down her cheek, then another. She squeezed her eyes shut and let them spill over. "Oh, Harland," she whispered. "I'm so sorry."

"Sorry for what?"

Her eyes flew open. Simon stood before her, a muscle twitching in his jaw, hands balled into fists at his sides.

"Everyone else is gone. You can stop your theatrics now."

"I loved him too," she whispered.

"Yeah, I'm sure you did," he said, his insolent gaze raking down the boxy gray pantsuit she'd worn for the presentation, and back up again. "Co-executor. You really did a number on him."

"What do you mean by that?"

"I had time to think last night. By law, executors are eligible for fees, a percentage of everything that passes through the estate. Did Dad show you his stock portfolio? Did you know just how wealthy he was when you figured out this gimmick?"

"I don't know anything of the sort!"

"I'm going to haunt you, Tamara. If you killed my father, I'll never let you forget it. Being forced to work together will be a constant reminder of what you did."

"Please stop," she said, her voice cracking. "I look at you and see the man that your mother fell in love with in those wedding pictures from forty years ago. I see Harland in the slant of your nose, the curve of your mouth, the way you take charge of a room just by entering it."

"Dammit, that's not what I meant! I want to be my father's avenging angel, not a stand-in for him. When you look at me, I want you to see me. I want you to think of me. I want—"

Simon snapped his jaws shut. How had she bewitched him? He'd wanted to be her conscience, a thorn in her side. Instead, God help him, he wanted her! Hadn't he learned his lesson? Hadn't a woman destroyed his family once before? Simon spun on his heel, digging a small divot in the sparse grass, and stumbled to another grave. His gaze traveled the obscenely tiny distance between Kevin's headstone and footstone. He should be on his knees, mourning his son and his father, not having flights of fancy about this woman he'd been trying to banish from his mind.

Sometimes, he thought darkly, it wouldn't hurt to take Jack's way out and drink himself to oblivion.

* * * * *

With trembling hands, Jack poured a shot of bourbon over an ice cube, then slammed the bottle back on the sideboard in his black-and-white, leather-and-chrome, decorator living room. He slugged down a gulp then growled, "Help yourself."

"No, thanks," Elliott said. "Too early for me."

"Goddammit, is this going to be a lecture? I get enough of those from Marta."

"No, it isn't. We have plans to discuss."

Jack glanced around. "Just us?"

"Just us." Elliott's gaze followed Jack's. The room was devoid of family photos and homey touches. Two ex-wives had disappeared from Jack's life, but the alimony payments hadn't. Half of Harland's assets could make a powerful motive for murder. He wondered when the police would figure that out.

Jack swirled the ice around in the glass then sipped. "We going to discuss what Harland wrote in his love letter to you?"

Elliott's voice was steely. "No."

"Dammit, Elliott, did he at least explain why he fucked you up?"

"Attorney-client privilege," he said tightly. How had Harland found the skeleton in his closet? He had to believe that someone else—Yvette?—was privy to that information. If he'd executed a new will under Elliott's nose, he was too clever by half to let it die with him. Elliott had no choice but to follow the dictates of the will or have his past opened up to public scrutiny. Scrutiny it couldn't withstand. "Maybe I will have a drop."

"What do you think we ought to do?"

"I'm open to suggestion," Elliott said, mixing himself a very dry martini. "Any ideas?"

"Legally, I guess she already owns the shares even though they haven't been transferred?"

Elliott nodded. No question as to who "she" was.

"So we look to her next of kin. Think she's smart enough to have a will? Or maybe she thinks she's too young to die."

"Go on."

"Suppose she dies without a will. What's the law say about next-of-kin? Would the step-brother inherit?"

"I don't know. I'll have to research if they aren't blood kin. I think there's a step-father too." Elliott sipped his martini. "That Vincent MacKinnon doesn't waste time. Carrie's already slept with him, would you believe it?"

Jack's eyes bugged out. "What?"

"They spent the night at the local hot-sheet place."

"That bitch! She's my private—" He clamped his mouth shut then decided to drain his drink.

"Jack, Jack. She'd go back to Simon in a second."

"He'll never take her back. Besides, all she wants is his money."

"When did you start fucking your sister-in-law? Before or after Simon filed for divorce?"

"How did we get on this subject? We're supposed to be talking about strategy. How to get Hart out of the way."

"I need to know everything about everybody so I can decide what information to use when and how."

Jack snorted. "Lawyers."

"Right. Without lawyers your project would be up shit creek and you know it. I have to figure out how to get Yvette on our side. Did you read your copy of Harland's will?"

Jack shook his head "no" then took another healthy sip of bourbon. "I assume she hit the high points. If there were any more surprises, she'd have uncorked them yesterday."

"She did a good, thorough, airtight job," Elliott said with grudging admiration. "So we play by the rules."

"What?"

"On the surface. Underneath we dig up what we can from Vincent. Carrie will be a big help there." Elliott smiled the smile of a shark about to chomp a swimmer in two. "There are some things she's good at."

Jack's gaze jerked around to Elliott.

"I didn't sleep with her. I look on her as my daughter."

Jack drained his glass and returned to the sideboard. "Too bad Harland didn't feel that way about the Hart bitch."

"The thing to do now is to eliminate her from contention."

"Now you're talking."

Elliott took the glass and bottle out of Jack's hand. "We have some serious planning to do." He led Jack to the dining room table. "We're going to brainstorm every possible calamity that might befall her. Put your thinking cap on."

"Now you're talking," Jack repeated.

"Here's a pencil. Concentrate on this." He also wanted the handwriting to be Jack's if it was ever discovered.

* * * * *

Carrie's reflection stared back at her from the pier-glass mirror between two floor-length windows in the dining room of the carriage house. As she'd expected, Simon had moved his clothes into Harland's home when she refused to vacate. She hoped he'd stay there for good. She wanted this place for herself — she coveted the low-key, golf-course lifestyle, all the rich, available men she rubbed elbows with, all the cock available to her.

Behind her, Jack nibbled on her ear as his trembling fingers unbuttoned her black silk blouse. Slowly the black demi-bra, which exposed the heavy crowns of her breasts — all natural, she was proud to tell anyone — came into view.

He slid the blouse off her shoulders, scooped the hard brown nipples out from the confining fabric and tugged on both of them. She felt the sexual pull all the way down to her pussy, already as wet as her mouth. The tiny part of her mind that wasn't engaged in pleasure wondered when she should ask him to do what Elliott had suggested, wondered if Jack would do it.

Jack pulled the straps down to where the folds of her blouse trapped her arms. Thus holding her hostage, he rucked up her black skirt. Then drew a harsh breath at finding nothing but skin. "Jesus, Carrie. Were you like this at the cemetery?"

Carrie gave him a sly look over her shoulder. "What do you think?"

She heard the rasp of his zipper, felt his hot cock rubbing between her naked ass cheeks. "Good thing I didn't know you were commando," he bit out, ramming home with one hard thrust. "Oh God, Carrie." He began pumping his hips with fervor.

With Jack's harsh breathing sounding in her ear, a movement in the mirror snagged Carrie's attention. Vincent. At any other time, she'd eagerly want her dream to come true, a sandwich of male bodies with her between them. But right now things were in a delicate balance.

Her gaze locked with Vincent's, willing him to be silent. She remembered that they hadn't locked the front door. Had he rung the bell and they hadn't heard it? Or had he just barged in hoping to catch them fucking?

She looked down to Vincent's crotch as Jack continued banging her. He grasped the base of his cock through his trousers, showing her how much it had grown in the minute or two he'd been watching.

She licked her swollen lower lip with a wet pink tongue. Already she could imagine herself pinned to the dining room table, legs pointed to the ceiling, Vincent's cock inside her, Jack sucking one nipple and pinching the other —

With a muffled curse, Jack climaxed. Half miffed that he hadn't waited for her to come first, Carrie gestured with her head for Vincent to get out of sight until she gave him a signal.

"Sorry, babe, I couldn't hang on. I'll make it up to you," Jack mumbled as he pulled out.

"It's okay, Jack. We've all had a rough day." Carrie straightened her spine and let her black skirt slither back down over her hips. Seeing Vincent's impatient hand signal, she pulled her bra and blouse into some semblance of coverage and nodded.

He strolled from the front hallway into the dining room, shifting his cock so the hard tip of it caught in the waistband of his Jockey shorts.

"What the hell are you doing in here?" Jack growled, fumbling his own cock back inside his trousers.

"Hi, folks," Vincent said jauntily. "The lights were on and I didn't see any cars, so I figured the lady was alone." He knew Carrie had expected him this evening. He was never wrong about that kind of signal. But he hadn't expected she'd offer him a *ménage a trois*. He could handle it. He wondered if Jack could.

Jack's bloodshot eyes raked him up and down. "Get out."

"Excuse me," Vincent retorted, "but isn't your house the next one down?"

"Get out."

"Not until the owner of the house tells me to." His glance sliced to Carrie, who was slowly buttoning her blouse, her eyes glowing with barely suppressed excitement.

"You lay your hands on her again and I'll—"

"Again?" This guy was drunk, Vincent assessed in a flash. He advanced a menacing step forward. "I haven't touched her."

Jack frowned then turned unsteadily to Carrie. "Where were you last night?"

"Right here," she retorted.

He grabbed her by the arms. "Don't stand there and deny that you two checked out the local motel last night."

"How dare you!" Carrie's eyes flashed fire.

"Are you saying you two didn't spend the night together?"

"Damn you, Jack. I was here. Alone."

"And I slept on the floor of my sister's living room. In a sleeping bag."

Jack focused with difficulty on Vincent's face. "You spent the night at...Tamara's?" His voice raised on the last word, as though the thought was too incredulous to believe.

"Where's your phone, Carrie? Call her. Call my sister."

Uncertainty filtered into Jack's expression. "But Elliott said—" He looked from Carrie to Vincent then back again. "Elliott said you told him you'd spent the night together."

Carrie's eyes narrowed. A steely hardness glimmered through the slits. "I don't know what game Elliott's playing, but he's trying to drive a wedge between us. I swear I spent last night alone. Right here."

Jack buried his face in his shaking hands. "I don't know what to think."

"Why don't you go into the kitchen and put on a pot of coffee?" Gently she pulled his hands away and looked into his eyes. "I'll join you in a minute." When he didn't move, she said, "Do it for me. Please? I need a shot of caffeine."

After a deep, shuddering breath, Jack shuffled off into a room that Vincent assumed was the kitchen. Carrie turned to him. "I wish..."

He cocked his head and waited.

But she didn't say what he expected her to. "It disturbs me that our lawyer could make such an accusation." Her mouth curved downward. "This thing about my father-in-

114

law's will has us all upset. There's a lot of money involved, and I can't alienate my brother-in-law."

Vincent knew that the look he was giving Carrie spoke loud and clear. It said he didn't care about any will, he wanted her, wanted to fuck her until she yelled stop, that he had the stamina the older, obviously drunken man didn't.

She glanced in the direction of the kitchen then back to him. "I've got to talk to him now. To defuse whatever Elliott planted in his head. Do you understand?"

He shrugged. "Whatever."

"I'll get him home somehow. He's only next door." Her gaze dropped to Vincent's mouth. "Come by around eleven. I'll leave a light on in the right front bedroom if it's safe. Use a golf cart. Tamara keeps one by her house. They all look alike, so no one will know whose it is. But park in back, just in case."

She took one step backward, then another. She looked down at his crotch for a long moment, licked her lips again. Then said, "I have to go."

Vincent watched her disappear behind the same door that Jack had, then turned on his heel and walked out the front door, whistling.

* * * * *

Bloodshot eyes stared blearily back at Jack in the mirror. Dammit, he'd been too drunk even to climb his own steps. He'd had to use the guest bathroom on the first floor.

He staggered into the kitchen. Carrie had had the right idea, making him drink coffee. He fixed another pot and leaned against the stainless steel counter as it perked.

Good ol' Carrie. A great fuck, better than either of his wives. But more than that, a friend. She'd gotten rid of that upstart Vincent. What right had he to look at her like that? He'd seen the lust on his face, saw what his hand was doing around his zipper. If that young punk thought he was getting into Carrie's pants, he, Jack Sutcliffe, firstborn twin, would set him on his ear, even if he had to pay someone to do it.

Firstborn.

The thought straightened Jack's spine a little. He was the head of the family now. Harland had actually done Jack a favor by dividing everything in half instead of giving him the shares and Simon the money. God knew, Jack could use some cash. Two ex-wives were two too many. When they heard about the bequests, they'd probably haul him into court asking for more alimony. They wouldn't get another red nickel if he had his way.

Firstborn.

The words conveyed strength, dignity. Traits he'd been sorely lacking for most of his adult life. Booze could leach out any good traits. Maybe he didn't have to hide behind his bourbon now that Harland was gone. Maybe he could become respected like his father. Maybe he could convince all the shareholders to vote with his project.

All but the Hart broad. She wouldn't vote to save him from the fires of hell. She'd spurned him, done everything she could to embarrass him. Who was she, anyway? A cripple.

He gulped down the first of several cups of strong, sweet coffee and pulled the piece of paper out of his shirt pocket. The words danced pleasantly in front of his eyes. Met up with bear in the woods. Automobile accident. Drowned in swamp. Kitchen fire—bacon? And a dozen more scenarios.

He poured another cup to get sober. He wanted to savor every possibility, think about how to execute each one.

* * * * *

Elliott swore softly. According to New Jersey Statutes Annotated, only blood relations were mentioned to inherit from an intestate decedent. That meant even if they got rid of Tamara, her shares wouldn't necessarily go to the step-brother.

It would go even to cousins twice removed if same could be dredged up. If there were no relatives, it would go to the state.

Disastrous. Although it didn't negate the reasons for getting rid of her in the first place.

He sat down at his home safe and twirled the combination. He couldn't resist reading the list once more. A duplicate list written in the shaking hand of the distraught Jack Sutcliffe.

Chapter Eleven

ဢ

"Oh God, Vincent. Please. Now!"

On her hands and knees before the pier glass, with Vincent grasping her waist from behind, Carrie watched their naked reflections with hot eyes.

"Don't tease me, Vincent, please!" She wiggled her hips, desperate to have him ram it home again. His young, sinuous body hid muscles of steel, and he held her on the edge of madness.

"I'll make you forget every other man you've ever fucked," he promised. "Especially that over-the-hill playboy I saw you with earlier tonight."

"He means nothing to me. I'm just keeping him happy until we get our development approved." She squeezed her inner muscles to remind him of what she wanted. "Don't stop. Please don't stop."

"You like?" Perversely he stayed motionless, as deep inside her as he could get.

"Yes, dammit! Give it to me! Give me, give me, give me give…" Her litany trailed off as he complied. His hips pumped like pistons gone amok. She closed her eyes and lost herself in a climax that made the world compress into a tiny ball and disappear into a vaporous mist.

Minutes later, she became aware of her surroundings, of the continuing heat between her legs, of Vincent's smug face watching her in the mirror, of the sweet, hot rhythm of his cock slowly pumping her—still pumping her. Instantly she was horny again.

"Short fuse, honey? No stamina?"

"I'll show you who has stamina, *honey*," she ground out. Her inner muscles closed around him, squeezing the thick shaft in a hot satin vise.

He groaned and began to move, slowly at first then faster and with more vigor, until they were both gasping.

Carrie shuddered. Yes! This was what she wanted, to be ravished, dominated. With one hand she reached between her legs to grasp his balls, cupped them, squeezed them as he moved inside her until he arched against her and she felt his scalding essence shoot deep inside her. He collapsed against her, buckling her knees and bringing both of them down to the Aubusson rug on the floor.

"No stamina?" she purred as she wiggled her ass against him.

"I'll get you for that."

And he did. Five more times. Jack could go to hell.

* * * * *

Sipping her first cup of coffee in the soft clear light of a pink dawn, Tamara stared out the kitchen window at the edge of the Atlantic white cedar forest two hundred feet away. She loved the Pine Barrens, but could she stay here? Should she allow her loyalty to Harland to keep her here as co-executor when she knew how volatile her feelings toward Simon were?

To say nothing of his feelings for her.

Sometimes the waves of hostility emanating from him were enough to make her hair curl. Other times she felt as ensnared by his innate sexuality as a fly caroming into a spider's web and being stuck fast by forces beyond its control.

He frightened her. How could she work with him?

Dammit, she refused to be intimidated by a mere man! So he'd kissed her. So what? Hadn't she been kissed before?

But the remembered feel of his velvet tongue sliding against her lower lip made her mouth soften with desire. The look of naked longing he'd given her before snapping back to hostility could melt the iceberg around her heart—if she'd let it.

Which she wouldn't. Couldn't. Not a man with that kind of baggage. She had enough of her own.

With a sigh she looked around the kitchen, a long rectangle with a dining area brightened by a window wall that spilled morning light into the room. Above an eating counter separating the two rooms, open shelves held a few dozen fragrant pinecones she'd collected during her forays into the woods.

She poured a refill into her mug, a covered contraption that wouldn't spill as she hopped from kitchen to table. Her unbraided hair cascaded over her shoulders as she bent forward to set the pot back on its hot plate. Should she care about that one little provision of the will that if both executors didn't work together, everything would go to charity? Could she live with her conscience if she made the twins lose their heritage?

She'd go see Yvette. Yvette would be able to give her some insight into Harland's thinking, and maybe into Simon's.

Not that she cared about Simon's thinking.

But if she had to work with him, she wanted to be prepared.

Lifting the mug of coffee, she hopped into the living room. The thin yellow cotton of her thigh-length gown swirled around her leg. A soft soughing in the corner caught her attention. Setting the mug on the nearest surface—a table whose legs were knobby branches chosen for their eye appeal—she spied the lump inside the sleeping bag, half hidden behind a plump easy chair.

Vincent. A tender smile warmed her face. She hadn't heard him come in, as she hadn't the previous night when Yvette stayed over. He was like a cat, nocturnal and stealthy. And just as sleek. Asleep, he looked like the little brother she'd

First to Die

tended a dozen years before, the tawny lock of hair fallen over his closed eyes. She stifled the urge to smooth it back.

His clothes had been folded and neatly piled on the sofa, jockey shorts on top. Vincent had told her nude was the only way to sleep, and she secretly agreed. For other people. For herself, long nightgowns gave the illusion of wholeness.

Vincent snuffled and shifted in the down-filled bag. Then his eyes flickered open. "Hi, sis."

"Did I wake you?"

"I was dreaming about coffee."

"You must have smelled it. Shall I get you a cup?"

He yawned hugely. "No, I think I want forty more winks."

"Late night?"

Vincent smiled, and all traces of innocent little boy vanished from his face. "You might say that." He snuggled deeper into the bag. "You always were an early bird, sis."

"And you were—are—a night owl," she said affectionately. "What are your plans for today? You came here to visit me, yet we haven't had an hour together. Did you ever get a job? If so, how much time off do you have right now?"

"After I wake up at noon," and they both laughed at that, "I'd like to borrow the Miata for a few hours, then take you out to dinner and we'll catch up. We never did get that lunch."

"What's the matter with your car?" She already knew the answer. Vincent had driven up in a four-year-old subcompact, something affordable. He loved the heady feel of driving her small sports car, and with Vincent behind the wheel, the combination would make female heads turn.

"It's down at the clubhouse. I used a golf cart to come here. I need a few things from the drugstore. Also a few shirts and maybe a new suit."

"Where'd you get that kind of money?"

121

Vincent's smile turned into a Cheshire-cat grin. Stretching luxuriously inside the bag, his bare, muscular arms reaching over his head, only reinforced the image. "Earned it."

"Doing what?"

"Now, sis, I'm old enough to fend for myself."

"Knowing you, it was probably for stud service."

Usually the bantering line drew a routine protest from Vincent. Now he just closed his eyes, his expression one of pure sexual satisfaction. Tamara clamped down on the instant thought of Simon's comment that Vincent looked predatory when he'd met Carrie. It was none of her business. Vincent with Carrie. Should she warn him about Carrie's claws?

No. He was old enough, as he'd just reminded her. And she herself was old enough to accept her baby brother as a sexual being, just as she herself was. If only men could get past her disability. Unconsciously she raised her hands to her hair and lifted the silky strands high off her neck, letting them sift down like rose petals against her neck.

"You look powerful sexy," Vincent drawled.

Being forced to stand on one leg had honed her balance to a sharpness matched only by old sea captains, but the comment knocked Tamara off balance. She'd been imagining Simon's mouth on her neck where she'd lifted her hair.

She reached out behind her. Her hand found the top of the TV and she stabilized. She realized she was standing in the brilliant rays of morning sun thrown across the living room through the dining room window. Vincent could probably see every curve of her body through the thin cotton.

A peremptory knock on the door startled her. She jerked her head to the sound. The house had no front hall. The entrance opened directly into the living room, only a few feet from where she stood limned in the morning sunlight.

Heat flashed from her face down to her toes when she saw him. Simon. Staring intently through one of the glass panes that were too high for her to see out of. Staring through the translucent cotton of her gown.

Jesus, that woman could make a marble statue come to life, Simon thought. His eyes had been greedily drinking in the lush sight of her silhouette beneath the gauzy fabric, her full breasts topped by nipples like acorns, the slight curve of her belly, and lower, where her pubic hair covered the spot he wanted to taste.

She'd been posing for a while, as though she'd known he'd been watching. As he had been, he acknowledged guiltily. The sight of her lifting her hair had turned his mind to mush, and he watched her stretch and preen as though for a male audience.

Her eyes flashing fire, she spun and hopped to the door. Briefly he admired her courage, recognizing that she was standing her ground instead of retreating to get a robe when the damage had already been done. But Jesus, if the sun didn't move out of that window damn soon, his body would override his brain and he'd forget what he came there for.

"What do you want?" she growled through the begrudging inch that she'd opened the door.

"I thought we'd get an early start on Dad's papers." He was proud of the forceful texture of his voice.

"I'm not ready."

"I'll wait. Is that fresh coffee I smell?"

She didn't take the hint, but stood her ground.

"The sooner we get done, the sooner you can leave. My guess is it will take two weeks, no more."

After throwing him a furious glare, she hopped aside and opened the door. *Oh yes, lady, I know what buttons to push,* he thought smugly.

Unfortunately, he discovered, she had a few buttons of her own. One of them stood in the living room, watching him with penetrating green eyes. An almost nude Vincent MacKinnon, hands fisted at the low-rise waistband of a pair of skimpy navy blue Jockey shorts, was a button he hadn't counted on. The ends of Simon's ears burned. She'd been posing for Vincent!

He cursed inwardly, remembering the comment that they weren't blood relations. Had it been more than innuendo?

"This man bothering you, sweetcakes?" Vincent asked in a husky voice.

"No, it's-it's okay, Vincent."

Simon marveled at how fast Tamara could move without her crutches when she wanted to. In an eyeblink she had disappeared into the bedroom hallway, hopefully to dress. It wouldn't do to think about how her breasts bounced and swayed as she hopped, how her hair cascaded around her face like lava fire.

"You keep away from her, you hear?"

Simon turned to find Vincent's hostile eyes boring into him.

"She's the most important thing in the world to me," Vincent continued. "You hurt her and you answer to me, understand?"

Simon almost laughed. He had a good four inches on him, although the lad's body looked well honed. Then Vincent walked right by him and disappeared into the same hallway.

Simon's mouth clamped shut. What did he care if they shared the bedroom? He stalked into the kitchen, jerked open several cabinet doors before he found a cup, and poured himself a black coffee. What the fuck did he care?

A minute later Vincent sauntered into the kitchen, a well-fitting white terrycloth robe snugly tied around his lithe body. He opened the correct cabinet door on the first try, took a mug and poured himself coffee with lots of fresh light cream.

"Cholesterol," Simon grumbled, unable to say anything sociable.

"The young are invincible, didn't you know that?" Vincent said between sips. "My cholesterol count is under one eighty. My stamina is superb." Glancing toward the bedroom, he smiled a secret smile that Simon itched to wipe off the boy's mouth.

He was goading him, Simon knew that, but it didn't help, knowing he was competing with someone more than a dozen years younger than himself.

Competing with? Dammit, was he crazy? He didn't want Tamara Hart! He wanted her ass in a sling! He wanted her punished for what she'd done to his father.

And he couldn't let a stray sunbeam divert his attention.

"I'm ready." Tamara stood between her red crutches, wearing loose jeans with one leg pinned up, a bulky sweatshirt hiding her curves, her spectacular waterfall of hair pulled back in a ponytail with an elastic band at her nape.

He couldn't find any indication of makeup. Dammit, did she think she'd look frumpy? She looked kissable, is what she looked like, scrubbed clean, wholesome, just-woke-up-and-ready-for-a-morning-quickie adorable —

"I said, I'll be along in a minute," Tamara announced, glaring at him.

Simon snapped out of his reverie. His glance sliced between brother and sister. They obviously wanted to be alone for a tender moment. Dammit, what did he care?

He stalked out, leaving the front door wide open behind him. Not that he expected to hear anything. He'd merely left it open for her to follow him out. He stood fuming on the porch, squinting at nothing in particular.

"Come here, you," he heard Vincent say. Tamara's answer was a giggle. Simon took a quick step off the porch and onto the scraggly grass. He didn't want to know what they'd say.

"You're bad," Tamara admonished. "You made him think—"

"Damn right." Vincent chucked her under the chin. "If he wants you, he's damn well going to have to fight me for you."

"Wants me? You silly goose."

"Doll, that man's nuts are aching right now. Trust me."

"I suppose you know all about aching nuts."

"That I do, sister dear, that I do. And his are in a nutcracker's mouth and we're pushing the lever down—"

"Stop it!" Tamara shuddered. "That's enough."

"Made him think exactly what I wanted him to think. Did you see the sleeping bag when he walked in? Did you see my clothes? Hell, no. I pushed everything behind the sofa and appeared in my French-cut shorts, and he thought I'd just gotten out of your warm bed and was watching you strut in a natural spotlight."

"It's all in your head. Simon thinks I was responsible for his father's death. He can't stand to be near me."

"That may well be, but not for that reason. He doesn't want to be near you because then he couldn't keep his hands off. If the man's anything like me, he'd be stroking a really hard cock right now."

Tamara punched his arm. "That's enough. If you want to use my car, you take that back."

"I take it back," he said promptly.

Which caused them both to giggle.

Standing with a foot on the golf cart's hood, Simon gritted his teeth and clenched his fists. He could ignore the indistinct murmur of soft voices, but the giggling was too much. He tossed away the pinecone he'd been idly hefting in the air and took a step toward the porch to drag her out.

Tamara stood in the doorway, a jacket over her sweatshirt. "Are you planning to come back in? I'm ready to go out."

He spun on his heel, sat in the driver's seat, and waited wordlessly while she maneuvered herself into the golf cart.

Cris Anson

Chapter Twelve

ॐ

"Damn, that isn't it, either." Simon crouched at the safe built into an inner wall in the den. A panel matching the waist-high wainscoting around the room had concealed it. Years ago his father had shown him the lever that opened it. But the combination he had used—the twins' birth date—didn't work.

"So call a locksmith." Tamara sat at Harland's desk, listing contents and numbers of passbooks on a form Yvette had provided. "It's not a safe-deposit box. You have a right to open it without the Surrogate present."

Simon gave her a scathing glance before returning his attention to the lock. She wouldn't understand. Simon prided himself on knowing how his father thought, as Jack never could. He knew that he should know the number.

"What numbers did you try?"

An exasperated sigh escaped him. "Birthdates. Death dates. Wedding dates. Everyone in the family." Simon was embarrassed that he'd had to look up Kathye's dates—two pitifully short months of life—in the family Bible.

"Who, specifically? Let's write it all down and see if there are any holes."

He shot her an angry look, then sat on the floor with his back resting against a panel. Eyes closed, he rattled off every date and its meaning. He'd even tried the date the course opened and the date Harland bought the farmhouse.

Tamara had to scribble fast to keep up. After Simon finished, she was silent for so long that he opened his eyes and looked at her from underneath his lashes.

In a very quiet voice she said, "What about your son?"

Stillness settled over Simon. "He wouldn't remind me of something so—" He turned his head aside.

"Painful?"

Simon's head jerked back. "What would you know about it?"

"I've known my share of pain."

His stomach clenched. He struggled to keep his gaze from the kneehole of his father's desk, where he knew he'd see one sneaker under one baggy jeans leg.

"I didn't mean—"

"What was Kevin's birth date?"

A muscle worked in Simon's jaw. Then he turned to the safe and tried it, left 4 for April, 30 right, 5 left for 2005. It opened. Simon rested his head against the cold steel of the safe's opening. "Kevin," he whispered.

A whiff of something warm and citrusy told Simon that Tamara had come up behind him. She placed a gentle hand on his shoulder. He resisted the urge to shrug it off. Kevin's death still pained him so much that the small comfort it offered was like a balm to his soul.

"Harland was remembering the joy, not the sorrow."

Dammit, why did she have to be so perceptive? He didn't want to approve of anything she said or did. He didn't want her to have any good traits at all.

"Let's see what's in here," she said briskly, as if to allow him the privacy of his thoughts. She bent over his shoulder. Her thick ponytail slid forward and dangled between them. If he moved a few inches, it would stroke his cheek. He remembered how her hair this morning had shimmered like gold in the sunlight.

How her yellow nightgown had clung like a halo around the lush silhouette of her body.

Dammit, he refused to think like that!

129

Abruptly he stood. "Dig all that stuff out." He reached the desk in two strides and snatched up the mahogany file tray. "Toss it all in here and we'll spread them out on the library table." He spun around for something else to occupy his hands. The fireplace. He'd started the fire when they arrived, but had been so intent on opening the safe that he hadn't checked its progress. A green log had fizzled out and the fire was almost gone. With a brass and iron poker he jockeyed the log off the andirons, then tossed some dry cherry logs on. When the fire caught, he stared as if hypnotized by the dancing flames.

How long he stood there, he didn't know. Tamara's irate voice roused him from his reverie.

"Are you trying to heat the whole house?"

The library table, strewn with papers, sat parallel to the fireplace. Tamara's back was to the roaring fire. He turned toward her voice. And almost groaned. Her hands were raised in the act of pulling off her baggy sweatshirt. He held his breath.

Underneath she wore a Nature Conservatory T-shirt in what must have been a men's extra-large. Inexplicably disappointed, he said, "Don't you have anything of your own to wear?"

"This is mine. I like them roomy." Then her chin came up. Sparks from her eyes rivaled those in the fireplace. "Except for evening. Then I like to be more feminine."

The memory of Tamara's plump breasts exposed above the low-cut blue gown seared Simon's brain. He remembered his father leaning over her as he held her chair, adoring her with his eyes, planting a kiss on her cheek. He felt a vein pulsing in his temple and took a deep breath. He must never forget that this woman was responsible for his father's death. "Just keep recording every document," he ordered. "I'll be back."

"That's it," she said. The pen flew out of her hand, bounced off the table and onto the rug. She hoisted herself out of the chair. "I've had it with your caveman tactics. I'm doing you a favor, remember? Whatever happened to 'please'? You haven't said one civil word to me since you banged on my door at six o'clock this morning."

"It was after seven."

"Too early to sneak up on someone."

"I wasn't sneaking. And you were awake."

"And busy."

The memory of Vincent in his skimpy briefs caused a flare of jealousy so sharp that Simon almost put a hand to his heart. "Right. With your so-called brother. Not a blood relation, as he took great pains to inform us. You knew damn well you were silhouetted by the sun under that piece of gauze you were wearing, yet you posed like a shameless hussy, lifting your hair off your neck and letting it spill down like you were teasing him."

"Hussy?" Her eyes flashed fire and venom.

The front doorbell chimed. Simon's head jerked toward the sound. He grabbed one of Tamara's crutches as hostage and jabbed the tip in her direction. "Sit down. If you try to leave, I'll only come after you. You're going to honor Dad's last wishes if I have to tie you to the chair."

"Big strong man. As if I could run away on one crutch."

Simon ground his back teeth together. This exasperating woman could teach a porcupine how to be prickly. He looked in disgust at the crutch in his hand and made a move to fling it aside. Had being away from civilization for ten months made him forget everything he knew about being a gentleman?

In two seconds she was at his side, one hand yanking at the crutch, the other pressed against his chest for leverage. "Don't you throw my property around!"

"Easy," he said. He had visions of her tugging so hard that she'd lose her balance, as she had the night of the board dinner when Jack had caromed into her. With his free hand he captured her around the waist and pulled her toward him, harder than he'd intended to, he later told himself.

She bounced against him, her breasts flattening against the hard wall of his chest. Her shiny blonde hair had pulled out from the elastic, probably when she'd yanked the sweatshirt over her head. It spilled over her shoulders and one side of her face in a golden fall. He noticed her thick dark lashes were tipped with blonde.

"Let go," she said in a strangled voice.

He released his hold on the crutch. When it slipped to the floor, he realized both of her hands were pushing against his chest. She had probably meant for him to let go of her.

No way. He brought his newly empty hand to the side of her head and splayed his fingers through her hair, gently combing it away from her face. Her hands on his chest curled into fists, grabbing the fabric of his black turtleneck sweater. *Put your arms around me,* he wanted to say. *Feel what you do to me.*

The doorbell chimed again. It brought him to his senses like a bucket of glacier melt tossed into his face. He grabbed Tamara by the upper arms just long enough to assure her balance then turned like a drill sergeant. His loafers clicked against the parquet floor as he marched down the hall to the front door.

Tamara groped for the doorjamb to steady herself. She'd girded herself for the kiss she'd seen building in his eyes, steeled herself—no, if she was honest, she'd admit she'd wanted that kiss. The feel of him against her breasts, her thighs, was hotter than the fireplace. The bulge of his cock against her pubic bone knotted her insides, made her forget that this man was definitely not the sensitive kind of guy she needed. Dear God, if he wanted a one-night stand with her, she didn't know if she could resist.

The sharp crack of Simon's footsteps sounded in her ears a second before he reappeared in the doorway of Harland's office.

"Here," he said, edging past her and carrying a tray with a domed lid in one hand and a carafe in the other. "I asked Chef to send something. I didn't see any breakfast dishes when I was in your kitchen this morning."

Tamara glanced at her wristwatch. Almost noon. No wonder her stomach had been making small sounds of distress.

He set the carafe and tray on an uncluttered spot on the library table. Tamara's mouth watered at the artfully arranged, bite-sized platter of melons, kiwi, pineapple, and three kinds of cheeses, with a holder of toothpicks shaped like miniature sabers, and soft poppyseed rolls.

She came to the table and sat in the chair he'd pulled out for her, noting with satisfaction that it was opposite the heat of the fireplace. "It looks wonderful. Thank you."

"Truce?" The rich baritone of his voice just above her head held a husky timbre. His breath tickled the hair at her temple. She hesitated to lean back for fear his large hands still rested on the edges of the chair.

"I'm starved," she said, glad to hear her voice sounded normal. She reached forward and grabbed a roll.

Apparently her ploy to break the spell worked, for Simon went wordlessly to a cupboard and returned with two glasses. The carafe held minted iced tea, she discovered when she took a sip from the glass he poured her.

He slid into the chair opposite hers. They ate without speaking. Tamara kept her eyes downcast, afraid that if she looked up she would find him staring at her.

"You're right," he said, breaking the silence. "It's too hot next to the fireplace."

A smile touched the corners of her mouth, but she resisted an "I told you so".

The sound of chair legs being dragged against the carpet caused her to drop a chunk of melon off its toothpick. Simon had moved his chair to the narrow side of the table, catercorner from her. "Much too hot."

Tamara swallowed hard. He had removed his turtleneck. His own T-shirt snugged against sculptured muscles. Now it would also be too hot on the far side of the table. She reached for her glass and quickly downed the rest of her tea.

In her peripheral vision she saw his hand come up. He stroked her bruised cheek with a knuckle. "Does it still hurt?" he asked softly. "Looks like it's healing nicely."

The last gulp of tea threatened to lodge in her windpipe at the gentleness of his touch. "It's fine," she managed.

"Good."

Another silence. She felt a different kind of heat as she realized he still gazed at her profile. Nervously she nudged the tray toward him until it touched a pile of papers, just out of his reach. "Are you still hungry?"

"Starved." The word was a caress.

"Do you—" her bravado faltered a moment, "do you want cheese or fruit?"

He skewed the chair until his thighs straddled the table leg. His knee was inches from her thigh. "Either."

Damn, she should have looked before she spoke. No fresh toothpicks remained. The tiny swords lay in a single pile in a corner of the tray. Was he squeamish about a used toothpick?

"Your hands are clean," he murmured as if reading her mind.

Trying to ignore the dry spot in her throat, she picked up a juicy square of pineapple and ferried it to his mouth.

It was a mistake to look. The sensuous curves of his upper lip beckoned to her. He opened his mouth, revealing strong, even teeth as white as any shirt a businessman ever wore. Then his tongue inched out, thick and dark and glistening. Oh God, what that could do between her legs...

She shoved the fruit into his mouth. Her index finger grazed his tongue. The contact was electric.

His mouth closed around the digit. The heat surrounding it burned through her hand, up her arm, down her torso, and centered between her legs like a branding iron. Her eyelids fluttered closed. Was this what it was like for a man to feel a woman's soft innards closing around his hard cock?

He sucked gently, stroked her fingertip with his tongue, released the suction. For a moment her hand stayed immobile, cocooned in the indescribable heat of his mouth. When she opened her eyes, his face was inches from hers. Slowly she withdrew her finger and traced a wet line across his upper lip. Their gazes met, held. His eyes darkened.

She whispered his name just before his mouth captured hers. His tongue slicked across her lips, nudged them open. Then all thought deserted her except the velvet heat of his tongue, the exquisite clinging of his lips against hers. She tingled in anticipation of a deepening of that kiss, a repetition on her tongue of the gentle sucking he'd performed on her finger.

But he didn't. He drew back.

She blinked a few times and roused herself to focus on his eyes. His face wore an odd expression.

He cleared his throat. "I'll start looking up stock prices. I saved Wednesday's Wall Street Journal. How far from done are you on that list?"

So he wanted to play games, did he? Tamara's spine straightened, her eyes narrowed. She turned toward the pile of papers she'd been working on and handed him one of the completed worksheets. Later, when Simon leaned in her direction to remove the fruit tray from the table, she skittered to the edge of the chair and grabbed hold of the armrest for balance.

She would not be jerked around. She would not!

Focus, focus, focus, she repeated silently like a mantra. Don't think about the blinding heat of his mouth around her finger, the aura of virility he radiated. His taste ran to simpering, petite brunettes like Carrie, not feisty, independent blondes, she reminded herself.

Focus! The sooner they finished this damn list, the sooner she'd be absolved of responsibility as co-executor.

"This is the last of the stocks," she said finally. She stood and reached for her crutches. "I need a break."

She swung down the hallway, stopping to gaze at a wall of photographs she'd seen many times before. Harland with Arnold Palmer. Harland in a golf cart with someone who had to be famous, for it was inscribed with an illegible signature. The twins when they were teenagers, grinning from ear to ear, holding golf clubs and looking as though they'd won a tournament. An aerial of the course from years ago, after a stand of Atlantic white cedar edging the back nine had been decimated by a forest fire.

Inside the lavatory, she frowned at how disheveled her hair was. But she wouldn't give Simon the satisfaction of thinking her vain by going back for the comb in her fanny pack. After washing her hands, she splashed warm water on her face and ran damp fingers through her hair. It would have to do.

Returning, she stopped in the doorway, studying him. Simon's head was bent forward over a calculator. His hair really was marvelous, she found herself thinking. Thick and wavy, with just a glint of gray here and there. She was glad the barber had left it long enough to graze his collar, long enough to grab hold of in a moment of passion.

"I don't believe it!" he exclaimed as he finished punching numbers. The sound of his palm slapping on the desk was as crisp as a rifle shot. Tamara drew a startled breath.

Simon jerked his head up at the sound. "You knew all along," he bit out.

Her eyes widened. He was referring to her!

"You're quite clever," he said, rising slowly from the chair and coming at her like a stalking panther.

"What are you talking about?"

"Don't play games. Are you going to tell me you didn't have any inkling of how much your share of the fee would be?"

"What fee?"

"I read up on estate law. The executor is entitled to six percent on all income that comes into their hands. These stocks alone come to over two million dollars. Six percent of two million is a hundred twenty thousand dollars. Naturally I'll waive my half of the commission. Will you?"

"I didn't know he was going to do this!"

"There's plenty of other assets too."

"Stop it! I didn't know, I tell you!"

"You figured with me away and Jack drunk, you had a clear shot at Dad's money. Well, it isn't going to work, lady."

"I didn't know—"

"I heard you the first time. But did you hear me?"

"What?"

"I said I'd waive my commission. Will you?"

So he thought she was after the heirs' money, did he? He thought he could kiss her until her brain fogged and then as much as call her a gold-digger?

She stuck her chin out. "No, I won't. By the time we've filed the last return, I'll have earned every penny of it, working with a bastard like you."

Grabbing her fanny pack and crutches, she stalked down the hall to the front door. She was going to Yvette's right now and see how she could extricate herself from this damnable mess Harland had gotten her into. Halfway down the front porch steps, she realized she would have to take Simon's golf cart.

So what? How else would she get home? Certainly not with that pigheaded barbarian. She damn well couldn't be expected to hobble the mile to her bungalow.

She just hoped he'd had it plugged in overnight to charge the battery. One of the things she especially liked about The Pines was electric golf carts. Less noise, less air pollution. She also hoped that the Neanderthal back in the house wouldn't remember how she'd gotten here until she was out of reach.

Back inside the den, Simon ripped the tape out of the calculator, crushed it into a tight ball, and pitched it viciously into the fireplace. Tamara Hart would come out of this like a rock star with a platinum CD.

Jesus, hadn't he learned anything from Carrie? Why had he thought this one would be different? Because of her disability? Put a beautiful woman near an impressive net worth and she behaves according to type. Oh, Tamara played it exactly right, stroking his lip, offering her finger for him to suck, staring heavy-lidded at him as though she'd been drugged after he broke the kiss.

Which, if he'd admit it to himself, was one of the hardest things he'd ever done. The soft promise of her mouth, the gentleness of her touch, the compassion when they'd talked about Kevin, had almost undone him.

Who was he kidding? She, too, had known which buttons to push. They learn fast, these scheming women who think their beauty entitles them to unearned income.

And Tamara was as beautiful a woman as he'd ever seen.

And as mercenary, he had to remind himself.

With a bitter sigh, he gathered up all the negotiable instruments and returned them to the safe. Then the phone rang. The caller's message made his blood cold as ice.

*   *   *   *   *

Marta immediately sensed the tension between Jack and Carrie as they entered the boardroom where she and Elliott awaited them. No doubt Jack was jealous of the cocky young man who'd burst into their lives. Tamara Hart had been a disruption since she arrived. And now the step-brother was causing damage. It wouldn't surprise her if Carrie had already done what Jack's expression accused her of doing, the slut.

At least Carrie was tractable. Tamara was a thorn. Tamara was the reason they convened this shareholder meeting without two of the major shareholders having been invited. The problem would be resolved soon, she vowed. It had to be.

Her gaze met Elliott's and she nodded. Although Elliott had called the meeting, Marta was as eager as he to make some decisions that would remove a major obstacle to Jack's plan.

"I still say Jack should contest the will," Carrie said as she sat down next to him.

Elliott smoothed the lay of his perfectly knotted Countess Mara tie. "Probate of a will cannot occur until ten days after death. We have time to come to a decision on that."

He looked pointedly at Jack. "If a will is contested, that means every provision is questioned. We're talking about more than Hart's shares. Can you live with a judgment that takes away your half of Harland's other assets?"

"They couldn't do that!"

"Why not? The will in my possession, which I assume would be the binding document if the new one is declared invalid, gives you the land and Harland's shares, but gives Simon all the rest, as Harland had told you innumerable times."

Jack pulled out a handkerchief and swept his forehead with it. "How much money are we talking about?"

"The co-executors are charged by law with listing all assets and liabilities. I wouldn't be too hasty contesting."

"How long after a will is probated can it be contested?"

"After a judgment of probate is issued, an aggrieved party has four months to file a Complaint seeking an Order to Show Cause."

"Four months?" Jack jumped up from his chair and began pacing. Marta noted that he hadn't brought his ever-present glass of bourbon with him. No wonder he was nervous.

"We'll make a decision well within four months," Elliott assured him. "We have two avenues for contesting. One, the testator lacked sufficient mental capacity to execute a will, and two, the will was a product of undue influence exerted upon a testator."

"There's a third option," Marta observed.

Elliott's eyes narrowed. "Which is —?"

"What Jack threatened at the last meeting."

Jack's face paled. "Hey, I didn't mean —"

"Your exact words, I believe, were, 'You're dead meat.'"

The words hung in the air. The shareholders looked uneasily at each other. No one wanted to be the first to voice agreement.

Finally Marta spoke. "Let's stop pussyfooting around. Elliott, did you speak with everyone individually?"

"I did."

"And?"

"Individually, and privately, everyone has the same goal."

"And here in this room when we're all together?"

Jack jiggled his coins. Carrie fussed with her short skirt. Marta stared at Elliott, who stroked his chin.

"God, what a bunch of pansies you all are," Marta declared. "We all want her dead. What are we going to do about it?"

"Hire a hit man?" Carrie asked hopefully.

All eyes snapped to Elliott. "How would I—?"

"Who but the lawyer could find out?" Carrie said.

"Harland must have had something on you to make you swallow the dirty trick he played on you, Elliott. You took it without a whimper." Jack stopped jiggling his coins and leaned, palms down, on the table. "Maybe you were a hit man in your past."

"Not funny," Elliott snapped. He glared at the others. "I won't take the rap. I only have ten percent of the shares."

"And a million in fees," Jack reminded him.

"Less than what a law firm with five names in its title would charge, I assure you."

"What about Marta?" Jack swung around to face the controller. "She wants to be CEO so bad she can taste it. Maybe I should just be chairman and let her take the day-to-day reins."

"First sensible thing you've said recently," Marta said. "Shows how well you can think when you're not drinking."

"Dammit, get off my case about that."

"I'm making a point, Jack. Between nine and noon you can be brilliant. Your handling of the planning board chairman was nothing short of inspired. Your decision to replace the gas golf carts with electric ones received a ninety-percent approval rating in the member survey. These ideas come in the morning. Then, every afternoon and evening you piss away your great ideas along with all the booze you guzzle."

Jack rounded the table and glared down at Marta. "If you were a man, I'd—"

Marta shot to her feet and stood toe-to-toe with Jack. "I'm man enough to take you on. Just because I occasionally wear skirts doesn't mean I can't shingle a roof or install a bathroom fan or throw the first punch in a slugfest with a drunk."

"I'm not drunk, dammit!"

"Can we get back to the matter at hand?" Elliott's voice was well modulated but carried like a stage actor's to the last row of a packed theater.

Sheepish, Jack took a step back. Marta stared him down. Jack broke eye contact first. Both returned to their chairs.

"Jack, where's that list you made?" Elliott asked.

"Wait a minute, don't pin this on me!"

"I'm not doing anything of the sort," he replied smoothly. "It's just that you have custody of it."

Jack's eyes hardened. He could look fearsome when he was sober. But Carrie, as far as Marta could see, contributed nothing except discord. She wondered if Carrie had a will. Would she leave her shares to Jack? Would Elliott know? If she didn't have a will, would Simon get her shares?

She put on her mental brakes. Even with Carrie out of the picture, they still were shy ten votes. They had to convert either Simon or Tamara. On the other hand, if they got rid of Simon and he died intestate, Jack would be next of kin...

She wouldn't let anyone leave until they made a decision, Marta vowed. She strode to the door to lock it.

* * * * *

Life was good, Vincent thought as he perked a fresh pot of coffee after catching another forty winks. Or maybe it had been eighty. He glanced at the kitchen clock. Nearly noon.

Carrie had been everything her eyes promised. He couldn't remember another night like it. No holds barred, no idea too repulsive. And it was his for the asking.

The five C-notes she'd given him at some point during the evening couldn't have come at a better time. Sipping his coffee, he smiled remembering how she'd presented it, not like a woman paying for services, but like a coquette playing a game. She'd wrapped them around his limp cock and tied them together with a red ribbon, trying to coax one more performance out of it.

He'd gotten the message. She'd gotten her performance.

If things kept up this way, he'd have a down payment on a seventy-thousand-dollar Dodge Viper in no time flat. He wolfed down two peanut butter and jelly sandwiches with several cups of coffee then dressed. In the posh men's clothing store downtown was a silk suit with his name on it, and he intended to find it.

Whistling, he snatched the keys to Tamara's Miata from the hook inside the pantry and sauntered out the door into the midday sun. Parked next to his old clunker, the little two-seater that cornered like a race car and purred on straightaways beckoned to him.

But it was two years old. The Viper would be brand new.

And it would be his.

He was done coming back to his old man with his tail between his legs when he ran out of money. He thought he'd make it in Atlantic City, but they recognized him as a card counter and he was barred for life from the casinos. He'd found a forty-year-old woman at Harrah's and thought she'd be good for a couple of years of freebies, but she went back to her husband. Ike was only a way station until Vincent caught his breath.

Carrie was his ticket now. And fun besides. His well-used cock perked up at the thought. "Not yet, boy," he said as he slid behind the wheel and inserted the key into the ignition. "Tomorrow's plenty of time for her to miss us."

Vincent adjusted the mirrors, slid the seat back a notch, buckled himself in, and smiled.

"Lady Luck, here I come!" Laughing, he turned the key.

The explosion blew the firewall into the cab, blasting the steering column violently forward. The concussion shattered the windshield and zapped through Vincent's brain. He was dead before a lick of flame found the fuel line and fed into the tank. In moments the fireball could be seen above the line of Atlantic white cedar.

Chapter Thirteen

ဢ

"Vincent! Vincent!"

Simon heard Tamara's grief-stricken cry above the chug of the fire engine's pump as he squealed to a halt and jumped out of the Lexus. The smell of scorched metal seared his nostrils.

When the head groundskeeper had called to tell Simon of the fireball he'd seen, Simon thought the bungalow had exploded. His relief on seeing Tamara almost buckled his knees.

Firemen trained their hoses on the bungalow to keep it from igniting. Steam still rose from the Miata, but the flames had been doused. Its white paint was either blistered or burned off. The tires had blown from the heat. The demolished car looked like it belonged in Belgrade or Bosnia, not rural Columbus County, New Jersey.

Restrained by a pair of strong hands, Tamara fought to reach the charred body in the driver's seat. The man holding her, Lieutenant Kyrillos, glanced at Simon, nodded a greeting of recognition then returned his attention to the wild gyrations of the woman in his grip. Simon walked into Tamara's line of vision, deliberately blocking the sight.

She lashed out at him, punching and scratching. "Get out of my way! I have to get to him! He needs me!"

Kyrillos relinquished his hold as Simon's arms came around her. "There's nothing you can do for him," he murmured.

Like a house of cards touched by a gust of wind, she collapsed against him, sobbing brokenly. He felt her shivers through the baggy T-shirt. He realized the sweatshirt she'd worn earlier still hung over one of the chairs in the den. Suddenly she struggled against his hold. "Jack did this."

"What?" Shock laced Simon's voice.

"Vincent was with Carrie last night. Jack must have found out and he did this."

"I can't imagine Jack being sober enough—"

"Then he paid someone else to do it." Her voice held a flat certainty.

Simon glanced uneasily at the detective, who asked casually, "Any idea where Jack might be right now?"

"Either on the course or at the club," Simon hedged.

Kyrillos spun on his heel, strode to an unmarked police car, and spoke to the uniform behind the wheel. A minute later the car headed toward the club and the detective returned.

"Miss Hart, can I have a few words with you?"

"Can't you see she's in shock?" Simon tightened his hold on Tamara's shoulders.

"Mr. Sutcliffe," the detective said quietly, "your father's death may have been an accident, but this is definitely a homicide. I would expect everyone to cooperate."

Their gazes locked. "We should talk first," Simon said.

The detective pursed his lips, considering. A tall, thin man with a strong nose and thick black eyebrows, he wore a raincoat over a dark suit. He looked out of place among the firemen purposefully bustling about in their yellow slickers and hats. The hosing had stopped and they were packing their equipment.

Kyrillos signaled to one of the men, who retrieved the crutches that someone had thoughtfully leaned against a tree trunk, out of harm's way. "Ms. Hart, why don't you go inside and make yourself a cup of tea?" he said gently. "I'll talk to you in a few minutes."

After Tamara was out of earshot, Simon gestured to the smoldering hulk. "That thing was meant for her, not Vincent."

"Oh?" He raised an eyebrow inquiringly.

Swiftly Simon outlined recent events—the development plan, Harland's dramatic revealing of Jack's victim, Harland announcing the new will then dying the next day, the hostility toward Tamara. In a rare burst of concern for his brother, he left out the implied threat Jack had issued, *You're dead meat.*

"People have killed for far less than two hundred million dollars," the detective observed.

Simon stared for a long moment at what was left of the Miata. "It couldn't be Jack," he said at last. "He doesn't have a fire in his belly."

"Do you?"

"Me?" Simon's hands clenched into fists. With an effort he relaxed them. "Ask my attorney how much two hundred million dollars would mean to me. Ask him what I did with my holdings after my son died. Ask him—"

"It was just a question." The detective gave him a narrow look. "Which of the shareholders does have a fire in the belly?"

Simon noted the absence of a gender-specific pronoun. He thought a moment. Carrie wanted to quash the divorce, but was it his money that she wanted? Or did she see Tamara as an obstacle to be removed in her quest to remain Mrs. Simon Sutcliffe?

What about Marta? He'd felt no hostility from her toward Tamara. In fact, when he considered it, she almost acted as though Tamara were invisible.

That left Elliott. Fire in his belly? Absolutely. Harland had told him in confidence of Elliott's humble origins, although the lawyer had skewed tales of his past to make himself seem less ignoble. Simon assumed the Sutcliffes and the corporation weren't Elliott's only clients, but he'd never mentioned any dealings outside The Pines. He realized that he knew nothing of Elliott other than what Elliott had carefully fed them. "I think it would make sense for you to question all of them," he said at last.

"Exactly. I have an idea and I need your help."

Listening, Simon frowned. He didn't like it, but he had no choice. "All right. Let's go round up the board members."

* * * * *

As Marta reached the door of the boardroom to lock it, it opened and Simon stepped in, a grim expression souring his face. He glanced around. "Is this a board meeting? Why wasn't I invited?"

"I was just heading out to call you," Marta improvised. "We're trying to decide whether to contest Harland's will."

"Marta!"

Marta scowled at Carrie. Would the stupid broad rather they admitted the real reason—deciding how to eliminate some of the shareholders?

"On what grounds?" Simon hadn't moved, but it seemed to Marta that he'd gotten taller, harder, more menacing.

"There are none," Elliott said, rising to draw attention away from Marta. "I believe we've just about convinced Jack to be happy with half of everything instead of all of the golf course."

Simon's penetrating stare caused Jack to look away.

"Of course," Elliott continued, "it also depends on the progress of the development. Now that you're back, you must join in the decision-making process. After all, with thirty percent share—"

"Never mind that. Someone wants to speak with you."

"With me?" Elliott echoed.

Simon's glance rested on each of them in turn. His gaze was so harsh that they shifted uncomfortably. "With all of you."

He stepped aside. "Lieutenant?"

Carrie gasped when she saw the detective fill the doorway. "We didn't do anything illegal!"

"Shut up," Jack hissed.

"Carrie is quite correct," Elliott said blandly. "Whether or not we decide to contest Harland Sutcliffe's will, no stigma should be attached to it."

Shedding his raincoat, Lieutenant Kyrillos gestured to Simon to take a seat. The twin walked to the Chairman's chair at the far end of the table and slid in. Kyrillos sat a hip on the credenza at the back of the room near the door. From there he commanded a view of each of the board members, a view, he realized, that Simon had also chosen.

He waited in silence, absorbing the body language. The sexy brunette looked extremely nervous, glancing at the lawyer every few seconds as if seeking guidance on how to behave in a new situation. After displaying a split-second of some unpleasant emotion that Kyrillos couldn't identify, the lawyer regained his aplomb and settled his face into the mask of a poker player. Or a lawyer, he reminded himself.

He watched the other twin's hands. They shook. Kyrillos remembered that he was a heavy drinker and wondered if the tremor resulted from the absence of booze at the table, the subject matter ostensibly under discussion, or his unexpected appearance.

Or something more sinister.

Had Jack arranged the car bomb? Was it meant for the poor bastard who'd caught it?

The controller moved to the door and closed it, then sat down. "You have our attention, Lieutenant."

Kyrillos held back the smile that threatened to turn a corner of his mouth. Simon was correct. Marta Chudzik took charge of the meeting as if she were already CEO.

"I hope you'll bear with me," he said. "I would like to ask each of you a few questions. Who would like to be first?"

"Ask away, Lieutenant," said the controller.

Kyrillos stood. "Fine. Would you step outside?"

She blinked. "Outside?"

"Yes. Surely you are aware of police protocol. Private interviews?"

He didn't miss her quick glance to the lawyer. "Fine," she said, walking to the door he held open for her.

"Of course, none of you will leave," he said as he followed Marta out and closed the door behind him.

Inside the boardroom, Simon sat stone-faced as the remaining group bombarded him with questions. "I don't know any more than you do," he said, annoyed to realize it was the truth.

What he did know was that Kyrillos would question them as to their whereabouts from yesterday morning until the current meeting, then place each of them in separate rooms under police guard until he called them all back to the boardroom. Only then would Kyrillos play his next card, whatever it was. Simon wondered how long Elliott would stand for these tactics before complaining their constitutional rights were being violated. He also wondered if Jack would accuse Carrie of spending the night with Vincent and thus set himself up as a suspect.

Finally he was alone in the room. Elliott had been summoned second, apparently to defuse all the legal strategies Elliott had been spouting to the Board. He was grateful that the last to go had been Jack and not Carrie. Being alone with her for even a minute brought bile to his throat. Still, the time he'd spent alone with Jack had been heavy with silence.

His thoughts turned to Tamara. He hadn't been allowed to talk to her since she'd hobbled into her bungalow for that cup of tea. Would she be up to this?

Hell, she'd weathered Harland's dramatic announcement of how she lost her leg. She'd bounced back from the tumble she took off Jet Star. Her shell was as hard as his own. She'd survive.

Her shell might be hard, but the feel of her soft breasts pressing into his chest, the delicious clinging of her lips when he kissed her made him want to do more than kiss her. For the first time since his son died, he'd found a woman who made him at least think of giving up his self-imposed celibacy.

Wake up, stupid! He could never let himself forget that this woman could be responsible for his father's death.

The door opened. The Board was shepherded back in amid mumbling and grumbling.

"We're not all here," Elliott noted. "Ms. Hart holds twenty percent of the shares. Why is she excluded from this little gathering?"

"Yeah, how come she didn't get the third degree?" Carrie said, giving the pronoun an inflection that equated it with horseshit on a boot heel.

"All in due time," Kyrillos responded calmly.

They settled back around the table. Their backs were all up, Simon noted. No doubt Kyrillos hadn't been gentle in his questioning, and if they were all innocent of a car bombing, they were taking rightful umbrage. Simon's gaze tried to penetrate into each soul. Had one of them been capable of murder?

"Having you all here at once makes my job easier," Kyrillos was saying. "Earlier today I was called by the Fire Department to the bungalow that Ms. Hart occupies."

"Fire Department?" Marta echoed.

"When I arrived, the firemen were fighting the blaze."

"What blaze?" Elliott said, clearly annoyed at being fed information in mini-doses.

"A car parked in front of the bungalow was in flames. As near as we can ascertain, it was a 2006 Mazda Miata, white in color. The license plate is being run through the DMV computer."

"Why bother?" Jack asked. "If it was parked in front of the bungalow and it was a white Miata, then it was hers."

"Formality."

"So this is why we were all treated like criminals?" Jack stood up and began to pace. His hand slid into his trousers pocket and the sound of jingling coins echoed around the room.

"I fail to see why a car fire initiated such a Draconian sequence of events as you have promulgated," Elliott said.

"That's because we haven't identified the body yet."

"Body?" Carrie's face turned as pale as the tight white sweater she wore.

"Body?" Jack's voice was a whisper. He staggered a step then gripped the chair back. "There was a body in the car?"

"I didn't say the body was in the car," Kyrillos said.

"But—but where else would—?" Jack lurched to the door. "I need a drink."

"No one leaves."

Jack's voice was hoarse. "I'm only going to ask Hank to bring up some Old Granddad."

"There's no phone in this room," Marta explained. "Harland didn't want meetings to be interrupted."

"No one leaves." Kyrillos rose from his perch on the credenza and poked his head out the door. Simon caught a glimpse of a uniform, heard the murmur of low voices. He hoped the detective was requesting a carafe of coffee as well as Jack's order. His own nerves were raw from waiting.

During the lull, one of the board members expended a great deal of effort to keep from gloating. One of them cast smug, surreptitious glances at the others. One of them thought, *All you sissies talked about it, but I'm the one who did it! I'm the only one with enough guts to put action to words. Tamara Hart is dead and I did it!*

* * * * *

Lieutenant Theo Kyrillos, seventeen years an investigator for the Columbus County Prosecutor's Office, felt the excitement of the chase welling up in him. Each of the people he'd questioned had a motive. None was too squeamish, in his opinion, to have carried out the murder, or at least ordered it.

All of them, it seemed, had something to hide. The lawyer's background would be thoroughly checked back to when his mother had first changed his diaper. He'd been too glib. Things he'd said hadn't jibed with information volunteered by others.

The sexpot, too, resented his digging into her past. Her nose went way out of joint when he'd hammered at her insistence that she'd spent the previous night alone.

But the biggest nugget was the fact that Jack Sutcliffe had worked on a road crew one summer during college. Could he have learned how to use dynamite? Kyrillos was sure the lab guys would verify it as the cause of the explosion.

On the other hand, the controller had been with The Pines for nearly twenty years. Cooking the books? Blackmail?

Kyrillos watched Simon toss back his second cup of black coffee with a nervous energy that seemed tightly leashed. Was he as innocent as he pretended? Sure, he'd just returned after a year traipsing around the world. He'd denied any affection for his wife, insisting that the divorce would go through as planned, had likewise denied any attraction to the blonde amputee. Yet Kyrillos didn't miss the tenderness, the possessiveness, when the twin arrived at the fire scene and scooped her into his arms.

It was time to begin Act Two. Kyrillos set down his empty cup and sauntered to the door. He spoke to the uniform then returned to his perch on the credenza.

"Everyone, please take your seats." He almost smiled. In a way, it was like a play. He was the audience and the actors were about to perform. They looked at him expectantly.

The door opened and Tamara Hart entered.

"Jesus Christ!" said Jack, spilling his drink.

Marta seemed dumbstruck.

Elliott pushed back his chair and held up his hands, as though warding off a demon.

Carrie screamed then fainted.

Chapter Fourteen

∞

Tamara flinched at the odd reactions to her entrance. Her nerves had been scraped raw by the events of the past few hours. She didn't need an autopsy to tell her Vincent had been behind the wheel of her burned-out Miata. Her brother, devil-may-care Vincent MacKinnon, who only wanted everyone to love him, was dead.

The policeman who'd helped her to her bungalow had been extremely polite, but adamant—sorry, she'd have to wait, he couldn't do anything until he was given further instructions. Then he'd brought her here with not a word of explanation, just the terse direction to go in.

She watched with scant interest as Elliott fussed over Carrie, who'd done a good job of pretending she'd just fainted. Marta's mouth opened and closed like a hinged shutter in a strong wind. Jack drank straight from the bottle, amber liquid dribbling down his chin. Against her will, she allowed her gaze to settle on Simon. His lips were tightened in a grim line.

Carrie's eyes fluttered open. She caught sight of Tamara and made a gurgling sound.

Tamara tightened her hold on her crutches. Why should the simple act of her walking into a room give Carrie the jitters?

"Vincent! It wasn't her, it was Vincent!" Carrie jumped to her feet. Her gaze skewered Elliott. "You bastard!" She swung around to Jack. "Bastards! Both of you!"

"Now, Carrie—" Elliott took a step toward her.

"Don't you come near me, you mealy-mouthed pig! No one said anything about Vincent! Just because he—" Her teeth snapped shut so fast that Tamara heard them click.

Tamara turned toward the door. Spying the detective lounging against the credenza, she lobbed him a glance that might have burned through asbestos. "I don't know what you're trying to do but I don't need any more harassment. I'm going home."

Carrie's screeching voice stopped her. "You killed him! You killed Vincent!" She rounded on Jack. "You jealous bastard, you couldn't share, you wanted it all, you—" Carrie's head snapped back at Elliott's slap. Her cheek blossomed a bright red with the mark of his palm. She staggered from the impact, but stayed on her feet.

"Carrie, you don't know what you're saying."

"You're in on it, too, you piece of shit!" Her violet eyes flashed like molten steel as her gaze ricocheted between Elliott and Jack.

Elliott's hands on Carrie's arms tightened. "Get a grip!" His voice lowered to a harsh whisper. "You're not among friends."

Belatedly Carrie's gaze found the detective. His dark eyes pinned her to the spot. Wordlessly, patiently, his face clean of expression, he watched them.

Carrie swallowed hard. Her face paled, making the outline of Elliott's hand stand out more vividly. "Coffee," she managed.

Jack poured her a cup then added a shot of Old Granddad and handed it to her. Carrie took several greedy sips. Her fingers shook as she placed the cup back on the table.

"I think it's time for more questions," Lieutenant Kyrillos said. He went to the door and ushered in several policemen. "Keep them apart until I'm ready for them." He turned to Carrie. "Mrs. Sutcliffe? Could you come with me, please?"

His arm on Carrie's elbow, Kyrillos threw a challenging look at the lawyer, a look that dared him to say, "Don't answer any questions without your lawyer present."

But Elliott Grosse was apparently too astute for that. Perhaps he was merely doing the gentlemanly thing and protecting a lady's reputation, Kyrillos mused.

Or perhaps he had his own neck to preserve.

* * * * *

"Hungry?"

Simon had been watching Tamara doze, head tucked against the angle made by the back and side wing of her sofa. When she stirred and blinked her eyes open, he'd finally spoken.

It took her a moment to focus on him. Simon slouched in the green-striped easy chair, his long legs sprawled in front of him, elbows on the armrests, chin leaning on his stacked hands.

"What time is it?"

"Almost sunset." He rose, went to the front window, pulled the drapery cord to let in the sweet light from the red ball that hovered just over the stand of Atlantic white cedar that began where her front yard ended.

When he turned back to her, the sunlight had bathed her glorious blonde hair in molten gold. The pupils of her eyes had contracted from the sudden light. Her irises were almost totally blue, a bottomless pool a man could drown in.

She pushed aside the afghan he'd tossed over her, sat up, and finger-combed her hair off her face. His fingers itched to do that chore for her, to stroke away, with his knuckle, the marks on her cheek from pressing against the corduroy upholstery.

"Are you hungry?" he asked again.

"How long have you been— How long did I sleep?"

"A couple of hours. You've had a traumatic day."

Tamara braced her arms on the seat cushions to lever herself up. "Thanks for bringing me home."

"No problem. Stay there. I'll fix you an omelet."

She pulled a wry face. "I'm not thinking of an omelet right this minute."

"I'll bring in some firewood." He gave himself credit for being sensitive enough to give her a few minutes of privacy.

Once outside, he breathed deeply, reveling in the tangy smell of cedar, of a fall nip in the air, smells that almost washed away the lingering odor of charred metal. The police had impounded the remains of the Mazda as evidence. She'd need a car now, at least until the insurance was settled. He made a mental note to drop his father's Mercedes off for her tonight.

He wondered if Lieutenant Kyrillos had tried to reach them. When Tamara had collapsed on the sofa, he'd disengaged the phone jack. Sleep was a healing balm for the kind of trauma she'd just experienced.

After a few minutes, he lifted some oak logs from the bin on the porch and brought them into the living room. Belatedly it occurred to him that Tamara wouldn't want a fire, wouldn't want to be reminded of the earlier fire. He cursed himself as twelve kinds of a fool for not thinking first.

He smelled the welcome aroma of coffee, heard the burble of water through the filter. Although he'd wanted a cup earlier, he hadn't wanted to make any noise that would wake her, so he'd spent a pleasant few hours just watching her sleep. It jolted him to realize what he'd been doing—protecting her in her most vulnerable state.

He set the logs in the hearth basket, dusted his hands on his jeans, and moved to the kitchen. With a pang of regret he noted that she'd wrapped a blue paisley scarf around her glorious hair at the nape. Still clad in the baggy T-shirt and jeans from the morning, she was pouring coffee into two mugs.

"You didn't have to stay with me," she said, not looking at him as she slid a steaming mug toward him. He sat on a stool on the dining-area side of the counter.

"You need a friend right about now. I share your pain."

"Do you?"

"I lost my father in an accident."

Tamara had the grace to blush. "I'm sorry. I wasn't thinking—"

"Of course you weren't. You're in shock." He smiled. "Which is why I want to make you an omelet."

"You don't have to."

"Hey, I grew up with a chef in my backyard."

She gave him a small answering smile.

"Besides," he said, "what's there to need besides eggs?"

"Chives."

He gave her a woebegone expression. "I couldn't just yank out every drawer and open every cabinet door, now, could I? You were sleeping so peacefully, I didn't want to make any noise."

"Just outside the back door. Any chef knows fresh herbs are the best." She pulled open a drawer and handed him snub-nosed scissors. "Go clip whatever you want."

After washing his hands from the logs, he did. A moment later he returned, scissors tucked in his jeans pocket and both hands full of green snippets of a half dozen fragrant herbs. "This is great. Not only chives, but parsley—Italian broadleaf, no less—thyme, sage, dill, rosemary, oregano—"

She laughed out loud. "You aren't going to put it all in at once, are you?"

His eyes darkened. "Your wish is my command."

He was fascinated to see the blush start at her chin and work its way upward. Even her delicate ears turned scarlet. It was all he could do not to toss the snippets away and grab her in his arms to reap the promise in her eyes.

"Bread," she rasped. "We'll need some bread. It'll have to defrost. I keep it in the freezer."

He fought to get his breathing under control. "Go sit—" He tried again, consciously lowering his voice an octave. "Sit down. I'll have everything done in a jiffy."

A shaft of disappointment lanced through him when she went to the round table after pulling out a loaf from the freezer. He'd hoped she'd sit at the counter, closer to him, watching him.

"I'm not really a good cook," he said louder than necessary for the ten feet separating them, "but I do a mean breakfast. You should try my French toast. The secret is to use fresh crusty bread, not that white pap you buy for a buck and a half. And you have to mix the powdered sugar into the egg, not sprinkle it on top. And use only fresh grated nutmeg, of course."

Damn, that woman had his tongue flapping like a chicken trying to escape a fox. He zipped up his lip and concentrated on the omelets. He'd be eating crow instead of eggs if he flipped it onto the floor.

In minutes he slipped a perfectly cooked dill-chive omelet onto a plate then garnished it with chopped parsley. He was inordinately pleased when she moved to the counter to direct his search for the cutlery.

"Start eating," he said, cracking three eggs into a bowl for his own omelet. "They get cold fast. Mine'll be done in a jiffy."

It was. He slid his own omelet onto another plate, piled on three slices of defrosted seven-grain bread—he approved of her eating habits—and poured another cup of coffee.

Only when he sat down did she seem to tense up. As long as the counter had been between them, she'd been fine. Brilliant deduction, Sherlock.

Twilight descended around them, until the only light in the kitchen came from the work light over the range. They finished their omelets in silence. From a corner of his eye, Simon saw Tamara aimlessly pushing around the last bit of omelet with her fork. *I know how you feel, lady,* he thought. *I want you too.*

"Simon..."

His groin tightened. If she was reading his mind, he didn't know whether to be overjoyed or nervous. He turned his stool toward her, his left knee brushing her right thigh. Curls of desire shafted through him. He wasn't sure he'd get out of here tonight without making a fool of himself if he hadn't read her desire correctly.

"Mmmm?" Play it noncommittal until he saw what developed.

"I know you think I'm responsible..." She hesitated.

Hell, yes, she was responsible for the sudden raging of his hormones. Sitting beside him in the dusk, the elusive scent of her, the pungent pine from the cones on the shelf above them, the myriad herbs strewn on the counter. All those scents swirling around him, joining with the memory of her breasts crushed against him, her mouth soft and yielding under his.

"But if you'll just open your mind..."

She wants you to make the first move. He slid his left hand so it rested on her seat back. She didn't flinch. *Good start.*

"Simon, this is hard for me to say."

And making it harder for him. In more ways than one.

She lifted her eyes to him, eyes rimmed with tears. "In light of what happened to Vincent, could you consider the possibility that Harland's death wasn't an accident?"

For a moment he was too stunned to speak. He furiously backpedaled in his mind. He'd been ready to lean forward and lick the stray crumb from the corner of her mouth, to untie the scarf from her hair and run his fingers through the golden strands, to stroke—

With an effort he removed his hand from her chair. "What do you mean?"

"I didn't goad him. Harland had never sat a horse better than that day. His back was fine."

A tear escaped the corner of her eye. She took a deep breath then plunged on. "I want you to listen, and please, don't interrupt. I've had this feeling something was wrong and couldn't put my finger on it. But I can't keep quiet about it."

Simon ground his teeth together. When her gaze fastened on his throbbing jaw muscle, he forced himself to relax.

"Just before we jumped, I thought I saw a—a wire. Please, let me finish."

He hadn't been aware that he'd moved. He schooled his features into stone. "Go on. I won't interrupt."

"We were going fast. If you remember the trail layout, the trees narrow to a chute just before the two wooden jumps. Jet Star had already committed to the jump when I saw—thought I saw—something. It was as though someone had drawn a line with a laser beam. For a split second I saw light shimmer in a line parallel to the top board of the jump. Then Blackwing stumbled."

"I spent several hours there yesterday," he said tightly. "I went over every inch of that area with a fine-toothed comb. Your shimmering light was a piece of cassette tape that had gotten caught between the boards."

She jerked back as though he'd slapped her. "Then why did Jet Star stumble too? I thought I felt a kind of a jerky motion just before we went down, as if he'd tripped on something."

"Why didn't you tell this all to Lieutenant Kyrillos?"

"I just kept thinking about it and trying to figure out what happened. This is the only thing that makes sense."

Simon just stared at her, unconvinced.

Tamara's chin went out, an action he recognized as the equivalent of putting her dukes up. "I know the groundskeeper uses high-tensile wire to keep deer out," she said. "If it was that strong, it would have had to be wrapped around a tree on both sides of the chute. Which means it left a mark if half a ton of horseflesh knocked against it. If it's there, I'll find it. I've decided to go riding tomorrow, to recreate the run."

He glanced at her leg before he could stop himself. "You're not up to it."

"That's beside the point. I'm going to get to the bottom of this. I loved Harland too."

She loved Harland. How could he have forgotten she'd been his father's mistress? He was only grateful she hadn't maneuvered him to the altar and finessed his entire estate from them. Simon slid off the stool and went around the counter to the sink, clenching his jaw. "I'll clean up the mess I made."

"You did the cooking. I'll straighten up."

He could take a hint. She wanted him out of here. "I can find my own way out. Thanks for the snack."

Simon cursed himself all the way back down the gravel road leading off to their private road, the Lexus handling the mild curves easily. When would he learn not to be a sucker for a beautiful woman in distress?

He went straight to the den and poured himself a cognac, nursing it as he stared endlessly into the cold fireplace. Reaching for the bottle again, he noticed the blinking red light on the answering machine. He strode to the desk and punched the button. Three messages, all from Lieutenant Kyrillos. With the last, the detective had left his home number. Simon dialed.

Kyrillos answered on the first ring. "I've been calling Ms. Hart all afternoon, but there's been no answer."

Simon grunted. "I forgot to plug the phone back in."

"What do you mean?"

"I stayed with her after we left the boardroom. She fell asleep in her living room."

Squelching a sigh, Simon realized he had no choice. He had to go back and tell her, in case someone else needed to get in touch with her. "She'll be all right."

"Maybe not when she hears what I have to tell her."

A prickle slithered across Simon's nape. "Tell her what?"

"Dental records came back. The body in that Miata was definitely Vincent MacKinnon."

* * * * *

Tamara slammed the plates, the mugs, the iron frypan, into the dish drainer after she washed them. What a chauvinist! Did Simon think she was helpless like his wife pretended to be? He didn't have to say it. One unguarded glance at her stump told her what he thought of her. Gimp. Geek.

Damn him! It had given her a warm fuzzy feeling to awaken to see his eyes on her, tender, possessive, protective. And to think he knew the names of her herbs, even the Italian parsley.

Wearily she hobbled into the bathroom. It had been a long day. She turned the tub faucets on full force and stripped out of her clothes, pinned her hair in a topknot, then poured several capfuls of bath oil into the steaming water. Easing herself in, she inched down until her shoulders were covered. The warm scent of Shalimar cocooned her. Her eyes drifted shut.

Against her will she remembered how good it felt to have Simon's protecting arms around her when she'd stood staring at the burned-out hulk of the Miata. Vincent. Dear God, why?

The loud knock on the front door startled her. Chills chased themselves down her wet limbs in the cool water. Was it an omen that she'd been thinking of Vincent at this very minute?

"Just a minute," she called out. Struggling to balance on her good leg, and belatedly remembering why she usually chose showers rather than tub baths, she managed to scramble onto the bath seat a hand's reach away. Quickly she toweled herself off, wrapped an ankle-length navy blue terrycloth robe around her still damp body, and hopped to the door. "Who is it?"

"I forgot to tell you. I pulled out the phone jack so you'd nap uninterrupted. I couldn't call you to tell you to fix it."

Tamara swallowed hard. Simon. "I'll do it right now."

She waited, her heart pounding, to hear his footsteps on the porch steps that would signal his departure.

"Tamara?" His voice was lower, almost seductively so.

She put her hand against the door, as if the tactile sense of it would transpose into his flesh. "Yes?"

"I have something else to tell you. May I come in?"

Don't panic. Disregard that underneath the robe she was damp and naked. Disregard that her bones turned to jelly when he looked at her with a lust he tried to hide.

With trembling fingers she turned the deadbolt knob and opened the door. Belatedly she realized she hadn't switched on any lights. A trapezoid of dim illumination from the bathroom spilled across the braided carpet, casting a faint glow on Simon's face. His pupils were so dilated they looked black.

She stepped aside and he entered the living room, closing the door behind him. His glance gave her a thorough

165

inspection down to her bare toes. He seemed to grit his teeth together.

"Here," he said, producing a keyring with the distinctive Mercedes logo and a black-topped key. "Dad's wheels. He'd want you to use it until you get settled with the insurance company."

The unexpected kindness melted her resistance. "Thank you."

He dropped the key into her outstretched palm. She stared at his big knuckles, the wide wrist, the black hairs curling around the edges of his stainless steel watch. For the life of her, she couldn't close her fingers around the gift. She held her hand open, vulnerable, waiting.

As though sensing her ambivalence, Simon touched his fingers to the fragile underside of her wrist, drew a line across the delicate bones. Suddenly the room felt too small to her. He filled it with his presence, blotting out what little light filtered in from the tiny bathroom hall. His broad shoulders strained against his oxford-cloth shirt. He'd changed his clothes to come here, a tiny coherent part of her brain registered.

"I—I think we'd better sit down." Simon's voice sounded like a file grating over a strip of metal.

In answer, she leaned toward him. *I'm not doing this,* she thought even as she let the keys fall to the floor. Her hands pressed against the firm wall of his chest. The heat from his body blasted though her palms and rocketed up her arms, her shoulders. "Simon," she whispered.

His mouth crushing against hers absorbed the sound. Without prelude his tongue stabbed in imitation of another, more elemental movement. She caught his tongue at its deepest penetration, sucked on it, clung to it with her mouth. His arms came around her. His big hands dragged down her back, her waist, her hips, coming to rest on her buttocks. Each place he touched branded her with fire. She clung to him mindlessly, her good leg so wobbly it was as useless as her stump in holding her up.

Suddenly he lifted her into his arms. Dazed, lips bruised and swollen, she wondered if he would seduce her in her own bed. He strode to the sofa and placed her down gently. Then he flicked on a table lamp and got down on his haunches before her, carefully avoiding any physical contact with her. "I'm sorry," he rasped. "That wasn't my intention when I came here."

"Then what—" She couldn't form a coherent sentence. His kiss had been totally unlike the tender moment they'd shared when she fed him the chunk of pineapple. This time he'd plundered her mouth as primitively as she wanted him to plunder her body. Her desire left her a quivering mass of jelly, left the juncture between her thighs wet and needy. The withdrawal of his hot, hard flesh tied her insides into knots.

Simon held himself in check only by the biggest effort of will he'd ever had to summon up. Seeing her all sleepy and rosy, damp from a bath and smelling like something from a sultan's harem, her blonde hair piled on her head except for strands that tickled her neck, had jackhammered an explosion of heat and blood into his cock. He knew without a doubt that underneath the robe she wore only soft skin. He also knew that she'd be his for the taking.

Count to ten. And then to twenty and thirty and a hundred, he ordered himself. Kyrillos would be here any minute. Police had to make all death notifications. Simon had insisted on being present. "I'm sorry," he said again.

She was pulling herself together. He could tell by the narrowed look that she gave him. Her hands clutched at the lapels of her robe, holding it like a shield in front of her soft breasts. As if it would keep him out if he was determined to have her, skin to skin.

Stop thinking about it!

He stood, picked up the forgotten Mercedes keys and set them on the side table then thrust his hands into the back pockets of his jeans. The few seconds that passed before he heard a car seemed an eternity to Simon. He didn't dare look to see if Tamara heard it.

The soft knock startled a gasp from her. Simon turned then, saw the uncertainty on her face. "I'll get it," he said.

Her eyes went wide and luminous with fear when she saw Lieutenant Kyrillos. "Vincent," she whispered.

Kyrillos came in, sat next to her on the sofa, and took her hands in his. "I'm sorry, Ms. Hart. Based on dental records, we identified Vincent MacKinnon as the person in the car."

Standing a little aside, Simon watched all the blood drain from her face. She seemed to shrink inside the robe. Then her back straightened and she drew on a reserve from deep within. "Thank you for coming out to tell me."

"I was able to get hold of Ike MacKinnon. We'll notify you when we can release the body for burial. It will probably be several days to a week."

"Thank you," she said again. Her gaze stayed on their clasped hands, as though deriving strength from the detective.

"If you need anything…"

She nodded wordlessly.

Kyrillos squeezed her hands, then stood and turned to Simon. Simon could only imagine how difficult it was for the detective to deal with death day after day. He walked out onto the porch with him. "Thanks for letting me be here."

"It's never a good idea to be alone when dealing with something like this." Kyrillos glanced back to make sure Tamara wasn't listening then lowered his voice. "If Ike MacKinnon is her only support—"

Shaking his head, Kyrillos stopped abruptly, as though knowing he'd overstepped his bounds. They shook hands.

Simon turned and went back into the house as the detective's car made a U-turn and headed out.

Tamara sat where they'd left her, hands folded across her lap, lips pressed together, gaze unfocused. Gingerly he sat down beside her, cradled her cold hands between his warm ones.

A great shudder went through her. "He's gone. He's really gone." Her lower lip trembled. One tear spilled over her lashes and trickled down her cheek, then another.

Gently he lifted her onto his lap. "Go ahead and cry," he murmured. He tucked her head into the hollow of his shoulder and began making soothing circles on her back. He could feel the silent tremors go through her as he held her close, rocking her.

Suddenly the dam burst and she began sobbing brokenly, keening, moaning her brother's name over and over. She cried for a long time, wrapped in his arms, clinging to Simon mindlessly.

When the sobs died down, she hiccupped a few times. He eased her to a more comfortable position on his lap. She snuggled into him with the trust of a baby as her eyes fluttered closed.

She was anything but a baby. To his chagrin he felt his cock stir under the pressure of her warm ass. He wanted to pull the pins out of her hair and comb it with his fingers. He wanted to push open the lapels of her robe and feast his eyes on the soft breasts that pillowed against him. Hell, he wanted them in his mouth, wanted to feel her nipples harden at his touch. He wanted to plunge into her, make her forget Vincent, make her forget death, make her remember her own vitality, her sensuality.

He did none of those things. He merely ached more with each innocent movement she made in his lap. Eventually she pushed away from him. His hands loosened their grip, but he held on to her arms.

"Simon?" Her mouth curled into a ghost of a smile. "Thank you for letting me slobber all over you."

"My pleasure." Damn, her mouth was all soft and dewy, her long lashes spiked with tears. The tip of her pert nose was rosy from crying, as rosy as he imagined her nipples to be.

Abruptly he shifted.

"I'm sorry, I must be awfully heavy," she said, then scooted back onto the sofa. She took one of his hands in both of hers. "Thank you for being here." She brought his hand to her cheek. It was almost his undoing. "And thank you for your concern, your friendship."

He bit down a groan. *Lady, I want more from you than friendship.* But it was a start. Gallantly he asked, "Can I make you a cup of tea before I go? Cocoa? Anything?"

"I'm all right now."

He stood, hoping she didn't notice the bulge of his cock still taunting him under his jeans. "Lock up behind me. I'll see myself out." He stooped over and kissed her on the tip of her reddened nose.

All the way home, and far into the night, he vibrated from the remembered feel of her, warm and clinging, vulnerable and trusting, on his lap.

First to Die

Chapter Fifteen

∞

"You're sure this is the tamest of the bunch?"

"Yes, ma'am. Zelda here don't know how to jump. She's quiet enough for a five-year-old to ride."

"Thanks, Cliff." Old Gray Mare described Zelda perfectly, Tamara thought as she mounted. The effort made her wince. Her stump hadn't quite healed yet, but Simon's casual dismissal of her ability had stirred her ire. She'd inspected the limb carefully this morning and decided she could do it. The bruises along the stump were still there. The bleeding had been caused when her thigh had struck a rock on the way down. The fourteen stitches would be removed soon. The socket of her cosmetic leg caused the least discomfort, so after the powder and the stump sock, she'd pulled it on.

She vaguely remembered the detective saying last night that he'd gotten in touch with Ike. There was no love lost between her and her stepfather, but she supposed she had to call him, had to offer her help in making funeral arrangements. Yet she simply wasn't ready to face that sleazebag. Maybe she'd wait for Ike to contact her.

And maybe the cheap bastard would do nothing, expecting her to arrange and pay for the funeral.

She'd call Lieutenant Kyrillos when she got back, ask what were Ike's exact words, ask if they had a clearer idea of when she might claim Vincent's body.

Having decided on a course of action, she tucked it aside and urged Zelda onto the trail. A gray dawn had turned into a promising morning. Bits of blue peeked out through dissipating clouds. Tamara breathed deeply. The smell of dry leaves permeated the crisp air. Here in the so-called highlands, away from the swampy areas, hardwoods flourished. Occasional splashes of maroon from black gum vied with scarlet from red maples and orange from sassafras to beguile her senses.

Her thoughts turned to Harland as the horse plodded along the trail. How he loved his Pine Barrens! And he'd transmitted his love of the land to her. Should she sell her shares? Or fight for the proposal Harland had approved? By granting her life rights to the bungalow, he'd obviously wanted her to stay here.

Was it worth the hassle? Was Simon worth it?

Unbidden, the previous evening's tumultuous feelings crashed down around her. Her mouth tingled from the remembered feel of his tongue caressing hers. Her nipples hardened in response to the memory of her explosive desire. Even after her crying jag in his arms, when she'd thought of nothing but Vincent and her loss, she remembered, with a twinge of embarrassment, the moment she'd become aware of the hard, hot bulge in his lap that she'd been sitting on. Then she'd moved subtly to deepen the contact between them, had smiled to herself at the indrawn breath he tried to disguise.

But when he'd shifted in obvious discomfort—pain?— she'd had to move away or suffer the consequences.

She'd hardly consider it suffering, she mused. His shoulders were as broad as a doorway, his chest hard as oak, his mouth sensuous, his eyes laser pinpoints of promise. And she knew, just by the way he kissed, that he'd be an exquisite lover.

Her seat on the horse shifted and she automatically leaned forward. With a start Tamara realized that Zelda was plodding up a slight hill. She looked around to get her bearings.

The wrought iron of the cemetery plot came into view. With a wry smile she realized she must have unconsciously directed Zelda here. She'd been thinking of Harland and instinctively had come to him with her problems.

She reined in and dismounted with a bit of difficulty then tied the placid horse to a sapling.

The slash of raw earth mounded atop Harland's resting place stood out obscene and ugly against the neatly manicured grass around the other headstones. The stonecutter had already finished his work, carving the date of Harland's death into the large headstone uniting husband and wife for eternity.

For a moment Tamara stood at the gate, absorbing the peace of the area. A shaft of sunlight threw a wide beam of shimmering light across an autumn palette of reds and browns. A ragged Vee of honking Canada geese passed overhead. Ironically, the earth smelled rich and fertile, the result of death and decay.

The cycle of life.

Tamara couldn't bring herself to enter the tiny graveyard. She stood with her hands clutching the gatepost as her eyes filled with tears. "Dearest Harland. I miss you so much. You were my anchor, my rock."

Her hands twisted back and forth across the knob of the post. "Did you expect something like this to happen? Is that why you laid such a heavy burden on me? Co-executors." She let out an unladylike snort. "Do you know your son thinks I'm a gold-digger? That I was your mistress, for heaven's sake! Why, that would be like incest. You made me feel like your daughter. It was an honor to be part of your family.

"Would you believe Simon all but called me a liar?" She sighed. "No, you wouldn't, would you. You think the sun rises and sets on him. I don't know how I can work with him. I don't want your shares. You've given me so much of yourself that I keep here." She brought the palm of her hand to her heart. "I'm grateful for the bungalow, yes. It's comforting to know that wherever I am, I can come back here and be part of you again. But the shares, I don't want them. I'd give them, and the bungalow, and my other leg, to have you back again."

Her voice rose in agitation. "It wasn't an accident. You know it and I know it. But that son of yours accused me of goading you to jump! As if anyone could make you do anything you didn't want to! When I told him about the wire, he thought I was just trying to deflect his suspicions. Dammit, no fluttering cassette tape could trip up a horse. Spook them, maybe. But not make them stumble the way both Blackwing and Jet Star did."

She swallowed hard. Her fists tightened against the gatepost. "I'll play your game, Harland. I'll be your guinea pig. Whoever did this to you, they want me out of the way too. I'll take the shares and flush somebody out. I swear, on your grave and your grandson's grave, I'll make them pay."

Zelda's whinny sent Tamara's head whipping around. The horse's ears had pricked up. Bridle straining at its tether, she was looking toward a thick stand of birch a dozen yards away. Tamara squinted against the sun, which now shone brightly, casting the woods into deep shadow. Then her gaze searched the perimeter of the area, seeking the reason for the horse's unease.

A deer, perhaps. Tamara gave one last, long look at Harland's grave then walked slowly to Zelda and mounted. A while later she approached the jumps. She guided Zelda to the left, where the beginner's trail bypassed the jumps.

"I thought you'd come here."

Simon strode onto the path from between two robust oak trees, wearing jeans and a thick turtleneck sweater. His gaze flicked across her ivory-colored shirt and tweed jacket, the black riding pants, and lingered on her left riding boot. Tamara thought she saw a spark of admiration in his eyes.

"Let me help you down," he said, raising his arms to her.

She should ignore him, should put all her weight on her prosthesis in the stirrup and swing her right leg behind her and dismount, as she had at the cemetery.

The look in his eyes decided her. She lifted her right leg over the pommel and sat side-saddle. His large hands came around her waist. He lifted her effortlessly, holding her at eye level. With bated breath she anticipated the feel of her body sliding down the hard length of him. From the flare of awareness in his eyes, she judged he had the same idea.

Instead, he set her gently on the soft leaf bed and dropped his hands. "I figured you might need some help."

Her chin went up. "I'm glad you're here. I want to see the look on your face when you discover I'm right."

For a long moment Simon stared at her. It was on the tip of his tongue to admit that he'd seen her on Zelda and followed her in the noiseless electric golf cart, that he'd eavesdropped at the cemetery. The quiet fall air had rung with her honesty and sincerity. She couldn't have known he'd come up behind her to the birch grove and hear her impassioned vow of vengeance. She hadn't been grandstanding for him, she'd been talking to his father. He'd seen how white her knuckles had been as they gripped the gatepost, had seen the grim set of her mouth.

Simon ran a hand through his hair. He believed her now. But he couldn't tell her that. The moment had been so private, so intimate that he instinctively knew she'd be embarrassed to hear it. So he merely said, "I hope you are right."

"Where's the cassette tape you said you saw?" she demanded, scrutinizing the boards of the jump.

"Gone. Probably blew away."

He saw the flash of anger in her eyes and rushed to forestall an outburst. "Look, I—I've had second thoughts about that. If somebody really strung a wire heavy enough to trip up a horse, they could have left the cassette tape to play mind games, to make you think you were mistaken." It was the best he could do and not come right out and say he'd overheard her. "Did you hear a twang or anything that might clue you in?"

Understanding widened her eyes as she realized he was taking her seriously. "No. We went down so fast, both horses whinnying, I don't think I'd have heard if there was one."

He took her arm and guided her away from the path. "Come here. I think I found something."

They stopped at an oak about eighteen inches in diameter, on a plane a couple of inches before the second jump. "See where the bark is scraped? It fits the scenario. Right height, horizontal gouge." He bent down to align his vision from tree to jump about three feet off the ground. "If we find something on the other side, I'm bringing Kyrillos here."

Tamara put a hand to her heart. He knew just what she was thinking. It really looked as though someone had deliberately caused his father's death.

Simon's hand on her elbow nudged her forward. Better she shouldn't dwell on the possibility of murder. They walked across the trail, heading for the sturdiest of the trees. The fat trunk of a flaming red maple had scrapes going in several directions along the side opposite the trail. He swore. "Can't tell. Some of these marks might be a buck scraping his velvet."

"You believe me," she murmured.

The vulnerability in her eyes made him want again to confess. Instead, he said, "If someone is trying to send a message, I think we should listen."

She shivered.

"Are you okay?" His arm came around her shoulder.

She shrugged him away. "Just thinking about the shares. It's like taking blood money."

"Dad wanted you to have them."

"I know. Let's get the paperwork done."

They turned, Simon's big hand resting lightly on her shoulder, and headed for the horse, which was contentedly browsing on the grasses at the verge. He untied the reins from the shrub and gave it a whack on its gray rump. Startled, Zelda began trotting toward the stables.

"She'll find her way back," Simon said. "I've got a golf cart on the other side of the fence. I'll have Chef send up some lunch. Maybe by the end of the day we can put a dent in all those forms Yvette gave us to fill out."

And maybe she'd feed him from her fingers again. After last night, he wondered how he'd be able to spend the entire afternoon with her and not want to kiss her again.

* * * * *

"Well, that's that." Tamara handed Simon the four-page information checklist that she'd filled out in her tidy handwriting. They had worked on it all day, stopping only to munch on the chicken salad sandwiches Chef had sent over with a thermos of lobster bisque. She had managed to keep her mind from straying too often to the handsome man behind Harland's desk.

"Tomorrow's Monday," Simon said. "We'll go to the Surrogate's office and fill out the power of attorney forms. While we're in town we can put the notice to creditors in the newspaper and open an estate checking account. You'll have to sign signature cards." He scanned the checklist. "You didn't fill out 'safe deposit box'."

Tamara's brow arched. "I didn't know there was one."

A sheepish look skittered across his face. "Oh, that's right. Yvette and I went after the funeral. I was too angry to bring you along. She assured me only one signature would be necessary if the estate attorney was present."

"She interprets things differently on any given day, don't you think? She's obviously following Harland's instructions. They must have had a number of conversations." Tamara stared thoughtfully at the papers in his hand. "Simon, how long was Elliott the family's lawyer?"

"Years."

"Can you be more specific?"

Something in the tone of her voice must have alerted him. Simon looked up. "Fifteen, sixteen years."

"Exclusively? Harland never used another attorney?"

"Not to my knowledge." A smile curled one edge of his mouth. "But obviously I don't know everything. I never met Yvette until I walked into the board meeting."

With his Wild-Man-from-Borneo hair, looking positively uncivilized. And now, she thought, now he looked just as uncivilized, and more dangerous, because the veneer of refinement barely covered his primitive edges. She had to get her mind back to the subject at hand. Fast. "Then why would Harland turn to Yvette for something as crucial as changing a will?"

Simon stroked his strong chin with a long finger. "I've been trying to figure that out. Obviously he didn't trust Elliott."

"After fifteen years? When did Elliott get his shares?"

"Originally Mother and Dad each held forty shares. Jack and I had ten each. When she died seven years ago, Dad gave ten more to each son. A few years ago he gave ten each to Elliott and Marta as a bonus for outstanding service."

A fleeting look of distaste passed across Simon's face. "Then I made a misjudgment. I gave Carrie half my shares when she was carrying Kevin."

"Misjudgment? Simon, you couldn't have known what would happen to your son."

His eyes glittered. "She wouldn't marry me unless I did. She called it a prenuptial agreement. I called it blackmail. She'd have let my son be born without my name."

Dear God, no wonder he hated her so! Tamara's tongue was a lump in her mouth. "Do you think Elliott could have…"

"I don't know. I told the detective that we didn't really know too much about Elliott's background. I'm sure he'll dig up any hidden skeletons."

Tamara stretched in her chair, arms raised over her head. "Well, we've done the hard part. I have a headache from bending over paperwork all day." Her stump was throbbing, but she wouldn't admit that to him. She'd been wearing the prosthesis too long, had been sitting in one place too long.

"Thanks for your help." Simon's voice came from directly behind her. She stiffened warily, every nerve ending exquisitely aware of him. Long fingers gently curled around her neck. His thumbs made slow circles along the bones of her upper spinal column then moved to her hairline under the braid. Lord, it felt good.

"You're all knotted up." His voice was a husky caress. His hands swept outward over her shoulders, massaging the trapezius muscles.

Tamara's eyes fluttered then closed. It felt too good to protest. She braced her hands, fingers splayed, against the library table and allowed him to stroke away the tension. The rational part of her mind told her that he was only doing this because she'd helped him, but all her synapses were responding to the lulling, sensual effect of his warm palms against her rapidly heating skin wherever he touched.

"Just relax." His breathy command against her ear fanned the stray locks that had escaped the braid. Resisting the urge to lean back into the solidity of him, she did as he requested. His strong hands swept in arcs from her spine outward, loosening the taut muscles. How wonderful it would be to be lying on the bed, two sets of clothing discarded, and feel his strong hands massaging the tiredness from her naked body.

A delicious moan escaped her before she could catch it.

Abruptly he withdrew his hands. "That'll do it," he said, his voice sounding like he was talking through a strainer.

She almost protested that it wasn't a sound of pain that she'd made—she could spend another hour absorbing the explosive sensations of his hands roaming across her body—then realized his withdrawal was for that precise reason.

Her fingers itched to repay the favor, to learn the feel of velvet over steel, to find the source of the heat that he'd transmitted through his long fingers.

"Come on, I'll drive you home." Simon's voice was rougher than he'd expected. But he couldn't control its timbre after a few minutes of caressing this woman who was by turns rugged, vulnerable, argumentative, flexible, adamant. She'd worked without complaint for almost six hours, helping him sort through insurance policies, deeds, business papers, appraisals and purchase certificates.

His father had left an impressive legacy. Aside from The Pines, his holdings included stocks and bonds, paintings, his mother's jewelry, the brand-new Mercedes. The list reminded Simon of his own holdings. It was time Elliott accounted for his stewardship. So much had happened since his return that he'd forgotten Elliott still held his power of attorney.

A feeling like a burning stone lodged in the pit of Simon's stomach. Was Elliott responsible for the car bomb? Or worse yet, for his father's death? He could only hope that Kyrillos was more than merely competent.

"I'm ready," Tamara said, shaking him out of his thoughts.

The Corvette made the short trip to her bungalow smoothly. He swung the car around so the passenger side was near the porch, shifted into park, and let the powerful engine idle.

Tamara hesitated, nervously fingering the door handle. She turned to him, those big blue eyes wide and uncertain.

God, if she looked at him like that much longer, he knew he'd be lost. He forced his attention to the luxurious smell of the car's leather appointments, the fresh pine scent of the air outside, anything but the tantalizing hint of her Shalimar perfume and her slightly musky essence swirling around him in the confined space.

"Would you like a cup of coffee? Or something?"

The "or something" was so artlessly stumbled over, Simon could only surmise she'd meant it in a straightforward manner, like, "Would you like tea instead of coffee?" But with his cock suddenly hardening, he read all sorts of nuances into those two words, like, "Would you like to kiss me senseless? Would you like to fuck me until I explode?"

His left hand gripped the steering wheel so tightly he felt a fingernail digging into his palm. He wondered if he could melt the leather-covered plastic with his bare hand. Outside, dusk was turning into dark and the porch light, apparently on a timer, came on to limn her profile with its golden light.

"Simon?"

His name was a beseeching whisper on her lips. That was all it took. He fumbled the ignition off and reached across the center console. One knee banged against the gearshift. He hardly felt the pain. His right arm curling around her shoulders, he drew her toward him. He cradled her chin in his left hand and grazed her lips with his. She squirmed closer, her mouth seeking a greater melding. He allowed her to take the lead, opening his mouth in invitation. She took it, stroking his tongue with hers, sucking on it. She grabbed a fistful of his hair and pulled him even closer.

The curl in his groin turned into a tidal wave. He was drowning in her, in the incredible heat from her mouth, the softness of her skin, the unique scent of her in the cocoon of the small car. With their mouths firmly, hungrily meshed, his left hand drifted down to stroke the smooth column of her neck. In a quick movement he flicked open the top three buttons of her ivory blouse beneath her jacket. He slipped long fingers under the silky fabric to trace her collarbone, her throat then lower to feel the smooth, plump skin under the lacy bra.

She moved against his hand, encouraging him to glide his fingers across her breast. Her nipple beaded under his touch. He undid several more buttons and pushed the concealing fabric aside. In the porch light, her bra shimmered, the pale skin peeking out from peach-colored lace. Her hard nipple looked like a strawberry ripe for plucking.

"God, you're beautiful," he breathed. He bent down and stroked the hard nub with his tongue. She arched into him, raking her hands through his hair. He cupped the fullness of her breast then closed his mouth around it, sucking it, tonguing it. Tamara thrashed against him, her hands stroking his neck, his back, shoulders, arms, anywhere, it seemed, that she could reach.

Her frenzied touch inflamed him. He fumbled for the closure of her riding pants, unhooked and unzipped it. Her skin underneath was as hot as noontime in July. His fingers splayed across the silky skin, dipped briefly into her navel, then stroked lower, finding the heat underneath her bikini pants. He could feel her arch against his hand, could smell her feminine essence, and he knew she wanted him with the same mindless frenzy that gripped him.

He skimmed the curls of her pubic hair, teased the edges of her swollen pussy lips. She pushed her hips up, straining against his hand. His fingers dipped into the soft folds, finding her hot and wet and ready. He touched her clit, stroked it in small, damp circles. In seconds she exploded, writhing against his hand, raining kisses on his face. She grabbed his neck and wrenched him closer, kissing him with an intensity that singed his soul.

Her spasms against his fingers slowed. Her head fell back against the seat. Her eyes were closed, her lips bruised and slick. A slight smile turned the edges of her mouth upward.

His cock throbbed with a fierceness that surprised him. He wanted to bury himself in the hot, moist place where his fingers had just been. He wanted to fuck her until he exorcised this hold she had over him. Instead, he settled for trailing soft kisses on her downy cheek, her jaw, her ear. He marveled at the thick fan of lashes resting against her flawless skin, the fine arch of her brows.

"Simon," she murmured, turning her mouth to his. Her soft lips languidly met his hot ones. He stabbed his tongue into the sweet recess in a forceful reminder of what he wanted. Her body went taut. Her eyes flicked open.

"Inside," she breathed.

He needed no more encouragement. In seconds he was outside and around to open the passenger door. He handed her out of the low-slung car, then pulled her to the hard, hot length of him. Her arms went around his neck. She molded herself to him as firmly as her mouth molded to his. He wedged a thigh between her legs, grabbed her ass cheeks and lifted her to ride his cock.

Thus welded together, Simon brought her to the porch. He slid her down the length of him until her feet touched the floor. "The keys," he growled.

"Oh. I, uh, my purse is still in the car."

Simon found the bag after feeling around on the floor in the dark. Tamara groped inside the purse and retrieved a keyring. She couldn't find the keyhole. His hand closed over hers, and together they managed to open the door.

The pungent smell of cigarette smoke assailed them. She flicked a switch. The soft glow of a table lamp lighted the living room.

"It's about time you came in," snarled a leathery voice. "I thought you were going to fuck right in that little car."

Chapter Sixteen

80

Tamara gasped. "Ike!"

Her muscles tensed. She felt, rather than saw, that Simon came instantly alert, his weight on the balls of his feet, ready to pounce, to protect. His hands made loose fists at his sides.

"How'd you get in?" she croaked.

"That's a hell of a greeting for your father." Ike pushed himself off the sofa, a cigarette dangling from a mouth that curved up in a sneer.

"I can toss him out," Simon said.

"No." She set her purse on an end table and stood facing him, back rigid, hands on her hips. "What do you want, Ike?"

Tamara noted that the traces of Vincent in Ike's eyes, the shape of the bones underneath the double-chinned face, had almost been obliterated by his lazy lifestyle. His gut hung obscenely over a belt that hooked on the last eye. He wore dirty jeans and an unzipped jacket with a gun club logo over the left breast.

"I want to know who's responsible for my son's death."

Simon wedged himself between Tamara and Ike. "So do we. The police are working on it. Now answer the lady's question."

"I just did."

"Her first question. How did you get in?"

Ike shrugged. The ash from his cigarette fell to the braided rug. He ground it dead with a scuffed work boot. "Back door's a piece of cake."

"We can haul you in for breaking and entering."

"Not in my daughter's house. She's happy to see me, ain't you, honey?"

Her mouth tight, Tamara turned and walked to the kitchen, holding herself together with supreme effort. She flicked on another light, picked up the teakettle and filled it.

Ike followed her. "Don't give me your back, daughter. We ain't talked in a while."

"I have nothing to say to you."

"There's the little matter of my son."

Tears sprang to Tamara's eyes at the thought of Vincent lying dead in the police morgue. She fought them back. She refused to cry in front of Ike. In a carefully controlled voice she said, "I suppose you talked to Lieutenant Kyrillos."

"That creep doesn't know his ass from his ear. I wanna know who killed Vincent."

"Where's your car?"

He jerked his head toward the wall. "Around the side."

"Why? So you could surprise me?"

Ike chuckled. "Shoulda waited. It woulda been better than an X-rated movie." He reached a knuckle to her cheek. She barely stepped back in time. "I've dreamed about seeing my daughter naked ever since Vincent told me he did."

"That's enough, you sick bastard." Simon charged into the kitchen and grabbed Ike by his gun-club jacket. "State your business and get out of here."

Ike's eyes narrowed. "Get your hands off me. This is between me and my daughter."

"Wrong. This lady is under my protection."

"Who're you?"

"Simon Sutcliffe. I own this land and I'll have you arrested for trespassing."

Simon released his hold on the jacket. Ike stumbled backward. His hip banged into the counter. "And I'll have you arrested for assault and battery." A glint appeared in his eyes. He adjusted the lapels of his jacket as carefully as if he were wearing a thousand-dollar suit. "You own this land. As I see it, you're responsible for my son's death."

"That's outrageous!" Tamara exclaimed.

Ike turned to her with a smug grin. "The man admitted owning this land. The car exploded right outside this here love nest. My son was in that car. Therefore, mister smart-mouth, I'm going to file a fifty-million-dollar wrongful death claim against you."

The teakettle emitted a shrill whistle. Tamara jumped then spun to remove it from the fire. With shaking hands she poured boiling water into the teapot over two chamomile teabags.

"I noticed you got some steaks in the freezer. What say we have a nice quiet dinner, just the two of us," he glared at Simon as at a snake, "and have a long chat."

"She already told you, mister, she has nothing to say to you."

"She certainly didn't look grief-stricken in the car a few minutes ago," Ike said, his sneer getting more menacing. "She giving it out for free again?"

"Out! Get out of here!" Tamara trembled with the effort to keep from slapping her stepfather's face. If she never saw him until Judgment Day, it would be too soon.

"Not until we get a few things straight. My son's going to have a first-class funeral. Mahogany casket with brass fittings, two rooms full of flowers. A big stone that says 'Here lies the only son of Ike MacKinnon, cut down in his prime.'" He stabbed a dirty finger at Simon. "And this guy's gonna pay for it on account of he's responsible for Vinnie's death."

"You're out of your mind! There's no way Simon will do that."

"He will. Or I'll go see my lawyer tomorrow. When I get done hitting that smartass and his fancy golf course with lawsuits, he'll find his legal fees costing him a helluva lot more than a decent funeral."

"Are you finished?" Simon's question was spoken with quiet menace.

Ike glared at him. "For now. But I warn you. You haven't seen the last of me." He tossed his cigarette butt into the sink then threw a malevolent glance at Tamara. "She never could keep her legs together." He stalked out, slamming the front door behind him.

Tamara stood rigid, her hand gripped around the teapot handle, until she heard the noise of an untuned engine disappear down the lane.

"He's gone." Simon pried her hand loose and nudged her into the living room. "Here, sit down. I'll make a fire."

"No."

"Come on, you've been on the go all day. Sit down and relax."

"No." She shrugged his hand off her elbow. "Simon, please, I-I need to be alone."

"And wait for that maniac to come back?"

"He won't come back."

"Pack a few things. You're staying at Dad's house tonight."

"No."

"Then let me call Marta. She has a spare bedroom."

"I'm not running away. Ike won't do anything tonight."

"I don't like it."

"You're not my keeper, Simon."

He clamped his mouth into a tight line. "I'll pop by the club and have someone nail the back door shut. And tomorrow, it gets a new deadbolt."

"I don't need—"

"I'm the landlord. I make whatever repairs I deem necessary for the safety of my tenants."

She looked down at the spot on the rug where Ike ground the ash in. "Suit yourself."

"If you need me tonight, call or come over, you hear?"

"For God's sake, Simon. I'm twenty-nine years old. I've handled that poor excuse for a man since I was fifteen. I can take care of myself. I don't need you."

Glowering and frustrated, Simon finally left.

Tamara sank into the nearest chair, her last words echoing in her brain. I don't need you.

It was the biggest lie she'd ever told.

* * * * *

The next morning passed in a blur for Tamara. Simon had driven her in the Mercedes to the Surrogate's office, the bank, the newspaper. His demeanor was all crisp business, co-executors attending to estate details. He'd called her at seven to ask politely if she'd be ready by nine. He apologized for waking her, but she'd been up since dawn, a detail she refused to share with him.

While Ike's visit had disturbed her, she was accustomed to his innuendoes, his threats. More distressing was her complete and utter capitulation to Simon. And in a car! Her cheeks burned every time she remembered that Ike had seen her wanton gyrations against Simon's fingers. Her passion had been so mindless and all-consuming that he could have screwed her right here in the center of town and she'd have reveled in it.

"Are you coming?" In well-tailored brown slacks and camelhair jacket over a white tieless shirt, Simon stood outside the car's open door, hand reaching toward her. He had parked outside a distinguished Federal-style building painted vivid blue with white trim. Yvette's office. They were to drop off the estate checklist and get their next assignment.

Tamara was tempted to stay in the car and pout like a child whose toy was taken away for some infraction. But she needed to talk to Yvette, needed some perspective for her inexplicable feelings. She wanted Simon with every atom of her being, wanted his strong, lean body on top of hers, wanted him hot and thick inside of her.

Yet he'd put distance between them since Ike's appearance. Was he disgusted at her family tree, notwithstanding that Ike wasn't related by blood? Or maybe he'd simply had second thoughts about screwing a gimp. It wouldn't be the first time a man got turned off when confronted with the reality of her stump.

Ignoring his offered hand, she swung her legs out of the solid sedan and hoisted herself up. She strode to the entrance and, without waiting for him to open the door, walked in. Either he'd come in behind her or he wouldn't, she didn't care which.

"Tamara!" the secretary greeted enthusiastically. A sturdy woman approaching sixty, Dottie favored Western shirts and cowboy boots with denim skirts. When she retired, she and her husband planned to move to Arizona to their son's dude ranch. "Yvette said you'd stop by today. She said to tell you to go right in."

Then her eyes widened. "Excuse me, sir?"

Tamara followed Dottie's gaze. Simon had already walked past her desk and looked as if he were deciding which of the two closed doors in the small hallway he would barge into.

"It's all right, Dottie. He's with me." Sort of.

Tamara brushed by him and entered one of the doors.

"Is Simon with you?" Yvette greeted her.

"That's a fine hello," Tamara responded, unaccountably annoyed. "Dottie led me to believe it was me you wanted to see."

Yvette's laugh was musical. "I'm delighted to see you, my friend. We have a long lunch ahead of us." Her gaze rested on Simon as he walked into the room. "Ah, you did come with her."

Tamara opened her mouth to protest. Yvette quickly said to Simon, "Elliott's called twice looking for you. Something about one of your properties that he can't handle. Wants you to call him right away. Here, use my phone. Tamara and I will get some coffee. Can I bring some back for you?"

With a negative shake of his head, Simon approached her workspace. It was modular, light gray, with a computer in a corner unit. Two neat rows of papers marched down one ell, four inches showing of each document for ease of finding the correct file. A vase of fragrant freesia, Peruvian lilies, and gerbera daisies graced the top of a three-drawer filing cabinet that abutted the workspace. Sunlight streamed through two floor-to-ceiling windows draped with sheer curtains. The room, Tamara thought, was much like Yvette herself, understated elegance.

"Come," Yvette said. "I just bought a new flavor of coffee that I'm dying to try. Let's brew a pot."

The two women walked out of the room, Yvette quietly closing the door behind her as Simon reached for the phone. She led Tamara past Dottie's desk into an alcove containing a tiny refrigerator, hot plate, and coffeepot. "From Ethiopia," she said as she opened a foil packet of grounds.

The rich smell of coffee and hazelnut brought a smile to Tamara's face. "I can't wait to try it."

While the coffeepot burbled and spat, Tamara constructed and discarded any number of opening gambits to broach the subject of Simon. In the end she decided to wait. He might return any moment, and she knew that once she admitted the intensity of her interest, any interruption would be intolerable.

Perhaps sensing her reticence, Yvette filled the silence with lighthearted comments about her son, a college freshman far enough away that he couldn't come home every weekend with dirty laundry, and about the new legal software she was learning that would make much of her law library obsolete.

The door to Yvette's office opened. Tamara spun around, spilling coffee from her china cup into its delicate saucer.

Simon's brows were knitted together in a fierce scowl. When he saw the two women, he seemed to make an effort to wipe his face clean of emotion. "Smells good," he said as he approached them. "I think I'll have one after all."

A gracious hostess, Yvette poured. "Cream or sugar?"

"Black."

"It's a character trait of strong people," Yvette observed with a smile. "Both Tamara and I drink it straight as well."

The look Simon gave Tamara made her good knee weak. "Strong isn't the half of it," he murmured.

Puzzling over just what he meant by that, Tamara lagged behind as Yvette ushered them into her law library behind the second door. Books covered three walls. The fourth, like her office, boasted sun-washed windows. A well-polished oak conference table dominated the room. Yvette sat at its head, gestured for them to sit on either side of her.

Simon handed Yvette the portfolio of estate documents he and Tamara had completed over the weekend.

"These can wait," she said. "I'll cut to the chase. The Pine Township Planning Board meets twice a month. One meeting is a work session, the other the actual meeting at which the public's views are solicited and recorded. Work sessions are a vehicle for developers to work with the board to iron out any problems, to offer compromises. Part of my duties as attorney for The Nature Conservancy is to monitor these meetings."

Yvette looked pointedly at Simon. "Tonight's work session includes Jack's proposed development. They are close to an agreement." She slid a piece of paper toward him. "These are the board members. Do you know any of them personally?"

Simon scrutinized the list. "I've bought stuff from the mayor's hardware store when I was renovating the carriage house, but I can't say I know him personally. The Realtor, she's come to me with some properties, but they haven't been to my liking so we never did business. Solana is a member of The Pines." He handed the paper back. "Don't know the others."

"Here's my take," Yvette said. "The chairman is a stockbroker who's buddy-buddy with Jack. That's a vote for him. Ethel Clark has been on the planning board for twenty years. She's an outspoken environmentalist. She'll vote no.

"Graham is a corporate type who's up for a promotion and a move to Ohio. Owns two hundred acres of cranberry bogs. I think he'll vote no. Vera Anderson's hoping to become the exclusive Realtor for the project. That's a definite yes for Jack. Ollie Upson owns a gas station. Macho redneck type, five kids, heavy gambler. I have no clue about him."

Yvette stroked her chin thoughtfully. "Although Phipps is retired, his son is at the same bank. My guess is he'll vote with Jack in the hopes of getting big business for his son."

"But isn't that conflict of interest?" Tamara asked.

A wry smile turned up Yvette's mouth. "Every one of them is a conflict of interest, or they wouldn't be on the board. The environmentalist is a NIMBY—Not In My Back Yard. The Realtor, the banker, the stockbroker, they all have a personal interest."

"What about the mayor?" Tamara asked.

"I don't know," Yvette confessed. Her eyes bored twin brown holes into Simon. "Which brings us to the crux of the matter. I need to know where you stand on Jack's project."

Simon shrugged. "I haven't given it any thought. Too much has happened since I left Kamchatka."

"Yes," she sympathized, allowing a moment of silence before zeroing back to the topic at hand. "I count four in favor of Jack's plan. It only needs a majority of a quorum, or three votes, so they can be missing a vote and still pass the project.

"You heard Tamara's presentation. Her facts regarding the aquifer, the density, were right on. If you had to choose between her million-dollar housing and Jack's condo plan—and one day soon, you will have to choose—which would you take?"

"Am I on the spot here?"

"No. As attorney for The Nature Conservancy, I intend to see that Jack's proposal is blasted out of the water. I guarantee you'll see newspaper headlines tomorrow. His plan is nothing less than a rape of the land."

One black eyebrow arched up.

"Yes, it's a passionate subject with me. As it was with Harland. Our affiliation began before I met Tamara. We shared a deep, abiding respect for his land. Tamara was the catalyst that brought it all together. Her proposal doesn't compromise the irreplaceable aspect of the property, yet still leaves room for substantial return on investment."

Tamara felt Simon's gaze on her. Yvette's public compliment warmed her, but the look in his eyes all but melted her prosthesis.

"Will you come with us tonight and lend your support?" Yvette asked.

"I can't."

Tamara swallowed hard. She didn't realize until just this second how much Simon's support meant to her self-esteem. She should have known. What mattered to him was bottom line, not the fruit of six months of her labor on behalf of The Pines.

"The reason Elliott was so eager to get in touch with me is the reason I can't come tonight," he continued. "It seems I have a court appearance tonight at eight o'clock. In Vermont."

Tamara's gaze snapped to him. Sincerity was etched across his face. And...regret?

"This isn't one of my investment properties," he explained, "or I'd let Elliott handle it. He still has power of attorney over my holdings. This one has personal significance for me. I can't let the claimant win simply because I didn't show up."

"Surely Elliott can get a continuance?" Yvette asked.

"He's exhausted every delaying tactic known to man or lawyer while I was out of the country." Simon's smile was taut. "And he did this out of the goodness of his heart. It's the one property that wasn't included in Appendix A."

"Appendix A being the attachment to your power of attorney agreement?"

Tamara was grateful that Yvette had smoothly answered her unasked layman's question. They were talking legalese, and it was out of her league.

"Yes." Simon stood, dug a twenty-dollar bill out of his pants pocket, and laid it on the table. "I took the liberty of making some toll calls from your phone. For one thing, I had to let my caretaker know I'll be staying over tonight." He looked at his watch. "If you want me to sign anything, I can wait ten minutes, but I have to pick up some documents before I hit the road."

A frown of distaste briefly creased his features. "Damn. They're in the carriage house." He looked at Yvette. "I need to make one more phone call. To Elliott."

He strode to the door. "To make sure it's empty when I get there." And closed it loudly behind him.

Tamara felt her mouth gape. She snapped it shut. "He hates her so much, he won't even be in the same house with her."

"Never mind that." Yvette stood. "If he meant what I think he meant, it's too good to pass up. Stay here. I'm going to dictate something urgent to Dottie."

Long minutes later, she returned with a gleam in her eye. "He signed it!"

Tamara craned her neck to see behind Yvette.

"He's gone."

"Gone?" Tamara felt like a parrot. "Simon's gone?"

"He said to tell you good luck." Yvette waved the document in front of Tamara's nose. "Here. Read it."

Tamara took the paper and read, "'I, Simon Sutcliffe, do hereby give Yvette Kai power of attorney to vote my twenty shares in any matter before the Pine Township Planning Board which concerns any proposed development of The Pines, a golf course located in Pine Township, Columbus County, New Jersey.'"

She turned and stared through the doorway of the law library, as if seeking any remaining essence of Simon after he had passed through the hallway on his way out.

He was gone. But his ability to render her speechless remained.

* * * * *

"Tell me all!"

Yvette squeezed Tamara's hand as they sat across from each other in a corner booth of *Die Forelle*, a trendy restaurant within walking distance of Yvette's office. Its specialty, as its name implied, was trout. She had removed her double-breasted gray power jacket, revealing a white charmeuse blouse with long sleeves. On anyone else the unadorned jewel neckline would look severe, Tamara thought, but its simplicity made Yvette look more regal. In contrast, Tamara felt underdressed in a gold cotton poor-boy sweater with loose-fitting slacks of a deeper gold, her hair held at the nape by a gold paisley scarf.

Tamara's insides turned liquid at the mere thought of Simon. "I-I want him, Yvette."

"It shows."

"What do you mean?"

"There's something, I don't know, vital about you this morning. Did you…uh, is he as virile as he looks?"

An uncharacteristic shyness fluttered Tamara's eyelashes downward, and she felt her cheeks heat. "We didn't get very far. We were like horny teenagers. I've never been kissed so thoroughly." She unconsciously touched her lips, which had softened just thinking about the barely leashed passion he'd displayed last night.

She lifted her lashes, allowing her friend to glimpse the vulnerability that only Yvette knew about. "I'm afraid. What if he— Oh, Yvette, this morning he was so distant, I was sure he was having second thoughts about taking a gimp to his bed."

"I forbid you to speak that way about yourself!"

"That's what I am. A freak. An amputee. Why would he want me when he had Carrie, could still have her?"

"For God's sake, woman, have you ever looked in a mirror? Have you looked inside your soul? How dare you equate yourself with that…that tramp! She's not worth the effort it would take to step on her face. Besides, it would mess up your shoes."

A tiny laugh escaped Tamara. Underneath the table she opened and closed her grip on the linen napkin. "I haven't felt this vulnerable in years. Maybe it's just Ike's visit."

"Ike was here?"

Tamara reached for her glass of chardonnay to erase the sudden bitter taste in her mouth. After a sip, she relayed the essence of Ike's visit the previous evening.

"No wonder you've lost some of your confidence. That worm belongs under the same rock as Carrie."

"He makes me feel slimy."

"Don't let him have that power over you, Tamara. If you want to surrender to anyone, do it to that hunk of a twin."

Tamara felt the corners of her mouth lift. "He is a hunk, isn't he? God, those eyes. Sometimes I feel like he's undressing me with them."

"Sometimes? As in, more than once?"

"Yeah. Several times, in fact."

"There you go then."

"What do you mean?"

"I assume he's done this visual undressing since the dinner at Harland's, when he saw you without your prosthesis?"

Tamara thought back to the look on Simon's face when she threw the water glass at him in the hospital and the sheet slipped to reveal the Victoria's Secret negligee that barely covered her breasts. She remembered his hot mouth capturing her finger in Harland's study, his eyes burning twin holes of desire into her. And most of all, the previous evening in his car just before he'd unbuttoned her blouse and suckled on her nipples, with the promise of more in his eyes.

"Yes," she said weakly, her finger sensuously tracing the mouth of her wineglass as if it were his warm, demanding mouth.

"Then he's undressing you in the full knowledge of what he'll find, wouldn't you say?"

Tears stung Tamara's eyes. "Oh, Yvette, do you think…"

"I do think. More than that. I know he wants you."

"How do you know that?"

"I doubt if he would have signed that power of attorney if it hadn't been for you."

Tamara shook her head. "He knows I'm Harland's spokesman. It's nothing personal."

"Honey, if it comes to choosing between Jack and you, I have absolutely no doubt who he'll choose. And Harland knew it. That's why he made the seventy-percent rule. It's up to you and Simon to change Jack's mind. Your twenty, Simon's twenty, and Jack's thirty. That's the seventy-percent voting block he envisioned. All the others are extraneous."

"I can't see Jack giving up his plan, and I refuse to vote my shares for it. If Simon feels the same way, and obviously he does or he wouldn't have signed your power of attorney, then I don't see anything being built. And I'd be just as happy."

"You wouldn't want ten million dollars?"

Tamara made a rude noise with her lips. "Will that give me back my leg?"

"No," Yvette said softly. "But it was Harland's intent to give you some recompense. And I think he would want you and Simon to find each other."

"How do you know so much about Harland? How did he turn to you when he already had a lawyer?"

"Harland came to The Nature Conservancy at the first inkling of Jack's plan. I've been giving him informal advice for more than two years."

"Whose idea was it to hire me?"

"His. Although he did ask my opinion. Harland knew all along who you were, of course. He thought it would be poetic justice to have Jack's victim give him his comeuppance."

Tamara ran a hand across her face. "So I'm stuck with this family."

"There are worse fates."

A grudging smile played about Tamara's mouth. She thought again of the power of Simon's kisses, the fire he engendered between her legs with his mere touch. "Yes, it could be worse," she agreed.

Chapter Seventeen

❧

"She's been a thorn in my side for years."

"How so?"

Ike needed no more encouragement. He could rip Tamara Hart up one side and down the other when he had a good listener. And the member offering him shots of rare single malt scotch listened with eyes and expression and body language.

"She don't appreciate me. I bust my hump for her after her Ma died, try to scrape up enough dough to get her into college. But after her accident, she didn't want nothing to do with me. It was like she wanted to wipe me out of her past, you know?"

His listener nodded, nudging a fresh Glenfiddich in Ike's direction. Ike picked up the amber liquid, smelled it with appreciation then sipped it as though he were a connoisseur. He could get used to living like this, yes sir he could.

"Why would she do that? You seem like a concerned father."

Ike grunted. "Stuck her nose in the air when she found herself a…" he almost said Sugar Daddy, but remembered that Harland Sutcliffe was a well-loved figure at The Pines, "a knight in shining armor. Didn't have the time of day for me."

"Because you're a laborer?"

"Yeah. And honest labor it is too. You ever lay bricks on the second story of a building when it's a hundred in the shade? I sweated bullets for her. But now that I'm unemployed and she's coming into money, she don't want nothing to do with me. Just yesterday, she kicked me out of her house."

"You were at the bungalow?"

"Yeah. Interrupted me a hot little scene too."

"Hot scene? With —?"

The question hung delicately in the air. Ike enjoyed drawing out the suspense. "Like father, like son?" he asked instead, letting the idea insinuate itself in the other's brain.

"She was humping Harland? You know that for a fact?"

"Wouldn't be surprised." Ike sipped his scotch before elaborating. "After all, she done it before with the boss."

He had his listener's attention now. The back straightened, the look sharpened, and Ike could just imagine how the gears shifted and meshed in that steel-trap mind.

"Yup. Ever wonder why she left that job in Philly? Weren't no accident that she was free when Harland offered her that job."

"I never heard. Why did she?"

"It wasn't because she was humping the boss. Although she was. It was because she fucked up so good and royal that they didn't have any choice. Even the boss couldn't save her ass."

"What did she do that the boss couldn't stand up for her?"

"It was the same kind of dumbass idea as that campaign for the new Coke. Remember they had to turn around and bring back Classic Coke because the public wouldn't go near the new stuff? She sold some cockamamie scheme to the company's biggest client. They damn near lost their shirt before they pulled it off the market. And Miss Tamara Hart had to take the heat."

"She told you all this?"

"Hell, no. Even with her tail burnt, she wouldn't come home to lick her wounds. No, I had to hear it from my son."

"My condolences. I only met Vincent once, but he seemed like a nice guy. A chip off the old block, you might say."

"Damn right. He was the spitting image of my own self at that age." Ike sucked in his gut and remembered the gravy years when he looked like a movie star, before the bad times when he was saddled with a wife and child who didn't pay him no mind, when he started preferring a cold six-pack to a cold shoulder.

"But Tamara—?"

"Was a bitch. Still is."

His listener picked up a glass similar to Ike's, sipped with as much appreciation as Ike did then said out of a clear blue sky, "You know something peculiar about the Pine Barrens? The soil is so sandy and porous that water flows right through it. Know what that does to the dead leaves on the ground? What it does to the shrubs growing under the taller trees?"

Ike's eyes narrowed. "What?"

"Moisture helps leaves decompose. In most forests, it makes rich compost. Here, it's so tinder dry that the leaves just lay there and dry out and pile up. A real fire hazard."

Fire hazard. He picked up his glass again and nonchalantly brought it to his mouth then sipped. "I'm listening."

"There's a practice in the Pine Barrens to minimize forest fires. It's called controlled burning. The object is to set a small fire of five to ten acres to clear out the understorey without it getting to the trunks of the trees."

"Interesting."

"Very. That stand of white cedar around the bungalow? It's scheduled for controlled burning this Thursday. One wonders if our little Tamara would be interested in seeing it close up."

"I might be able to convince her to take a look."

"It would be a never-to-be-forgotten lesson. It would be worth quite a bit for someone to teach her."

"I spent a good number of years making sure Tamara learned to mind me," Ike said, hoping his eyes would convey how eager he was to continue teaching her without coming right out and saying so in the unlikely event this conversation would be overheard.

Apparently his companion had the same thought. A glance at the clock over the bar. "You know the gas station at the crossroads on the south side of town?"

Ike nodded.

"There's an air pump behind the bays. At exactly six o'clock, pull up there, check your tires. We can talk further and maybe reach an understanding."

Ike's eyes were drawn to the movement of the member's thumb and forefinger rubbing together in a gesture Ike understood.

It would make him rich.

And it would remove the thorn from his side. Permanently.

* * * * *

"Sorry I'm late," Marta yelled out her window as she rolled her stately sedan past the twelve-year-old clunker in her driveway. She parked in the garage and walked in the gathering dusk to where Cliff's upper body was hidden under the hood. One of the groundsmen had sold the piece of junk to him for fifty dollars and Cliff was trying to get it in shape for inspection.

When Cliff had his head buried inside the bowels of a car, she knew he forgot to keep track of time. She'd been unavoidably detained at the Club and had asked Chef to pack two roast chicken specials. "Dinner's ready. All it needs is sixty seconds in the microwave. How soon can you wash up?"

"Few minutes. I still can't figure out why it won't start."

She was proud of Cliff. As did most teenage boys, he had a love of mechanical things. He'd learned car repair at the special school he'd graduated from last June, but now he had no supervisor to turn to. Marta herself had a fair knowledge of car maintenance—she'd had to, living alone all these years—but she knew he needed to find his own answers. The stable job was just a transition until he found an opening as an auto mechanic.

Marta looked at him with a fierce kind of loving. He'd grown up understanding that his parents had died when he was two. He'd spent ten years with foster parents who reminded Marta of the dour couple in the American Gothic painting. Then the live-in school, with no family but her to write to him. She'd spent the last few years working on adopting him, and now it was up to her to try to compensate for all his lonely years.

Cliff eased out from under the hood and stood up, rolling his shoulders to loosen the muscles. "It's turning over, but won't kick on. Wait. I'll show you."

He slid behind the wheel and turned the key. A wavering noise, like a siren whose batteries were almost dead, floated in the still dusk air. He switched the key off then got out. "It's not the battery. Water's fine, terminals aren't corroded."

"You took off the air cleaner to see that the choke isn't stuck? Checked the fuel pump fuses?"

"Yeah."

"It's almost dark. Want to call it a day and have dinner?"

"Just let me check a few more things."

Shaking her head in mock dismay, Marta went back to her car to retrieve the two Styrofoam-boxed dinners. At least he had persistence, she thought. She locked the garage and entered the kitchen through the connecting door, stored the dinners in the fridge, and went upstairs to change.

As she slipped into old jeans and an Eagles sweatshirt, she heard the purr of an engine. Much too quiet to think Cliff had found the problem. She looked out the bedroom window. Elliott's car.

It reminded her that tonight was the last work session before The Pines made the official agenda. The next meeting would be advertised in the paper and all the environmental nuts would descend. She raked a strong hand through her bowl-cut gray hair, to settle the cowlick the sweatshirt had raised, and clumped downstairs. She wanted Elliott to reassure her they had the votes.

He wasn't in the living room. She opened the front door.

Her eyebrows rose as she surveyed the scene. Elliott, in his thousand-dollar suit, and Cliff, in grease-smeared T-shirt, both huddled over the engine. "You won't be late for the planning board meeting, will you?" she called out.

Carefully Elliott stood and glanced at the watch that, Marta knew, was solid gold. "Half an hour yet. Did they deliver those color renderings of the townhouse façades?"

"I have them. Come on in."

He followed her through the front hallway and into the living room. Was that liquor on his breath? She abruptly turned to him. "Should you be drinking before the meeting?"

Elliott leveled a steely stare at her. "I was gathering important information." A smile twisted up the ends of his mouth. "Very important information."

"Such as?"

"All in due time."

You want to play poker? Marta thought. Fine. She wouldn't tell him what she'd done today. When he found out, he'd wish he'd thought of it himself.

"How many votes do we have?" she asked.

"Four. More than enough."

The answer was so definite, so certain, that Marta relaxed.

"When do we eat?" Cliff burst into the living room. "You were right, Elliott. The rotor had a crack in it. I'll have to get a new one tomorrow. It's under the distributor cap," he explained, turning to Marta, "so I didn't see it right off."

Marta considered this new information about Elliott. She'd never known him to soil his hands under the hood of his German luxury car, yet he knew to look at the rotor. He was just a little too slick for her, so she'd hired an investigator to dig into his past. She didn't trust him. Never did. While Jack hung onto Elliott's every word, Marta took his advice only after careful consideration.

Elliott was beginning to get on her nerves. Always playing big shot when he'd come from nothing. When she was in charge, he wouldn't have as much influence over Jack as he had now.

And she was doing whatever she had to, to make sure of it.

* * * * *

Jack shifted nervously in his chair. For the past half hour he'd watched Elliott play to the Planning Board like an actor in an Academy Award-winning performance, but Jack wouldn't be comfortable until it was behind them.

His gaze rested on the chairman, Ray Ramsey, whose son graced a copy of a photo in Jack's pocket. It showed Ricky Ramsey, age seventeen, with his grubby hands on the bare tits of the banker's wife. If Solana ever got hold of that photo, he'd call in Ramsey's half-million-dollar balloon mortgage in a flash.

This was the hardest part, Jack thought. The waiting. He wanted to stand on the chair and say, "Let's take a vote!"

The mayor, Norm Baldwin, would make out like a bandit on The Pines. Jack had mentioned to him that the general contractor would buy ten percent of their stock, at retail, from Baldwin's hardware store, without going through the bidding process.

He studied Vera Anderson covertly. The Realtor's hands trembled slightly. He could tell she needed a drink. Hell, he sympathized with that need. He'd vowed to cut his consumption in half. He knew it took more grit than he had to stop altogether, but he longed to become the man Harland had thought he could be.

Ollie Upson was fingering his tie as if it was a foreign object. Ollie was more comfortable with grease under his fingernails and a dolly under his back. A native Piney, he had a fatal weakness. Gambling. Jack knew Elliott held a lot of his chits and wouldn't hesitate to squeeze him.

Another solid vote would come from Ed Solana. Jack had cultivated Solana on the golf course for almost two years now. Solana's son was up and coming at the same bank from which Solana had retired. Financing a major project like The Pines would make him a Vice President at age thirty-two.

Elliott's imposing voice stopped in mid-sentence. Jack followed his gaze. Then swore under his breath.

The gimp had just walked in.

"The last problem I see," Mayor Baldwin was saying as Jack watched Tamara Hart walk toward them without a hint of a limp, "is the buffer zones. The zoning ordinance calls for twenty-foot buffers. Your plan specifies ten."

"Your honor," Elliott replied, "the area you've indicated abuts state forest land. Its remoteness from populated areas will be an additional buffer. Besides, the structures themselves honor the twenty feet. The encroachment is strictly patio usage."

"The zoning ordinance also requires berms and screen planting on that twenty feet of buffer zone," Tamara interrupted, coming to a stop in front of the chairman.

Ramsey stood. "And who are you, young lady?"

"My name is Tamara Hart and I own—"

"Mr. Chairman, with all due respect," Elliott jumped in, glaring at Tamara, "I have the floor."

"Sit down and wait your turn," Ramsey ordered, pointing to a chair. When Tamara sat in the first row directly opposite the chairman, Ramsey sat down. "Mr. Grosse, please continue."

"Mr. Chairman, I have a question." This from the corporate hotshot, Graham.

Grudgingly, the chairman said, "Go ahead."

"What standing do you have as regards this property?" He was looking at Tamara.

"I own twenty percent of the property in question."

"I think we should ascertain just who the players are," Graham said. "Mr. Chairman, I would like to ask Ms. Hart a few more questions."

Sweat breaking out on his upper lip, the chairman glanced worriedly at Elliott. They had the votes, Jack reminded himself. They could afford to make a show of allowing everyone to speak.

Apparently Elliott felt the same. A smile stretching his lips, he settled a hip on a corner of the table where the blueprints lay and swept out a hand in a gesture that said, *Ask away.*

"Why haven't you appeared before now?"

"Some background first. I'm an image consultant. I've been working for—" Tamara stopped to take a deep breath, "the late Harland Sutcliffe for the past six months. I only made my recommendations a week ago. When Harland died—" Her voice cracked. Very good, Jack thought, Tamara was a good actress, "I was the recipient of half of his shares."

"I see. The other half?"

"Was split ten to each son."

Graham's eyes bored into Jack. "Just how much of this property do you represent, Mr. Sutcliffe?"

"Mr. Graham, allow me to speak for my client." Elliott stood and walked to the dais, looking every inch the successful lawyer in his expensive suit. "During these lengthy proceedings, Mr. Jack Sutcliffe owned twenty percent of the shares. In all that time Mr. Harland Sutcliffe made no negative comment whatsoever as regards the proposed development, but led Mr. Jack Sutcliffe to believe that his forty percent would be bequeathed to him as the older son, giving him majority control."

Elliott paused, giving each board member his jury stare. "After Mr. Harland Sutcliffe's will was read, and I stress it has not been probated yet so we cannot be sure that it will stand, it is true that Mr. Jack Sutcliffe owns thirty percent. However, there are three minority shareholders of ten percent each, which vote he controls, giving him sixty percent."

At the sound of footsteps, Jack turned then stifled a groan. The lady lawyer for The Nature Conservancy entered the room with a young woman with thick eyeglasses and curly hair that sprang out at every angle. Yvette nodded in the general direction of the board. She sat down next to Tamara, murmured something, then Tamara shook hands with the bespectacled woman.

"If I may be permitted to continue this work session," Ramsey said, glaring at the three women.

"Mr. Chairman," said Yvette, "may I present Tara Hollis of the *Columbus County Observer*."

Jack's breath stopped.

With a dazzling smile, Yvette continued, "Since the development is scheduled for formal presentation at the next planning board meeting anyway, Ms. Hollis thought it might be a good idea to give the public some background in advance of the meeting."

Ramsey gave the reporter a look that should have had her slinking to the back row. Instead, she opened up a steno notebook and produced a pen from her jacket pocket. "We're not going back over any prior decisions just for latecomers," he said with asperity. "Now where were we?"

"Ms. Hart was discussing berms and screen planting," said Graham, turning to Tamara.

"Thank you," Tamara said. "May I point out to the board that if you plant the required trees five feet on centers according to good landscaping practice, in a few years the trees will overhang the patios and the occupants won't be able to use them. Besides, a berm of the height required in the ordinance would be unstable in a ten-foot base."

Her gaze rested on the board members, one at a time. "And, notwithstanding the township's zoning ordinance, I'd like to point out that the Pinelands CMP—that's the Comprehensive Zoning Master Plan," she explained to the reporter, "requires a three-hundred-foot buffer zone around all wetlands."

"Mr. Chairman," Elliott interrupted, "having an interest in the property is one thing, but Ms. Hart is not an expert witness."

"And this is not a trial," said the mayor mildly. He turned to Tamara. "You were with Harland when he took that fatal jump. I remember the story the *Observer* wrote about your background. Even without expert qualifications, your statement makes sense."

"Mr. Chairman, it is not my intention to belittle the enormous amount of work that you've already done on the proposed development," Tamara said. "Yet I must ask your indulgence."

She took a deep breath. "As you've just learned, I only recently became a part owner of The Pines. Prior to that time, I spent six months meeting with the shareholders and members of the golf club, visually surveying every square foot of the property, and studying the CMP on the Pinelands. While the property is technically outside the boundaries of the Pinelands Area, much of it shares the same fragile ecology. There are a number of discrepancies between this plan and my findings, which I would point out at the regular meeting as necessary.

"Having this development come up for a vote at the next meeting, however, could be premature. Harland Sutcliffe's will stipulated that seventy percent of the shareholder votes agree. Even with Board approval, the project couldn't build."

She turned, looked Jack in the eye. He had a sudden strong need for the Old Granddad he'd denied himself all day. "It was Harland's hope," she said softly, "that his two sons would agree on the highest and best use of the property."

Damn her, trying to use Harland against him! He was trying, dammit, trying to prove something to Harland, to himself with this development. Jack's fist clenched inside his pants pocket while he fought to school himself against showing any emotion.

"My recommendation," Tamara continued, "is radically different from the plan before the board, a plan more in tune with Harland's thinking and more in harmony with the fragile ecology of the property."

Ramsey banged his gavel. "We've been over the development point by point, and we've made compromises that we felt were in the best interests of all parties. The development will be sewered, so there's no septic seepage into the aquifer. As you said, we're not bound by the Pinelands CMP. Even if we were, the guidelines for the Regional Growth Area aren't exceeded."

"I understand there's no requirement to deed-restrict the open space in perpetuity," Tamara said. "That's an oversight on the part of both the board and the developer. Without such a restriction, further development can occur. In fact, even the golf course can be plowed over."

"You're throwing up a smokescreen because your own project isn't going to make it," Jack countered.

Tamara's back stiffened as she walked to the side table containing the stack of blueprints. "If I may," she said, looking through them until she found one to pull out, "I'd like to show the board some of the areas where perhaps more study is needed. In some places where development is indicated, the water table is too close to the surface."

She returned to the dais and spread a blueprint over the papers strewn on the table in front of the chairman. Jack and Elliott edged behind her, craning their necks to see what the Planning Board would see.

"Here, for example, an existing horse trail runs about like so." Her index finger sketched a line in a curve along a proposed crescent of three-story buildings housing, if Jack remembered correctly, a hundred forty-some condo units.

"Granted," Tamara continued, "the actual location of the proposed buildings is on what is called uplands. Test borings verify that. However, the infrastructure—driveways, streets, sewers—" here she looked directly at Ramsey, "are at the edge of wetlands. How can you approve underground utilities when they'll be lying so close to the water table?"

"Mr. Chairman," said the retired banker, "our own township engineer verified the findings of the respected architectural firm that drew up the plans."

"Then they should have known enough to obtain a Letter of Interpretation from the State of New Jersey before any plans were developed."

"Just who is this Avante Consultants?" Ramsey asked, scowling at her as if a child had made an impertinent remark.

"That's Ms. Hart's company," Elliott responded. "May I point out to the board that the primary thrust of her company, which, by the way, is a sole proprietorship with only one employee, is image consulting," he said with an undertone of sneer, "not engineering. Ms. Hart presented ideas to enhance the image of The Pines, such as redecorating the pro shop and catering to women. Her company has no credentials to judge the adequacy of engineering drawings or conduct test borings."

"Avante Consultants didn't do any borings," Tamara said heatedly, ignoring the "redecorating" slur. "We used an engineering firm from Mercer County. Here are copies of their data." She passed out small bound booklets with a cover page showing a name and logo that Jack recognized. Nervously he gauged the reaction of the board to the firm, rumored to be above reproach. How many of the board knew of their reputation?

Tamara was still talking. "Ladies and gentlemen, there are numerous similar instances of questionable placement of structures, all of which are set forth in this report. In light of that, and because seventy percent of the shareholders have yet to agree to the highest and best use of the property, I respectfully request that you remove The Pines development from the agenda of the next public meeting."

"Now see here, Tamara—" Jack said.

Elliott's hand on his arm stopped his temper from exploding. Jack barely held himself in check when Elliott gave him a warning look. Then he understood. The press was here. They couldn't seem as if they were running roughshod over the environment. They couldn't hint that they had the board in their pocket.

"I'll see you in hell, gimp," he growled just loud enough for Tamara to hear. Then he stalked out, leaving Elliott to deal with the legal niceties.

* * * * *

"We did it!"

"You did it, you mean."

"No." Tamara's eyes sparkled like the contents of the glass she raised to Yvette's at *Die Forelle*. "I couldn't have spoken so forcefully if you hadn't prepared me as though I was a witness getting ready for cross-examination."

"And you did an exceptional job."

Tamara sipped her champagne in celebration of the planning board's postponement of a vote on The Pines. Only one glass, she had cautioned. She was driving an unfamiliar car, Harland's Mercedes, and needed her wits about her. Besides, it had been a long day, considering the sleepless night she'd spent thinking about Simon's kisses, his hands, his body.

Simon. How she wished he'd been there! Would he have been proud of her? Would he be sitting here now, plying her with champagne and giving her soul-searching gazes? Would they celebrate privately by continuing their—

"I thought Ramsey would pop an artery," Yvette said, interrupting her wayward thoughts. "We talked about conflict of interest earlier, but he almost acts as though he's being paid under the table to ram the project through."

"Do you think Elliott would do anything illegal?"

"I wonder. They had to know the project would be news after the public hearing, and if your findings are correct..."

"They are."

"It was a rhetorical statement, dear heart. I think that little coterie at The Pines is running scared. They thought all you were capable of was redecorating the Pro Shop. They didn't see your backbone. Without knowing it, you validated all of Harland's concerns. I hope Jack realizes that and comes to his senses before he's made a laughingstock in the *Observer*."

"Maybe you should talk to him."

Yvette's eyes narrowed. "Not I. You're the one with all the details at your fingertips."

"Me? Didn't you hear him threaten me? I don't know that I'd ever willingly be alone with him again."

"But you have Harland's wishes on your side."

Tamara felt the sting of tears at the backs of her eyes. "Who would have—?" She stopped. Any of them could have wanted Harland dead. What was it the detective said? People have killed for a lot less than two hundred million dollars.

But Jack? Could Jack arrange his own father's death?

No. Of course not. But the reason why Harland left her the shares—to fight the project and to reconcile the brothers—overwhelmed Tamara.

* * * * *

Tamara strapped herself into her seat belt and fumbled with the unfamiliar controls of Harland's Mercedes. Her sudden change of mood had cast a damper on the celebration and Yvette had ordered her to go home and get some well-deserved rest.

The headlights illuminated the slick macadam surface as she pulled into the two-lane road leading out of town. She found the switch for the windshield wipers. The single arm cut a wide swath across the glass. Applying gentle pressure to the accelerator, she felt the surge of power. *This kind of luxury I could get used to,* she thought, *leather upholstery, burl walnut inserts, the smooth ride like sitting on a sofa.*

Since the car was practically driving itself, she turned her attention to the audio system. AM, FM, CD, Tune, Seek—maybe she shouldn't fiddle with all those buttons in the dark.

Yikes! She hadn't even seen headlights come up behind her. Yet a monster pickup truck perched unnaturally high on the chassis was trying to pass her on this narrow, high-crowned road. She slowed down.

The truck slowed down too.

"Make up your mind," she muttered as she sped up. So did the truck.

In seconds the truck and the Mercedes were neck and neck.

Tamara hazarded a quick glance to her left. All she saw was black. Tinted windows, dark metal, the driver wearing wraparound sunglasses, dark hat, dark jacket. Chills scratched down her spine when she realized he was driving without headlights.

She jerked her attention back to the road. Although there were no hills to speak of in the Pine Barrens, she knew the back roads meandered to follow property lines. It wouldn't do to run into a ditch in the rain, after midnight, with a maniac—

Dear God, was he trying to run her off the road? Her fingers gripped the steering wheel so hard her knuckles whitened. Perspiration pooled under her arms. The moisture in her mouth disappeared.

She felt a harsh bump against the left front fender. The impact jerked her hands from the steering wheel. The right tires knifed through soft shoulder muck. She grabbed the wheel, eased it to the left, felt rubber bite into pavement.

Another bump, harder. Metal screeched against metal for an agonizingly long second. This time she hung onto the wheel.

Lord, The Pines was still several miles away. Could she make it home before he— No! She couldn't lead this lunatic to her house! Think! Monday—damn! The clubhouse was closed.

Panic seeped through the edges of her control. Where was the police station? Oh God, she didn't know! She tried to conjure up a mental map of the area. Her mind went blank. Simon was away. Would Jack be home? Awake? Sober?

Up ahead, a sharp curve to the left. Could she get past the truck?

She floored the accelerator. The car leaped like a panther hunting weakened prey. Her head snapped against the headrest.

As the car clung to the curve, her headlights illuminated several drained cranberry bogs. God, if he forced her off the road, she'd land in one of the depressions and slam into a dike.

Just then she spied two red eyes in the roadway. A deer! Her reflexes worked before she could think them through. She jammed the brake pedal to the floor, pulled a hard right then jerked the car back on the road.

Something slammed into the driver's side window. The glass shattered, showering her with shards. *Hang on! Don't get hysterical.*

It was the deer. The truck had apparently taken a straight line to catch up and had smashed into it. The animal's body wedged between the two vehicles. Its head poked through the opening, bobbing like an obscene carousel horse inches from her face as the vehicles careened through a black hell. Its lifeless eyes seemed to be staring at her, accusing her of its death. Tamara fought the bile rising in her throat.

The truck veered to the left. The deer disappeared. Tamara swallowed hard, trying to muster up a drop of saliva.

The vehicles clashed again. Instinctively she knew he'd merely maneuvered to get rid of the cushion between them. She hung onto the steering wheel, desperately trying to force the heavier vehicle to give her breathing room.

Another sharp left. She almost missed seeing that curve, distracted as she was by hurtling too fast through the pelting rain and the black monster at her side. She forced the Mercedes into the path of the devil truck, an unconscious prayer on her lips.

What happened next seemed to Tamara to be firebursts of impressions, disjointed vignettes her mind couldn't coherently process. Metal shrieked. Tires screamed. The seat belt bit into her shoulder. Her head snapped sideways. Rain hissed in her ears. The smell of burning rubber assaulted her nostrils. Her teeth snapped shut on her tongue, the metallic, sickly taste of blood filling her mouth. She felt herself upside down.

Then, mercifully, nothing.

Chapter Eighteen

ॐ

The Corvette sped down the Garden State Parkway toward home. Simon rotated his cramped shoulders under a woolen shirt but kept the speed at a flat seventy-five. He'd pulled off the interstate for coffee and a bagel shortly after crossing into Massachusetts at dawn but decided he could make The Pines without another stop.

Last night's court appearance in a Vermont hamlet could have been avoided with a couple of phone calls and a reasonable offer of compromise. Because he'd been unavailable and Elliott had used his lawyerly tactic of obfuscation for close to five months, the judge had been ready to jail Simon for contempt of court.

The property adjoining Simon's used his driveway for a right-of-way to his residence. An old bridge crossing a small creek had collapsed after an oil truck had delivered fuel to the neighbor. The municipality had wanted an environmental impact statement coupled with an industrial-strength replacement. He'd wound up agreeing to a stone bridge that could accommodate an eighteen-wheeler.

That property held special meaning for him. It had been his first acquisition twenty years ago with a bequest from his grandfather. One beautiful fall weekend of his freshman year at Middlebury College, he'd explored the rolling hills and noticed a "For Sale" sign. Glimpsed through heavily wooded frontage, the Alpine-style chalet had intrigued him. He'd driven up the long driveway and handed over a deposit as soon as he'd seen the picture-postcard views from the living room's wall of windows.

Over the years its value had skyrocketed as he'd added acreage. He'd had a number of offers, but it was the one property he refused to sell. He considered it his talisman because it had set him on the path of his life.

Damn, that tempest in a teapot last night was something Elliott should have been able to handle long-distance. He'd fire him as soon as he got back.

No. First he'd see Tamara and finish what they'd started the other night in this very car. His groin stirred at the mere thought of the way she shattered into a million pieces at his touch, the sinuous, urgent way she moved against his hand. His mouth hungered for the taste of her full, soft breasts, the nipples hard against his tongue. He wanted to lick every inch of that satiny flesh, trace her generous curves with his palm, taste the cream, between her legs, that had oozed against his fingers. The feel of his tongue encircled by her hot, enveloping mouth had given him a foretaste of what it would be like to sink himself into her sweet pussy. He wanted her. Desperately. He shifted in the seat, adjusting the sudden hardness of his cock inside his jeans.

He almost missed the Parkway exit. Swearing softly, he cut across three lanes and steered down the ramp. He paid the toll and automatically asked for a receipt. Over the years he'd gotten accustomed to recording every expense for the IRS.

Shortly before noon the 'Vette turned into the driveway of the farmhouse. Simon tensed to see a nondescript black Chevy in front of the porch. That could only be an unmarked police car.

Simon pulled up behind it, killed the engine and got out. Inhaling the unique piney aroma of home, he stretched his arms up and out, flexed his muscles to unkink them, and walked toward the Chevy. He could hear the muffled squawk of the police radio when Detective Kyrillos opened his door.

"You're a hard man to get hold of," Kyrillos greeted him. His glance took in Simon's unshaven jaw, rumpled hair and clothing, and, Simon had no doubt, the look of too little sleep.

"Had some business to attend to out of town."

"That explains why you haven't answered my messages."

"I've been driving since three a.m., Detective. Can we talk over coffee?" Simon didn't wait for a response but took the porch steps in one stride and unlocked the door.

"Sounds good." Kyrillos followed right behind him down the center hall to the kitchen. "Where were you?"

"Is this an official inquiry?" Simon asked, tossing his car keys into a small wooden bowl on the counter. He turned his attention to the coffee maker.

"Yes and no."

The cryptic response jerked Simon's head around. The detective had made himself at home, coat on one chair, slouched on a second, his foot on the stretcher of a third.

"Mind telling me where you went?"

"Vermont." Simon plugged the pot in. "Why?"

"You can, of course, substantiate your whereabouts."

"Hell, yes. Just call up Municipal Court Judge Dennis Matlock in Middlebury. I'm about eight thousand dollars poorer after I promised a structure as sturdy as the Brooklyn Bridge."

The relief in the detective's eyes piqued Simon's interest. "Why?" he asked again.

"I didn't think it was you, but I had to ask."

"Why?" he asked a third time. "Dammit, don't play games."

"A little accident last night on rain-slicked roads. Car overturned. Sideswiped a row of trees and flipped over."

Simon's blood ran cold. "What car?"

"Great safety advances in today's cars. Probably the safest car on the road, a Mercedes."

"Tamara." It was barely a whisper. Simon felt the hairs on his arms rise. His tongue thickened so he could barely force the words out. "Is she okay?"

"If it hadn't been for the air bags, she might not have lived to tell about it."

Simon's legs felt like thistledown. His knees gave way. He barely got the fourth chair pulled out when he collapsed into it. He was stunned at the feeling of relief, of possessiveness, toward Tamara. "What happened?"

"She says a big pickup truck souped up with a lifter kit ran her off the road. Tinted windows, no headlights."

"How bad—" Simon caught the panic in his voice, cleared his throat and tried again. "How bad was she hurt?"

"Both the front and side airbags deployed. Her biggest problems were glass slivers and the bruise from the seatbelt. She was released this morning. I drove her home and then came over to see if you were here."

Simon closed his eyes in silent prayer. He didn't stop to dissect his feelings. She was all right. He'd stop by to see her as soon as Kyrillos left. No, first he'd order some flowers. Roses. Two dozen. Five dozen. Hell, he'd buy out the store.

"Someone means business."

Simon looked thoughtfully at Kyrillos. "The shares."

"Her take would be something like twenty million dollars?"

Simon's mind reeled with the frightful possibility that someone on the board of The Pines tried to kill Tamara. No!

"No, it isn't twenty million dollars?"

Simon hadn't realized he'd spoken the negative aloud. The detective raised an eyebrow at the bleak expression on his face. "No, it couldn't be someone on the board." Simon raked a hand through his rumpled hair. "Could it?"

"That's what I'm trying to find out. Since our first discussion after the car fire, my team has been investigating. Found some interesting tidbits. Shall I run them by you?"

The last gasp of the coffeepot claimed Simon's attention. "First things first." He poured two cups, black, and brought them to the table. Simon took a few sips of the scalding brew then sat down heavily. "Go ahead."

"Where do you want me to start?"

"Any place."

"Your wife?"

A shudder raced through Simon before he could discipline himself. "Ex-wife soon, I hope."

"What do you know about her background?"

"Her father was killed in a plane crash ten years ago. He was a businessman whose company carried heavy travel accident insurance on executives. They lived on the insurance money. Her mother died after—" He didn't know whether to reveal this. It was so private, so poignant.

"Go on," Kyrillos prodded.

What harm would it do now? All his feelings toward Carrie were gone. "Her mother, Cornelia, found herself pregnant at age forty-something. Carrie urged her to—" *Steady, Simon, you can say it!* "To have the baby. But she hadn't married again and the insurance money was running out. She'd have to get a job and couldn't be saddled with a child. She—she had an abortion and contracted toxemia. She died shortly before we met."

Kyrillos had a strange look on his face. Simon averted his gaze. He didn't want the detective to see the moisture in his eyes. Carrie had told him, with a catch in her voice, that she wanted children so much she'd have taken her mother's child to raise it as her own. That was when he'd decided to marry her. He gritted his teeth remembering how he'd had to pull the story out of her. Had she been playing him for a fool even then?

"How did you meet?"

"At the club. Elliott introduced her as his client—he was probating her mother's will—and asked us to join them. She looked so—so vulnerable, all alone in the world except for Elliott."

Kyrillos stood, made a show of pouring himself another cup of coffee. He positioned himself to look out the window. "Carrie's mother's name is Corrinne Black. She's never been married. She's alive and living in Hoboken. She was—is—a hooker."

The cup shattered against a wall. Hot coffee splashed in every direction. "Damn her!" Simon, on his feet, looked perplexedly at his hand, wondering who had directed it to act so violently. He let his arm drop to his side. "Damn you, woman," he said more softly. "Damn your lying soul to hell."

He collapsed back on the chair and buried his face in his hands. "Kevin." A prayer formed on his lips for the son whose bitch of a mother had never loved him, who was the innocent pawn to transform the father's yearning for a son into the mother's share of the golf course.

Another cup of black coffee appeared in front of him. "Got anything strong to put in this?" Kyrillos asked.

Simon took one deep breath, two, three. "I'm all right."

"There's more."

Simon met Kyrillos' gaze reluctantly. He schooled his emotions into a tight package. "I'm ready."

"Elliott Grosse and Corrinne Black go back a long way. He might have been her pimp."

Rage boiled over in Simon. He bolted out of his chair, grabbed the keys to the Corvette. And bumped smack into Kyrillos.

"You're not going anywhere."

"The hell I'm not. Get out of my way."

"Sit down."

"That bastard's going to need more than a plastic surgeon when I'm done with him. Now move!"

Kyrillos reached behind his back and pulled out a pair of handcuffs. "Do you want me to place you under arrest for attempted assault?"

The handcuffs dangling from the detective's hand winked eerily in a ray of weak sunshine. Simon watched them sway slowly, like a hypnotizing device in an expert's hands.

"Sit down."

With a deep sigh, Simon set the chair upright and sank into it. His gaze fastened on the starburst of coffee stains on the wall of the breakfast nook. Here and there a drop had dribbled down. Like tears, he thought.

He had shed the last of his tears for his son. Now he would seek revenge. If it was against Elliott as well as Carrie, fine. In fact, he welcomed it as an outlet for his rage. The detective was right. He wasn't going anywhere. Yet.

"Ready for the next little secret?"

Simon's gaze snapped back to the detective. Their gazes held a long time. Finally Simon said, "In the living room, the sideboard nearest the hallway. Stolichnaya."

"I'll get it."

In a minute the detective was back with two bottles, the vodka and a Glenfiddich. Both Elliott and Marta occasionally sipped the special single malt scotch. "Damn good stuff, both of them," Kyrillos observed as he poured one of each into Waterford glasses.

"So you're off duty?" Simon asked wryly.

"Extenuating circumstances." Kyrillos handed him his drink.

Simon downed the Stoly in one gulp. "Okay, let's hear it."

"Jack Sutcliffe routinely handled explosives when he worked on a road crew twenty-one years ago."

The Stoly hit Simon's stomach like a Molotov cocktail. No. His brother couldn't— "Jack didn't do it."

"He could have been drawn out. Someone, say, a lawyer with expertise at depositions, could have asked him how it was done."

Simon seized on that possibility. His brother might be a slacker, a drunk, but he wasn't a killer. A shudder ripped through him. His twin. No way could his twin have set that car bomb. Even though they'd grown apart, surely Simon would have instinctively known if Jack was evil.

But Elliott? After having set Simon up like a lamb ready to be fleeced, after being a pimp, for God's sake, a pimp to Carrie's unmarried prostitute mother— "Did Elliott really pass the bar?"

"Yes. But not until he was in his mid-thirties. At first I figured he was so late because he went back to school on the G.I. Bill of Rights after 'Nam."

"I didn't know Elliott was in Vietnam."

"He wasn't. Seems that back in 1965, when President Lyndon Johnson announced the doubling of the draft, Elliott had a mysterious accident. He supposedly was a guard in a warehouse and was shot in the foot while trying to apprehend an intruder."

"Really? I never noticed a limp."

"Apparently it all smoothed out after the war."

Simon's eyes narrowed. "What are you getting at?"

"He had a low draft number. One way to not get called up was to become 4-F. Getting shot in the foot would do it."

"Son of a bitch."

"Precisely. I served. Got scars on my leg from shrapnel to prove it. I had three buddies who didn't make it back. If he—"

Simon could finish the unspoken sentence that Kyrillos choked off. A coward like Elliott Grosse would get no quarter from a Vietnam vet with a badge. A sense of rightness, of finality, came over Simon that justice would be done.

"The doctor who certified his physical status died several years later. His records disappeared."

"How could Dad have been so hoodwinked?"

"I'd say he'd had some inkling of Elliott's duplicity. Why else would he have turned to Ms. Kai to rewrite his will?"

That reminder of his father's death triggered a memory of the wire Tamara saw. "I should have told you this before," Simon said slowly. "I don't think Dad's death was an accident."

The detective snapped forward in his chair. Simon related Tamara's suspicions, their discovery of tree gouges. "It was only on one side of the jump, so we discounted the evidence. If they were on the other tree as well, they were distorted. It might have been caused by a buck rubbing velvet."

"I'll send a forensics team out there to poke around."

"I wish I'd told you earlier. At the time, I felt we were overreacting. But now, with all that's happened —"

"I understand."

"Can we go after Elliott for pimping?"

The quick change in subject didn't faze the detective. "He apparently stopped when he hung out his shingle. The statute of limitations doesn't extend that far back."

"You're sure he graduated law school? He did pass the bar?"

"I don't think he could have gotten two institutions to falsify records. And yes, he did pass the New Jersey bar."

Simon grunted. Elliott had made some oblique references to his "time at Harvard", but Simon couldn't remember whether, among the certificates on Elliott's office walls, he'd hung any diplomas. All he remembered were photos of Elliott with famous personalities, including the New Jersey Governor and both its U.S. Senators.

His mind began sifting possibilities. Elliott had a special interest in Carrie, his whore's bastard daughter, so he'd introduced them with a specific aim. As Simon's wife, she would be entitled to half his assets. When Kevin died she'd lost her hold on him but didn't want to settle for a mere ten percent of golf course shares. Elliott still had Jack under his thumb, but with Harland giving Tamara twenty shares, Elliott saw his opportunity for control slipping away. He had to get rid of Tamara.

That didn't make sense. Why wasn't Simon himself the target? His thirty percent that would devolve to his widow would give the Elliott-Carrie-Jack-Marta consortium control. They wouldn't need Tamara's shares.

The obvious answer was even more chilling.

Someone wanted Tamara dead.

Chapter Nineteen

ဆ

Ollie was getting more nervous by the minute. He hoped he wouldn't lose his license. If anyone knew what he'd done, he might as well close up shop. He'd have to leave his family and move further into the Piney woods where there was no neighbor for ten miles. Or maybe he'd disappear into Long Island's Pinelands.

What if they found his fingerprints on the truck? Well, hell, he argued with himself, it would be unnatural if they didn't. Hadn't Ollie himself driven the truck into the storage area behind his chain-link fence when it came in for repair?

A big man with a beer gut that no amount of heavy work could shed, Ollie Upson had owned his auto repair shop for fifteen years. In all that time he'd never made enough to put by. That, he told himself, was why he'd taken to gambling. Not because he had to bet on every game that was played. Football, basketball, college or pro, you name it, Ollie would bet it.

When that slick lawyer came to him with fifty-two grand in IOUs, Ollie like to have choked on his own spit. Hell, it would have taken two lifetimes of dollying under trucks to pay that off. That's why he'd jumped when offered a way out. Years ago he'd gotten on the planning board to spite his neighbor after a little dispute about what he could put on his property. In hindsight, it looked like the smartest thing he'd done in his life.

The phone on the wall of his tiny, grease-stained office jangled. He grabbed it. "Yeah?"

"They found the truck," Ike MacKinnon said.

Ollie's gut twisted. He reached in his drawer for a swig of Mylanta. The past few months had given him an ulcer.

"When they hoisted the Mercedes up out of the muck," Ike continued, "they found black paint on it. They also got matching Mercedes paint chips on the passenger side of the truck."

"They can't pin anything on me," Ollie said plaintively.

"Right," Ike soothed. "Because you already called them to say your holding area was broken into last night, didn't you?"

"Yeah, I did."

"What'd they say when you called?"

"Said they'd put out an A.P.B. on it. Said whoever sawed through the padlock did an amateur job."

Ike snickered. "Don't matter what kind of a job it was. The truck got stolen, didn't it? No way will they figure out what part you played if you just follow instructions."

Ollie reached for more Mylanta. He could taste that five grand he'd been promised for knocking the Mercedes off the road.

"But you didn't really follow through, did you?"

"What do you mean?" Ollie croaked.

"She was supposed to hit the bridge abutment, not a bunch of saplings that didn't do diddly-squat to the car."

"Wait a minute, I took all the risk—"

"You don't produce, you know what you get?"

"Hey, that wasn't our—"

The dial tone buzzed loudly in Ollie's ear. Suddenly his stomach turned over. He jumped to his feet and high-tailed it to the john. He didn't need more Mylanta. He needed a basin.

* * * * *

Parked on the verge, Simon watched the delivery truck pull out from the cutoff to Tamara's bungalow then drove the golf cart toward her home. He wished he could have seen her expression when she'd been handed forty-two red roses, the entire supply from the local florist shop.

He touched the envelope in his jeans pocket. Kyrillos had given it to him when they parted. The locksmith had been finishing up the new security arrangements when Kyrillos had driven her home from the hospital. When he'd flashed his badge and said he'd be stopping by Simon's next, the man had asked him to deliver the envelope.

With the bill—time-and-a-half for urgent work—was a set of master keys to the bungalow. Simon had requested double deadbolts front and back, removable metal pegs inserted through the window sashes, and a bar for the sliding patio door.

He only wanted the keys because he was the landlord, Simon told himself. It had nothing to do with his fantasy of slipping into the house in the middle of the night and seeing Tamara sleeping in the nude. With the covers having slipped off her delectable body, her magnificent blonde hair spread out on the pillow, a soft smile on her face from dreaming about him, he'd undress, climb into her bed and slip into her wet pussy, watching for the moment of awareness as she awoke with him fucking her.

His fantasy had stopped there. It had been too painful. That was when he'd taken a cold shower and shaved off the overnight stubble. If he was going to seduce her, he didn't want to scratch her tender skin.

Well, maybe just a little. Where it wouldn't show.

He'd like to unlock the door and walk in, surprising her, maybe catch her with her face buried in the bouquet, inhaling their heady fragrance, or perhaps rereading the card.

And he'd meant it. *You're more important than the car.*

The Mercedes could be replaced. Tamara was one of a kind.

Standing on tiptoe on her porch, he peeked through the small pane of glass at the top of the door. He couldn't see her. He rapped lightly, then called, "It's Simon." With the midafternoon sun at his back, his face would be in shadow. He didn't want to frighten her into thinking MacKinnon had come back.

Tamara came from the bedroom hallway into the living room, a bemused expression on her face. She held a single rose to her cheek. Her gaze locked with his through the glass. Her mouth moved. He hoped she had whispered his name. She walked seemingly without pain toward him. Simon tossed off an unconscious thank-you to the airbags. The door opened. "Simon." His name on her lips was like a caress, throaty, soft.

Less than a foot separated them, but he was strangely reluctant to breach the gap without invitation. Surely she could interpret the naked longing in his eyes, the desire to hold, to protect, to possess this magnificent woman.

Then her attire registered on his consciousness. She wore a kimono type of wrap, white shimmery silk, accented by a narrow red binding that skimmed around her throat, dipped into a vee at the start of her cleavage, and ran down the length of her body. A wide red sash emphasized her tiny waist, the fullness of her breasts. He allowed himself the fantasy that she had become his private geisha.

Her hair had been casually pinned up, as if inviting his mouth to skim down her graceful neck. Stray wisps had escaped to feather around her perfect oval face. She wore no makeup. This was a vision he could wake up to every day for the rest of his life. The thought rocked him.

Wordlessly she reached out to stroke the velvety petals against his mouth. The erotic sensation sent blood rushing straight down to his cock. He clenched his hands into tight fists.

She took a single step backward. He needed no further invitation. He slipped inside and kicked the door closed, then with only a part of his conscious mind gave the lock setup a quick scrutiny. One had a thumb-pad. He flipped it. The other needed a key to engage the lock.

As if reading his mind, Tamara turned to a dried-flower wreath she'd hung on the near wall. "I keep them here," she said in a husky voice, handing him a keyring with a shiny Yale key.

"But it wasn't—" She hadn't used it. Because she expected him? Simon couldn't ever remember having been so fumble-fingered in his life. He finally snicked the lock into place. Flipping the keyring onto the nearby table, he turned. His arm bumped into the softness of her breast. The contact burned through his shirtsleeve and snapped all his nerve endings into red alert.

They were so close he could smell her familiar perfume— had she dabbed some on in anticipation of his arrival? So close that he could see a dozen small red slashes on her neck and left cheek, no doubt from glass shards. He raised a hand and stroked a knuckle around them. "Do they hurt?"

Her gaze never left his. She shook her head, *No.*

"Are you all right?"

A nod, *Yes.*

"Does anything hurt?"

She shook her head, *No.* Then, "Yes."

"Where?" He wanted to throttle the bastard who had done this to her, wanted him strung up by his balls and horsewhipped.

"Here." Slowly she lowered her hand, dragging the rose between her breasts, across the red sash, down her stomach. The blood-red flower stopped where her thighs met.

Simon's pulse rate doubled. He dropped to his knees, nudged the flower aside with one hand, and kissed the indicated spot.

The rose fell to the floor.

His hands reached behind her and cupped the firm curves of her ass. His tongue stroked where his lips had kissed, moistening the silken fabric.

"Would you—" Her soft gasp pleased him, inflamed him. "Would you like to see the rest of the flowers?"

Simon got to his feet reluctantly. The crushed petals released their fragrance under his heel as he turned and followed her. He knew the bedroom contained a queen-size bed, an armoire, a dressing table. She had turned the room into a bower—cabbage roses on the quilted bedspread, on swags at the windows, on a chaise longue. One wall was papered with ivy climbing a trellis. Sunlight filtered through sheer white curtains.

On a cloth-covered round table near the bed sat a huge glass vase. Some buds were still tightly furled. Others had relaxed in the warmth of the room. Several had opened to their full, complex beauty, releasing a heady aroma.

She was like those roses, Simon thought. Tightly coiled but destined to unfold her beauty under the inexorable tide of his heat. Liquid fire rushed through his veins at the thought of her opening under his touch. His cock throbbed painfully. He wanted to throw her on the bed, rip open that white robe and plunge into her, wanted to lose himself in her ripe softness. But he just stood there, mesmerized by her artless beauty.

Tamara picked up the card from where it had been propped up against the vase at an angle that could be seen from the bed. "I was touched," she said simply, looking at the unsigned note.

She stood on tiptoe and grazed her lips against his, like the brush of a butterfly's wings. "Thank you."

"I'd give the entire flower shop to keep you from harm."

Then they both moved at once, as though a starter gun had been fired for a footrace. Their hungry mouths meshed, then their bodies. Her arms slid up behind his neck, her fingers tunneled through his thick hair. He held her head captive with one hand. With the other he pressed her even closer to the unmistakable heat of his rampant cock. Their tongues found each other and stroked, tasted, melded. He moved his hips rhythmically, suddenly frantic to finish what they'd started the other night in his car.

The last vestige of sanity fought with his savage desire. *She deserves more than a back seat quickie.*

He broke the kiss and took a deep breath. Sliding his hands to her waist, he rested his forehead against hers. "I want to do this right," he whispered on a groan.

Slowly, methodically, he began pulling out the pins holding her hair up and set them on the bedside table. Then he combed his fingers through the shimmering strands, letting them drift down to her shoulders. "Beautiful," he murmured. "Like spun gold. You sure Rumpelstiltskin isn't hiding around here?"

Her thick eyelashes were downcast, throwing feathery shadows on her skin. With a small smile on her lips, she moved her head sideways in a wordless *No*.

Gently cupping her face between his hands, he dropped kisses on her hairline, the perfect arch of her brow, the corner of her eye. He trailed his lips across her cheek to the delicate shell of her ear, then darted his tongue inside.

She gasped, but held still. Her eyes remained closed.

His hands dropped to the collar of her robe, spread the opening a little wider. His tongue licked a path down the smooth column of her neck. Every few inches he stopped to nip her skin between his teeth and relished every shudder he evoked in her.

"No good," he said against the hollow of her collarbone. "I can't reach…"

He nibbled at her neck while his hands dropped to her sash. He loosened the red silk that had held the opening to her robe tight against her curves. His fingers traced the red edge of her collar, each downward swoop bunching the silken fabric further apart, each upward swoop stroking her satiny skin. The twin swells of her breasts came into view. He was inordinately pleased at how he'd induced her nipples to jut out under the filmy fabric. He skimmed his knuckles over the tight peaks.

She made a sound deep in her throat and arched into his touch. He bent forward and laved a nipple through the material. She groaned again, grabbed handfuls of his hair with both hands and held him against her. He sucked gently then pulled away. Through the damp fabric he could see the puckered areola surrounding the coral peak.

"Don't stop," she said in a half-whisper, half-moan.

"I don't intend to."

He dragged the silk off her breast and blew a light puff of air on the exposed nipple. It tightened even more.

"Please."

Drawing back to drink in the sight of her, he muffled a curse at the ugly diagonal bruise on her shoulder, her chest.

From the seat belt. The accident.

No! he shouted inwardly. He wanted nothing to intrude. He had to make this perfect for her, make her forget the ugliness.

His fingers caressed her shoulders, slipping the silk down to her elbows. Both breasts stood exposed to his view. He cupped their heavy weight in his hands, kissed each one lavishly, then in one swift movement swept her off her feet and gently set her down on the bed. The movement unraveled the sash. It lay in a rippling red swath across her waist. The white silk parted at her hips, exposing the dark blonde curls.

Simon could feel every hard beat his heart took, pumping blood into his throbbing cock. He wanted to nudge her thighs apart and sink into her sweet pussy, wanted to fuck her until she shattered in his arms.

"I'm going to drown you in rose petals," he said in a hoarse voice, reaching for a stem from the vase. He plucked the petals and released them one by one. They drifted downward, landing on her flat stomach, between her breasts, on her pubic curls. Some blended in with the red sash. Some stood out vividly against the white silk that had slid off her shoulders.

Her eyes glazed with passion, Tamara watched him pull out petal after petal, watched them float down. She was burning with need and he hadn't touched her in what seemed like hours. Every place a petal landed felt as though he had kissed her there. She thought she'd go crazy if he didn't touch her soon. It was as though he was playing a game of tug-of-war, seeing who would break first.

"Please," she moaned, arching her back in invitation.

A slow smile spread across his face. "Please what?"

She raised her arms. Rose petals cascaded onto her bare breasts. Their lavish scent intoxicated her. "Please come here."

Simon yanked his navy polo shirt over his head and tossed it aside. He toed off his shoes—she barely noticed he was sockless—and knelt on the bed. Nudging her thighs apart, he planted himself between them.

She managed to unsnap his jeans, but he gently pushed her arms back down. His hands held hers captive on the quilted spread. "Now I'm going to count the petals," he said.

He bent low to her body. His warm breath caressed an exposed patch of skin below her navel. "One," he said, kissing the spot. His mouth hovered over her hipbone then dipped. "Two."

Tamara was mindless with need. She lifted her hips and gyrated against his mouth. Releasing her hands, he skimmed his fingers along her damp slit and gently probed the nest of curls, seeking the bud that could make her shatter. "More rose petals down here," he murmured. "How do they taste, I wonder?"

He lowered his head. His tongue found and licked her clit, slowly then with more force. She thought she would explode from the sensation. He slipped two fingers inside her pussy. Her moist inner walls contracted around him. Her head thrashed from side to side on the pillow. She shut her eyes to concentrate on the exquisite sensations he was coaxing out of her. "Please," she moaned. "Please."

Simon grabbed under her knees and slung her legs over his shoulders. He slipped his hands under her buttocks, lifted her hips to his mouth, and raised himself to his knees. "I want you to look at me when I kiss you," he growled.

She opened heavy-lidded eyes. The contrast of his dark hair against her blonde pubic curls was wildly erotic. With her hips high in the air, gravity had shifted her breasts toward her, rose petals pooling between and over them.

Simon's mouth descended again to her slit, his eyes locked with hers. The intimacy of their gaze while his mouth caressed her most private parts branded her. His expression became fiercely possessive.

Sensation crowded out all self-consciousness. She gave herself up to the delirious feeling of his mouth on her clit, sucking, nibbling, his fingers rhythmically stroking inside her pussy. Electric currents zapped every nerve ending in her body and she cried out his name again and again. The contractions shook her until she thought she would dissolve into a pool of her own juices.

Long moments later she felt her hips being lowered back to the bed. She wanted to lift her arms to invite him into them, but a great lassitude filled her.

The mattress shifted. Lazily she opened her eyes and saw through lowered lashes that Simon was on his feet. Ropy muscles in his arms and legs bunched as he bent forward to pull his jeans off. Her lassitude vanished with the sight of his naked body as he straightened to his full magnificent height. Her eyes snapped to the thick shaft jutting out from the black curls at his groin.

He wanted her, stump and all! Suddenly she found the energy to raise her arms in invitation. He eagerly knelt between her opened thighs and covered her body with his, then slid with a delicious friction up and down, crushing the rose petals between their warmed bodies. Their newly released fragrance melded with the lingering smell of their passion.

His mouth found hers and he kissed her hungrily. The taste of her juices on his tongue, tangy, sweetly musky, aroused her anew. He rubbed his hard cock against her belly, teasing, taunting her with its heat. She spread her thighs wider, hooked her good leg around his for traction as she arched her back, begging for more contact. She was too hungry for the feel of him to tell him it was easier for her to be on top, to remind him that she only controlled one of her legs.

Her hands explored his body everywhere she could reach—across his broad shoulders, up and down his spine, his taut ass cheeks. She wanted to know every inch of him with her fingers, her eyes, her mouth. She wanted to pleasure him the way he'd pleasured her. She squirmed beneath him, telling him with her body how much she needed him inside her, now, how much she wanted him slamming into her with the same mindless desire she had for him.

Something was wrong.

He had grown still.

"I'm sorry. I have to go."

"What— Why?"

"I tried—" Simon swiveled his legs to the floor and stood. He grabbed his jeans and, showing her his back, yanked them on. He slipped into his loafers and snatched up his polo shirt on his way to the door. "I'm sorry. I just couldn't—"

His words were muffled as he pulled on his shirt in the hallway. Seconds later Tamara heard the front door slam.

The throbbing between her legs was all-consuming. Her breasts screamed with desire. Her lips felt swollen and well kissed. She sat up in the bed, untangling herself from the white silk robe.

And saw her leg.

The cosmetic prosthesis that was made to look like human skin. She barked out a harsh laugh. It had happened again. Through the haze of his passion, the man she wanted had remembered what was wrong with her and found he'd lost the stomach—or should she say hard-on—for making love to a gimp.

She'd been humiliated before by an insensitive lover, but never had she so wanted someone to be different.

Because she couldn't avoid the truth. She loved Simon.

A tear trickled unnoticed down her cheek. She'd been a fool, as usual. Letting her heart and her body rule her head.

She'd known the exact moment he'd changed. He'd scraped his shinbone against the edge of her prosthesis and let out a hiss. And then it had happened.

His thick, magnificent cock had become flaccid.

Because she was unlovable. She was marred. She was an amputee.

Chapter Twenty

🔊

"May I come in?"

If she hadn't been holding herself so tightly together, Tamara might have chuckled at the blank look she received when Jack opened the door to her knock and saw her on his porch. As it was, she hoped she had enough adrenaline left to speak her piece before getting as far away from The Pines as she could.

"Come to gloat?" he said at last.

Tamara's chin went up. She noticed the *Columbus County Observer* in Jack's hand. The banner headline leaped off the page. RAPE OF THE LAND? PLANNING BOARD TABLES VOTE ON PROPOSED DEVELOPMENT. The look in Jack's eyes made Tamara shiver, as though he had been thinking up ways to kill her. Or at least put her out of commission.

She resisted the urge to rub her damp palms down her jeans. She couldn't allow him to see a trace of weakness. Adjusting the collar of her raincoat to hint that it was chilly outside, she repeated, "May I come in?"

Jack stared at her a moment—she forced herself to meet his gaze—then spun around and started down the hall. "Sure."

Tamara stepped onto the black-and-white tiles, pulled the heavy door shut with a solid thunk, and followed him into a cathedral-ceilinged living room. She'd never been inside before. They'd always met in the boardroom. She was struck by how impersonal the room was, even with an unmistakable decorator's touch. Chrome-legged tables and twin black leather sofas flanked a white marble fireplace. Austere vertical blinds shielded large expanses of plate glass. But no homey accents like mashed-in pillows, family photographs, books or magazines graced the room. Sterile was the only word that came to mind.

Suddenly she pitied Jack Sutcliffe.

He stopped at a massive black lacquered unit that she guessed held an entertainment center. "Drink?"

"No, thanks." She hadn't smelled liquor on his breath and hoped he was sober enough to listen with an open mind.

"You came to talk to me. So sit down and talk." He clinked several ice cubes into a tall glass, then sliced a lemon wedge and squeezed it in. With an expert flick of his wrist, he opened a bottle of club soda. The sound of it gurgling as he poured was loud in the silence of the cavernous room.

Tamara perched on the edge of a sofa. Club soda? Was he going sober?

Glass in hand, Jack sauntered from the bar and stood at the fireplace, one elbow casually draped on the mantel. "So talk. Convince me to drop my plans."

"I didn't come here about the development."

Jack eyed her speculatively. "Then what?"

The question hung in the air. She had rehearsed any number of opening gambits, but they'd all seemed forced. Still, she knew she couldn't just walk away without trying. She swallowed hard. "I'd like to speak to you about Harland."

A scowl darkened Jack's face. "Missing your lover?"

"I never slept with him." She felt her lower lip quiver and rushed on before it betrayed her. "Harland was the father I wish I'd had. My father died when I was eight. I had no one to look up to when it was most important to me." Unconsciously she rubbed the spot where the cuff of her prosthesis met skin.

Jack caught the movement and snapped his gaze away to hide the guilt. He took a sip of club soda. "You have Ike."

Tamara couldn't quite suppress the shudder that ran down her spine. "If I never see him again, it would be too soon. That man was no more father to me than—than John Wayne Gacey."

"Hear him tell it, he raised you after your mother died."

"He's slime. He's only here because he smells money."

The smile on Jack's mouth looked like a sneer. "And you?"

Tamara felt her hands fisting. She relaxed them with an effort. "Don't attribute Ike's qualities to me."

"So why are you here?"

"I— Harland loved you."

"Don't give me any hearts and flowers."

"Jack, please. He was your father."

"Yeah, so what?"

"Don't throw away the most precious thing you have!"

"I'm not throwing anything away. Harland's dead."

Tamara's voice quivered. "What about your family?"

Jack grunted. "Who's left except Simon?"

"That's precisely who I'm talking about. When I see you together, the animosity just rolls off you. He's not just your brother, he's your twin. Your father wanted you and Simon to work together. That's why he changed his will. Don't you see?"

She licked suddenly dry lips. This wasn't coming out right. "From what I gather, the original will gave you all his shares in the golf course and Simon all the other assets. Why did he change it? Have you asked yourself that?"

When Jack didn't reply, she went on. "I've thought about what Harland wanted. He gave you cash, liquidity, to get out of your personal problems. It doesn't matter which development you finally wind up with, as long as you work together."

First to Die

Jack raised an eyebrow. "So all I need to do is convince Simon to vote with my plan and we don't need your shares. Is that what you're saying?"

Tamara turned her face away from his stare, so unnervingly like Simon's. "Yes." It was almost a whisper.

"How do you propose I do that? I've seen how he looks at you, all male hormones. All you have to do is tell him how to vote and he'll do it. Then we're deadlocked again."

"Not true." Her voice cracked. She took a deep breath and continued. "I'm leaving. I came here to sell my shares."

Jack was raising the club soda to his mouth. His hand stopped in midair. "Yeah, right. A million dollars a share."

"No. I'll sell them for exactly sixty-six dollars."

"Sixty—how did you arrive at that off-the-wall number?"

Tamara stood on wobbly knees. She couldn't take him looming over her, mentally and visually dominating her. She had to convince Jack, she couldn't bear to face a repulsed Simon again. "That was Harland's age when he—he gave me the shares."

"And the catch?"

"Simply that you and Simon agree on a proposal. Whether it's your proposal or mine or none at all. That was Harland's wish. It's what he told me on the day he—" She bit back a sob. "Almost his last words were, 'Twins, work together.' And since both you and Simon want me off the property, I've arranged to move this weekend. I'm going back to Philadelphia."

Jack gave her a thoughtful look. "To your old firm?"

"No. I'll still be freelancing. I have some great leads."

He snorted. "That newspaper article gave you good publicity, I guess."

Lying went against her grain, but it was better than anyone knowing that she was simply running away. Tamara grabbed at the excuse he'd thrown her. She lifted her chin. "Yes. I'll have my pick of jobs."

"Sit down." Jack went to the sideboard and poured another glass of club soda, then came back to where she was still standing. "Please." He handed her the glass, then sat down on one of the sofas. "What did Harland say about me?"

No, please, she'd had a hard enough time saying what she had to say. She just wanted to get away from the memories. Away from the man who reminded her so much of Simon. His eyes a shade darker, his face fuller, more jowly, but the mouth, oh the mouth, the full lower lip, the pronounced cupid's bow on the upper, the way he crooked his head to one side when thinking.

"Please sit."

Against her will, Tamara lowered herself onto the other sofa, averting her eyes. If she looked at him, she could see Simon's face instead, his eyes darkened by passion, his mouth wet from their kisses —

"Tell me what he said about me."

She swallowed hard. "You were his firstborn. Because of that, he made allowances, protected you when he should have let you suffer the consequences. Looking back, he wished that he'd used the 'tough love' concept on you."

"What's that?"

"It's primarily for parents with rebellious teenagers, but it applies to any age group. Its philosophy is that if your child does something wrong, he has to pay the price. It means not being embarrassed or guilt-ridden at your own perceived failure to raise that child correctly.

"Harland told me he fervently wished he'd been harder on you growing up. Anything you did, he let it slide. Consequently, you never had to toughen up, acquire a thick skin…"

"The way Simon did."

"He said you had everything handed to you. Simon always knew he was second, so he worked harder."

"So you think your little speech will show me the error of my ways, and I'll go to Simon hat in hand and say let's work together, I want to throw away a two-hundred-million-dollar project because my father wanted to 'tough love' me but never got around to it."

She set her glass on the table and stood abruptly. "You asked what Harland said. I told you. Now if you'll excuse me, I have some packing to do."

"Not so fast." He caught her by the arm as she tried to scurry past him toward the hall.

She stiffened her spine. She'd said all she was going to on the subject.

"The shares. How are you going to turn them over?"

"I'll give you a legal document."

"I want to see something now. If you think I'm going to go groveling to Simon, kiss ass, give up two hundred mil only to find out you're still against me, you must think I'm in my cups."

Tamara looked pointedly at the hard grip Jack had on her arm. Abashed, he let go. She opened her purse, retrieved an envelope, and handed it to him. "Will this do? It's notarized."

"Let's see it." Jack unfolded the brief document, scanned it then read it more carefully. He looked up at her with narrowed eyes. "Do I get to keep this?"

Tamara's stomach tightened. That document would cut off any further contact she might have with The Pines, with Simon. "Yes. Now may I go?"

"Be my guest."

He escorted her through the hallway to the front door. With his hand on the knob, he said, "One more thing."

Please, just let me get out of here before I embarrass myself and cry. "What?"

"If you're giving up your shares, if you don't want anything to do with The Pines, what about the bungalow?"

"I-I—"

Jack smirked. "Just as I thought. You're grandstanding."

"No, it's just that I haven't..."

He folded his arms across his chest. "You haven't what?"

How could she give up the Pine Barrens that she'd come to love as much as Harland had? Where would she live if she couldn't make it on her own? Where would she go? To Ike?

Never! She'd make it somehow. She just hadn't figured out yet how she was going to do it. "If you don't mind, I'll keep that option open for a few weeks until I find a place to stay."

"That shouldn't be too hard, with all the job offers you'll have to pick from."

"Right." She yanked the front door open. "As soon as I get settled, my attorney will send you the document. With Harland gone, there's nothing to keep me here."

With that lie hanging in the stifling air of the hallway, Tamara stepped onto the porch and out of the Sutcliffes' lives.

Both of them.

* * * * *

"Where the hell is that thing?"

In his attic, a highball glass of straight Old Granddad nearby, Jack rummaged through cardboard boxes. "I know it's here someplace. It was in Ronni's era." His first wife was a tall, stately blonde with slim hips and no boobs. But boy, could she give head. He'd married her when he was twenty-six.

The youngest of five children and the only girl, she was big on family. She took pictures of every outing, every gathering, and pasted them in scrapbooks. She had a thing about both families getting to know each other. She insisted on picnics every Fourth of July, and invited her brothers and their families and Harland and Mother and Simon and whichever broad he was humping at the time and made a record of their antics.

"Ah, here it is." He found two photograph albums at the bottom of a box of books on horticulture. He'd once learned enough about living plants to be able to talk to his mother about her obsession. He sat on the rough-planked floor and opened one of the albums at random.

"I remember this." An eight-by-ten photo showed Jack and Simon, arms around each other's shoulders, each holding golf clubs. "That's the tournament we won." Some college round robin at Simon's school, Middlebury. Jack had already been kicked out of Princeton. He fingered the edges of the photo. He'd seen it before. Where?

In the hallway off Harland's study.

He flipped to another page. In that photo he was helping his mother plant a Franklinia, a tree that had been found in the wild in Georgia in 1770 by a friend of Benjamin Franklin, who named it after him. Shortly thereafter, all the wild plants disappeared and every Franklinia existing today was descended from those first plants the guy had brought back.

Funny that he should remember such an insignificant detail. Jack reached for his drink and took a hefty sip. Mother was like that, he recalled. Full of trivia and so excited about a subject that she made you excited about it too.

"How'd this get here?" The photo that had caught his eye showed a very young Jack—he remembered it as though it were yesterday—on his first two-wheeler, Harland running beside him to steady the bike if he should need it, but his hands at least a foot away from the shiny metal.

Ronni must have gotten duplicates of things that she thought should be handed down through the family, he decided. He hadn't been ready for a family at twenty-six. Hell, he hadn't been ready for marriage, if truth be known. Still wasn't.

He turned back to the bicycle photo, staring at it a long time. That's the way it always was, he thought, emptying half the glass in three big swallows. Dad hovering over me to catch me if I fell.

Like the accident with the MG.

Christ, Tamara Hart. One-legged victim of Jack Sutcliffe. He guzzled down the rest of the Old Granddad.

He was a victim too. Of Harland Sutcliffe, if he wanted to get technical. Dad had been overprotective. Shit. Simon had never asked for, never gotten help learning to ride his own bike. One day he'd just said to Jack, look what I can do, and spread his arms out like eagle wings and ran that bike right down the driveway, steering with his body, and Jack still had training wheels on his bike.

Tough love. Dad should have shown him 'tough love' instead of coddling him.

Christ. He needed another drink.

Chapter Twenty-One

ഏ

Her heart was still pounding. It had taken every shred of energy she possessed to discuss Simon in as calm a manner as she might debate the typeface for a new business card.

The die was cast now. Tamara had no choice but to leave. Her heart ached at the thought of never seeing Simon again, never kissing him or holding him, never matching wits or crossing swords with him. Never making love with him.

She hadn't been mistaken. She'd seen and felt his engorged cock when he was in the throes of passion, just as she'd seen that he'd deflated like a punctured balloon when he'd remembered her leg. She couldn't stay here, catching glimpses of him from afar, yearning for him, loving him, all the while knowing he thought of her as less than whole, less than a woman.

It had been bravado, not common sense, asking for sixty-six dollars for her share of the course. How would she live? She had maybe three months' worth of living expenses in her savings account. She could sponge off Yvette, who'd be glad to have her, but Tamara had her pride. It was about all she had left. She wouldn't let Simon see how much his rejection hurt her.

The golf cart slowed as she approached one of the access roads to the woods. She gauged the position of the sun through the haze of far-off smoke. About two hours of daylight left to make a last trip, to indelibly engrave in her mind every sight, every sound, every smell of the Pine Barrens.

Memories assailed her as she drove. The previous spring Harland had taken her slogging through the bogs to search for the purple-striped, green Pine Barrens tree frog, no bigger than a thumbnail, whose croak, once heard, was unforgettable. Also unforgettable was the vivid blue of the fragile Pine Barrens Gentian, as blue, he'd said, as her eyes.

To some, the Pine Barrens were a dull blur as they whipped past on their way to the shore. But to Tamara, the subtle shades of green and brown, the vivid splashes of fall color, as now, were more beautiful than a rainbow arcing across the sky.

The path led through an uplands stand of oak that was being tended for later log harvesting, their bronze leaves still clinging to sturdy branches. Huckleberries flourished nearby. The smell of autumn-dried leaves permeated the air. She caught a glimpse of a red-winged blackbird perched on a bent reed.

As she neared a bog, with its rich, cedar-smelling muck, she remembered Harland telling her how native Indians used bayberry roots to treat toothache, wild indigo as a stimulant, wild cherry for tonic, and of course, harvested wild cranberries and blueberries. "Barrens" was a misnomer, he'd told her time and time again.

She stopped the cart and got out. Her sneakers sank into the spongy cedar bog as she walked a dozen feet downhill to a little thread of a creek. On the far side, a controlled burn executed last year had destroyed a patch of pine and scrub. Amid the blackened stumps, her eye picked out clumps of turkey beard, a type of rose whose roots grew deep into the soil and would patiently wait years for sunlight before they sprouted. She also saw new seedlings from the tight pinecones that needed the intense heat of a fire to flare open and scatter their seed.

The resulting sunlight on this side had coaxed into life a few curly grass ferns, a plant so rare it grew in the Pinelands and the Bolivian Andes and nowhere else.

Tamara inhaled deeply. She would carry the Pine Barrens in her heart the rest of her life, but she couldn't live here, not with Simon likely to pop into her field of vision unexpectedly to break her heart all over again. She'd relinquish her life rights to the bungalow in writing, mail it to Jack, and get on with her life somewhere else.

The decision to fulfill Harland's last wish lifted a heavy burden from her shoulders. If she faced a bleak future without Harland, without Vincent, without Simon, so be it.

Her gaze skimmed along the sphagnum that cushioned the bog surface as she walked slowly back to her golf cart.

The cart was gone.

The frown on her face concentrated her thoughts. The path was level, the cart couldn't have rolled away. She glanced around to the checkpoints she'd unconsciously noted—the dead swamp maple with woodpecker holes, that particular clump of wake-robin, the fire-red of that sumac, then back to the creek.

A sudden thought sent chills chasing across her skin.

Someone had followed her.

How else could a golf cart disappear in the woods? Its electric motor gave off only a soft purr, and she had been attuned to the rustle of leaves indicating tiny rodents scurrying along the forest floor, the chirp and flutter of birds in the canopy, the sporadic rat-a-tat of the woodpecker.

Whoever was after her, was he waiting on her golf cart? Behind that dense pine? Crouched within the thick snarl of blueberries?

With a shiver, Tamara pulled her raincoat closer to her. Move! She couldn't stand here like a victim. She had to get back to civilization. But which way? Ahead, she knew, was a groundskeeping road that would take her to the big barn where the ten-gang mowers were kept.

She bent down on one knee. Vague tire imprints in the soft sand showed the golf cart had backed up.

She started off at a lope toward the barn, constantly scanning the uneven path ahead. Tree roots jutting out or clumps of grass that the cart tires would roll over could trip her up. She wished she'd worn her athletic leg, which would allow her to run more easily than the cosmetic one, and would give her leg more "feel" for the terrain.

Suddenly she heard footsteps behind her, heavy, menacing thuds in the packed sand. She dared not look around to see how far away the threat was. She knew she was in good shape from her aerobics and weight training, but her breath came in labored gasps as she pushed herself to pump her legs harder, faster. The air around her darkened. Her next deep breath told her why.

Smoke.

Hackles stood up on her neck. They weren't supposed to control-burn until Thursday. Had it been deliberately set?

The realization made her stumble. In that split second, she felt herself being thrown to the ground. Her face landed in a squish of muck. She barely had time to move her head to clear her nose to breathe. A heavy weight pressed against her back.

"Got you now, you bitch. You're gonna die in that fire."

Ike MacKinnon wrenched her arm upward behind her back hard enough to make Tamara yelp. With his other hand he grabbed her hair and yanked her head up. "You're a threat."

"Why— Aaagh!"

"I'm doing the talking! You shut up!" He jerked her to her feet, one fist twisted in her long hair, the other pinning her arm at a grotesque angle behind her.

She felt as though her shoulder joint would pop. He yanked her toward him, slamming her buttocks into his groin. She could smell his breath, sour from drinking, smoking, and

First to Die

his own fetid stench. "Too bad I can't do what Simon did. I've wanted to fuck you since you came to live with me."

"No!" Tamara lifted her good leg then slammed her heel down as hard as she could on his instep.

Ike grunted and loosened his hold. She wrenched out of his grasp and began running.

He cut her down with a tackle to her ankles. With the breath knocked out of her, Tamara lay on her stomach, gasping. Ike planted his knees astride her waist, grabbed her neck with both meaty hands, and tightened his grasp. "I can strangle you right now, you bitch."

"Why?" It came out barely a croak.

"Your shares."

"I gave them up. Ask Jack."

Harsh laughter erupted above her. "Go on, lie as if your life depended on it. I waited fifteen years to see you grovel."

"It's true," she rasped. "Harland only gave me the shares to force Simon and Jack to work together."

"Enough! I gotta do what I gotta do."

He jerked her head up. With a great heaving gasp that seared her lungs, Tamara inhaled the hot, dry smell of forest fire. She could hear its roar in the distance.

"It'll look like an accident," he said. "Trust me."

She felt a knee in the small of her back. In her peripheral vision she saw him reach for a dead branch. He lifted it then swung down heavily, cracking her on the right temple.

The last thing she remembered was being dragged into the thick, dry brush in the path of the fire.

*　*　*　*　*

"You're drunk."

"'S'true. I am. I just want to—just want to—" Jack swayed toward the doorjamb where Simon barred the way.

"This is Harland's house. Yours is down the road." Simon deliberately used his father's given name as a reminder of how Jack had continually showed his disrespect.

"'S'Dad's house. Our house. Our home."

Simon's spine stiffened. His arm stayed across the open doorway. "What do you want?"

"C'n I come in?"

"I'm fresh out of bourbon."

"Not bourbon." Jack frowned. "Coffee. You always have a pot going. You're a coffeeholic."

Simon bit down on his inner lip to keep from retorting, *And you're an alcoholic.* He took in Jack's bloodshot eyes, the thick wavy hair that looked like an electric mixer had zapped it, the buttons buttoned crooked on the light-blue shirt under his bomber jacket. "Yeah, I guess I can scare up a cup of coffee."

"Atta boy, li'l brother." Jack reached out and put an unsteady hand on Simon's shoulder as Simon stepped back to let him in. "Knew I could depend on you." Stumbling over the threshold, he added, "Dad always did."

"Dad always did what?" Simon asked as he closed and locked the door. He strode to the kitchen, hearing Jack's shuffling footsteps behind him.

"Did what?" Jack asked.

Simon shook his head. The guy was drunk as a robin on overripe wild cherries.

Jack eased himself with calculated precision into a bentwood chair then propped his elbows on the edge of the round oak table and buried his head in his hands.

Simon kept one eye on his twin as he fixed the coffee maker for two cups. From the looks of it, Jack needed a quick jolt.

"Shit. Forgot."

"Forgot what?"

"Had a, um, had a package, a shopping bag. Front porch."

"So?"

"Can you get it? Not sure I could make it to the door."

Simon narrowed his eyes. "If you barf, you'll clean it up."

"Not barf. I'm fine. Fine. I'm fine," he reiterated.

A moment later Simon placed a heavy shopping bag at Jack's feet. "What's in this, books?"

"Books. Lotsa books."

"What for?"

"'Member Mom's hobby?"

"Sure." Their mother had used native plants to landscape around the farmhouse with such finesse that it looked as though the house had grown up magically in the middle of them. Of course, she hadn't dug the holes or moved the trees and shrubs—the twins had. But to this day Simon loved to view the building from any angle, in any season, and see a blossom, a color, a berry, a shape of leaf that she'd chosen for a specific reason.

"Found all her books in the attic."

"What were you doing up there?"

"Looking for what went wrong."

The light on the coffeepot glowed. Simon poured most of the two cups into a large mug and set it in front of Jack.

"Did you find it?"

"Find what?" Jack grabbed the coffee and gulped.

Simon rolled his eyes and set about making another pot. This promised to be a long night.

"Know what Tamara said?"

A muscle twitched in Simon's jaw at the sudden switch in topic. Had Tamara said something about his debacle? "What?"

"Dad wanted us to work together."

"Tamara told you that? When?"

"Few minutes ago. Hour ago. Sometime today. Before I started drinking."

"Are you saying Tamara made you turn to the bottle?"

"Swear. Ask her. She came by, I was sober. She tol' me some things, got me thinking, lookin' at myself, my life. Shit. Didn' like what I saw. So I got drunk."

The coffeemaker started rumbling. Simon swung a chair around and sat facing Jack, his arms folded across the backrest. "So Tamara told you Dad wanted us to work together?"

"Yeah." Jack sipped again. "Made me think of Ronni."

"Tamara made you think of Ronni? Why? Because they're both blondes?"

Jack looked at him as though Simon were a dummy sitting in the corner with a dunce cap on his head. "Ronni was the one so big on family, 'member? She was always taking family pictures?"

He bent down toward the shopping bag too fast, slammed a steadying hand on the table. After a deep breath, he pulled his hand away and moved the books around. "Yeah. Here it is."

An album? Jack got drunk because of a photo album? Simon glanced at the coffeemaker. The drip was only half done. He had a feeling he'd need a cup soon enough.

"Don't like myself when I'm drunk," Jack announced.

"That makes two of us."

Jack's head snapped up. He peered at Simon, squinching his eyes into slits. "Yeah."

Simon waited.

"All kinds'a things," Jack said as though in response to a question. He flipped open the album. "Look at this. I'd forgotten how proud I was. How proud Dad was."

Simon angled his head to see the photo Jack pointed to. It lay alongside a newspaper photo showing the same scene.

Something clicked in Simon's brain. It was one of the few times he'd felt jealous of Jack.

"It was a trophy trout," Jack elaborated unnecessarily, although Simon remembered it as vividly as though it had happened yesterday. The family had gone to Maine for the month of July, tenting in a trailer park. They'd been twelve and Jack had caught a twenty-five-inch, twelve-pound brook trout, the Maine state fish, and gotten his picture in the Augusta papers.

"The look on Dad's face," Jack said, a catch in his voice. "I didn't put it there very often, did I?"

"You didn't have to," Simon said, almost too soft to hear.

"I did have to. Only I didn't know it."

"He always protected you."

Jack drank the dregs of his coffee. "That's what I meant. That's what Tamara said. He protected me in spite of myself. I didn't have the pleasure of putting that look on his face."

Simon noticed the red signal light glowing. He stood up slowly and filled his own cup, then brought the pot and poured Jack a refill. "And now?"

"Now it's too late."

A muscle in Simon's jaw clenched. *No shit, Sherlock.*

"I mean, maybe it's not too late."

"Make up your frigging mind," Simon snapped.

"The shares."

Simon's patience was fast nearing its end. "Sober up, you big shit! You aren't making a lick of sense."

"Am too. The shares. Not too late. For Dad."

Simon gave him a narrow look. "What do you mean?"

"Which side are you on?"

"What do you think I am, a ping-pong ball? Stay on one subject!"

Jack straightened in his seat. "I am on the subject. Of Dad. Which side are you on?"

"You mean, between Dad and yourself, or what? Dammit, I drove seven hundred miles and had three hours' sleep last night and I'm in no mood to debate semantics with a drunk."

"The shares. How would you vote your shares? Tamara's project or mine?"

Tamara. Simon's groin tightened at the thought of the woman who could drive him crazy. Was driving him crazy. She had to have been devastated at his performance, or lack thereof, but he couldn't admit to anyone yet what he still hadn't accepted in himself ever since Kevin—

His gaze fell on the mug he'd grabbed for Jack, a duffer swinging a club, the legend around the sketch stating, "Golfers Have Stiffer Shafts." The irony of it almost caused him to smash the mug out of Jack's hand.

"Dammit, how will you vote your shares?"

Simon gulped his coffee from a mug that, thankfully, had no mocking slogan. "I don't care. Which way is the wind blowing?"

"Jesus, what's got into you? You spend ten months mucking around in every godforsaken corner of the earth to help the environment, Tamara tells the world that my development plan rapes the land—or didn't you see the headline in today's paper?—and you want to know which way the wind is blowing?"

"What headline? What happened last night?"

"Well, did I finally get your attention?" Jack bent down to the shopping bag and pulled out the first section of the *Observer*. "Here." He tossed it on the table. "If that didn't make me barf, nothing I drink will."

Simon sat down and scanned the story. It seemed a well-balanced article, quoting many sources, and encompassing much more than last night's Planning Board proceedings. "Tamara told us most of this stuff during her presentation."

"Yeah, but who listened?" Jack retorted.

"I did. I had an open mind. I didn't know anything about your proposal when I walked into that board meeting."

"What do you know about it now?"

"This engineering firm that did the test borings for Avante Consultants. Are they legit?"

Jack sighed heavily. "Yeah. Several club members told me of their excellent reputation."

"And your consultants are also well thought of?"

"So I'm told. You got any aspirin? This is too much thinking for me."

Then stop drinking, Simon wanted to say. He found a bottle of pain reliever in one of the cabinets and handed them to Jack with a glass of cold water.

"Thanks."

"You want a sandwich or something? When did you eat last?"

"Don't remember."

"Me neither." Simon pulled out four slices of rye bread, slapped peanut butter and raspberry jam on them, and served one to each of them. They ate for a while in silence.

"Simon?" Jack hesitated, washing down the last of his sandwich with the last of his coffee. "What do you do when you realize you made the grandmother of all mistakes?"

Simon rubbed his tongue on the roof of his mouth to get the peanut butter off, but it was just an excuse to procrastinate. He had no clue what mistake Jack was referring to, but his own was not confiding in Tamara about his impotence ever since the night Kevin died. Dammit, he wanted to share his life with her, wanted to hold her, give her pleasure, protect her, and the stiffness of his cock be damned. With the kind of uninhibited response she'd given him, the trust—

Jesus! What if she thought he'd run because of her leg? What if she thought that she, not he, was the problem?

He jumped to his feet. He'd go explain right now. If she felt a tenth for him what he felt for her, they could make a go of it, they could give each other emotional support, maybe they could heal each other—

"What's the matter? Where you going?"

Damn. Simon had forgotten about Jack. He backpedaled. "I thought I heard someone at the door." He theatrically cocked an ear, waited motionless a moment.

"No, guess not." He sat down again. Jack was handing him an olive branch of a sort. He had to give his brother his attention. "Sorry. You were talking about mistakes?"

"You know, this is the ugliest time. Half drunk, half sober. Drunk enough to say what's on your mind, sober enough to hate yourself for it."

Simon went still. He focused his gaze on his brother.

"I think maybe we bit off more than we can chew. About the development. I relied too much on the advice of others. Dad was right. I have no head for business. He was very wise to leave you half his shares. He knew you'd put the brakes on anything stupid. Or illegal."

"Are you saying there's something illegal about your proposed development?"

Jack looked into a middle distance only he could see. "I don't know. We did some things with the planning board. Elliott had answers for everything. Marta had the numbers. Between them, I heard so much about two hundred million dollars, I guess I got greedy. I went along. It was easier than taking a stand."

"And now?"

"This newspaper article makes me look like a dupe."

"How much truth in these allegations about effluent discharge, water tables and such?"

Jack's gaze turned to Simon. The haunted look in his eyes shook Simon. "Truth is, I don't know. I don't know a goddamned thing about any of it. They used my name, my position, my inheritance."

"'They' meaning Elliott and Marta?"

"Them and all of them. The planning board, the bank, the engineers... Jesus, I feel so useless! Dad was right. I don't know shit about development."

Simon kept silent. He didn't know what to say.

One side of Jack's mouth crooked up in a ghost of a smile. "You never did answer my question. Whose side are you on?"

"And the choice is—?"

"Mine? Or Tamara's?"

Simon felt like he'd been sucker-punched. His brother was reaching out to him, asking him to choose between his twin and the woman he wanted to spend the rest of his life with. "Does it have to be mutually exclusive? Isn't there some middle ground?"

"Tamara said that Dad gave her the shares so that you, me and her would make up the seventy percent. He wanted us to work together."

It finally dawned on Simon that in his half-drunk state where truth surfaces, Jack had been referring not to Harland, but to Dad. He leaned forward and gripped Jack's wrist. "I'd like that—big brother."

Jack looked away, but not before Simon saw moisture in his eyes. He cleared his throat. "According to the article, the planning board decided not to put it on the agenda for the public meeting. That gives us some breathing room. Why don't we both get a good night's sleep, and tomorrow you can give me a top-to-bottom review of your blueprints. Then we'll review Tamara's presentation, the engineers' recommendations, and go from there."

"Simon." Jack placed his free hand atop Simon's, which still gripped his wrist. Simon added his other hand, until they were stacked in an interlocking grip.

"Big brother."

"Twin brother."

They stood at the same time, and in mutual spontaneous gestures swung an arm around the other's shoulder.

"I'll walk you to the door. Did you drive up? Or take a golf cart?"

"Got the SUV. I was so drunk, I wouldn't have known if the motor was running on the cart."

They laughed at Jack's attempt at self-deprecating humor. At the door, Jack stopped, dropped his arm, and said, "While I'm baring my soul, there's one more thing that's been keeping me awake at night."

Simon's demeanor became somber as well. "Shoot."

"Don't hate me."

Simon swallowed hard. What kind of confession his brother was about to make, he couldn't guess. "I won't."

"The night Kevin died? Carrie in the poolhouse?"

Simon was still absorbing the unaccustomed closeness between them. He was slow to shift the gears in his brain to a subject he so loathed. "Carrie?"

"The guy with her…" Jack's voice trailed off.

A muscle twitched in Simon's jaw. "How did you know she—"

"Oh God, I couldn't help myself, she'd been falling all over me for weeks, and I just couldn't keep saying no anymore. I'd gotten divorced a second time, my main squeeze had left me, I was horny as hell, and she was like an itch I had to scratch."

Suddenly Jack's words penetrated Simon's brain like a two-by-four being dropped a dozen stories. "That was you out in the poolhouse? You son of a bitch! She should have been inside the house where she could have smelled the gas—"

Simon's fist shot out, missing Jack's jaw by inches, and smashed into the front door. "Get out! Get the fuck out of my house! You killed my son!"

Jack's face paled. "No! It wasn't like that at all!"

"Damn you, you might as well have held a blanket to his face! You were responsible for Kevin's death!"

"Jesus, Simon, how could I have known the heater would—"

"Get out! Out! Damn you to hell!"

Jack grabbed the doorknob and managed to jerk the door open. Simon dragged him across the porch by the collar of his bomber jacket. At the top step they both stopped short.

"Oh my God," Simon whispered.

"Holy shit," Jack said.

The sky was on fire.

Simon spun on his heel, darted into the kitchen and speed-dialed the groundskeeper's line. He knew that they'd have an open line to the fire warden with the fire so close.

After a terse conversation, Simon snatched some supplies from the front closet and tore back outside. Grabbing Jack by an arm, he broke into a run, dragging him along. "We're not done with this conversation, brother," he ground out. "Not by a long shot. But right now, if you want to show Carrie how fucking macho you are, there's a fire you can fight."

Chapter Twenty-Two

ഇ

To many day-hikers, the ladder effect of Pine Barrens woodlands is one of its most charming features. It consists of fragrant oak-leaf and pine-needle litter lying on the ground, an understorey of sheep laurel and blueberries, scrub oaks and laurel and young pines, then trees of intermediate age, up to the tallest, oldest Atlantic white cedars, which towered over the stunted pines.

Those charming features become an inexhaustible fuel supply when fire breaks out. Unlike oaks in damp forests, the Pine Barrens oaks growing in dry sand have protective oils concentrated in their leaves. The glistening pitch in pine needles is incendiary. An uncontrolled burn can produce crown fires, which consume the entire tree. The aim of controlled burning is to rid the forest of this dangerous buildup of fuel while sparing the tree trunks.

In a corner of her mind Tamara knew all this. Harland had told her often enough. So when the acrid stench of smoke penetrated her consciousness as she lay sprawled on the forest litter, she felt panic engulf her. The controlled burn was two days early. She took a deep breath to calm herself. Instead, smoke billowed into her lungs and she coughed harshly.

Small, shallow breaths, she reminded herself.

She pushed up onto her elbows and knees. The crackle of branches being consumed was overwritten with the general roar of the fire. She scrambled to her feet, glanced around wildly. The fire was a half-mile?—mile?—away and moving toward her.

The four-minute mile had long since been broken, but a fire can race along at five to ten miles per hour. Tamara knew she couldn't outrun the fire. She'd have to outwit it. One way would be to get onto blackened ground — stand fast in the face of the oncoming blaze, then dash through the wall of flame. The problem was, the headfire could be a foot deep or a hundred. There was no way of knowing.

Find the cedars!

She scrambled to her feet. Her eyes stung. Tears ran unchecked down her cheeks. Squinting through the smoke, she looked around desperately for the narrow, conical shapes of Atlantic white cedar. They grew with their feet in water, she knew. But they grew so close together that if a crown fire started, she'd be incinerated in minutes.

There! It was her only chance.

Tamara plunged through the brush. Dry branches pulled at her hair, raked deep scratches across her face. She tripped on a gnarled tree root, but managed to stay upright. Heat and smoke seared her lungs. The roar of the flames sounded like Niagara Falls at close range. The fire was at her back, devouring the underbrush, eating up the leaf litter, burning the turf underground.

Her sneaker squished into a spongy mat of sphagnum moss.

Water!

Fat cedar trunks sprouted from hummocks in the bog. She slogged between them, the adrenaline that pumped through her veins pushing her almost beyond endurance. The swampy bottom oozed like quicksand. It sucked a shoe off her good foot, tugged at her prosthesis, pulling her off balance. She landed hard on her good knee in the muck. Tamping down the terror that threatened to overwhelm her, she grabbed blindly at a clump of grass sprouting from a hummock. Just before its roots gave way, it gave Tamara enough purchase to scramble to her feet.

Just a few more yards! she prayed.

Her foot landed in a puddle with a splash. Taking one deep, hot, smoke-laden breath, she dived down into two feet of tea-colored water and squiggled her body into the muck.

* * * * *

"Grab a pulaski and start chopping!"

The fire boss barely glanced at the two new volunteers before riveting his attention back to the conflagration. Simon spun the SUV in a tight circle, aimed it on the sand road for a possible quick getaway then slammed on the brakes.

Jack wasn't sure he was up to this fire-fighting business. His head still pounded from half a bottle of Old Granddad, and his bladder was reminding him of all the coffee he'd drunk. But more to the point, Simon's reaction to his confession twisted slowly through his gut, making his stomach feel like an invisible hand had squeezed all the bile up to his throat.

Stumbling out of the SUV, he realized he hadn't done much in his life to be proud of. Hell, the last thing he could think of was that damn trophy trout he'd been reminded of in Ronni's scrapbook. But being responsible for Kevin's death? Christ. He'd never thought of it that way. It was the truth, if he wanted to look deep down inside that hole that used to contain his heart. He was a shit of the first rank.

He jammed a yellow hard hat on his head and grabbed a pulaski. He'd only used one once before. The preferred firefighter's tool, it had an axe on one end for chopping trees. The hoe side could break up soil, smother embers with dirt, or scrape down to the bare roots. Even he knew that sometimes roots smoldered underground for days after a fire was thought to be out, then flare up on the other side of a firebreak.

On a groan, Jack trudged through the tangled understorey in response to the fire boss's savage gesture. Simon already had his back bent to the job. Typical, thought

Jack, showing his older brother up by plunging into the thick of things.

At least Jack had had the sense to change from his loafers into steel-toed workboots during the ride up. Dad had kept several pairs in the front closet for emergencies—all the Sutcliffe men wore size twelve—and Simon had tossed two pair into the truck while Jack had stood, slack-jawed, staring at the lurid orange horizon.

The headfire seemed to be veering off to the right. Jack was, he hoped, in the backwater. His only other experience firefighting was when the clubhouse had been threatened nine years ago. Then every able-bodied person was pressed into service to dig the firebreak. An aerial of the devastation wrought by that fire hung in the hallway near Dad's study as a reminder never to be complacent.

Not that the homily had ever penetrated Jack's brain.

Until now.

Jesus, what a destructive force! The heat, even five hundred yards away, weakened his knees. His throat lost all its moisture, sucked up along with the oxygen that the fire fed on. Far to the right a tree exploded from the heat, showering the area with live coals and flaming branches. He could only hope they fell within the firebreak and not beyond.

Sweat poured off his forehead under the hard hat as Jack chopped at the base of a six-inch-caliper pine. Others had scraped forest litter backward and dug around roots. In minutes his arm muscles ached. His calf muscles went into spasms. It had been years since he'd pumped iron or even run a mile. On the golf course he used a cart. He was in terrible shape.

It seemed like hours before the pine toppled. Someone wrapped a chain between its branches and a 'dozer hauled it to an accumulating pile. They were going for a backburn, Jack realized. When conditions were right, as they were now with no wind, they could double the benefit of a firebreak by setting a fire forward of the clearing. The manmade fire would burn into the headfire and stop it in its tracks.

He sure as hell hoped so.

The second tree trunk he hacked at was smaller, but it seemed to take longer to fell. His breathing became labored. A tightness in his chest brought him up short. Oh God, was he having a heart attack?

The pulaski fell out of his hands. His knees buckled, he felt lightheaded. He looked around for his brother. Simon was tossing logs into the backburn. Jack tried to call out, but his breath came in shallow gasps. He crumpled into a heap and landed in a tinder-dry laurel bush.

A hundred yards away, Simon grunted as he and another volunteer heaved a log. It crashed into the flaming pile with a shower of sparks. Suddenly his knees gave way and he felt weak as a newborn kitten. He dropped to a squat and laid his head on his knees. Hell, he was no Victorian damsel about to swoon from a too-tight corset. He'd been through worse on Kamchatka.

Jack. When they were kids, they used to be able to finish each other's sentences, know when the other got into hot water, but they'd grown up so dissimilar that Simon hadn't had a twin instinct in twenty years. He stood up slowly and scanned the landscape for Jack.

He wasn't in sight.

Simon pulled out a handkerchief and wiped the smoke and tears from his eyes. Squinting, he studied each firefighter under the concealing hard hats. Most of them were in jeans and denim shirts. He had conscripted Jack with his gray gabardine slacks and light blue shirt.

Something caught his eye under a shrubby laurel. Something that looked wrong, misplaced. Jesus! That lump was Jack, face down in the forest duff, and the fire was creeping toward him. Simon burst into a dead run. "Jack!"

The fire had crept to within inches of the still figure by the time Simon grabbed him under the arms and dragged him away from the fuel supply. Jack's boot snagged on a tree stump. Simon cursed, set him down gently and unhitched it. Then he hoisted the dead weight over his shoulder. In seconds he had crossed the twelve-foot firebreak and headed toward the emergency vehicle.

"He needs oxygen!" he gasped, laying Jack down at the foot of the tank. He hovered over the technician.

Please, Simon prayed. *Let him be all right.*

* * * * *

"You're very lucky. Quick thinking too. It saved your life."

Tamara squinched her eyes shut and tried to block out the horror. The creek heating up until she thought she'd be boiled alive like a lobster. The slimy muck of creek bottom clogging her nose, her ears. Her lungs bursting from lack of oxygen, her fear that she'd pop her head up, gasping for air, and be charcoaled like a hamburger on a hibachi.

"You're safe now."

Safe. She'd felt safe in Simon's arms, but it wasn't Simon talking, wasn't Simon sitting in the hard hospital chair while veins in each of her arms pulsated to the drip of intravenous solution to combat the dehydration, the shock. She opened her eyes to Detective Kyrillos' gaze. "He tried to kill me."

Kyrillos leaned forward. "Who?"

"Ike. He followed me, hid my golf cart. When I started running, he tackled me, knocked me unconscious."

Kyrillos took out his ever-present notebook and began writing. "Did he give you a clue as to why?"

"My shares. I told him I gave them up, but he didn't believe me."

"You gave them up? To whom?"

"I went to see Jack this afternoon." She recounted her argument that Harland had wanted Simon and Jack to work together, that if they could agree on a plan, any plan, she'd sell her shares for next to nothing.

"But Ike hadn't known that."

"No."

Kyrillos thoughtfully stroked his chin. "When was the last time you saw Ike before this?"

With a weary sigh, Tamara brought her hands to her face and gently rubbed her eyes with the pads of her fingers. The backs of her hands had blistered and were dabbed with ointment. "A few days ago. He was waiting for me in the bungalow when I—"

Suddenly she sat upright in the bed, barely noticing that the sheet had dropped to her waist, exposing the skimpy hospital gown. "The bungalow. Did it—?"

"The fire wasn't anywhere near it."

She slumped back and whispered a prayer of thanksgiving. "The fire. It wasn't supposed to be until Thursday."

"I know," he said.

"Was it—was it deliberately set?"

"It's too early to tell. You can be sure the arson unit is going over every inch."

"How many acres were burned?"

"The fire crew was very good, lots of hands, and there was hardly any wind. We estimate forty, forty-five acres."

Tamara gave Kyrillos a tiny smile. "I'm sorry. You're the interrogator and I'm asking all the questions."

He smiled in return. "This isn't an interrogation, it's an interview. And I'd say after what you've just survived, you deserve to have your questions answered."

Her smile disappeared. "Do I need police protection?"

Kyrillos stood, walked to the window of the semi-private room. The other bed was unoccupied, its bed crisply made up. After a moment he turned back to her. "We found a body in the woods about a half mile from the creek you jumped into. We're in the process of IDing it with dental records."

He returned to the seat he had just vacated and sat down. He took her hand in both of his and held it carefully. "I won't beat around the bush. It was Ike MacKinnon's general size and shape. He was found face-up." His voice trailed off.

Tamara didn't need him to draw a picture. Her imagination vividly conjured up the sight of the fire sweeping across Ike's prostrate body, searing the flesh off the skull. A tear leaked out of her tightly closed eyes. "He didn't deserve–"

She couldn't talk. Her throat had squeezed shut.

"Perhaps justice has been done," he said gently.

The door to her room burst open. Simon filled the doorway. At the sight of him, Tamara's breath stopped.

"They said you were–" His quick, thorough scrutiny took in her condition. His tense muscles relaxed fractionally, his fists loosened. One side of his mouth quirked up. "We have to stop meeting like this."

Tamara scrutinized Simon also. His face looked like a damp washcloth had been swiped over it and had missed most of the dirt. The smell of smoke and charred wood clung to his clothes. His hair stood on end, as though he'd run through the air-dry blower at a carwash.

Kyrillos got to his feet and walked toward Simon, thrusting his hand out. "You guys did a helluva job."

Simon finally wrenched his gaze from her. He accepted the handshake wordlessly.

"I'll be in touch when we hear something," Kyrillos said at the doorway before leaving and closing the door behind him.

"Thanks." Tamara's voice was a mere whisper, a combination, she thought, of what Kyrillos would be in touch about, of having breathed too much smoke and hot gases, and of the man now advancing to her bed. Most especially the latter.

"You fought the fire?"

"How can you tell?" Simon let out a short, almost embarrassed laugh then raised an arm to his face, sniffing the shirtsleeve. "Guess I should have changed first, but..."

"But?" she prompted.

"I heard you'd been caught in the fire." His jaw muscle flexed. He shifted his gaze to her pillow. "I was afraid for you."

"You...were?"

Something in the husky way she said those two words pulled his gaze back to her. His amber eyes were lambent. "Hell, I wouldn't wish being caught in a forest fire on my worst enemy. Does anything hurt?"

Of course he'd be concerned. It was his property. He was probably worried about getting sued. Feigning nonchalance, Tamara shrugged. "The IV stings."

Simon looked at her blistered hand, palm down on the bleached hospital sheet. "How about your hands?"

"A little. The painkiller helped. They're more concerned about smoke inhalation. They took X-rays, and I think I OD'd on oxygen." She forced a smile. "I'll live."

Live? What I mean is, without you I'll merely exist.

But she wouldn't beg. If he didn't want her, she'd be damned if she'd go through another harrowing experience just to get him into her room. She took a deep breath and tackled the subject that would send her away from The Pines for good. "I don't know if you've seen Jack yet. I gave him a notarized document offering to sell my shares at a nominal price."

Simon was silent so long she thought he hadn't heard her. Finally he said, "He told me."

"That's it? No reaction?"

"He came to me drunk as a skunk. What'd you say to him?"

"Drunk? He was sober when I left. We drank club soda. I didn't do anything."

"But what did you say?"

"I told you. I offered to sell my shares. The only requirement was that you and he agree to a plan for the property. Any plan. That's all Harland wanted. For his sons to work together."

"Then why didn't Dad just give us all the shares?"

"My shares split equally between you would have given you thirty and Jack forty. Adding Elliott, Marta and Carrie's ten each, they could do it without you. Since you gave Yvette power of attorney, I assume you wouldn't go along with Jack's plan.

"On the other hand, if Harland had given you all my shares, he would have slighted Jack, who, after all, was supposed to get the whole thing. And that would have stymied any development at all because you'd have forty shares."

Simon's stare was unnerving. Tamara turned her head. Her gaze finally rested on the other bed, its bleached white sheets tucked in tightly, its restraining sides down, the call button clipped to the edge of the top sheet. Simon's voice brought her back to the question at hand.

"So by giving up your shares, you expect Jack and me to work together."

Tamara swallowed hard. "It's what Harland wanted."

"If you played your cards right, got us both to work for Jack's plan, you'd be sitting on a gold mine. I don't see you turning your back on twenty million dollars' worth of shares. I grew up surrounded by wealth, made a pile on my own and could do it again. But you? Judging from Ike, you didn't have two dimes to rub together. If it hadn't been for Dad, you'd still be—"

Simon snapped his mouth shut. The vein at his temple pulsed. "You feel you don't deserve what Dad did for you. This is your way of putting paid to the debt you feel you owe him."

Tears stung the backs of Tamara's eyes. *No, dammit, I won't cry!* She thrust out her chin. "I've fulfilled my contract. You can implement my recommendations or not."

"What if we asked you to implement them?"

"You don't need me for that. Everything is thoroughly spelled out. You can hire someone just out of design school."

"Aren't you selling yourself short?"

Just go away! "Maybe it's time for me to move on. If you've seen my résumé, you'll know I haven't stayed in one place too long." *It's a failing of mine, sleeping with the boss, then having him turn his back on me.* It would be the last time she made that mistake. Her heart was breaking just being in the same room as Simon. She closed her eyes. She was too tired to think.

Simon glanced at his watch. "It's after midnight. I shouldn't keep you up so late after your ordeal. Why don't I come by tomorrow and we'll talk more then? Say ten o'clock?"

"Visiting hours aren't until afternoon."

He favored her with his most devastating smile. "The nurses let me in tonight. They'll do the same tomorrow."

"Fine." She wouldn't be here, she'd be out at dawn. She'd run now, except she was exhausted and the burns on her hands stung and the medication was wearing off. No way could she hang around, be within touching distance of Simon and not be able to—

Don't think about it!

She rang for the nurse. A pain pill would make her drowsy enough to be able to sleep.

* * * * *

"Goddamn Ike. Goddamn him! What a fuck-up!"

Marta tossed back the shot of Glenfiddich that Elliott had handed her, then continued her diatribe. "You want a job done right, you do it yourself." She held out her hand for another shot.

Elliott obliged her then sank back onto the antique Sheraton settee in his living room. It was late, but both were wide-awake. "Apparently she's none the worse for wear. Only minor burns, singed hair. Keeping her overnight is only a precaution."

Marta pulled her mouth into a tight line. She stared at Elliott. The smug bastard. *He thinks I don't know why he set Carrie up with Simon in the first place. He thinks the way they all do, that a woman doesn't have the brains, the balls to be top dog.* Well, this one did. Add to that the female's instinct to protect her own and he'd know she meant business. She'd ram the development down the planning board's throat and Elliott would be right alongside her every bleeding step of the way. Or else.

"What do you propose to do now?" Elliott asked.

"I'm thinking."

"You mean you don't have a Plan B?"

"Don't mock me. You're in this as deep as I am. If your skeletons came out of the closet—"

Elliott shot to his feet and came to face her. "Don't you threaten me. You need me too. And I know your secrets."

With a calmness she didn't feel, Marta put a hand on the back of a Hepplewhite side chair for support. He was bluffing. He had to be bluffing. No one knew. She sipped at the

Glenfiddich, amazed that her hand didn't tremble. "Honor among thieves?"

"Why do we need to eliminate Tamara, anyway? Why can't we work around her?"

If he really knew her secret, he wouldn't be asking, Marta thought, and a great knot untied in her chest. "As long as she's there to influence Simon's vote, we don't have a development. And you said if a person dies intestate, the state distributes the estate. Ike would get something by virtue of being her stepfather. That would give us a cushion."

"So with Tamara out of the way, you think you can make Simon see the light?"

"Jack can."

"That drunken sot? He can't find his ass in the dark without two hands."

It disturbed her, even now, to have someone disparage Jack. When Marta had first come to The Pines, he'd been a boy on the verge of manhood. And he'd been kind to her. More than kind. He'd taught her a number of things she thought he'd been too young to know, things she'd never forgotten. On the other hand, he never acknowledged the part she played in his life.

"Don't underestimate Jack," she said. "Twins have an affinity."

"I haven't seen any affinity in fifteen years."

"It's there. If Jack stops drinking and whoring around, he could be a good administrator. If he made an effort, he could bring Simon to our way of thinking."

Elliott snorted. "You don't know shit about Simon if you think he'll do anything Jack asks."

"Why not?"

"The night his son died?"

Marta went still. "Yes?"

"Carrie was in the poolhouse fucking Jack's brains out."

Marta felt the blood drain out of her face. If he knew that, what else did he— "How do you know that?"

"I have my ways."

"Does Simon know?"

"He hasn't confided in me."

"Don't be sarcastic."

"Think back to before the accident. Jack's second divorce had just become final and he'd been seeing that masseuse—"

"Physical therapist."

"Uah. She was some floozy doing lap dancing on the side. Then she up and leaves him. Carrie knew he was as horny as a tomcat locked in a barn for three months. She brushed her tits against the poor slob every time they were together. Once Carrie set her hot little bod in action, he didn't stand a chance."

Marta's eyebrow lifted. "How do you know how hot her 'bod' is?"

"I've got eyes."

"Right. Meaning you haven't sampled her charms yourself?"

Elliott sipped his drink, as silent as the Sphinx.

"You fucked her yourself, didn't you?" Marta loaded her voice with disdain. "And you old enough to be her father." A woman like Carrie could take a deep breath and have every man in the room stare at her. Add an ersatz Southern drawl and the morals of a French whore, and she could have her choice of any man in the room, while Marta only had the one great summer—

"If it makes you feel better, I never fucked Carrie."

"Bullshit."

"Suit yourself."

Marta swallowed the last of her drink and slammed the glass down on a piecrust cherrywood table that Elliott prized. "I'll let you know what Plan B is. Tomorrow."

"Good."

After Marta left, Elliott sat back on the settee, crossed his legs, carefully arranging the crease in his trousers, and let his formidable legal brain sift through all he knew about Marta. She had a secret, all right. She had a Swiss bank account into which she made regular deposits. His contact at Marta's bank had, for a princely sum, given him access to her records. But where the money went from there, he had no clue.

Why would Marta Chudzik deposit ten grand a month into a secret account out of the country? Why not invest it here in the open? She lived frugally—the woman certainly didn't fritter it away on clothes or makeup or hairdressers—but a hundred twenty thousand a year? She didn't have enough left to live on if that was coming from her salary.

The Pines. Because the corporation was closely held, it didn't need to be audited the way stock-trading companies were. Marta could be embezzling.

How could he get the books audited?

Carrie.

Elliott reached for the phone on the side table. He smiled at the sleep-filled voice that answered with a throaty hello.

"Is it too late for me to come over?"

"Elliott? Of course not."

Ten minutes later he was pulling into a parking space next to her newly occupied townhouse. The front porch light was lit, the door unlocked. He entered, carefully locked it behind him and snicked the safety chain on as well.

Carrie, seated on a white nubby bouclé sofa, had applied lipstick and eyeliner but hadn't combed her sleep-tousled hair nor bothered to wrap a robe over the diaphanous negligee that clung to her voluptuous body.

"To what do I owe this pleasure?" she purred, her voice as sultry as he'd ever heard it, patting the cushion next to her.

"I need a favor." He sat down where indicated.

"Do you want a drink?"

Her breasts hung loose inside their shirred pouches of lace. He could see the coarse texture of her pubic hair underneath the silky fabric that lay like a benediction on her thighs. A drift of gardenias wafted over him—she had dabbed perfume on.

"No. I want you to ask Jack to do something."

"What makes you think I have any control over Jack?"

Elliott's eyes roamed over her body. He could almost feel her pulse accelerating at the frankly appreciative scrutiny. "You could always make him do things."

She gave him her best pout. "Not anymore."

"Why not?"

She shrugged, letting a strap slip down her shoulder.

"Maybe I should tell Simon what you and Jack were doing in the poolhouse a certain midnight about a year ago."

Carrie bristled. "You wouldn't. I came to you in confidence. You wouldn't betray me!"

Elliott had long ago learned to let silence speak for him. It spoke eloquently now.

She sighed. "What do you want me to do?"

"Tell Jack he should audit the books."

Carrie's eyes widened. "You don't trust Marta?"

"I didn't say that. It could simply show Simon how much business acumen Jack has."

"What do you expect to find?"

"You ask too many questions."

Taking that as an invitation, she slid closer to him on the sofa, snugging her thigh against his. The strap of her negligee slipped further down her shoulder. She leaned forward, putting a manicured hand on his knee. "How do you propose to shut me up?"

"That's another question."

Cris Anson

"Elliott? Kiss me."

"I didn't come here to get laid."

Carrie jerked back. "Don't be crude. It isn't like you."

"You only know what I let you see."

The sparkle returned to her eyes. Her hand teased its way up his thigh. "You mean you are crude? Let's see. You don't want to get laid. What might appeal to you?" She licked her lips slowly, trailed her fingers to his crotch.

He grabbed her hand, pulled it away. "You get more like your mother every day."

"What do you know about my mother?"

"She liked men. The more men, the more she liked it."

Carrie wrinkled her pert little nose at him. "I'm very choosy. I like my men rich and handsome."

"What about Vincent? He wasn't rich."

"Vincent was…" she shrugged, "like ice cream on a hot day."

"You mean he cooled you off?"

She laughed. "Oh, that's funny. He was a baby. I like my men more mature. Like you."

"No."

A frown marred her perfect face. "Then why did you ask that seductive question, 'Is it too late to come over'? Why else would you stop by at midnight?"

"I told you what I wanted. To get Jack—"

"You could have asked me that over the phone."

"No, I couldn't. I needed you to see my face when I asked you. To impress upon you how serious it was."

She ignored his last comment and returned her hand to his cock. "We think alike, you and I. We could be a great team. And not just in bed. I could be your trophy wife. All your lawyer friends would be pea-green with envy."

"If I were inclined to marry, I assure you, the offer would be most tempting. However, it's not an option."

"What are you, a fag?"

Elliott stood, adjusted his navy flannel blazer. "That's beneath you, my dear." He offered a hand, which she reluctantly took, and pulled her to her feet. Then he placed his palms on her bare shoulders and gave her a continental kiss, one on each cheek. "Be assured, you have a place of honor in my heart. But I can't marry you. We must continue to be, as you observe, 'a great team'. No more than that."

Marry her! He wouldn't, couldn't do anything of the sort. Her mother, Corrinne, would hang his balls out to dry if Carrie pursued that harebrained scheme. The scandal would ruin his standing in the legal community.

Corrinne had waited until he was on top of the heap before she'd told him. The conniving bitch. He hadn't believed her himself, still wouldn't believe her, if it hadn't been for the DNA results. He'd been suckered into volunteering a blood sample, thinking it would shut her up for good.

But fate didn't always play his way. So he'd swallowed hard and accepted the fact that Carrie was his daughter. Then he'd introduced her to Simon for safekeeping.

Chapter Twenty-Three

ဢ

"To The Pines, please. South entrance."

Her freshly scrubbed face shiny in the early morning sunlight, her newly washed hair billowing, Tamara ran to the cab parked at the curb of County Hospital. Her feet flopped around in a pair of too-big sneakers she'd snatched from a janitor's closet. She'd felt like a thief, sneaking down corridors and out the front door in a borrowed green scrub suit at seven-thirty in the morning. She wasn't breaking the law. She was perfectly within her rights to check herself out. And she wasn't running away from any ten o'clock meeting.

The short, tanned man holding open the rear passenger door wore a cap emblazoned TOWNE TAXI. The open door echoed the logo. He smiled hugely and handed her into the seat, then slammed the door shut. Clutching her muck-encrusted raincoat and equally dirty jeans and underwear as reminders of her trial by fire, she settled back gratefully into the seat and closed her eyes.

With a roar the cab shot forward. Her eyes snapped open like shades pulled up too fast. How had he gotten around the cab and behind the wheel in less than two seconds?

The driver's shoulders under a white shirt were as wide as the seat. His black hair curled out from under a TOWNE TAXI cap. She blinked at the reflection in the rear-view mirror. Simon! If this was his way of getting her to turn over her shares right away, she wasn't going to let him bully her. She'd do it when she was good and ready, and psyched into it so it wouldn't hurt.

She grabbed the door handle. It wouldn't budge. "What–?"

"Childproof locks," he said in such a calm, reasonable tone of voice that she almost hit him. "Only opens from the outside."

"This is kidnapping!" she sputtered.

"No, ma'am, you ordered a Towne Taxi at County Hospital for seven-thirty and you got one. It's not a federal offense if the driver is different from the doorman."

"Stop this car immediately!"

Instead, Simon shifted into high gear and pressed his foot to the gas, leaving the downtown district behind them.

"Simon, don't play games. Stop and let me out."

The car turned into a side road and coasted to a stop, the heavy engine idling in a purr. "Ma'am?"

"What on earth do you think you're doing?"

Removing the Towne Taxi cap, he turned around, rested his arm across the top of the bench seat, and gave her a look of such intensity that she was afraid he could see all the way to her soul. "I want to talk to you."

"Who was that guy on the sidewalk?"

"Golfing buddy. He owns the only cab company in the area. I simply asked him to let me know if he got a call for a hospital pickup. So he did."

"And he lets you take business away from him?"

"This cab is rented for the next five hours. Paid in advance. Besides, he gets to drive my Corvette in the meantime."

"Where—where are you planning to take me?"

"Where do you want to go?"

"Back to my bungalow."

"On one condition."

His deadly serious expression left her feeling weak. "What?"

"That we talk."

"About…what?"

"Anything and everything."

She didn't know how to respond, so she didn't. His arm flung casually across the backrest mesmerized her. His white shirtsleeve had been rolled back to expose a muscular forearm, the thick black hairs lying neatly like beaten wheat stalks. Long, tanned fingers lay splayed over the gray upholstery. His nails were blunt cut and clean.

She realized her scrutiny was getting too intimate. Her gaze skittered around the late-model cab. The meter, silent on its dashboard mount, stared at her.

After a long moment, Simon shifted into first and made a careful U-turn. When they were headed toward the golf course, she said, "Why did you do this?"

"I told you. I want to talk to you." But he said no more until he brought the cab to a halt in front of the bungalow. Then it was an innocuous, "Here we are."

He got out and swung around the hood to open her door. The action put Tamara in mind of the last time he'd done that. Her muscles tightened at the thought of his passionate kisses in the Corvette. The memory of their naked bodies clinging to each other yesterday hit her with unexpected force. She dug fingernails hard into her palms and hoped the pain would clear her head. She had to remember that he'd told her without words what he thought of her less-than-whole body.

When she reluctantly accepted his hand, tingles shot up her arm. She had to stop letting him affect her. He was just being polite. But he wanted to talk. She followed him up the porch, holding the bundle of dirty clothes loosely. "So talk."

"Out here?"

Goose bumps formed on Tamara's bare arms. A shiver zapped through her. On a cool, late October morning she was standing on the porch in a light breeze in thin scrubs and nothing else, yet she was strangely reluctant to open the door to seek the relative warmth of her home.

First to Die

"Did you lose your keys?" he asked.

She almost laughed out loud. Keys had nothing to do with her reluctance. The keys felt heavy in her pocket. Luckily they had been safely buttoned inside her raincoat pocket yesterday.

"I have one." Simon pulled out, from his jeans pocket, a keyring attached to a monogrammed silver disk.

Her eyes flashed murder. "How dare you! You made another set of keys so you can just pop in any time you want?"

"I'm the landlord," he said, unperturbed. "How else could I get in and clean the place or fix the damage if a tenant sneaks out in the middle of the night?"

Outrage snatched Tamara's breath at his insinuation that she would leave the place dirty or in a shambles.

"You know, that green outfit makes your eyes look bluer."

The comment, she knew, was meant to throw her off balance. Instead it called her attention to the way the well-washed scrubs caressed her breasts in the gentle breeze. Her peripheral vision picked up the disconcerting fact that the cool air had puckered her nipples until they were clearly visible under the thin green cotton. Her arms had been relaxed so the dirty clothes rested against her hipbones. Feeling her face flame, she jerked the bundle up to cover her chest.

"May I?" Unlocking the door, he pushed it open and made a sweeping gesture with his hand. "After you."

Tamara was acutely conscious that underneath the scrubs she wasn't wearing so much as a pair of panties. And Simon stood too near her, all tightly leashed male, freshly shaved, smelling piney and outdoorsy like the air around them, his gaze pinning her immobile. Talk? How could she talk when all she wanted was his arms around her, his mouth on hers, her body so close against his that dental floss couldn't fit between them.

A gust of wind made her shiver. She strode into the living room. "I've got to change into something warmer."

Simon followed her in, closed and locked the door, turned to where she stood at the kitchen doorway, her back to him, staring at the dirty clothes she'd just dumped into a pile on the floor.

"Don't bother," he said in a matter-of-fact voice. "I'm only going to take them off."

Goose bumps that had nothing to do with the temperature broke out on Tamara's skin. Her bones turned to butter and her blood to flowing lava. She grabbed on to the doorjamb for support, her mind reeling with the implications of his statement.

Simon's voice whispered against her ear as his hands touched her shoulders from behind. "I don't know what you thought of my performance, but I'm not proud that I ran away." He pulled her backward until her back nestled against his chest. "It wasn't you I was running away from. It was me."

Tamara swallowed several times to combat the sudden dryness in her throat. What did he mean by that? And what was that bulge he was pressing into her buttocks?

"I can't control what's been happening to my body, but by God, I want you more than I've wanted any woman in my life." He lifted the hair from one side of her neck and began nibbling at her ear. Tamara's knees threatened to give way. His lips felt so hot, so good, so right. She snuggled against the hard, warm wall of Simon Sutcliffe and basked in the sensations radiating outward to every part of her body.

"Whatever happens to me, happens." His voice was a hoarse whisper. "Let me love you. Let me kiss you, touch you all over. I want to feel your body next to me. I want to watch you explode in my arms. And I'm selfish enough to want to see the expression on your face when you open your eyes again and look at me, knowing I'd sent you to paradise."

"But my leg—"

"Your leg is what made you into the woman I love. You must have thought I ran away because I was repelled..." His fingers crept under the scrub top, splayed upward to the crease between her ribs and the heavy roundness of her breasts.

"Nothing about you repulses me, do you understand? I want you because of you. I ran away because I was ashamed of myself, not of you. I was repulsed by my damn male pride that refused to let such a vital, sexy, courageous woman see me vulnerable."

His thumbs grazed Tamara's nipples. Gasping at the electricity that thrummed down to her groin, she thrust her breasts into his touch.

"But you mean more to me than my pride. I need you, Tamara. I want to love you. All of you. Your long leg and your short leg, your beautiful breasts, your soft mouth—"

He spun her around. Mindlessly she grabbed fistfuls of his thick hair and pulled his head down. Her mouth eagerly opened to his savage assault. Then they were all over each other, hands touching, sliding, grabbing, garments ripping, buttons pinging against walls, until they stood naked and clinging to each other.

He swept her up, one strong arm around her back, the other under her knees, and carried her to the bedroom. Her arms went around his neck and she kissed him as though it was the last moment of her life and she wanted more—more of his mouth, his tongue, his taste, than sixty seconds could provide.

Awkwardly he bent forward, his precious burden still in his arms, and ripped the bedcovers back then gently placed her down. He tumbled in after her, landing on top of her because she hadn't loosened her hold on his neck.

His hard, heavy weight on her naked body was an aphrodisiac to Tamara. She arched her back to meet him, gloried in the feel of the rough hair on his chest scraping against her swollen nipples, sending splinters of need through her. As Simon ravaged her mouth, her hands skimmed over the smooth steel of his back and down to his taut ass then up the sides to his chest. Her thumbs slipped between their bodies to find his flat nipples and she gloried to feel them harden in response. All she could think of was more, more, more...

He groaned without breaking the kiss. It was like a duel to see who could suck harder, kiss deeper, feel more millimeters of skin, press closer to the other. It was like rain after a drought, melting sunlight after three feet of snow.

It was heaven and at the moment Tamara didn't care whether Simon could sustain an erection. She greedily absorbed the feel of him with every inch of her body that she could connect with his. With her prosthesis on, she had as much traction as she needed. She writhed under him, demanding more, feeling the heat of his cock at the entrance to her pussy. Primitive sounds escaped from her throat. Finally she managed to say, "Please—"

"I'll try," he said hoarsely.

With one savage stroke, he entered her. The feel of his cock inside her slick shaft drove her over the brink. The explosion ripped her apart and reformed her into floating molecules that melded with him, clung to him like bath oil on skin. Pinwheels and stars and angels danced behind her closed eyelids because this man had wanted her for her, disability be damned, had said—

Her eyelids drifted open. Hadn't he, somewhere along the line, said I love you? And not in the heat of passion. She became aware of Simon looking down at her, on his unguarded face a look of pure love such as she'd never seen. He was leaning on his elbows, holding the bulk of his weight off her. Her awareness shifted to the heat between her legs, the juice of her passion hot against him, his cock now soft and pressed against her thigh.

"Did you…" She almost bit her tongue trying to stop the thought. If he couldn't—he didn't—

"Not yet," he said, a cocky smile hiding whatever insecurities he had to be feeling. "I have some more tricks I'd like to show you first."

He slid down an inch at a time, kissing her neck, the valley between her breasts, her navel…

"No, Simon." She grabbed his hair and lifted his head up. "You gave to me this time and last time. Let me taste you, kiss you. Let me explore you. I have to touch you to believe that you're real, that you're here, letting me do this to you. I don't want you to do a thing. Don't move a muscle, understand?"

Reluctantly, Simon sank back onto the mattress.

"Relax and keep your hands right…there." She lifted his arms up over his head as if he were surrendering.

And he was.

As his gaze captured and held hers, she straddled him, her knees astride his hips. With her fingers, she traced his mouth, the smoothly shaved planes of his jaw, his neck. She bent forward to kiss the throbbing pulse at his throat. Her hair fell down around her face, puddling on his shoulders. Slowly she moved her head from side to side. Her gloriously shiny hair skimmed across his skin like dandelion thistles, barely touching him yet unbearably erotic. She cradled her full breasts in her hands, thrusting the hard nipples outward, and dragged them erratically across his chest.

"Pretend these are pencils," she said. "I'm writing my name on your chest. Branding you."

The idea of her branding him appealed to Simon mightily. Pencils, hah. Fat crayons, maybe, in all shades of the rainbow. His fingers flexed with the need to cup them, to touch those hard points. But this was her show. He wanted her to feel relaxed and free with him, safe to do whatever she willed.

While she was tantalizing him with her luscious breasts, her thighs alternately tensed and relaxed, bringing her sweet, damp slit into fleeting, teasing contact with his cock. He felt blood and fire flow into it.

"I told you not to move a muscle," she said, an impish gleam in her eye.

He flexed his fingers again, but kept his hands upraised. Never had control been harder to exercise.

She shifted her stance, edging downward toward the foot of the bed, nudging her way between his knees. Her hair trailed down his flat stomach like leprechaun kisses. Then her mouth replaced the hair. She nipped a bit of skin where his thigh met his torso, her cheek brushing his pubic hair. He hissed in a breath and reminded himself not to grab her.

"Does it hurt?" she asked, the glaze of passion in her eyes revealing that she knew exactly what emotion she was evoking.

"A little," he breathed. "But I deserve all the pain you care to inflict."

She took his half-hard cock into her hands, stroked it, then bent down and took him into her mouth. He grabbed fistfuls of the pillow to keep himself from bucking his hips against her. She stroked him with one hand, cupped his aching balls with the other, eased him in and out of her mouth with a clinging suction that made his eyes roll back in his head and growling noises come out of his throat.

He'd had women who'd sucked his cock, but before it had just been another sensation. Never had it felt so loving, so intimate, as having Tamara's mouth on him, bringing him so close to the edge—

He reached for her, wanted to impale her on him, wanted not to waste a single precious second of whatever state of hardness she'd coaxed him to.

Tamara shrugged his hands away, shook her head, and continued doing magical things with her mouth. He stopped fighting, knowing that she needed to do this for him, to bring him to climax even though he couldn't do so inside her. His balls tightened unbearably, his cock throbbed with need for her, and he reached the point of no return, his semen gathering, strengthening as it boiled upward and shot out of his cock and into her throat with the force of a fire hose.

The top of his head burst open like a volcano, and out spewed his desire for revenge and his hatred for women in general and Carrie in particular, and his anger at Jack for diverting Carrie from watching over Kevin. There was only this woman, this beautiful, perfect woman, Tamara Hart, whose mouth was even now capturing his essence and clinging to him as though he were a lifeline and she a drowning sailor.

And only he knew that it was the other way around.

Chapter Twenty-Four

ॐ

She couldn't stop admiring him. A wide, well-muscled chest, sprouting a black lawn of hair, tapered down to a corrugated stomach and narrow hips. Her fingers traced the black line that arrowed from his chest to a snarl of black curls at his groin.

"How come your chest hair isn't curly?" she asked lazily. "Not wavy like your head or…wild like here…" She gave his limp penis a playful squeeze.

"Good genes," he murmured, nestling her head inside the hollow of his shoulder.

Tamara had never experienced such a peaceful aftermath of lovemaking. Face it, she told herself, never before had she made love. All she'd ever done was have sex. If she never had a hard cock inside her again, she wouldn't regret it as long as Simon treated her like a cherished, desired princess. He'd brought her to climax twice more with his talented mouth and fingers, until she was wrung out…and smiling.

She stroked the unprepossessing little fellow. "Do you want to talk about it?"

Under her cheek she felt him tense then relax. "Yeah, I guess you deserve to know." His hold around her shoulder tightened. "You know about Kevin, of course."

"Yes, I'm so sorry—"

"Don't." His head turned away from her. "That's when it started. The night Kevin…died, I came home unexpectedly. I found Carrie—well, let's just say it was with a guy. If she had been watching Kevin, as she should have, she'd have smelled gas long before it became lethal, but she was fu—"

His voice broke. Tamara unconsciously stroked the arm he had flung around her waist, as one might comfort a crying child.

"Anyway. After that I couldn't even bear to look at her. I told Elliott to get me a divorce and signed up with Earthwatch. Everyone said I ran away, couldn't face that my son died. No one knew why I ran except Carrie and me and—"

He snorted. "I ran away, all right. Worked myself to exhaustion in every godforsaken Earthwatch site I could find. Lost twenty pounds. I was at a dig in Queensland, the boondocks of Australia. One dusk I was bathing in a stream when this woman comes on to me. She was everything Carrie wasn't. Tall, slender redhead, society type, I got the impression she was slumming. She pulled off her T-shirt and safari shorts, and waded toward me in the water. Asked for soap. Asked me to wash her back.

"I thought, why not? I'd been celibate for six months by then, halfway to a divorce, or so I'd thought. She made me horny, walking nude like that. The fact that it was anonymous appealed to me."

His hold on Tamara tightened. "It didn't work. After a couple of strokes I just slipped out of her. Didn't learn my lesson, though. A few months later I was on a tiny Indonesian island. Natives helped with the cooking. One of them was very nubile. She tried to serve me. Lifted her sarong, bent forward like a bitch in heat waiting for a dog to mount her from the rear. I couldn't even get hard enough to stick it in.

"It was then I realized I was blaming all women for what Carrie had done. Then I came back and saw you at the board meeting in that silk blouse, your nipples sticking out like an advertisement for sex, your hair inviting men to run their fingers through it, that sexy sway to your hips when you walked—"

He took a deep breath. "I didn't know you had to walk that way because of the short leg. I thought at first that you were Jack's latest. Then I saw the way Dad looked at you. I thought he was lovestruck. I don't know whether I was angry or jealous." He turned toward her, absently placed a kiss on her eyebrow. "I know better now. He did love you. But not the way I assumed."

Finally he looked at her, saw tears rim her eyes. "Before," he continued, looking away again, "I didn't care whether I ever screwed another woman again. Now I want only to please you. I want to be hard for *you*, not because of some macho posturing."

"It doesn't matter," she said. "You've given me more than just sex. You've given me self-respect."

When he started to speak, she covered his mouth with her palm. "It's my turn." She shifted. Now she couldn't look at him. "Before, I was ashamed of my body because all the men I'd met made me ashamed. When they found out I was an amputee, they'd either do what Jack did when I flailed my short leg at him—run away and throw up—or they'd get off on humping a crip. I got to the point where I flaunted my sexuality, made their nuts ache to get to me, just so I could lift my skirt or drop my slacks and watch their cocks fizzle away to chicken wings. The only relief I could get was if they didn't know, which meant keeping my clothes on. Like your anonymous couplings.

"They didn't work, either. I hated myself. Then you walked into the boardroom, all testosterone and swagger and insulting visual inspection. You got my back up. I was damn well going to flaunt my boobs at Harland's dinner and make you burn for me."

"But Harland asked you to show your disability."

"Yes."

"You looked so vulnerable, I think I fell for you right then and there."

"Then Harland died. You accused me—"

Simon's arms tightened like steel bands around her. "I wish I could think it was all over, that whoever made Dad's horse stumble got his just desserts."

A shudder ripped through Tamara. "Do you think it was more than just Ike? Surely he wouldn't kill his own son."

"That car bomb was meant for you," he said flatly. "Vincent simply got in the way. Think of the timing. I fly in from Russia, you deliver a bombshell, Dad delivers one, the next day he gets his neck broken. Vincent appears after Dad's funeral, the car explodes, and Ike pops up."

"But they both knew where I was long before you came back. Vincent and I spoke on the phone at least once a month. He knew more about what was going on here than you might think."

"So Ike could have masterminded it."

"Yes." Even though she didn't think Ike was that brilliant or that vindictive, she wanted to believe it was him, to believe she didn't have to go through life looking over her shoulder.

After a moment when each was absorbed in private thoughts, Simon said, "You think we could scare up a few eggs? It's got to be past noon and I haven't eaten yet today. After all," he said, giving her a Groucho Marx leer complete with waggling eyebrows, "I've had a very busy morning."

An hour later, when they had showered and dressed and wolfed down eggs and home fries and a ham slice, they lingered in her dining room over coffee, enjoying the view of the pine woods they both loved.

"There's something else you should know," Simon began.

Tamara set her mug down and gave him her full attention.

"Who Carrie was with that night."

"You don't have to—"

"Yes I do," he said. "It was—" She sensed a tenseness in him that was stronger than when he'd first admitted his vulnerability. "It was Jack, curse his black soul to hell."

"Oh, Simon," she breathed, feeling hot tears form. "No wonder you ran. What a burden you carried!" She took his hand, brought it to her lips. "How hard it must have been for you to come back, to look him in the eye and know that he—"

"I didn't know before. He just admitted it last night."

Tamara blinked. "How did he happen to tell you?"

Simon was silent a moment, as if struggling with inner demons. "He came staggering to my house, drunk, after your visit. He'd gotten maudlin, went up the attic, dragged out some photo albums and brought them over. Either he was drunker than he realized, or he thought by reminding me of our happy childhood he was softening me up. Anyway, he said it'd been on his conscience and he couldn't live with it anymore.

"It was hard enough accepting Kevin's death and Carrie's part in it when it happened. I thought I'd gotten over the pain of losing both my son and my illusions of a happy family. Hearing his confession almost ripped me to pieces. I knew we'd grown apart since we decided on separate colleges, but Jesus! We're twins. I should have had some inkling. And I've been torturing myself with the question, was I that bad a husband that Carrie turned to my mirror image?"

"Jack's weak. He's like seaweed. Flows whichever way the tide pulls him." She resisted the urge to disparage Carrie. Carrie's behavior, then and now, spoke for itself. But something was askew. Tamara tried to piece together the sequence of yesterday's events. "When did he tell you? Before the fire? Or after you came to see me in the hospital?"

"Before. I was tossing him out of the house when we saw the flames lighting up the sky."

"And still you saved him." When Simon said nothing, she added, "Detective Kyrillos told me you pulled Jack out of the fire after he'd collapsed."

Simon shrugged. "I had to."

A tear trickled down Tamara's cheek. "Then there's hope."

He turned his face away, as though unwilling to see anyone shed a tear for a wife-snatcher, home-wrecker, and baby-killer.

"Simon, don't you see? In your heart you've already forgiven him."

"No, I haven't." Vehemence laced his voice. "I can't."

"He's your brother, your twin! He's Harland's son, just as you are. Harland had to have known, or guessed, what drove you away. You aren't the type to run away from pain, from tragedy, from your father. Deep down, you were afraid it was Jack and you didn't want to know. So you fled from all the pain. Harland let you go, hoping you'd work it out of your system. But when you didn't return, he sent that telegram. To start the chain of events that would force the two of you back together."

"No wonder Jack tried to lose himself in drink. To have that burden on him, to be responsible for the death of his brother's son." She unconsciously squeezed Simon's hand harder. "Don't you think he's paid for his crime? He couldn't have had a single good night's sleep since it happened. When I offered him half my shares, he acted as though... Oh, Simon. He knew you wouldn't want to work with him. Even my notarized statement didn't sway him. No wonder," she repeated.

"What did he say when you gave it to him?"

"He thought I was grandstanding." Tamara shifted in the chair. "He wanted me to give up my life rights to the bungalow as well."

"And?" Simon had gone very still.

Panic flashed through her. Did Simon, too, expect her to relinquish her last link to Harland? "I told him I wanted to keep that option open until I found a job and a place to live."

"I see."

"But if that's what it takes to make you forgive Jack, I'll do it."

"You're asking me to forgive Jack?"

"That was Harland's purpose in hiring me, in giving me the shares. To bring the two of you together once and for all."

"I can't. For God's sake, Tamara, he killed my son!"

"Then why did you pull him away from the fire? So he could spend the rest of his life feeling guilty? So that every time he looks in the mirror, he'll see a man his brother can't forgive? Simon, your brother drinks because he's seeking oblivion—relief from the bitter knowledge of what he did."

She raked fingers through her hair in frustration. "Sometimes I think Catholics have the right idea. They go to a priest, confess their sins, get forgiveness, and then they can go on with their lives without an albatross around their necks."

"You neglect one little nugget of truth with that parallel."

"What's that?"

"The priest is a disinterested third party."

Tamara gritted her teeth. She had no answer to that. Biting back a resigned sigh, she stood up purposefully and gathered the dishes from the table. Then she put a plastic pan in the kitchen sink, squeezed detergent, ran hot water.

"Let me do that," he said. His voice was rough and low behind her.

Her back stiffened. "You did the cooking."

"Can your burns stand being in hot water?"

She'd forgotten her burns. The endorphins that Simon's thorough, exquisite lovemaking had released in her had completely overwhelmed any lingering pain. "They're fine. Like everyone says, I was lucky." Just the same, she adjusted the water to lukewarm and pulled out a pair of rubber gloves from a drawer.

"Tamara, I—" His hands caressed her shoulders, reminding her how masterfully he'd touched her just a short while ago.

"You know, I think we both need to be alone for a while," she said. "You need to think about the future. About Jack, about what Harland wanted. And I need to rest. After all I've been through in the past twenty-four hours..."

He snatched his hands away as though he'd touched a red-hot cooking element on her electric stove. "Of course. You must be exhausted."

"Yes. Thank you for understanding."

Tamara kept her gaze locked onto the vista of fragrant pines outside her window until after she heard the front door open and close. When the growl of the taxi's engine told her Simon was leaving, her shoulders slumped. "Harland," she groaned. "Why did you give me such a Gordian knot to untie?"

Then she forced some iron into her backbone, dried her hands and went to the bedroom. She had to make good on her promise to Jack when she'd given him the notarized document. On her promise to Harland. She had to leave so the twins could see they had no choice but to work together.

What she couldn't fit into two suitcases she'd have shipped. Whatever place she found to land would be devoid of sunshine. That was the only thing she was sure of.

That and her love for Simon.

Chapter Twenty-Five

&

He couldn't do it. Not even for Tamara. He couldn't forgive the man who had killed Kevin. Simon drove on autopilot back to town and exchanged the taxi for his 'Vette. He had half a notion to just zip back up to Vermont, to his hideaway.

Hide. Yes. That's exactly what he'd be doing. Hiding.

The pain gripped him again, as sharply as it had when the fire department had had to pry his fingers open to take Kevin's limp body away. He saw again his son's one-toothed laugh, the sparkle in his brown eyes, the black curls that one day would have looked like Simon's own.

He saw the tiny casket that he alone had carried to the gravesite, refusing any help, ignoring his father's protests. He heard the first clod of dirt hitting the polished cherrywood.

"No!"

The car screeched to a halt in response to Simon's stomping on the brakes. He was in no condition to drive to Vermont. Hell, he wasn't even mentally fit to drive back to The Pines.

"Dad," he croaked. "What are you asking of me?"

Suddenly he knew what he needed to do. He shifted into first and roared up the road to the tiny cemetery that had come with the farmland, where his father was buried.

Inside the intricate wrought iron fence, the grass was kept neatly clipped around modest headstones. Outside, a meadow stretched for a hundred yards to a perimeter of oak trees that stood in silent tribute. In late April, his mother's beloved spring beauties and trout lilies grew in bright profusion. Now the stately oaks had strewn withered bronze leaves that crunched under Simon's Docksiders.

"Kevin," he whispered. He closed his eyes and allowed an inarticulate prayer to filter through his mind.

"Simon."

Simon whirled around. His hands clenched to fists at the familiar voice. "Jack." The word sounded like an accusation. "What are you doing here?"

"You may not believe it, but I come here often."

"To reassure yourself that Dad's really dead?" Simon couldn't help that it came out sounding like a sneer.

Jack got off the golf cart slowly, like an old man, and walked to the gate but didn't enter. His gaze traveled the obscenely tiny distance between Kevin's headstone and footstone. "To punish myself."

Simon had to lean forward to hear the whispered words. As soon as he'd seen Jack come to under the oxygen mask at the fire scene, Simon had put him out of his mind. Had tried to.

His brother looked like he'd aged a decade since then. Simon's immediate thought was, he'd gone back to drinking with a vengeance. Then he narrowed his eyes, obscuring everything except the sight of his twin, staring grief-stricken at Kevin's resting place. He noted Jack's hands clutching the finials at the gate until his knuckles were as white as his face.

Something was wrong with Jack. Had he had a heart attack at the fire and no one told him?

Jack turned slowly, like a zombie. The haunted look in his eyes as he stared at nothing knocked the breath out of Simon.

"Tamara was right, you know."

Every muscle tightened in Simon's body. "About what?"

"About what Dad wanted."

"What did Dad want?" As if he didn't know, as if Tamara hadn't tried to convince him.

"But I'm not...worth..." Jack's gaze strayed around the meadow, to the iron fence, to the golf cart. He seemed reluctant to meet Simon's eyes. He reached a hand inside his rumpled jacket, fumbling as if unable to find what he sought. "Here. Tamara gave me the idea. This is what Dad really wanted."

When Simon didn't move to accept the envelope Jack held out to him, Jack stuffed it into Simon's jeans waistband. "I don't deserve it." With that cryptic remark, Jack shambled off to the golf cart and started cautiously down the hill.

It took a moment for Simon to react. What the hell was that all about? He snatched the envelope and ripped it open.

"Jesus, no," he whispered.

He jerked his head up. The golf cart was just disappearing behind a stand of native rhododendron. "No!" he shouted, dashing to the Corvette. "That's not what Dad wanted!"

Gunning the motor, Simon tore down the same path Jack had taken, passed him on the verge and slammed the car to a stop diagonally on the road. He knew damn well the golf cart could maneuver around it, but he hoped the visual impact of the roadblock would impress upon Jack that Simon wanted— needed—to talk.

The golf cart stopped. Simon jumped out and ran around the car to it, waving the paper Jack had given him. "What are you trying to do, be a martyr? What the hell's gotten into you?"

"I finally took off the rose-colored glasses. What I saw sobered the hell out of me."

"If you think you're going to take the easy way out, you're going to have to get past me first."

Jack's weary gaze met Simon's for the first time since they'd met at the cemetery. "That's just it. I'll never get past you. I'm tired of trying. You take my shares. I'm going to sell my house, take my half of Dad's assets, and start over someplace else. I could probably get a job as a golf pro any place in the country with a handicap of three, wouldn't you say?"

"What about Dad's will? What about him wanting us to work this out between us?"

"I'm tired of being compared to you and coming out at the short end of the stick. I want to go someplace where no one knows I'm the ass end of the horse."

"Damn you, stop feeling sorry for yourself! You're a Sutcliffe! Your place is right here, at The Pines. If you try to leave, I'll blackball you to every club on the Tour. You'll have to play in some rinky-dink municipal course that has crabgrass for fairways."

Jack lowered his eyes. His shoulders slumped like an old man carrying a hundred pounds of firewood on his back. "You hate me that much?"

Simon's arms had been flailing the air to emphasize his anger. Now they flapped helplessly around as though a lethargic breeze had tried to stir the air but failed. "Hate you? I'm trying to convince you not to go!"

Slowly Jack raised his head.

"Hell, Jack, you're my brother. My twin brother. How would it look if your handicap was lower than mine and I didn't even know it? How'm I going to win your money at Bingo Bango Bongo if we're playing on different courses?"

Comprehension was just starting to put a spark back into Jack's eyes. Simon threw his arms around him. "Listen, you stupid shit, anybody can run away from a problem. It takes a Sutcliffe to stay and face it. And when you have two of them making a stand together, why, I'll bet we can even find a compromise that will make everybody—the planning board, the shareholders," his voice cracked on the next word, "Dad—
"

"Simon." Jack's voice cracked as well. And then they were bear hugging so awkwardly that Jack lost his footing and slipped and Simon fell on top of him and they began wrestling and tickling each other and laughing like they used to in high school until they both had to stop to catch their breath.

Then they started wrestling again. Simon gave Jack a slight advantage by subtly letting his right arm go limp. Alertly, Jack flipped Simon onto his side and wrenched that arm behind his back. Simon tasted grass, felt the blades tickle inside his ear. Holding the arm rigid, Jack knelt with a knee on his brother's back and crowed, "Gotcha!"

And that's how Elliott found them.

* * * * *

"Gentlemen, gentlemen! What are you doing?"

Simon felt the sudden release of pressure on his shoulder socket as Jack scrambled to his feet. Simon rose more slowly. He was trying to figure out what Elliott was doing this far from the club, on this out-of-the-way road leading to the cemetery.

"We were just communicating," Jack said.

Simon noted Elliott's raised eyebrow in response to the wry comment but made no elaboration. Simon still wasn't convinced that Ike was the only one behind all of their recent troubles.

"I've been looking all over for you, Jack. Hank told me to try here."

"Ah, yes. A good bartender knows at all times where his best customer is."

Under his tan, Elliott flushed slightly. "I'd wait for you at the bar, except that reporter from the *Observer* is breathing fire to do a follow-up story. I don't like what she's leading up to. We have to pull her focus back where it belongs."

Jack caught Simon's eye under the pretext of dusting grass off the seat of his tan golf slacks. Their long dormant twin instinct roared into action. *Let him think we're still at odds.*

He gave Simon a wink before turning back to Elliott. "Is Marta still at the office?"

"Yes. She's as eager as I to head her off."

"Tell her I'll be in the boardroom in a half hour. Make sure Carrie's there too. I'll swing by and pick Tamara up."

Elliott's gaze shifted to Simon, whose impassive face gave no hint of his thoughts.

"I'll see you in a half hour, then." Elliott returned to his black BMW, made a K-turn, and headed sedately back to The Pines.

"I don't trust him," Jack said.

"Good. I don't either."

They both smiled with the knowledge that they hadn't had to voice their suspicions aloud.

* * * * *

"I tell you, something's up between those two. They acted like they were still at odds, but there's some undercurrent I couldn't put my finger on." Elliott paced the length of the boardroom, a frown etching a deeper line into his forehead. "I don't like it at all."

"Sit down," Marta snapped. "You're making me nervous."

She had seated herself symbolically at the head of the table. Elliott didn't like her unspoken statement that she was in charge. "You'd be nervous, too, if you saw a two-hundred-million-dollar project evaporating before your eyes."

Marta's face paled. She ran a hand through the helmet of her gray hair. "Then we have to stop them."

"How?" Carrie had been silent until now, her nervous glance darting from one to the other. At her question they both looked at her as though they'd forgotten she was there. "How could it evaporate? You said you had the planning board in your pocket."

"They could withdraw the development from consideration. But don't you worry your pretty little head about anything," Elliott said, sitting down next to Carrie and taking her dainty hand in his manicured one. "You just vote along with us and everything will turn out fine."

"Is that what the reporter said?" Carrie persisted. "That we're withdrawing it?"

"Apparently that lawyer who did Harland's new will suggested it. And you know how reporters are, tenacious when they get an isolated bit of information, they want to win the next Pulitzer Prize, so they —"

"The what prize?"

Elliott tamped down a flare of annoyance at Carrie's ignorance then mentally shrugged. That's what happened when a prostitute saw to his daughter's education. He wondered how Marta would use that hot potato of information. The fact that he'd changed his will leaving everything to Carrie may or may not raise eyebrows. They'd think he was her lover. That would be better for his image than having an illegitimate daughter out of a hooker.

Look at him, thinking of his own demise! The problem at hand was not Carrie Black Sutcliffe. It was Tamara Hart.

The door opened. Speak of the devil, Elliott thought.

Tamara walked into the room, chin high, shoulders squared as though facing a firing squad. Jack handed her into a chair opposite where he and Carrie sat then sat next to her.

The door remained open. No one else entered.

"Where's Simon?" Carrie demanded.

"He said something about going to the house," Jack said, shrugging as if his brother's attendance was of no importance.

Elliott bristled. "I thought you were coming together."

"I'm not my brother's keeper," Jack tossed back. Elliott didn't miss the fact that Jack patted Tamara's shoulder as if reassuring her of his presence, his support.

"Dammit, Elliott, didn't you stress how important this board meeting was?" Marta asked. "We can't do anything without Simon's twenty votes. Unless —"

All eyes turned to Jack, who had taken hold of Tamara's hand, a "trust me" look in his eyes as he gazed at her. The thought that Jack had her twenty votes sewed up, that they would have eighty percent of the votes, gave Elliott a moment of comfort. But the look in Tamara's eyes made him wonder, with a sense of growing dread, if it was she who had swayed him.

A noise in the hall captured everyone's attention. Simon barged in then wordlessly took the chair at the foot of the table. He ignored Tamara, ignored the fact that his twin was holding her hand.

Elliott grabbed control of the meeting. He stood and made his way to a corner near Marta, where he could see everyone. He'd long ago learned, standing was a position of power when everyone else was seated. "The reporter from the *Observer* asked me to comment on the possibility that our development would be withdrawn and we would let our approvals expire. I've called this meeting to hammer out a statement that reiterates in the strongest possible terms that The Pines expects to have the first certificate of occupancy in two years."

"As I've tried to tell this bully who strong-armed me here," Tamara said, "you don't need me. I've given Jack a legally binding document giving up my shares in The Pines."

"You'll stay until your offer is accepted or rejected in a similarly binding document," Jack snapped, dropping her hand.

At this double-barreled blast of Tamara's statement and Jack's take-charge attitude, Elliott's eyes widened before he caught himself. A lawyer should never let his emotions show. "May we inquire as to the contents of this offer?"

"Yes," Tamara said, cutting Jack off. "Harland wanted his sons to work together. I offered to give half my shares to each if they agree on a proposal. That would give them the seventy percent Harland's new will required. I don't care which proposal they support. They could agree to leave The Pines as is, as long as they agree. Then I'm out of the picture."

"Why would you do something that stupid?" Carrie asked.

The glance Tamara gave Simon before lowering her eyelashes told Elliott the answer. She was in love with him and it wasn't reciprocal. Simon resolutely gazed at a spot on the wall.

"Her reasoning doesn't matter," Elliott said quickly. "Obviously it was a decision she made after great deliberation, and we should honor that decision."

He turned to Tamara. "Could I look at it? To make sure it's legal? That it says exactly what you mean it to say?"

"It's legal and binding. Yvette made sure of that."

"Ah. Then we know it's all in order," Elliott said graciously, although he was furious at being upstaged by that environmental lawyer. "If you wish to leave this meeting, you may do so."

"She stays." Everyone looked at Simon. "She stays until she tells us how she would vote."

Tamara gazed at him with pain etched on her face. "It doesn't matter," she said in a tremulous voice. "I'm leaving The Pines. In fact, Jack pulled me and my suitcases out of the taxi and forced me to come here."

Sharp breaths were drawn around the table at the admission.

Simon stood then, placed his palms on the table, fingers splayed out, and leaned forward. "Be that as it may, Miss Hart, my father entrusted you with certain responsibilities. One of them was to see that Jack and I work together on this project. I'm asking you, in the name of Harland Sutcliffe, what you suggest Jack and I do with the project if we were to accept the shares you have so unselfishly offered us."

Her heart was in her eyes as she looked at Simon. Even Elliott could see a love of a lifetime in her naked longing for this man who was so coolly asking her for a business decision when she'd obviously made an emotional one.

"I—I would do just as my presentation suggested, a smaller development that respected the environment, that made an enclave of million-dollar single family homes."

"You're not making this recommendation simply to justify the consultant's fee?"

"Certainly not!" Her eyes flashed fire at Simon. She might love him, but she wasn't going to let him intimidate her, Elliott thought. She was a very obvious threat to their well-laid plans.

"You wouldn't leave The Pines in its current state?"

"No. It's too beautiful a place to be selfish with. The type of buyer a million-dollar golf-course dwelling would draw will find himself loving the same things about this area that Harland did, that I—"

She turned away from Simon as her voice broke. "Besides, Harland meant for his sons to have more. My proposed development, any development, would mean more money in your pockets."

"But if you kept your shares, you would vote for your own proposal. Is that what you just said?" This from Jack.

"If," she said, her voice so low they had to stop breathing to hear her, "if both brothers voted for my proposal, and if I were voting the shares Harland left me, that I am trying to give away to you and—and your brother—" Apparently she was so lovesick and heartbroken that she couldn't even speak Simon's name, Elliott thought. "Then yes, I would vote for my proposal."

"Then it's settled, isn't it, little brother?"

Simon smiled hugely. "That it is, big brother."

"Tamara, will you stay and see that Simon and I follow through with your plans?"

Elliott's head jerked in disbelief toward Jack. The little prick was defecting! He jumped to his feet to rescue what he could. "Tamara," he said in a carefully modulated voice, "you don't have to. If you want to leave The Pines, don't let them intimidate you. If you're giving up your shares because of..." how could he say this delicately? "bittersweet memories of Harland, or unhappy memories of the way your step-brother—well, we would all understand, and we thank you for your honesty."

"Honesty? Who are you to talk about honesty?" Jack was on his feet, rounding the corner of the table toward Elliott. He grabbed the lawyer by the hand-finished lapels of his suit jacket and pulled him to his feet, towering over him a good four inches. "All it took was a cursory examination of the books to see there were a number of large unexplained withdrawals over the past two years. And I'm sure I'll find more when I have time to dig through the files that have already been stored."

He relinquished his hold. Elliott struggled to restore his dignity by resettling his jacket on his trim shoulders and said coolly, "I don't know what you're talking about."

"You might think I've been a lush. But even drunk, I've absorbed enough to know what expenses The Pines incurs."

He slashed an accusing look at Marta. "I'm sure you didn't act alone. I'm sure Elliott told you how to code the accounts, how to hide the fact that over a hundred thousand dollars a year has been siphoned out of The Pines to phony vendors, to cash deposits in dummy accounts. Oh, don't look so shocked. I knew of it even before a little birdie told me to go on a witch hunt."

"But—but—" Marta sputtered. "I saw them too. I just assumed—" Her face mottled. "I thought you were doing it. You had so much alimony to pay, your bar bills were so high, I simply turned my head, thinking it would be yours one day anyway."

"You thought I—? Marta, I'm disappointed in you. I thought we were special to each other over our long association."

Marta's eyes burned. "You don't know the half of it."

Tamara's head was spinning. It sounded like Simon and Jack had reached some sort of understanding. Dare she hope...?

The noise level in the boardroom was escalating. With Marta and Elliott ganging up on Jack, she had to leave so she could clear her head, could find a quiet spot and absorb what she thought she'd heard. She stood on unsteady legs and made her way to the door.

"We have some unfinished business, lady."

It wasn't the gentle hands on her shoulders that held her immobile. It was Simon's hoarse, emotionally ragged voice in her ear. She swallowed hard, tried to put the accustomed iron back into her posture. He had to spell it out for her. She couldn't risk making a fool of herself again. Her heart would break if he rejected her.

He nudged her into the hall and closed the door behind him. Then he turned her around. "Look at me."

Tamara couldn't raise her eyes past the strong column of his throat, at the pulse pounding there, at the little hollow in the center of his collarbone that his unbuttoned white shirt revealed. She tried not to think of how the black hair peeping out of that shirt arrowed down to his groin...

Her knees turned to mush. Her phantom foot itched. She felt his finger crook under her chin and lift her head up.

"You did it," he murmured, his intense gaze burning hers. "You got us all to do what Dad wanted."

"Oh Simon, truly?"

"Don't leave. You have to stay to make sure we follow your plan."

As though they had minds of their own, her hands lifted up to his chest. She felt heat surge through him, felt the strong, slow beat of his heart beneath her palm, felt his arms go around her back. Then she was crushed against him and all reservations fled from her mind and she opened her mouth, her mind, her soul to him.

"Tamara," he groaned against her devouring mouth. "I want you. God, how I want you."

She pushed away just far enough to look into his eyes. The same naked longing she'd glimpsed earlier, after she'd brought him to climax with her mouth, burned in them.

"I know I don't have the right to saddle you with half a man," he said, his voice low and full of pain, "but if you could be satisfied with half a loaf, I want to feed you forever."

Forever. She loved him mindlessly. But passion wasn't enough. He had to understand what it was like to be an amputee. A half-baked idea formed. If Simon could agree to that, he truly loved her, even though he'd never said it except that throwaway line before their passion had even erupted.

"Let's go away for a while and talk about it," she said.

Joy leaped into his eyes. "Yes! Good thing you're already packed. I have just the place. In Vermont. I'll take Jack's SUV so we have enough room for your suitcases. We'll—"

"There's only one condition."

Simon's voice trailed away. His eyes narrowed. His arms banded around her like pincers. "What's that?"

She told him.

After a long moment, he said, "Agreed. I'll do anything to convince you."

Tamara hoped with all her heart that he could keep his end of the bargain.

* * * * *

"Dammit, how could you have sat there so coolly and not even twitched?"

"Because I am a professional, and you are not."

"The hell I'm not," Marta retorted as she paced the length of Elliott's cherished Aubusson rug. Elliott sat on his leather chair with a martini on the coffee table before him. She'd barged in, unannounced, to Elliott's house several hours after the board meeting broke up and set her attaché case on the Hepplewhite table behind him. She was so agitated she hadn't removed her thigh-length swing coat or her leather gloves. "I have an MBA, I've been controller of a multimillion-dollar organization—"

"And got caught with your finger in the pie."

"Jack's full of shit! I saw those withdrawals, and I reacted just the way I said. It'll all be his someday anyway."

"You forget one minor detail, Madam MBA."

"What?" Marta glared at him.

"Take your coat off if you're going to stay here and wear out my rug. I hope you at least wiped your boots off."

Elliott's reference to her boots unnerved Marta. She'd worn slacks and boots because she'd taken a horse from the stable and come through the riding trails. Everyone knew she hated riding. The horse was tied up behind Elliott's property. She hoped Elliott wouldn't realize he hadn't seen her sedan when he'd opened the front door. "I'm not staying. And don't change the subject."

"Then say what you have to say and let me enjoy my martini."

Marta returned to his previous comment. "What minor detail?"

"Until last week when that ball-busting Yvette Kai produced Harland's new will out of a hat, Jack thought he was getting the golf course and Simon the stocks and bonds."

Marta waved away his argument. They were getting off track. She had to pick Elliott's brains before doing what she had to do. "The real detail is that we have a mutiny on our hands."

"You have a mutiny on your hands," Elliott corrected her. "Regardless of which plan is eventually developed, I am the attorney of record. If you aren't satisfied with ten percent of the profits, I can draw up papers forcing any judge in New Jersey to make you sell your shares according to their present value."

"You're out of your mind if you think I'm giving anything up. Even more so if you think you can cheat me out of the pot of gold five years down the road after all I've done to get it."

"You won't have a choice if you force my back to the wall."

"Are you threatening me?"

"No, but I might if you don't listen to me."

"No, you listen to me, buster. I've had it with all you macho creeps trying to play Monopoly on my ante. Jack's original plan will go through if I have to steamroller over you."

Elliott snorted. "Don't mix your metaphors. And while you're at it, be sure to roll your little steam machine over Simon and Tamara. Do you know what that pair's doing right this minute?"

"Probably fucking like rabbits. They practically raped each other across the table and thought we were too stupefied by their collusion to notice."

"If I were Simon, I know what I'd do," Elliott said with a smug look on his face that Marta wanted to wipe her feet on.

"Yeah. You'd stand in line with your dick in your hand."

Elliott turned up a corner of his mouth. "My dear Marta, how gross you can be. One would think you're jealous."

"Go to hell. Not Simon. Never with Simon."

"As I was saying, I know what I would do with the delectable Miss Hart."

"What?" She knew Elliott was simply being Elliott, goading her. He would, with his logical, legal mind, point the way to Plan B.

"Take her away from all of this and go to Vermont."

Marta felt the blood leave her face. They couldn't leave. She turned her back to Elliott and kept pacing at the same speed only by a sheer effort of will. She'd never bothered to ask Simon where his chalet was. But Elliott would know. "Nice time of year for that," she said, pleased that she'd regained enough control so that no emotion showed. "The foliage must be spectacular."

"No, that far north they're past their prime."

"Oh? How far up is it?"

"About midway between Stowe and Killington."

Oh, great. Marta wasn't a skier. She'd have to finesse him. "On a secondary road in the middle of nowhere, no doubt. A cozy little chalet hidden by trees and invisible from the road."

"That's pretty accurate. It's about ten miles from Middlebury, the nearest town. When I went up there I thought I'd never find it. But when I passed the landmark, I remembered that Simon had told me that's how he knew when to turn off."

"What landmark?"

"Somebody had a row of six boulders, each taller than a man, moved to the edge of his property to make it look like the receding glaciers had deposited them. Didn't fool anyone."

"And it's what, the next property after that?"

Elliott eyed her. "Why are you so interested all of a sudden?"

That was probably all she'd get out of him, she couldn't make him suspicious. He had to be sitting right there in that chair for her plan to work. She shrugged. "Just making conversation. And speaking of conversation, I have something that will make you speechless."

Elliott chuckled and leaned back, relaxed and supercilious as usual. "My dear, I have yet to see the day."

Marta snapped open the scuffed attaché case. She picked up the lab report with still-gloved fingers and slipped a .32 pimp special into the side pocket of her bulky coat.

"Read this." She thrust the paper at his left side. He had to take it with his left hand. When he did, she maneuvered behind his chair and positioned herself just even with his right shoulder, as she'd carefully researched on the Internet.

He snapped fully alert. "You bitch, where'd you get—?"

Marta slammed the barrel of the semi-automatic pistol against his right temple and pulled the trigger. The impact drove his body sideways. His head smacked against the curved edge of the backrest. She braced for the splattering of brains and blood. Nothing. Nothing but a neat little hole an inch from his hairline and a faint tattooing of gunpowder around the hole.

She'd bought the gun on a grungy back street in New York City. The illegal hollow-point bullet would do the most damage, they'd said, bouncing around the skull and fracturing it like a cracked egg, leaving little or no mess.

She stepped in front of the lawyer who'd thought he was better than she, who looked down at her, a dowdy woman with no life but The Pines. She'd considered telling him about her family, so he'd know why he died. But, as she expected, he'd reacted with laser swiftness to the DNA report linking him with a prostitute's daughter, and she'd reacted just as swiftly.

Impassively she stared at the dead body staring sightlessly back at her. His right eye had hemorrhaged. Should she close his eyes? Would he have squeezed them shut at the last minute, knowing that what he was doing would be irrevocable?

No. She decided Elliott Grosse would go out of this world as he had through life, arrogant and unblinking.

Don't pick up the ejected cartridge, she reminded herself. Where did it land? Suppose it bounced off her and landed some place that a good cop would know was at an impossible angle?

There it was. She eyed the trajectory. Looked okay to her.

She knelt at his feet, thinking with grim satisfaction that she'd never, even figuratively, done that during his lifetime. Gently she pried at his fisted right hand, then harder.

It won't open! Rigor mortis wasn't supposed to happen for a couple of hours! What was wrong?

Don't panic. Taking a deep, calming breath, Marta worked methodically, pulling back one finger at a time. Sweat beaded on her thick brows but she ignored it. She worked the .32's grip into the opened fingers, then forced the fingers closed, almost as tightly closed as the left hand around the DNA report.

After a careful scrutiny of the room to be sure everything was as it should be, she set her mind to the last, most important task. The demise of Tamara Hart.

Chapter Twenty-Six

Sunlight filtered through the bare branches of the maple tree through the wall of windows and into Simon's consciousness. Morning. He sat up with a jolt. The sleeping bag moved with him and he remembered. Tamara.

He lay back into the canvas-covered down bag with a soft sigh and closed his eyes. They'd started driving before dusk, arriving at his Vermont chalet around three in the morning, stopping once to fill the SUV's tank with gas and himself with wake-up coffee. Tamara dozed until he'd braked for a stop sign in downtown Middlebury.

Now she was in the master bedroom upstairs and he on the planked living room floor near a fire that had gone to ashes.

The peaceful sound of silence greeted him. His nose discerned the residue of woodsmoke, a lingering aroma of lemon polish from the caretaker's efforts, the elusive scent of a certain woman. And coffee.

His eyes flew open. That's what had awakened him. The sound of the coffeepot sighing the end of its brew cycle.

He sat up again and cast an eye around for his jeans. He usually slept in the nude. Tamara had seen him nude, had kissed and stroked him in all his normally covered places. Still...

Slipping into his jeans, he zipped them and sauntered barefoot and bare-chested into the kitchen.

Tamara was leaning with both elbows on the center island, gazing out the window, sipping coffee. Her shiny hair had been twined into a loose topknot. She wore a snug, cut-off

T-shirt that stopped mid-rib, exposing a tiny waist that flared out to sweetly curving hips. Her bottom was thrust outward, her firm ass clearly outlined under clingy, flesh-colored tights. Almost as though she knew what a picture she'd make to his sight.

His balls tightened painfully. She knew exactly what a picture she made. Clearing his throat, he asked, "May I have a cup?"

She straightened, turned. Her eyes scanned him from naked shoulders to unsnapped jeans to bare feet. Then they went to his face. Something like disappointment flicked across hers. "Didn't you forget something?"

His grin at seeing her in his kitchen disappeared.

"You promised."

Her outthrust chin made Simon turn on his heel and return to the living room. He didn't know how he'd manage.

But that was the point, wasn't it?

Last night he'd carted everything inside. She'd sweet-talked the medical supply house into staying open late for them. Simon picked up the wide weight-lifter's belt that closed with thick bands of Velcro and a heavy buckle. He placed his left knee and calf on the sofa, sat back on his haunch until his heel touched his butt.

He hesitated. He'd be strapped up for a four-day weekend.

Do it, he ordered. Taking a deep breath, he immobilized his leg with the belt. Good thing his leg muscles were so supple from all the climbing he'd done in the past year.

She'd argued that if he merely immobilized his leg as though it were in a cast, he'd be able to balance and walk and climb steps almost as well as a normal person. So she'd insisted on the simulation of an amputated leg.

The crutches lay at his feet. Foot. How was he going to reach them with one leg?

Bending forward at the waist, he stabilized himself against the sofa then bent his "good" leg until his knee almost touched the wooden floor. At the last inch his ankle gave way and he landed on both knees. But he'd reached his target. Grabbing the crutches, he lumbered to his feet like a clumsy elephant and balanced himself between the metal sticks.

He swung into the kitchen. Tamara sat in the breakfast nook window seat, gazing at the rolling hillside beyond the deck, a vista that stretched for miles in three directions. It was one of the reasons he'd fallen in love with this place.

"I wouldn't mind that omelet now," she said, keeping her eyes on the view.

He gave a curt nod, managed to get to the refrigerator and open the door. He rested the crutches against the counter, balanced one hand on the jamb then reached down to the bottom shelf for the carton of eggs. Carefully he set it on the counter and swung the door closed. His hand went to the crutches. No, first he needed a bowl. He hopped the two paces to where they were stored and brought it down.

Hell, he'd forgotten the milk. Should have gotten it out with the eggs. He hopped, using the counter as a balance point.

Then he remembered the fresh dill that had been on his telephoned shopping list. While his head was inside the fridge, he groped for the countertop to set the milk down. The crutches clattered to the floor. Biting back a curse, he straightened and fought the urge to kick them out of his way.

But he had only one leg.

Although Tamara hadn't said a word, he could feel her eyes boring into his bare back.

He bent down, picked up the crutches and set them aside, feeling a small measure of pride that he hadn't come crashing down on his knees as before, and set to work cooking.

Minutes later he slid a perfect omelet onto a plate.

"I'd like to eat here, if you don't mind," she said, still seated on the window seat beyond the breakfast table. "And I'll have a refill on that coffee. And two slices of toast."

Holding the plate, Simon pursed his lips. If he hopped, would the omelet slide off? If he had to use both crutches, could he carry the plate?

"Tell me how you'd do it," he finally said.

She turned and met his uncertain gaze. "Any way I can," she said in a neutral voice, and turned back to the view.

After a moment's thought, he reached to an upper cabinet and withdrew a soup bowl. He slid the omelet into it, wrapped a knife and fork inside a napkin, and hopped to the window. "Your breakfast, madam," he said.

"Thank you." She handed him her empty coffee cup.

"Black, if I remember?"

"Yes, please."

Simon hopped back to the counter. Aware of how his bare toes flexed and grabbed at the floor, he wondered if he'd be as well balanced if he were wearing shoes, and decided, probably not. Decided, too, that she'd make sure he found out.

The toast popped up. "Butter? Jam? I have some homemade strawberry stuff that my caretaker made."

"Strawberry would be fine."

He sandwiched the jam-topped toast sloppy side in and wrapped a napkin around it. The coffee, he realized, would spill, so he poured Tamara half a cup.

After delivering that, he hopped back and poured himself a full mug of black coffee. A fine sheen of perspiration had slicked his bare chest, less from the exertion than from concentrating on simply doing it.

When he'd made himself a similar breakfast, he brought it to the table then looked at the chair in dismay.

"You can take it off for a half hour," she said.

"Thank you." He couldn't quite contain his sigh of relief when the belt had been removed and his leg was straight again.

"I'm sorry. I imagine your muscles are cramped."

"They are that," he admitted. "And I can finally scratch that itch inside my knee joint."

"Good for you."

He'd heard about phantom itches on limbs that no longer existed. Would he spend this long weekend tiptoeing—or, rather, hopping—around minefields of semantics?

As he drained his coffee, he realized he'd been so eager to see Tamara that he hadn't used the bathroom. His bladder was talking to him loud and clear. He stood. "I...er, I have to—"

"You have to put it back on before you use the bathroom."

Was it that obvious? But of course. She'd caught him staring at his empty mug with a bemused look on his face.

Okay. No sighs, no groans, no self-pity. The belt went on. He hopped to the crutches, already sensing that two or three hops around the kitchen, with the counter or table within reach to stabilize him, was one thing. But to hop the twenty-foot length of the living room to the guest bath downstairs—

Against his will, his mind took a different tack. When Tamara hopped, how much did her breasts bounce?

The sudden tightness in his jeans had nothing to do with his bladder. He found himself thinking of the soft fullness of her breasts, their weight in his hands, their taste against his tongue. Grabbing the crutches, he headed for the bathroom.

Usually he just spread his legs, balanced, and aimed. This could be a project. He was delighted that the only problem he encountered was dropping a crutch while yanking up his zipper.

When he came out, she was leaning against the back of a stuffed chair near the stairs. He got a good look at her abbreviated T-shirt. She damn sure wasn't wearing a bra. He wanted his fingers to be stroking her breasts instead of gripping the handles of crutches.

But their agreement had been, she said when. And that wouldn't occur until she was satisfied he understood her point of view. Sunday had been her prediction. Forcing his mind to something less erotic, he said, "Want to play a board game? Cards?"

"Let's go for a walk and enjoy the fresh Vermont air."

For a moment he just stood there, knowing she was turning her big guns on him. He glanced around the living room, at the empty spot where he'd left his shirt, shoes and socks, last night. Somehow he knew she'd taken them upstairs while he fumbled in the bathroom.

Resigned, he swung himself to the stairs then stood, thoughtfully considering his options. Do the crutches go first and then the leg? Or vice versa? He tried it both ways.

A more tedious climb he'd never endured, even in Kamchatka. With every step, his respect for Tamara increased. No wonder she had such a chip on her shoulder. It was well earned.

But he'd make her feel loved. She was loved. He loved her for herself, for the steel in her spine, the brains in her head, and yes, the courage she'd had to display simply to get as far as she had. Not just for her perfect face, the centerfold figure. Not just for the way her body had wrapped around him when he'd plunged so briefly into her sweet pussy. Or the way she matter-of-factly accepted his impotence and made him come anyway.

He hobbled into the master bedroom, hoping to see the indentation her head had made on his pillow. The king-size bed was neatly made. His gaze swept the room. No clothes strewn on a chair, no makeup on the dresser. He wanted her to feel at home here, wanted to see her lacy bra dangling on a doorknob.

What was he doing to himself? She wasn't wearing a bra now. He didn't need to see a bra on a doorknob to imagine the feel of his tongue against her hard, tight nipples.

Need slammed into him. He wanted this woman. Now. Under him, astride him, lying on her side, however was most comfortable for her. With a pang of regret he realized he hadn't asked her which way that might be.

Dammit, what was wrong with him? Was his cock doing his thinking for him? He wanted Tamara so desperately that he'd forgotten the reason he'd agreed to this scheme. This was how he'd prove his love.

Leaning against the dresser for balance, he yanked a T-shirt and a crewneck sweater over his head. Cheating, he removed the restraining belt to put thick woolen socks and hiking boots on both feet then strapped his leg up again.

Going down was even worse. He'd rappelled down a Russian mountainside without hesitation, but on these fourteen steps in a Vermont chalet he felt as though the next one would be his undoing. Again he had to make a conscious decision to put the crutch first, then the foot.

Tamara stood at the front door. She'd changed from the distracting tights and T-shirt. Over a butter-yellow turtleneck she wore a woolen hunter's plaid shirt, its long tails covering her curves. Her left jeans leg was neatly pinned up. She balanced easily between her crutches.

He felt suddenly humbled. She'd removed her prosthesis in sympathy for him!

Her gaze poured over him like melted butter. "It's such a beautiful morning," she said. "Let's not waste it."

The love Tamara felt for Simon as she'd watched him awkwardly come down the stairs on crutches overwhelmed her. Never had a man made such an open, if unspoken, declaration to her. She could stop him right now and know he understood.

But that wasn't her only goal. She meant to taunt him, entice him, seduce him until he forgot all about being impotent.

Her only problem was not jumping him herself. When he'd walked into the room with those snug, unsnapped jeans riding low on narrow hips, his broad chest naked and enticing, she'd been hard-pressed to keep her eyes off him. She'd wanted to pull him right to the floor and take him inside her for however long he'd last before losing it. But she was determined to get him past the hatred for all women that had festered since his son's death.

But not now. Now they were going for a walk. "Show me what you like about this location."

Simon hobbled up and stood close, towering over her. She could see him shift to balance on his good leg. Then he put both crutches in one hand and leaned into her. "First, a kiss."

Tamara's mouth twitched. "That's not in the —"

His mouth absorbed the rest of the sentence. He kissed her softly, just skimming her lips, then feathered tiny kisses along the corners of her mouth, up her cheek. Her eyelids fluttered closed. He kissed those, kissed the space between her eyebrows. His free hand caressed her throat, the hollow between her collarbones, then skimmed down her shoulder. His knuckles brushed against her breast. Her nipples jumped to attention.

His mouth found hers again. His tongue traced a line across the seal of her lips. Automatically her mouth opened. His tongue slipped in and out, softly, slowly, then with more authority. She knew what he was doing. He was echoing a more primitive rhythm that was making her good leg weak. She was grateful she had both her crutches under her armpits.

Suddenly he withdrew and said, "I like everything about this location. Come. I'll show you."

Her mouth felt pleasantly violated. Her breasts tingled. Warmth had spread from her pussy outward. It took her a moment to understand. He was playing her game.

She squared her shoulders. "I'm ready."

Outside, puffy clouds like unbaked meringue dotted a cerulean sky. Tamara felt the warmth of sunlight on her cheeks. Fallen leaves cushioned a gently sloping path that led through a small stand of birches, vivid streaks of white with black striations, with occasional strips of peeling bark. She stopped and took a deep breath. "Different, yet the same."

Simon came up behind her. "I know what you mean. The cleanness, the freshness, of the air. Back home the smell of pine is all-pervasive. Here it's just one of many. Pine, dried leaves, grasses."

"Listen." Tamara cocked her head to concentrate on the rustling of dried leaves. "Sounds like the same scurrying little feet as at The Pines."

"Yeah. Squirrels, probably, and other rodents, getting ready for winter."

Walking leisurely, they allowed the peace of the morning, the sweet bird trills, to settle over them. The birches thinned, and Tamara could see a patch of blue ringed by vivid green grass. "Is that a pond?"

"Yes. Stocked with trout."

"Is it yours?"

"Yes. I own down to that line of trees. That's national forest land beyond. I picked up parcels here and there over the years. There's about eight hundred acres here."

They walked through the clearing toward the pond. Tamara turned to admire the view of sharply rising hills. "Nice place for a ski resort."

"No," he said softly, "I've done enough developing."

Tamara gave him a speculative glance. "Does that include The Pines?"

He stopped, leaned on his crutches, squinted against the sunlight as he looked out into the distance. "No. We'll build your plan, Jack and I. We think that's what Dad wanted."

"I'm glad you've reconciled."

"It feels good. Like a burning porcupine's been removed from inside my chest."

"Dropped a few jaws when you backed each other up."

"Serves them right. They were out to line their pockets, all of them."

"What do you think Carrie will do after the divorce?"

Simon snorted. "Take the money and run, I hope."

"She strikes me as the kind who can't live without a man. She should have no trouble attracting one. She's young, beautiful, vivacious."

"And she'll be rich."

Tamara searched Simon's face. The comment was wry, but his expression showed no animosity. "You need a good lawyer."

"You're telling me. Elliott's dragged his feet long enough. How's Yvette on divorce?"

"Not her strong suit. But I'll bet she'll recommend the bastard who represented her ex-husband."

They started walking again. Simon set down a crutch-tip on the soft, uneven terrain. With his weight on it, it sank into the ground. He went sprawling onto the grass with a curse.

Tamara took a few steps forward, her gaze focused on the shimmering blue of the pond. From bitter experience she knew that an amputee didn't need the additional humiliation of people staring at his clumsy attempts to regain his footing. She heard Simon grunt. A few words of what might have been Russian escaped as he hauled himself upright.

"Damn gopher hole."

"Yes, things like mud, stones, soft dirt can be a hazard," she agreed, then deliberately moved toward the pond. "Your other properties. Did you develop them yourself?"

She was gratified to hear him right behind her. "No. I handle office buildings. A couple along the Route One Princeton corridor, some in downtown Philadelphia, others in Jersey. I bought money-losing properties, refurbished them, found Class-A tenants. I try to fix what's already out there. I built a couple of smaller ones, but they were in-filling between existing structures. I never took farmland or bulldozed woods."

Tamara agreed with his philosophy. Until her stint at The Pines, she'd never thought about land preservation. But now she'd rather live in the simple bungalow on The Pines than in Jack's densely packed original plan even if it meant tons of profit. The thought made her smile. Ike would have tried to browbeat her into —

Ike. Vincent. Her throat constricted. Guilt washed over her and she shuddered. She'd been so wrapped up in Simon that she hadn't given her family a thought.

"What's the matter?"

She felt Simon's arm around her shoulder. "Ike."

"Don't think of him. It's over. You're safe."

"But I'm lollygagging in Vermont and Ike and Vincent are lying on slabs in the police morgue. I should be down there. Suppose Detective Kyrillos releases the bodies for burial and I'm not there to make funeral arrangements?"

"Jack knows where we are."

"So much violence."

"Don't think about it. Think about what you'd like for dinner tonight. There's steak and there's steak."

The comment had the desired effect. Tamara chuckled. They had reached the pond. The warmth of the sun brought out the season's last long-legged skate bugs to dapple the water's surface. In the distance a trout leaped, then splashed back into its depths.

By unspoken consent they settled down on the thick grass. In one seamless motion Tamara bent forward, dropped her weight onto her right hand then shifted her hip to the ground. Like an expert tumbler, Simon thought. He awkwardly mimicked her motions, coming to rest with a thump.

"I'm balancing differently than you," he observed. "With my big foot dangling out behind like a dinosaur tail."

"We could make your leg more like mine," she said quietly.

"I'm sorry. I wasn't looking for sympathy. I was just making an observation."

But it sounded like the former. Chagrined, he changed the subject. "This looks like somebody's lawn, doesn't it? The caretaker has a few sheep. Brings them here to feed. Cuts down on lawn-mowing."

"You really are environmentally attuned." Smiling, Tamara lay on her back, her crutches at arm's length, her stacked hands cushioning her head as she looked at his stork-bent leg. "You can unbuckle while we're resting."

He did. Then easing his long length onto the grass, he shifted to his side, propped his head on his hand and gazed at her clean profile, the flawless skin that glowed in the warm sunlight. "Your eyes are the exact color of the sky," he said.

She turned the full force of those eyes to him. "At first, yours reminded me of whiskey. Now, when I look at them, I see the color of the cedar streams at The Pines."

"I hope I'll always remind you of home," he said softly.

"Home," she repeated. "I haven't had a home since my mother died."

"Tell me about her."

"I have her hair. It was long and thick and shiny blonde. I used to watch my father brush it. He'd get this look on his face that I was too young to understand. But I knew it meant she was loved, that I was loved." She closed her eyes. "I was eight when he died. But I'll never forget that image."

Simon understood all too well her father's desire to brush his love's hair. He wanted to do the same to Tamara's.

"My mother didn't have many skills, but she was an expert seamstress. She could have gone into business for herself, but she was adamant that she wanted the fringe benefits, like medical insurance, to protect me after my father died. So she worked in a sweatshop, sewing clothes assembly-line style.

"The irony was, she died before I lost my leg. Ike wasn't working, so we had no insurance. If it hadn't been for Harland…"

"You loved him like a father." Simon swallowed hard against the sudden knot in his throat. "Like I did."

"Yes."

"Did I ever apologize for thinking otherwise?"

"I don't remember."

He leaned toward her, pinning her arm between his chest and the grass. "I apologize." His mouth hovered over hers. "I want to love you the rest of your life. I want to protect you, to cherish you. I want to erase all your bad memories. I want to give you good memories. But I don't have the right to ask."

"You have every right." She tilted her head and captured his mouth with hers, putting into it all the love she felt but couldn't yet admit. Years of vulnerability still had to be breached.

When the kiss ended, she said, "If you could do this for me," she indicated the wide belt lying beside his leg, "I'd say you're staking a claim that would be valid in a court of honor."

"Tamara," he groaned then rolled onto his back, flipping her atop him. Her thighs parted to straddle him. His fingers sifted through her hair, finding and discarding the pins holding the topknot in place. Her hair cascaded down like a waterfall, capturing them in a fragrant silken tent as their lips met.

There was no teasing, no tenderness. Their mutual hunger outran their promise to wait. He thrust his tongue into the hot recess of her mouth. She eagerly claimed it. She arched into him as he ground into her. She bunched her fists in his hair, trying to bring him into even closer contact. He held her captive, his hands moving, touching, molding to her contours.

Suddenly she felt him go rigid. "Don't make a sound," he whispered. "We have company."

Her eyes were wide as platters as she looked into his smiling ones. Then she felt the tenseness leave him and knew there was no danger.

"Very slowly, turn your head to your left."

She did. Through the fall of her hair, she saw them. A small "Oh" escaped her.

A deer with twin fawns had come to the edge of the pond not forty feet away. She watched them drink. The mother's head bobbed up every few seconds, as if searching for danger, then finding none, dropped down to sip again. When they were done, they backed away from the water's edge.

Tamara stared, fascinated, as the mother licked the fawns' faces. It was an instinctive gesture of maternal love so poignant that she felt something shift inside her. She wanted this man's child. Children, if he could manage.

And she knew she wouldn't, couldn't wait until the self-imposed restraint of Sunday. She'd have to seduce Simon tonight.

Chapter Twenty-Seven

ℰↃ

From the doorway to the living room, Theo Kyrillos stared at the body of Elliott Grosse in his expensive leather chair. The lab boys were meticulously combing the room taking samples, photographs and measurements.

"I'm done," said the medical examiner. "It's all yours."

The cleaning lady had arrived, as she did twice a week, just before nine o'clock, and entered with her own key. According to the badge who had answered her frantic call, she'd seen her employer as soon as she got into the hallway, screamed, dropped her handbag and keys and ran to the kitchen to call 9-1-1.

Kyrillos dearly hoped that was the case. This crime scene had to stay pristine. Too many deaths had revolved around the principals of The Pines for any evidence here to be tainted.

"Any guess as to time of death?" he asked the M.E. as he walked into the room around the lab techs.

"I'd put it somewhere between six p.m. and midnight. I'll narrow it down after the autopsy."

Kyrillos made a slow circle around the body, his keen mind absorbing details almost without conscious effort. Peering at the entrance wound, a small neat hole in the victim's right temple, he noted the tattoo the gunpowder left on his skin, which meant the weapon had been against his head when fired. The hemorrhaged eye was consistent with trauma of this type.

"Think it's suicide?"

"Could be."

Kyrillos leaned down to the table and sniffed at the colorless residue of liquid in a martini glass. Gin. Then he crooked his head and read the document clutched in Grosse's hand. A DNA report of paternity. The names jumped out at him. Carrie Black. Elliott Grosse.

Had Grosse killed himself rather than live with the knowledge in that document? Had someone tried to blackmail him?

Neither scenario made sense. If he wanted to thwart whoever hoped to smear his name, why wouldn't he have destroyed the DNA report first?

"Check all the wastebaskets for envelopes," he said to the tech in charge of the scene. "See if we can find out where this document came from."

"Roger."

Pulling out a pen from his jacket pocket, he poked the tip into the tightly clenched fist holding the paper. The cadaveric response was consistent with the neurological response of a body struck in the brain that resulted in instantaneous death.

He probed in the right hand, which held an Ivers Johnson .32, known as a pimp's gun because it was small enough to keep in their pants pocket. The grip was different. Kyrillos knew you couldn't mimic a death grip—it was either there or it wasn't.

In the right hand it wasn't.

He would keep his speculation to himself to see if the M.E. reached the same conclusion—that this wasn't a suicide.

Pulling out his notebook, he recorded his impressions then left the house. On the porch he noticed a clump of dirt and called to a tech. "I want a sample of this. Check the maid's shoes and those of the deceased. See if there's a match. Also, check all around the house for footprints. Grosse didn't strike me as the type to step into mud and track it onto the porch."

"Will do."

Kyrillos walked slowly to his car, studying the layout of the front yard. Ten or so heavily landscaped acres, a semicircular macadam driveway, no visibility from the road or from neighbors. The assailant could slip in and out unnoticed. He'd question the neighbors anyway.

But first, the shareholders.

Grosse's home was about a mile from The Pines' entrance. He glanced at his watch. Ten-thirty. He mentally reviewed the locations of the other shareholders. The closest one was the controller, Marta Chudzik. She'd probably already be at the office.

He aimed his unmarked Ford toward the southern entrance of The Pines. As he passed the stables, he braked to a stop. The kid, what was his name? Cliff something. Marta's nephew. Could he have done it? Why?

No, he didn't seem bright enough to pull off a murder and make it look like a suicide. He drove up the private road, where three of the shareholders lived.

No Jack, no Carrie, no Simon, and at the bungalow, no Tamara. He went on to the golf course office. Neither the bar nor the restaurant was open yet. He went upstairs and entered the office. "Hello? Anyone here?"

Jack came out into the small reception area, carrying a sheaf of computer papers. His striped tie was slightly loosened over a long-sleeved white shirt. For the first time since Kyrillos met him, Jack looked like a seasoned executive, with clear eyes and a spring in his step. "I'm the only one here right now. What can I do for you, Lieutenant?"

"I'm trying to establish some information in regards to an incident last night."

"What incident?"

Kyrillos gave him his blandest smile. "I'm the cop. I get to ask the questions."

"Okay. Come back with me." He led the way to an office whose large window overlooked the putting green. Neat piles of papers were stacked on a large cherrywood desk on which rested a brass nameplate with the simple legend, Manager. A dark suit jacket hung on a hanger in one corner.

"Make yourself at home," Jack said, gesturing to a padded office chair in front of the desk. "Coffee?"

"No thanks." Kyrillos sat down and waited for Jack to pour himself a cup and sit down behind the desk. He noted the relaxed gait, the casual stance. Was it a pose for his benefit?

"Now, Lieutenant, what can I do for you?"

"What did you do last night?"

"I had dinner with a colleague."

"Whose name is?"

He looked sheepish then said, "You'll find out anyway. Yvette."

"The lawyer?"

"Yeah. Why?"

"What time to what time? Where?"

"I picked her up about seven. We drove up to Princeton, to Lahiere's."

Kyrillos' eyebrow raised. "The food here's not any good?"

"Lieutenant, when you eat here every day of your life, you need a change once in a while."

"Okay. What time did you leave?"

"We lingered over a brandy. They kicked us out when the bar closed. It must have been two-thirty when I dropped her off."

"Then what?"

"I went home and jerked myself off," he said ruefully.

Kyrillos grinned. He could understand that the cool, unapproachable Ms. Kai would have that effect on a man's libido. And he knew that Jack Sutcliffe had an unimpeachable alibi.

"What about the rest of the shareholders? Do you know where they are? I drove up the road. Couldn't find anyone at home."

"Simon and Tamara are in Vermont by now. They have a lot to talk about, and didn't want to be interrupted."

"Vermont? Where?"

"Don't know exactly. I've never been to his chalet."

Kyrillos raised an eyebrow.

"It's a place he kept private. In fact, when he told me he was taking Tamara there, I knew it was serious. He's never invited anyone from the family up there. Not even Dad."

Jack reached for his Palm Pilot. "But I do have the phone number. If you need the address, Elliott probably has it. He had power of attorney while Simon was gone."

Keeping his face impassive, Kyrillos wrote the number down. Jack's offhand reference to Elliott in the present tense was another indication that this shareholder, at least, probably wasn't a suspect. "Do you know what time they left?"

"No."

"Would you know where Carrie is?"

Jack's mien visibly cooled. "No, and I don't care. She played me for a fool. And now I'm sober enough to realize it."

Kyrillos studied the man who sat behind the desk like a CEO. That's what was different. He was sober. "What about the controller?"

"She called me early this morning. Said she was taking a personal day. I told her, go ahead, you deserve one. She hardly ever takes vacation time."

"Did she say what she was going to do?"

"No, and I didn't ask."

"Tell me about her background." He'd finally gotten the report on her from when she first went to college. He wanted to see how it jibed with whatever résumé she'd given them.

Jack frowned. He wasn't sure what the detective was getting at. There were some parts of Marta Chudzik's past that he didn't necessarily want anyone probing into.

"How did she get the job here in the first place?"

"I'll have to look in the personnel records. I was just a kid when she arrived."

"She started as what, a secretary?"

"I believe so. Then she took a year off to get her degree. Dad thought that was great. In fact, he paid for her tuition. Said it was a fringe benefit. He was like that. He set up a scholarship fund for the caddies too.

"Anyway, a few years later she started studying for her MBA in a program tailor-made for working stiffs, every Saturday for several years. Brilliant mind. Had no trouble."

"When did she start? September?"

"I'd have to check."

"What was she like back then?"

Jack got up to refill his coffee cup. He didn't like the direction of the detective's questioning. "Just what are you looking for?"

"Did she have boyfriends in those days? She was what, thirty, thirty-one when she came here? Did she look as, uh, frumpy as she does now?"

Jack was slow to sit back down. "What are you trying to ascertain?"

"According to college records, Marta Chudzik matriculated in the January semester, had the summer off, returned in September and graduated the following January. She came back to The Pines with her degree in accounting."

"That must be right then."

337

"Did you know that during that summer between semesters, she had a baby?"

The coffee cup slipped out of Jack's hands and landed on the table, splashing black liquid all over his neat piles of papers. "A...baby?"

"She never told you? Never told Harland, her employer?"

Jack leaned back in his chair. Dizziness was only one of the effects of the detective's revelation. He wondered if the man could hear the furious pounding of his heart.

"So you don't remember her seeing anyone regularly? Being sweet on a co-worker perhaps?"

"N-no. But I was in high school then. I wouldn't have paid any attention to someone who was, what did you say, thirty?"

"Did she ever talk about family? Someone she might have given the baby to?"

"No." Jack's head was empty of every fact except that Marta Chudzik had had a baby a year after she arrived at The Pines. Dear God, could it be...

The detective's beeper went off. Jack jumped.

"Excuse me, may I make a phone call?"

"Help yourself." Jack gestured to the phone on his desk and walked to the window, staring blindly at the golfers who were practicing their putts on the meticulously kept green.

"I've got to go," the detective said, handing Jack his card. "Call my beeper if any of the others show up, will you?"

The message from the lab sent Kyrillos to the stables. Recent imprints of a horseshoe had been found behind Elliott Grosse's house. And horse droppings were mixed in with the soil sample taken from the front porch. Perhaps the killer had gotten there on horseback.

"Hi, Cliff. Remember me?"

"Yeah. You're the detective was asking about Mr. Sutcliffe when his horse threw him."

"Right. I'd like to ask a few more questions, if I may."

Cliff shrugged. "Sure."

"What time did you close up yesterday?"

"Around six."

"Has anyone been here this morning yet?"

"No. It's quiet since Mr. Sutcliffe died."

"Tell me, Cliff. What did you think of him?"

"He was great. Like a father."

"You lost your parents at an early age, didn't you?" His voice was gentle, encouraging.

"Yeah. My father died before I was born."

"I'm sorry for your double loss."

There was that shrug again. As if his shield against pain and loss was in place and every bad thing rolled off him.

"What about your mother?"

"She died when I was just a couple of years old. I don't even remember her. My Aunt Marta put me with a foster house because she couldn't take care of me."

"But now she can."

"Sometimes she's too..." He gestured helplessly, as though he had no words to describe it. "Clinging."

"Maybe it's the only way she knows to show she loves you."

Cliff just grunted.

"Does anyone come here after you're gone for the day?"

He shrugged again, a don't-know-and-don't-care attitude. The report on Cliff's foster parents was that they were stable but undemonstrative. The kid had probably bottled up all his emotions because they weren't reciprocated. Then for four years he boarded at the school.

"Does anyone else have keys to the stable?"

"Up at the office they do. Aunt Marta keeps a spare at home in case I lose mine."

"When you came in this morning, did you notice anything different? A horse that maybe was ridden and didn't get groomed afterward? Or a bridle out of place?"

"Didn't look."

"Could we look now?"

Cliff's response was simply to turn on his heel and lead the way into the stable. He looked around, but made no comment, so Kyrillos assumed he noticed nothing amiss. Horses occupied six of the ten stalls. He watched as the boy rubbed the first horse on its nose, murmured a few words then opened the stall. With a gentle touch he ran a hand over his back, down his haunches.

"Nope," he said as he went to the second.

At the fourth stall he made a sound then ran his hands over the horse again. "Where you been, Zelda, old girl?" He turned to the detective with a puzzled look on his face. "Feels like she's got dried sweat on her. Damn." His hand stopped on her left knee. "A burr."

Kyrillos kept the rising excitement out of his voice. "Can you check her shoes? Is there any soil in them?"

Cliff gave him a look that said, *boy, are you stupid.* "All horses have dirt in their shoes. It's what they walk on."

"Sorry, let me rephrase that." He pulled out several small plastic bags from a jacket pocket. "Could you get me samples of the dirt in her shoes?"

"What's up?"

"Just routine. We found a clump of dirt mixed with horse manure some place where it shouldn't have been, and we want to see which horse it came from."

"Oh."

Just that simple. No curiosity, no speculation. Just compliance. His hunch had been right. Cliff didn't have the guile to be a murderer.

He stuffed the filled bags into his pocket. "I went to the golf course office looking for your aunt. Jack told me she'd taken the day off. Know where she might have gone?"

Cliff followed him back out into the sunlight. "Nope."

"Or when she'd be back?"

"Maybe tomorrow. Or Saturday. She made a big fuss about me having enough to eat while she was gone. Made a pot of stew and told me twice how to heat it up."

Alarm bells went off in Kyrillos' head. If Marta Chudzik was behind this, he'd have to warn Tamara and Simon. If they were too, ahem, busy to answer the phone, he'd have to find the address and then call the Vermont State Police, just in case.

On the other hand, if he was wrong, he sure as hell didn't want to be sued for slander.

Chapter Twenty-Eight

ℬ

"I think maybe a shower would be in order."

Simon tried to make a joke. "That bad, huh?"

They stood in the hallway. It had been almost a mile to the pond, downhill all the way, but on the return, the crutches had made him conscious of the slightest incline. Sure, he'd worked up a sweat. It was a warm day and he wasn't used to walking one-legged, so he'd been extra careful. He didn't want to fall again. But the way she'd said it, briskly, as though trying not to wrinkle her nose, well, it was almost an insult.

"I'm just trying to give you the full experience." She looked pointedly at his short leg, still hooked up behind him. "If you do it right, maybe I'll wash your back."

"I accept." He grabbed at the offer before she could emphasize the "maybe".

Maybe he'd reciprocate. The idea of his soapy hands caressing every smooth inch of her skin made his balls tighten, his jeans snug. Hell, they'd been snug all day long, ever since he'd seen her ass all but offered up to him in those tight tights this morning.

"Don't forget to put the belt back on before you get in the shower. I'll be up later."

"What about my back wash?"

"You don't take crutches into the shower. You might like to find your balance first."

Understanding dawned. His pride had taken a beating, once in the kitchen, and once when he'd poked a crutch in that damned gopher hole. She was giving him breathing room.

With a nod he went into the spacious master bath, removed the thick belt then unzipped the jeans carefully until his cock sprang free. He was hard as a crutch, with the memory of her lying on top of him, the clean scent of grass all around them, her fragrant sun-colored hair cocooning them in privacy. But he had a point to prove.

He was tempted to adjust the water first, but that would be cheating. Even though she wasn't there to see, he'd know.

With a sigh he reset the belt to cradle his naked thigh and calf, and reached into the glass-enclosed stall. When the water was hot and the spray needle-sharp, he hopped in. Damn, but the tile floor was slippery. Good thing he'd been holding on to the edge of the enclosure.

He centered his weight on the one leg. The hot spray felt good on his skin, especially his thigh. He could feel the quadriceps muscle loudly protesting the day's work. He grabbed the soap and began scrubbing his chest. The soap slipped out of his hand.

He swore. How the hell could he bend down...

"I have it," Tamara said. He heard her slip in behind him and roll the glass door closed. Soon he felt her soapy hands drawing lazy circles on his shoulder blades, down to his waist, the small of his back, then his butt. His glutes clenched.

"Firm ass," she murmured. "Very nice."

Her touch was heavenly. He closed his eyes and savored.

Then her hands skimmed around to his hipbones, drawing more circles. A soapy finger dipped into his navel. Her hands slid up to his chest, across his nipples. He bit back a groan and pressed his hands against the wet tiles to keep his balance.

She leaned in to him. It felt as though she was wearing a T-shirt that was already drenched. Her hard nipples poked into his back. She edged around to his side, her thighs spreading to capture his leg, and the cradle of her sex made scorching contact with his bare skin.

Damn. This was all a game to her. He was as hard as a cop's billy club and she was teasing him, knowing that he'd agreed to wait until Sunday. Anger surfaced. He braced himself to hop around to confront her. Her hands dropped to his cock.

He forgot his next move. Her soapy fingers slid the length of him, traced the thick veins that stood out, skimmed along the hard ridge of the head. He clenched his teeth. She could make a statue melt.

Then her hands were cupping his balls, rolling them in her hands, kneading them as he had kneaded her breasts. He was on the verge of exploding.

Abruptly the stroking ceased. "That's enough," she said. "We don't want to use up all the hot water."

"Yes, we do," he said, his teeth still clenched. He grabbed the controls for leverage and hopped an about-face. But she had already stepped out of the shower.

"Don't forget to wash your hair," she said. The steamed glass door slid shut between them. Then he heard the bathroom door close.

He swore a string of silent oaths. He grabbed the shampoo from the shelf and roughly scrubbed the foamy liquid into his scalp, then stood under the needle spray until he felt the water turn lukewarm.

With a vicious snap of his wrist he shut off the spray and pushed the door open. "The hell with this," he said, and jerked off the wet belt and tossed it onto the sink counter.

In the full-length mirror, steamed but evaporating slowly with the overhead exhaust fan, Simon saw himself, on two feet, his cock fully engorged, rivulets of water running down his skin, hair plastered across his forehead. He reached for a towel.

There was none.

The door opened. "This isn't going to work, is it."

It wasn't a question, it was a statement. Tamara stood in the doorway between the bathroom and bedroom, the oversized white towel in front of her like a shield, her gaze on his two big bare feet on the tile floor and water puddling around them.

"The belt's wet," he said, feeling the accusation in her eyes at his weak alibi.

"You have five minutes to figure out something else." She tossed him the towel and closed the door, giving him a glimpse of apricot lace that barely covered her ass, her breasts.

He toweled himself off brusquely, giving his cock a couple of brutal swipes until it wilted. He scratched a comb through his thick hair, which was more unruly when wet. Gingerly he opened the door. Tamara wasn't there.

Guilt washed over him. He retrieved the wet weightlifter's belt from the bathroom and laid it out over the back of a chair to dry. Maybe he should ask Tamara for a hair dryer. Then he opened a drawer and found what he liked to call his cowboy belt, thick brown leather four inches wide.

A devilish smile tilted his mouth upward. The hell with clothes. He applied the belt, pulling it tight over his ankle so it wouldn't slip and draw another accusation, then reached into the closet for a white silk bathrobe.

Two could play at this game.

Grabbing the crutches, he centered himself over them, ready to beard the lioness. The bedroom door opened.

Tamara stood in the doorway, wearing an ivory slip that looked like a Victoria's Secret thing, all peek-a-boo lace and clingy silk. Held up by lacy straps, it skimmed across her breasts and hips, ending midthigh. He barely noticed that she hadn't pulled her prosthesis on, that she was on crutches.

He swallowed hard.

"Just wanted to make sure you're all right," she said sweetly. "You were taking so long."

"I…uh, couldn't figure out which belt to use."

Her gaze skimmed down the length of him. She nodded approvingly. Then her eyes made a slow trip back up. Simon could feel each millimeter of his flesh heat as her gaze touched his foot, his ankle, his calf, the knee-length hem of his bathrobe, the gap in the robe between his thighs where a strategic part of his anatomy threatened to poke out, the fabric bunched between his underarms and the crutches, the chest hair that was exposed between the white lapels.

"Dressing for dinner?" she said, her mouth quirked upward.

"I…uh—"

She swung into the room, sat primly on the side of the neatly made bed, set her crutches to lean on the bedside table. "I'll just hang around here and give you some, er, pointers. If you need them. About maneuvering, I mean. With the crutches."

He limped over to her, placed his crutches next to hers, balanced on his good leg. Without thinking the consequences through, he lifted her by the waist and crushed her to him. "I'll show you what kind of maneuvering I can do." His mouth came down on hers, hard and hot and demanding. Then in a dim corner of his mind, he felt himself tipping forward. In a reflex action he flung her onto the mattress and somehow managed to fall half onto the bed as his good knee hit the floor.

"I overbalanced," he said unnecessarily.

"I noticed."

Simon also noticed. He noticed Tamara's chest rising and falling heavily with each breath. He noticed how that bit of ivory silk and lace molded itself to her lush curves. Noticed how her mouth softened, how her hooded eyes dropped to his mouth.

Just the way he wanted her.

But not now.

"Cat got your tongue?" he said with a rakish smile. "You're hungry?" He gave her a look of unbridled lust, his gaze raking up and down her body, a look he hoped would let her know he was every bit as hungry as she. Then he patted her knee.

"You should be. It's almost dinnertime." He stood and reached for his crutches. "Go get dressed."

"Wh-what?"

"Not to worry. I had the foresight to pack one of Dad's great reds. A Merlot of rare vintage."

The fog in Tamara's brain dissipated. He'd done it to her again! The damp ache that centered in her pussy throbbed with wanting him. Her nipples had reached acorn hardness without his having to touch them. Who was seducing whom?

* * * * *

Should he or shouldn't he?

Jack sat in Simon's Corvette, which he'd exchanged for the SUV, at the edge of the road leading to the stable.

Dammit, he had to. He gunned the motor and pulled in.

"How'ya doing, Cliff?"

"Hi, Mr. Jack. You want Jet Star?"

"No, I-I just thought I'd stop by and talk."

Cliff looked at him in surprise. Jack resisted the urge to run a finger around his collar. He'd changed from the suit and tie into jeans and a golf shirt, but the open collar still felt tight around his neck. "Not very busy around here, huh?"

"Nope."

The kid wasn't making it easy. Well, why should he? He hadn't an inkling of what was racing through Jack's mind.

After some small talk about the weather and the Eagles, he asked, "Ever think about taking up golf?"

"Who, me? Nah."

"Why not?"

Cliff shifted on his feet, stared at the ground. "I ain't like you guys. I don't belong."

"Like hell you don't. Didn't Dad treat you like family? Isn't Marta part of the family? Why—" His voice cracked. He tried again. "Why shouldn't you be family too?"

Cliff shrugged.

"Tell you what. If you want to try it sometime, I'll be your private instructor. How's that? Would you like to?"

Cliff gave him a steady gaze, as if really looking at him for the first time. A small thrill shot through Jack at the connection. "Yeah. I would. I'd like to know what all the fuss is about. Mr. Sutcliffe, he loved it so much. Just like he loved the woods around The Pines."

"I know. I'm just now realizing how precious it all is."

Cliff shuffled his feet again. Apparently keeping a conversation going had never been part of his education. Jack had to remember that he'd gone to that special school. If the kid was going to have more to do with The Pines in the future, it was up to Jack to polish him up. He owed no less to Cliff if his suspicions were correct.

"Say, if your Aunt Marta won't be back in time for dinner, why don't we go out for pizza and beer?"

"Sure. Why not? And maybe shoot some pool?"

"Now that's something I've never done."

"I'll be your private instructor." Cliff's eyes held a hint of sparkle.

"Thank you. I'm a fast learner."

A slow smile split Cliff's face, the first Jack had seen from the kid. It took his breath away. It was like looking in a mirror. Although Cliff was a good three inches shorter and built solid like Marta, he had the Sutcliffe smile.

Damn, it had to be true. He'd been brash enough at seventeen to seduce Marta and go at it all summer, but had never thought of the consequences. After the detective's bombshell, he'd figured it out on paper. He'd stopped boffing her after Labor Day and gone back to prep school. Counting on his fingers, he calculated she could have just barely made it through the semester, as big as a house, had her baby in June, and gone back in September to finish as though nothing had happened.

He might just be looking at the smile of his own son. It was a humbling thought.

Chapter Twenty-Nine

80

She was enjoying this extended foreplay, Tamara realized as she watched Simon decorate the sizzling steak platter with a garnish of fresh parsley. Never had anyone taken so much time to make her feel so wanted, so desirable. Too, never had she met anyone with such iron control.

Simon's white Egyptian cotton shirt contrasted vividly with his black hair and tanned skin. A red-and-navy striped silk tie was perfectly knotted. Trim black slacks wrinkled slightly under the weightlifter's belt. He'd asked for her hair dryer, so she assumed he used it to dry the belt.

For her part, Tamara felt sexy and feminine. She'd given her luxurious fall of hair a few strategic hot curls that softly framed her face. A light hand with navy mascara enhanced her eyes. Her blue silk blouse was unbuttoned enough for Simon to glimpse the cleavage above her sexiest, lowest-cut, underwire bra. The tiny pleats and dense shirring of her cotton broomstick skirt clung to her hips yet allowed freedom of movement.

Freedom for Simon to discover the surprise underneath — a garter belt holding up black stockings.

No way could she wait until Sunday. He was going to get seduced good and proper after dinner. Whether he could sustain an erection didn't even enter into Tamara's mind. Her goal was to break through his every mental barrier.

Dinner passed in a haze of sexual innuendo and hot looks, with vintage Sinatra love songs as background. Tamara felt as though she'd stepped into a remake of *Tom Jones*, where the young, gorgeous Albert Finney and a lusty wench licked food from their fingers as they licked each other with their eyes, promising even more licking for dessert.

The wine, as he'd promised, was superb. She indulged in only two glassfuls. Seduction needed a clear head.

To that end, she unbuttoned one more blouse button then tackled the dozens up the front of her skirt as Simon, his shirtsleeves rolled up, built a fire in the massive stone fireplace. She felt not at all guilty that she'd worn her best dress-up prosthesis, the one built for a three-inch sandal, while Simon still hopped on one leg.

She sat in a wing chair near the fire and crossed her legs, the good one on top. The skirt parted thigh-high. She leaned forward, making the most of her cleavage, and stretched her hands, palms out. "Mmmm," she said. "Nice fire."

"Damn you, woman," he muttered under his breath. "What are you trying to do to me?"

"Do?" Her eyes were wide and innocent. "Nothing." She gracefully raised herself from the chair and spun around, the skirt twirling high enough, she hoped, for Simon to glimpse the tops of her stockings. "I'm just dancing."

"Tamara," he rasped, fists clenched at his sides. "I'm only human."

"Show me."

He was slow to respond. "What?"

"Show me how human you are."

The gleam in his eyes warmed her down to her phantom toes. He worked his tie until its two tails hung loose. "You asked me, I'll show you, but don't you dare throw it in my face later that I didn't wait until Sunday."

"I won't," she managed as he lumbered toward her. The thump of his crutches was drowned out by the thump of her heart.

At the last minute she adroitly sidestepped him.

He swore. "What's this, hide and seek?"

"No, I just want to see how determined you are."

"Lady, I wrote the book on determined."

She backed up, choosing a more open ground than the confining strip of floor between the roaring fireplace and the low coffee table. Relentlessly he set his crutches, then his foot, as he stalked her. Her derriere touched a wall. He stopped with only inches between them and planted his crutches on either side of her sandals.

His smile turned feral. "Any more moves, lady?"

Her gaze dropped to his mouth. Her tongue slowly traveled across her upper lip, sheening it with moisture. "I, uh, maybe a waltz?"

"The music's stopped."

"I'll go fix it."

She maneuvered a high-heeled foot outside his crutch. He tossed the appliance aside and swiftly curled his free arm around her waist. The other crutch fell as he tunneled his hand under her hair. His mouth sought and captured hers like a heat-seeking missile homing in on a target. With no support, he leaned all his weight onto her for balance.

The heat of her, arching into him, rubbing against him like a cat, exploded the last vestiges of his sanity. Without lifting his head from the kiss, he backed off just enough to slip his hands between their heated bodies. He grabbed at the opening of her skirt and ripped it apart. Buttons pinged against the wooden floor. He tossed the garment aside and fumbled with his zipper.

In his frenzied state he couldn't comprehend stopping to unbutton his waistband and work the weightlifter's belt off his leg. He yanked out his rampant cock from the zipper opening. The need to touch skin on skin drove him to the edge of sanity. His hands went to her hips to rip her panties off.

Finding bare skin under a garter belt pushed him over. With a feral sound, he broke the kiss, braced his forehead against the wall behind her shoulder, hiked her good leg up, wrapped it around his hip. He planted his other hand on her ass and lifted her clean off the floor, then propped his bound leg against the wall.

Tamara divined his intent instantly. He was doing what she'd goaded him to do, letting himself go beyond the brink. With trembling, eager fingers she guided his burning-hot cock to her slit, tightened her legs around his hips, and twined her arms around his neck.

With a single savage thrust he came home, home to her love, home to her heart, home to the very corners of her soul. Then he stood as still as night, eyes closed, breath coming in shallow gasps. She could see his neck muscles tauten, could feel him tremble with the effort to remain motionless.

She began to rock her hips.

"No," he groaned. "Wait!"

"Not on your life. I can't wait another minute."

Her hips quickened their rhythmic movement.

"No. I need a minute or I'll lose control—"

"Dammit, I don't want your control! I want you!" She grabbed fistfuls of his thick hair and dragged his head away from the wall. "Look at me! I want you to lose control. I want to watch your face when you shoot into me." She moved her hips again, priming the pump, feeling his cock thicken impossibly more.

Their gazes locked. She watched his pupils dilate, his eyes lose focus. With a dozen savage strokes he gave up his tenuous control and, hoarsely shouting her name over and over in a primal litany, pumped his seed so deep into her that she could feel his scalding juices all the way to her soul.

Her guttural roar was a sound of triumph. *This one was for you,* she thought with all the pent-up love he'd released in her. *To wash away the pain of the past. To give back to you what you've given me. To show you that not all women are alike.*

After a while she loosened her hold. She became aware of the discomfort—her splayed legs, the prosthesis hanging like an anchor from her stump. Her spinal bones, from her cervicals to her coccyx, had been slammed repeatedly against the paneling. She'd probably have bruises tomorrow.

A small price to pay for so precious a gift as he'd just given her.

A satisfied smile touched her lips. She reveled in the feel of him leaning slack against her, the thud of his heart against her breast, the heavy, uneven breathing in her ear, the clean, soapy smell mixed with his unique musky scent, the salty taste of sweat on his neck. She knew she would remember this moment the rest of her life.

Simon roused slowly. "Are you okay?"

"I've never had a Harvey Wallbanger before."

"My name isn't Harvey," he growled. "And don't you ever forget it."

Her stump was starting to throb. She tried to shift her position to lessen the pull. It felt like a ten-pound sack of potatoes tied to her knee.

"You're hurt!"

"It's just—it feels like my short leg went to sleep."

Simon's focus sharpened instantly. Jesus. He'd just slammed the woman he loved, the woman he'd give his life to keep safe, into a wall like a drunken sailor on his first shore leave in a year. "I hurt you," he said, alarmed. He placed gentle but firm hands on her waist. "I've got you. I won't let go. Ever." He eased away from her, allowing her legs to ride slowly down his hips.

When her feet touched the floor, her legs buckled. He pulled her close, vowing to do it right the next—

Slowly realization filtered through his brain. What he had done. What she had done. "Tamara," he whispered. He cupped her face in his hands with all the tenderness he'd felt when he first held his newborn son. He kissed her nose, her cheekbones, her eyebrows. Then he touched his lips to hers. In that kiss he put all the promise, all the protectiveness, all the love that welled up in him for this woman who had crumbled his self-imposed barriers.

"Do you think maybe we can sit down?" she asked.

Guilt flashed through him. What had he done to her leg in his frenzy? He made a move to turn then realized his own leg was still bound up.

The realization must have hit her at the same time. "I think we can dispense with this," she said briskly, and made quick work of the buckle and Velcro. "Let's get to that fire."

Simon shifted his weight tentatively on his newly freed leg, then swept Tamara up in his arms. "By all means."

It was only when he had her firmly in his grip that he noted her state of undress. He vaguely remembered having ripped off her skirt. She wasn't wearing panties. Had he ripped them off too? No, he distinctly recalled the added surge of lust on discovering the lack of that particular garment.

Lust surged through him now as he felt her bare hip softly bouncing against the cock that still poked out of his zipper — a cock that was already hard and ready to slip into her smooth, tight cunt again.

No, it was her turn. He shifted his attention to her silk blouse, which hung open to reveal the apricot lace bra he'd glimpsed earlier. The delectable memory paled before the real thing, her softly mounded breasts above the demi-cups offered for his eyes, his mouth.

He intended to take full advantage of it.

Gently he set her on the rug near the fire and knelt down beside her. "I'm going to undress you one stitch at a time."

"On one condition."

He groaned. "What?"

"Each time, you take off one stitch of yours."

His cock leaped in agreement. "I can live with that."

"I get to choose which stitch."

"I can live with that too."

His cock hardened further at the touch of her heated gaze on it. He saw the flame of desire in her eyes, waited for her to order his slacks to come off, but she said, "Your shirt first."

Glad he hadn't worn a T-shirt, he made short work of the buttons and stripped off the white shirt. His tie slid unnoticed to the floor. He knelt with his knees straddling her hips.

"I need to touch you," she whispered.

He leaned toward her, hands braced near her shoulders. "Touch all you want."

She reached up. Her palms flattened against his chest, brushed across his thick mat of hair, followed the contours of his muscles, skimmed around the sides, down to his waist. He could feel his cock swelling even further with the promise of her touch, the look of naked passion in her eyes.

"Isn't it my turn to take off a stitch of yours?" he finally managed.

She stroked his rampant cock with her gaze. "I think—" her mouth curved up in a teasing grin, "this poor little thing is being strangled. You'd better take off your pants."

Simon needed no further encouragement. He shot to his feet, toed off his sockless loafers, undid his belt and waistband, then shucked his slacks and boxer shorts in one swift movement.

"You cheated," she said, her smile telling him how pleased she was that he had.

"The fire's too hot." Kneeling as before, with his legs straddling her hips, he undid the last few buttons on her shirt that were still buttoned. "You'll get a fever with this on." He lifted her shoulders, slipped the blouse off her arms and tossed it aside, then set her tenderly back on the rug.

"You're right," she murmured, her body arching up to him. "I'm very hot."

"Speaking of strangling." His fingers unhooked the front clasp of her demi-bra. "How can you breathe with this thing on?" He pushed the lace cups aside, exposing the taut peaks of her peach-colored nipples.

"I know just the thing for fever," he murmured as he bent his head. "Water." His tongue laved her nipple, leaving it wet and glistening and even harder. Then he blew gently. The areola pebbled. "Better?"

Tamara's response was to pull his head to her other breast. "This one's getting too hot." Her voice was thick and sultry.

He sucked and tugged and kneaded and kissed one breast, then the other, until she writhed beneath him. He felt her fingers alternately skim through his hair and bunch up into fists as she reacted to his relentless attention.

"Simon." The single word was laced with need. She arched toward him, rubbing her flat stomach against his hard cock.

"Lady, you're just beginning to learn the extent of my control." He dipped his head to the blonde curls that marked her slit. His tongue found and stroked the bud that had unfurled into a damp flower of passion.

She moaned and lifted her hips in to him.

"What's this?" he asked in a mock-severe voice, drawing his body a few inches away from her. "More articles of clothing?"

"Simon!" Her arms reached up in a silent demand to bring him back where he belonged.

But he merely slid down lower, intensely interested in her black stockings. Gently kneeing her thighs open, he positioned himself between them. He unhooked each of her garter snaps, kissing and licking her inner thighs as his fingers moved. He made a tsking sound then said, "You're full of things that can strangle you." He unhooked the garter belt and lifted her hips off the floor to pull the belt out of the way.

Her provocative position prompted him to dip into her sweet pussy again. His tongue tasted, probed, darted inside to lick and nibble at her until she cried out his name again.

"Did I hurt you?" he murmured as he lowered her hips to the rug. "I'll stop."

"No," she managed to say in a thick voice.

"No, what? You want me to stop?"

"No, damn you!" She arched into him, wrapped her arms around his waist and pulled—tried to pull—him down against her.

He could understand the urgency of her need. After all, he'd already had one release tonight and she hadn't. They'd been teasing each other all day long. He'd never felt so hard, so ready, so eager to take and to give. But there was one more thing he had to do before he could please both of them.

He rolled a stocking down her good leg, unbuckled the sandal strap, and pulled off both shoe and stocking. He kissed the bottom of her foot, her toes, and worked his way up her calf, her inner thigh, stroking, teasing, lavishing attention on every inch of her smooth skin, paying special attention to her clit with his tongue.

Tamara squirmed with need under his tender assault. She thought she'd die if he didn't put his cock inside her right this minute. She'd done everything she knew how, pulling, pushing, inveigling, wriggling, and still Simon was like a juggernaut, following his own agenda.

Then his hands went to her left leg. She stilled. Her eyes squeezed shut. *He won't, he can't,* she prayed, but whether she was praying that he wouldn't expose her stump or he wouldn't freeze up at the sight of it, she didn't know.

Relentlessly he tugged the stocking down her cosmetic leg, exposing the cup of her prosthesis, then the smooth, flesh-colored plastic skin. When the stocking was down around her fake ankle, Simon began kissing the area where flesh met plastic, stroking her inner thigh as he did.

"How do you take this off?" he asked softly.

Oh, God, she didn't want to spoil the mood, couldn't bear to experience his rejection when he saw the stump. Not now, not when she loved him beyond life itself. Tears stung her eyes.

"Tamara, honey, I want to see all of you," he murmured. "I want to kiss every inch of you. Please." His eyes met hers with the most tender look she'd ever seen. "No secrets."

Not even when she'd hobbled into Harland's study in front of the shareholders and ignominiously fallen on her butt had she felt this vulnerable. When Ike had dragged her into the path of the forest fire she hadn't felt as defenseless as at this moment when the man she loved was asking her to lower her final barrier.

"I want you naked before me. As I am," he reminded her.

She swallowed hard. He'd confided his inability to hold an erection, a malady that struck to the heart of a man's pride. Just because he'd been able to climax in a dozen strokes after hours of foreplay didn't mean he was cured. He'd been rock-hard before and lost it. He was offering her his own vulnerability. Surely she could do such a small thing as take off her leg, something she'd done night after night for the past ten years.

"It just twists off," she said, her voice a mere whisper.

"Show me."

Reluctantly she took his outstretched hand to help her sit up. She grasped the flexible socket with both hands and gently pulled downward. The leg popped off.

Simon took over. He slipped her stump sock off, stroked the exposed skin, moved his long fingers over every inch as if to familiarize himself with a part of her that he hadn't seen before. He bent his head down and kissed the smooth scar where her skin had been sewn back together. "Is this sensitive?"

Tamara could barely breathe. She leaned back on her elbows and offered up her vulnerability to him. "Not really."

Simon began laying a trail of kisses, first on the inside of her knee, then an inch higher, then higher, and higher. "Is this sensitive?"

"I-I think it's starting." Liquid fire laced every spot where Simon's lips touched.

She could feel the smile form on his lips as he placed his fiery brand yet higher up her inner thigh. He licked, nibbled, nipped a bit of tender skin between his teeth. "Is this?"

"Y-yes, I think you're on the right track." She lay back on the rug, her fingers itching to grab hold of his hair, his arms, anything, just to pull him close to her, to feel the hard length of his body on her. But she knew he'd take his time, time in which he might drive out of her mind the fact that she'd just given him carte blanche over her flawed body.

His mouth stopped just short of her pubic curls and lingered there, teasing her with his control. "I think maybe...here." He lifted her short leg, hooking the knee over his shoulder and stroking the swollen lips he exposed by his action.

Now she was totally vulnerable, totally exposed to his view. She reveled in it, in the strength he'd given her to accept herself as she was. Her eyelids fluttered closed.

They flew open as he drove two fingers inside her, then slowly slid them back and forth, releasing honeyed juices from her. "Oh God, please!" Her voice held a hint of desperation. His magic fingers sent shock waves of electricity to every curve and corner of her body. Then he circled her swollen clit with wet fingers. She bucked against his hand, felt moistness seeping down her thighs.

Then he scrambled on top of her, entered her with one smooth, hard stroke.

Their gazes locked. The intensity of his held Tamara in thrall. With his eyes he told her he loved her, accepted her, wanted her. She poured her own emotions into her own gaze. Then a smile tilted the corners of her mouth upward and she began rocking her hips.

Heeding the prompt, Simon began moving inside her with deliberately slow strokes, almost withdrawing totally before sliding inside to the hilt, teasing her, goading her to prompt him to move faster. Then he stopped.

The tightness inside Tamara's throat threatened to choke her. Had he lost—

"I forgot," he said. "It's easier for you to be on top."

In a quick motion he reversed their positions and her legs straddled his. In that moment she knew he loved her as she loved him, totally, without reservation, regardless of disability or incapacity. He'd freely given up his control to her.

Savoring the dominant position, Tamara ground her hips into him, lifting then bearing down on him, watching the place where their bodies joined, his cock slick and covered with her juices as she accepted him deep inside her. She leaned forward and stroked his hairy chest with her breasts, captured his mouth in kiss after demanding, plundering kiss. She felt his large hands circle her waist, helping her, rocking with her, finding a rhythm that gradually built into a frenzy until there was one body, one heart, one universe, one love. That love exploded inside her, inside him, melding their juices, sending them to a higher plane where their souls fused into one being of light and love until the end of time.

* * * * *

A long time later, Tamara stirred in Simon's arms. She stretched luxuriously, like a cat waking in a beam of sunlight. "Some cocoa would hit the spot, don't you think?"

"Don't move. I'll make it."

She watched him put a few more logs on the fire, unselfconscious about his glorious nakedness, then move to the pile of his discarded clothing. A moment later he was back, his wrinkled slacks riding low on narrow hips. He held out his equally wrinkled white shirt. "Here, put this on. It'll keep my arms around you while I'm in the kitchen."

What a beautiful sentiment, Tamara thought as she slipped her arms into a shirt that came to her knees. What a beautiful man. She inhaled the lingering scent of him in the fabric and smiled at the sight of the sleeves dangling down beyond her fingertips.

Barefoot, he scooped her up in his strong arms, carried her to the sofa, and gently set her down. "The floor's pretty hard," he said. Then he disappeared into the kitchen.

Tamara snuggled into the sofa and gazed around. The living room was a box about twenty-five feet square, a window wall opening to a deck, the fireplace on a second wall, the other two sides of the box an open plan flowing into a book-lined alcove and a dining area that led to the kitchen. The sofa sat at right angles to the fireplace, its back to the dining area.

The sounds of a spoon scraping against a metal pot made her feel cherished—her man was making her cocoa!

She should get up and gather her clothes and prosthesis, she thought idly. But she was just too happy, too satisfied, too like a cat that had knocked over a bottle of cream and lapped up an unexpected treat, to make a move.

A great lassitude filled her. So this was what love was like. If she lived to be a hundred, she'd never stop loving this man. Her man. She smiled at the sound of his off-key humming.

Her ears pricked at another sound, far from the kitchen.
Like a door unlatching. She held her breath, hoping to hear—
hoping to not hear—another sound to pinpoint its location.
Mentally she catalogued the doors in the chalet. Upstairs only
the master bedroom and bath. Downstairs, the front door, one
to the bathroom, one between garage and laundry.

Uneasy, she folded the shirt cuffs back and rolled the
sleeves up to her elbows. If someone was trying to break in,
she didn't need to be impeded by a straitjacket. She was
vulnerable enough with nothing under the shirt and her
crutches upstairs and her prosthesis lying in the middle of the
floor with its black stocking dangling.

Then she heard Simon whistling, the sound of the
refrigerator door shutting. She relaxed back onto the cushions.
If someone was sneaking around, he'd have heard it.

Another sound, muffled, like a foot bumping into
something solid, caused her to sit bolt upright on the sofa. A
cold fear washed over her. Before she could cry out, she saw
the fire's glint on a gun pointed right at her heart.

Chapter Thirty

ஐ

"Don't move."

Tamara gasped.

"Shut up," Marta hissed as she crept into Tamara's line of sight, her grip sure and steady on the Smith & Wesson automatic she'd bought in New York along with the .32.

Tamara's eyes grew huge. Her mouth contorted in a rictus of fear, like a Halloween mask. Marta could hear her harsh rasps. She'd wanted to shoot them both while they were rutting, the blonde straddling him shamelessly, gyrating like a paid performer. But before they died, she needed them to know why.

She would shoot Simon at close range and then slit Tamara's wrists until she bled to death all over him. In Tamara's desk at the bungalow Ike had found a retractable razor gadget used to slash packages open. It gave her the idea for a tragic murder-suicide. Simon couldn't accept Tamara's stump and she shot him in a fit of rage then decided she couldn't live without him after all. Perfect.

Marta had climbed through the unlocked laundry-room window and threaded her way around a desk in the alcove. Now she eased into the shadows, her back to the window wall, and watched Simon stride barefoot into the room carrying two mugs, sexual satisfaction oozing from every pore.

"Stop right there."

Simon's head jerked up. His eyes searched the shadowy reaches of the room until he saw her. Some emotion skittered across his face then smoothed out to blankness. "Marta," he said neutrally.

In the flickering firelight shadows, the only illumination in the room, Marta noted the breadth of Simon's shoulders, well defined muscles of his bare chest, narrow hips, hair mussed and falling across his forehead. It reminded her so much of the youthful Jack in her bed, she thought her heart would break.

"Put the cups down over there." With the gun she pointed to an end table at the far side of the sofa.

"No! Walk behind the sofa." He had started coming around the sofa's side nearest to her. She didn't want him between her and Tamara. Marta had no doubt he'd try to play hero if given the chance. He'd always been the fearless one, the risk-taker. Not like Jack. Jack was the amiable one, and she'd guided him as much as she could without him realizing it.

"Real slow."

With his eyes focused on Marta like twin lasers, Simon bent down and fumbled the mugs onto the table, then straightened slowly. The play of firelight on his muscles as he moved momentarily distracted her. Again she saw Jack as he used to be. She blinked. This was Simon, the enemy. Her mouth compressed into a tight line.

"What is it you want?" Simon asked in a quiet voice.

She grunted. "What does it look like? I want you dead."

"Why? You're just like family."

"You don't know the half of it."

"Why the gun, Marta?" he persisted.

Marta angled her chin toward Tamara, who perched on the edge of the sofa, leg on the floor, stump dangling, white-knuckled fists clutching the cushions. She had managed to hide the fear Marta had seen earlier, but sweat beaded on her forehead and her lip trembled. Good. Marta wanted her to suffer while contemplating her future. Her very short future.

"Let's start with her. She ruined everything when she came to The Pines." Marta shifted the gun to point it at

Tamara. "You made Harland change his mind about leaving Jack the golf course. Then you changed both the twins' vote on the development."

Tamara's face turned as pale as her knuckles, but she looked Marta in the eye. "If they build my plan, you'd still have ten percent of—"

"Dammit, not my measly shares. I tell you, Jack should have gotten it all! Harland promised him the golf course. If you hadn't gone off the wall at the planning board meeting, they'd have voted our plan. We had it all sewed up."

"What do you mean, 'sewed up'?" Simon interrupted.

"I guess I could brag a little, seeing as how you won't be around to tell tales." Marta preened. "Jack has a red-hot photo of the chairman's son, who's a caddie at the course, with the wife of the banker who holds their mortgage. The Realtor gets exclusive sales for five years, the banker all the financing. And then there's Ollie. The truck driver who couldn't even run a car off the road. Elliott bought up all his gambling IOU's and gave him an alternative."

"So Elliott engineered it all—"

Marta barked out a harsh laugh. "You all think Elliott was the brains. He talked a good game, spent a lot of money on his image. But I'm the mastermind. I'm the one who deserves all the credit." She felt a smug smile break out, made no effort to stifle it. "Besides, Elliott's dead. Shot himself in the head."

A strangled noise escaped from Tamara. Marta's attention snapped back to her. The bitch looked ready to vomit. Good. Marta took a step toward her.

Simon's pulse rate shot up. With all the other violent deaths, it couldn't have been suicide. The look in Marta's eyes scared him. It was the look of someone with nothing to lose.

He had to keep her talking, focus her attention away from Tamara and on himself until he could disarm her. In a quiet, unthreatening voice, he asked, "Why did he kill himself, Marta?"

"He thought he was above the rest of us. But I found out about him and Carrie."

Simon swallowed hard. Nothing about Carrie surprised him anymore. "What about them?"

"I can see it in your expression. You think she fucked Elliott, too, like she fucked Jack behind your back." Marta laughed again, a crazed sound that sent shivers across Simon's neck. "What I found out is even better. Carrie's a whore. Like mother, like daughter. And Elliott was pimp to both of them."

"You're lying," he said evenly. He wouldn't let her bait him.

Ignoring his accusation, she said, "I made sure the police will call it suicide."

"But it isn't?"

The malevolent expression that crossed Marta's face chilled Simon to his marrow. "No. I pulled the trigger. For fifteen years he looked down his nose at me. I'm plain, but I'm smarter than he ever was. I found out his sordid little secret."

"Finding out that he was a pimp is enough to convince the police that Elliott committed suicide?"

Marta's maniacal laughter boomed like a funhouse gone amok. It made the hairs on Simon's arms stand up. She took another threatening step. "You're underestimating me again. The police will find a lab report in his hand. DNA proof that Carrie is Elliott's daughter."

The staggering allegation seared through Simon's brain. For a moment his synapses refused to process the information. Elliott had introduced Carrie as a client when he was handling her mother's estate. Carrie had wanted to take the child—

Elliott had set him up!

Bile seethed in Simon's throat. She was lying. She was trying to throw him off balance by spewing lies. "But why get rid of Elliott? Are you and Carrie working together?"

Marta snorted. "The only thing that whore likes more than a man's cock is cold hard cash. I'd buy her out in a minute."

"But why kill Elliott?"

"For Jack. And Cliff."

"Cliff? The stable hand? How does he enter the picture?"

Her chin lifted. Pride momentarily transformed her face into something radiant. "Cliff is my son."

"Your *son*?" The joy that Simon had known during Kevin's brief life flashed through his mind. "We didn't hear about Cliff until last summer. How could you have abandoned him all these years if he was your son?"

"I didn't abandon him!" Marta shrieked. "I provided for him as best I could. I found foster parents for him right after he was born. We made up a story about his mother and father dying when he was two. Then when we found out he needed special schooling, I paid all the bills. And I set money aside for him in a Swiss bank account."

"You wiped him out of your life." Simon's voice was flat.

"Put yourself in my place. I'd just gotten a job, my first job in ten years—"

"What!"

"I had to drop out of college to care for my father. Ten long years it took him to die, ten years of me chained to a bedridden, bitter man. When he died I found out he hadn't paid property taxes in all that time. They sold the house out from under me at a sheriff's sale. I had no money of my own. I took the first job I could find."

"The Pines."

"Yes. I couldn't believe it when Harland offered to finance my degree."

"Why shouldn't he? Dad did all kinds of good works behind the scenes."

"I mean, I couldn't believe how perfect the timing was. You see, I was pregnant. I had Cliff during summer break, went back to school in September, and got my degree the following January. I didn't have a choice, do you understand that? I had to give him up!" She took a deep breath. "But I never forgot him. Cliff always came first. He still does."

"What about the father? Why didn't you go to him for help?"

"I couldn't."

Simon realized that Marta seemed to have forgotten about Tamara. Apparently Tamara realized that, too, as she sat silent and motionless. She was hiding her fear well, but he sensed it was there. Sensed, too, that it was as much for him as for herself. Her alert vigilance told him she would attack Marta if the opportunity presented itself. He couldn't let Tamara do anything foolish. He had to keep Marta talking, had to get Tamara out of the line of fire. He would protect the woman he loved with his last breath.

He took a small step toward Marta. "Why couldn't you ask the father for help?" His voice was soft, like a psychotherapist talking to a deranged patient he'd just calmed down.

"He was seventeen years old! If I told him, his father would think I was just looking for a payoff!"

Something like barbed wire knotted in Simon's stomach. "Who was seventeen years old?"

Marta's eyes glittered. "Jack. Jack is Cliff's father."

"You're lying."

"Ask him! Ask him how much he loved me. All that first summer, we taught each other. He looked beyond my face and saw the woman beneath. He made me feel..."

The last word was whispered. "Beautiful."

Simon laughed, a biting sound of disbelief. "Then he went back to school and forgot about you."

"No! We've always had a special relationship."

"So you talked him into bribing the planning board—"

"Yes! All for Cliff. And for his father. When I got hold of Elliott's little secret, I knew I'd found the answer. When we do DNA testing on Cliff and Jack, I'll be able to prove he's the heir to the Sutcliffe fortune. Meanwhile, it was up to me to see that there was enough of it to pay him back for all he suffered growing up without knowing his mother or father. All I suffered at not being able to claim him as my son."

Her chin shot up. "But just in case, I had to eliminate the shareholders, one by one."

Simon's knees threatened to buckle. He willed himself to stand tall and unmoved. "My God," he whispered. "There was a wire at the jump. You killed—" Simon's voice broke. "You killed my father."

"And wired the Miata. Except the wrong damn person turned the ignition."

From his peripheral vision Simon saw Tamara biting down on her lips, trying to hold back her anguish. Marta had killed Vincent too.

"But there's more. Did you think Harland was the first to die?"

"What do you mean?"

"It's amazing what you can learn on the Internet," Marta said in a smug voice. "How to plant explosives, how to clog a valve on a gas heater—"

Simon balled his hands into fists. His heart missed a beat then slammed against the wall of his chest like a sledgehammer. "No. You didn't—"

"There could be only one heir. Kevin had to die."

The anguished cry that came from deep in Simon's soul was that of a wounded animal. Rage blotted out any thought of caution. He lunged at the monster who had killed his son.

First to Die

His unexpected move made Marta stagger backward. Her foot landed on an uneven surface. Instinctively she pulled the trigger as she toppled backward to the floor.

The impact of a bullet tearing through flesh sent Simon reeling. He crashed into the coffee table. It collapsed under his weight. A sickening crack rent the air as his head hit the edge of the stone hearth.

"You killed Simon!" Propping her stump against the front of the sofa for leverage, Tamara launched herself like a Saturn rocket, oblivious to danger, knowing only that her beloved Simon had been shot. All the excruciatingly long minutes of fear had pumped her veins full of adrenaline. She slammed into the older woman, heard the breath whoosh out of Marta as they sprawled on the floor in the center of the room, Tamara on top of Marta.

Get the gun!

Tamara managed to snag Marta's right hand—her gun hand—and get a grip on the madwoman's wrist. Tears pricked her eyelids from the ripping pain as Marta wrapped her free hand around Tamara's flowing hair and yanked.

Marta's thick thighs gripped Tamara's good leg in a scissor-hold. Marta had about five inches and forty pounds on Tamara, but Tamara's upper body strength was finely honed from years of workouts. Her left hand still held Marta's gun hand in a death grip. Tamara's weight kept Marta's back to the floor.

Her muscles strained. Beads of sweat rolled down her forehead and temple. She jerked their locked hands up and crashed Marta's knuckles down against the hardwood floor. Marta grunted in pain but hung on to the gun.

Tamara propped herself on her short leg. She locked the knuckles of her right hand into a straight line, fingers and thumb squeezed rigidly together, and in a karate-style chop, jammed them into Marta's jugular.

A garbled sound ripped out of Marta's mouth. Her scissor-hold on Tamara's thigh, the fist in her hair, loosened.

It was enough to give Tamara purchase with her good knee. She twisted to the left to clamp her other hand as well onto Marta's gun hand. Marta's left arm gripped Tamara's waist, squeezing the breath out of her. She flipped Tamara onto her right side. Tamara's stump flailed, trying to gain traction. The flip freed Marta's gun hand from the floor, although Tamara still hung on with almost superhuman effort. The gun waved in the air as they struggled for dominance.

Tamara's biceps bulged with the effort of pushing Marta's wrist up to where she could get a two-fisted grip on it. But Marta fought with the tenacity of a sumo wrestler, a heavy leg shoved between Tamara's bare thighs to hold her down.

Tamara's eyes stung with tears. Her muscles burned. Her breath blasted out in short gasps. Desperately she yanked Marta's gun hand down. An explosion ripped into the air between them. The pungent smell of gunpowder overpowered Tamara's nostrils. Hot blood splattered all over her. Bile rose in her throat at the sickly sweet smell, the slimy, sticky feel of it trickling down her face.

She fought down nausea as tremors shook every inch of her body. There was something she had to do, someone who needed her. She had to…

Her body went rigid. Her mind blanked out. She slumped to the floor.

"Tamara! My God, Tamara!"

Simon dropped the prosthesis he'd grabbed as a makeshift weapon and crawled the last inches to where the two women lay bloody and motionless. His thigh burned. It felt as though the bullet had shattered a bone. Blood dripped into his eye from the gash made when his temple had struck the hearth.

But he felt none of the pain as he pulled Tamara away from the corpse whose face had been blown away. He cradled

Tamara in his arms. Her eyes were closed, her breathing shallow. "Tamara, talk to me! Tamara, I love you. Please, God, let her be all right!"

Tears and blood mingled on his cheeks. Panic welled up in him at her stillness. He stroked her blood-spattered, feverish face, brushed back tendrils of hair that had caught on her lashes.

"You have to be all right," he murmured as he rocked her like a baby, his mind unwilling to accept any alternatives. He forced out of his mind the sight of all the blood saturating the oversized shirt that clung wetly to her. It wasn't her blood, it couldn't be hers, he told himself again and again.

Finally her lashes fluttered then lifted. Her eyes were blank, the pupils dilated. Then they focused on him.

"I love you, Tamara. I don't want to wait another minute to say it. I want—"

Her eyes widened as they zeroed in on the gash in his forehead. "You're bleeding!" She struggled to sit up. A quick glance took inventory of Simon's body. She saw the black slacks saturated with blood, rivulets of red dripping from his temple to his bare chest, the taut lines of his mouth, his pale skin.

"Marta shot you! Where's the phone? Is there 9-1-1 in Vermont?"

Scrambling on hands and knees to the phone, she dialed as he directed, then demanded instructions for on-the-scene first aid. She found Simon's silk tie on the floor and fashioned a tourniquet above the leg wound, then crawled to the kitchen for a clean linen towel, which she pressed to the gash on his temple to stanch the bleeding.

Not until they heard the faint wail of sirens did Tamara let go of her emotions. Shudders racked her body. Tears spilled over her eyelashes and down her blood-streaked cheeks.

With an effort Simon sat up, opened his arms. She settled into them and they collapsed to the floor in a tight embrace. "You know, if you weren't a gimp, we'd both be dead by now," he said, trying to make his voice flippant. Even in his excruciating pain, he knew he had to distract her to keep her from going into shock.

"Wh-what do you mean?"

He gestured to the cosmetic leg, still encased in its high-heeled sandal and black stocking, that lay where he'd dropped it when the gun fired the second time. "When I rushed Marta, I surprised her so much that she took a step back. She tripped on your prosthesis."

Tamara's mouth made a big wide O.

"Speaking of which, if you're going to be my wife, you have to understand that I love you whether you're on crutches or on your graphite leg or *au naturel*, like you are now."

Tamara moved back as far as his embrace would allow and blinked. "W-wife?"

"Speaking of which," he repeated, his head cocked, listening to the approaching sirens. "I wouldn't take kindly to anybody seeing my wife's private parts..."

"Oh." Tamara looked down at herself, at the ripped, blood-soaked shirt plastered to her body. Her head lifted, as though she'd just now heard the sirens. The pale skin beneath the blood on her cheeks pinkened. "Oh," she said again.

She scrambled to the sofa, pulled down the earth-toned afghan, and wrapped it around her like a sarong, from armpits to knees.

The doorknob rattled. "Simon! Tamara! Open up!"

Tamara struggled upright and hopped to the door. With fumbling fingers she unlocked it and threw it open. "Lieutenant Kyrillos! Am I glad to see you!"

His sharp glance raked over her. "Are you all right?"

"I'm fine. It was Marta. She shot Simon in the thigh."

"The ambulance is right behind me. Let's get out of their way." He scooped Tamara into his arms and carried her to the sofa, setting her down gently.

The EMTs barged in and zeroed in on Simon sprawled on the floor amid a pool of blood, his face grimacing in a rictus of pain.

Tamara's gaze lingered on him until they blocked her view. "Marta is Cliff's mother," she said, turning reluctantly to the detective. "She was responsible for Harland, Vincent—" A shudder stopped her. She closed her eyes then opened them at the sudden flurry of activity.

Simon, lying groggily on the gurney, gave her a weak smile.

She struggled to stand. "I'm going with you."

Kyrillos got to his feet. "I'll take you."

"No." Her gaze scoured the room. "There. My crutches. Please?"

Wordlessly Kyrillos handed them to Tamara. *You'll never again have to stand alone,* he thought as he caught the look of love that passed between those two people who had suffered so much.

Then he followed the procession to the ambulance.

Epilogue

ഇ

The festive pop of the champagne cork echoed their cheerful mood. Simon and Tamara sat on the terrace overlooking the eighteenth hole and watched the bartender pour Dom Perignon into their flutes. When he dredged the bottle into its bucket of shaved ice and withdrew, they raised their glasses to each other.

"To the final decree," Tamara said. "At last."

"To our wedding," Simon responded. "It can't come too soon for me."

Almost a month had passed since they had faced the terror of Marta's madness. On this Monday after a long Thanksgiving weekend, the Pines was closing down for the season. But when Simon received the divorce papers that morning, he asked Hank, Ilya and Danuta to help him with a private celebration.

The setting sun gilded the course. The day had been sunny, and the flagstones radiated warmth. They had decided to sit outside to enjoy the unique atmosphere of the Pine Barrens around them and wore suitably warm clothing. Leisurely they sipped in acknowledgement of the toasts.

"Jack's just about chosen the architect. He's eager to get started now that we have the votes." Simon smiled as he inhaled the fresh, pine-scented air. "You were right about using Yvette's ex-husband's lawyer. I'd never seen Carrie so meek. She sold her shares without a whimper. And agreed in writing never to harass me."

"Still, you were generous, considering the fact that Elliott left her a bundle." Tamara took a sip, wrinkling her nose as the bubbles danced. "I still can't get over his paternity."

"I'll never forgive him for his deceit."

Tamara laid a hand on his forearm. Underneath the heavy sweater, she felt his warmth, his vitality. "Never forget that she gave you Kevin."

His jaw muscle ticced. "And took him away."

"But you have wonderful memories."

"Yes." Simon's gaze seemed far away.

She ached for his loss, but looked forward to presenting him with a child of her own. Their wedding would take place in less than two weeks. She stroked her flat stomach. She was only a week late, but she hoped that soon she could ease his pain by sharing her secret with him, as soon as she herself was sure.

"Look at that. I don't believe it." Simon's voice called her back to the present.

Tamara's gaze followed his. Two duffers strolled onto the eighteenth green, toting their bags and marking their balls. "I do. Golfers are a crazy bunch. I've seen them out there in two inches of snow, using orange balls so they could find them."

Simon squinted into the hazy dusk. "That's Jack."

"And Cliff."

"Looks like he's teaching the kid how to play Bingo Bango Bongo."

Tamara groaned. "Another five-hour golfer."

"Cliff doesn't seem to have been bothered too much by Marta's death."

"No wonder. From what I gather, he didn't even know he had any family until the foster parents told him he had to go to that school. By then, I think he would have felt no one loved him."

"How she could have abandoned her own son all those years—" Simon left the thought unfinished.

But Tamara knew what he was thinking. Parental love for children, a child's love for his parents, were sacred concepts. To both Simon and Tamara. They had both benefited from the unconditional love and support of nurturing parents. Tamara knew that Simon would be a wonderful father and looked forward to sharing the experience with him.

"I think he's going about it right," Simon said.

"Yes. A big brother is what he needs now, not a father he didn't know he had. Or knowing his aunt was really his mother and that she was demented enough to kill."

They watched as Cliff sank a three-foot putt. Joy suffused his features as he retrieved his ball. Jack threw an arm around his shoulder in congratulations. They gathered their bags and walked toward the lockers, punching each other's shoulders like a pair of jocks.

"Are you and Jack going to try to recover the Swiss bank account that Marta embezzled?"

Simon raised an eyebrow. "What do you think?"

"Of course you wouldn't. I don't know why I asked. I think you're as kind and generous as Harland. And just as handsome."

"Wait until my hair turns white like his. And with this damn thing on my leg, it'll be any day now." He shifted in his chair, seeking a more comfortable position. His left leg was sheathed in stainless steel from groin to heel. Marta's bullet had shattered his femur. So many pins had been inserted that he could set off an alarm at airport security.

Tamara hid a smile behind her glass as her gaze traveled the length of his Hulk-size leg under gray sweatpants she'd had to sew a gusset into. "Ironic, isn't it?"

"Fitting." His expression turned somber. "It's helped me understand the reason for the chip you had on your shoulder. I respect your courage. I'm proud of your accomplishments. I want to share in your future triumphs."

My biggest triumph was helping you heal. While Simon was in the hospital, Tamara had nightmares that awoke her in the middle of the night. Now that they slept in each other's arms, the nightmares had dwindled to bad dreams that merely made her restless. When she awoke now, it was usually because Simon had been touching her with his mouth, his hands, his body. The first time she had awakened in the dark to find him hot and hard inside her, the deliciously slow friction had caused her to climax in seconds. She had come a second and a third time before he allowed himself release.

Yes, Tamara thought with a smile, Simon Sutcliffe was healed. And so was she.

They had healed each other.

The End

Also by Cris Anson

෩

Second Best

If you are interested in a spicier read (and are over 18), check out the author's erotic romances at Ellora's Cave Publishing (www.ellorascave.com).

Candy Cravings
Dance of the Butterfly
Dance of the Crystal
Dance of the Seven Veils
Discovery
Mischief Night
Tantalizing Treats

About the Author

෩

Cris Anson firmly believes that love is the greatest gift...to give or to receive. In her writing, she lives for the moment when her characters realize they love each other, usually after much antagonism and conflict. And when they express that love physically, Cris keeps a fire extinguisher near the keyboard in case of spontaneous combustion. Multi-published and twice EPPIE-nominated in romantic suspense under another name, she was usually asked to tone down her love scenes. For Ellora's Cave, she's happy to turn the flame as high as it will go--and then some.

After suffering the loss of her real-life hero/husband of twenty-two years, Cris has picked up the pieces of her life and tries to remember only the good times...slow-dancing with him to the Big Band sound of Glenn Miller's music, vacations to scenic national parks in a snug recreational vehicle, his tender and fierce love, his unflagging belief in her ability to write stories that touch the heart as well as the libido. Bits and pieces of his tenacity, optimism, code of honor and lust for life will live on in her imaginary heroes.

Cris welcomes comments from readers. You can find her website and email address on her author bio page at www.cerridwenpress.com.

Tell Us What You Think

We appreciate hearing reader opinions about our books. You can email us at Comments@EllorasCave.com.

Why an electronic book?

We live in the Information Age—an exciting time in the history of human civilization, in which technology rules supreme and continues to progress in leaps and bounds every minute of every day. For a multitude of reasons, more and more avid literary fans are opting to purchase e-books instead of paper books. The question from those not yet initiated into the world of electronic reading is simply: *Why?*

1. *Price.* An electronic title at Ellora's Cave Publishing and Cerridwen Press runs anywhere from 40% to 75% less than the cover price of the exact same title in paperback format. Why? Basic mathematics and cost. It is less expensive to publish an e-book (no paper and printing, no warehousing and shipping) than it is to publish a paperback, so the savings are passed along to the consumer.

2. *Space.* Running out of room in your house for your books? That is one worry you will never have with electronic books. For a low one-time cost, you can purchase a handheld device specifically designed for e-reading. Many e-readers have large, convenient screens for viewing. Better yet, hundreds of titles can be stored within your new library—on a single microchip. There are a variety of e-readers from different manufacturers. You can also read e-books on your PC or laptop computer. (Please note that

Ellora's Cave does not endorse any specific brands. You can check our websites at www.ellorascave.com or www.cerridwenpress.com for information we make available to new consumers.)

3. *Mobility.* Because your new e-library consists of only a microchip within a small, easily transportable e-reader, your entire cache of books can be taken with you wherever you go.

4. *Personal Viewing Preferences.* Are the words you are currently reading too small? Too large? Too... ANNOYING? Paperback books cannot be modified according to personal preferences, but e-books can.

5. *Instant Gratification.* Is it the middle of the night and all the bookstores near you are closed? Are you tired of waiting days, sometimes weeks, for bookstores to ship the novels you bought? Ellora's Cave Publishing sells instantaneous downloads twenty-four hours a day, seven days a week, every day of the year. Our webstore is never closed. Our e-book delivery system is 100% automated, meaning your order is filled as soon as you pay for it.

Those are a few of the top reasons why electronic books are replacing paperbacks for many avid readers.

As always, Ellora's Cave and Cerridwen Press welcome your questions and comments. We invite you to email us at Comments@ellorascave.com or write to us directly at Ellora's Cave Publishing Inc., 1056 Home Avenue, Akron, OH 44310-3502.